The Doomsday Key

ALSO BY JAMES ROLLINS

Subterranean

Excavation

Deep Fathom

Amazonia

Ice Hunt

Sandstorm

Map of Bones

Black Order

The Judas Strain

The Last Oracle

The Doomsday Key

A Σ Sigma Force Novel

James Rollins

HARPER LUXE

An Imprint of HarperCollinsPublishers

Schematics provided and drawn by Steve Prey. All rights reserved. Used by permission of Steve Prey.

HarperCollins books may be purchased for educational, business, or sales promotional use. For information please write: Special Markets Department, HarperCollins Publishers, 10 East 53rd Street, New York, NY 10022.

FIRST HARPERLUXE EDITION

HarperLuxe™ is a trademark of HarperCollins Publishers

Library of Congress Cataloging-in-Publication Data is available upon request.

ISBN: 978-0-06-177475-1

09 10 11 12 13 ID/RRD 10 9 8 7 6 5 4 3 2

To Mom
With all my love

Acknowledgments

All authors need a bedrock of support. Without a firm footing, there would be no foundation to build on. And I'm no exception. I wanted to take this moment to acknowledge those folks who've been my bedrock over these past years. I'd first like to acknowledge my critique group who still keep me both honest and productive: Penny Hill, Judy Prey, Dave Murray, Caroline Williams, Chris Crowe, Lee Garrett, Jane O'Riva, Sally Barnes, Denny Grayson, Leonard Little, Kathy L'Ecluse, and Scott Smith. And an extra big thanks to Steve Prey for all his great help with the introductory maps and schematics. Beyond the group, Carolyn McCray and David Sylvian keep me moving forward through the best of times and the worst. And for all the many years of help with stories and articles and things that explode, a special thanks to Cherei McCarter. And because I must (because he is forcing me to write this), I wanted to thank Steve Berry for some key plot advice, but I'll freely acknowledge that he's a great writer and an even greater friend. Lastly, a special acknowledgment to the four people instrumental to all levels of production: my editor Lyssa Keusch and her colleague Wendy Lee, and my agents Russ Galen and Danny Baror. They've truly been the foundation under this author. And as always, I must stress that any and all errors of fact or detail in this book fall squarely on my own shoulders.

Northern Europe and Arctic Circle

DOOMSDAY VAULT

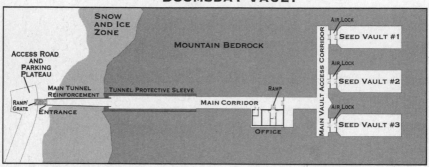

Notes from the Historical Record

During the eleventh century, King William of England commissioned a comprehensive survey of his kingdom. The results were recorded in a great volume titled the Domesday Book. It is one of the most detailed accounts of medieval life during that time. Most historians accept that this grand accounting was done as a means to gather a proper tax from the populace, though this is not certain. Many mysteries still surround this survey, like why it was ordered so swiftly and why some towns were inexplicably marked with a single word in Latin meaning "wasted." Furthermore, the strangeness of this census and its exacting detail earned the tome a disturbing nickname by the people of its time. It became known as the "Doomsday Book."

During the twelfth century, an Irish Catholic priest named Máel Máedóc, who would eventually be named Saint Malachy, had a vision while on a pilgrimage to Rome. In that ecstatic trance, he was given knowledge of all the popes who would come until the end of the world. This grand accounting—a cryptic description of 112 popes—was recorded and safeguarded in the Vatican archives, but the book vanished, only to resurface again during the sixteenth century. Some historians believe that this recovered book was most likely a forgery. Either way, over the intervening centuries, the descriptions of each pope in that book have proved to be oddly accurate—up to and including the current head of the Catholic Church, Pope Benedict XVI. In Saint Malachy's prophecy, the current pope is listed as *De Gloria Olivae*, the Glory of the Olives. And the Benedictine order, from which the pope took his name, does indeed bear the olive branch as its symbol. But most disturbing of all, Pope Benedict XVI is the 111th pope. And according to this oddly accurate prophecy, the world ends with the very next one.

Note from the Scientific Record

During the years 2006 to 2008, one-third of all honeybees in the United States (and much of Europe and Canada) vanished. Thriving hives were suddenly found empty, as if the bees simply flew away and never returned. The condition earned the name Colony Collapse Disorder. This massive and mysterious loss generated sensational headlines and fears. So what truly happened to the bees?

Within the pages of this novel lies an answer . . . Most frightening of all, it's true.

In the final persecution of the Holy Roman Catholic Church, there will reign Peter the Roman, who will feed his flock among many tribulations; after which the seven-hilled city will be destroyed and the dreadful Judge will judge the people.

—PROPHECY OF SAINT MALACHY, 1139

The power of population is indefinitely greater than the power in the earth to produce subsistence for man.

—THOMAS MALTHUS,
AN ESSAY ON THE
PRINCIPLE OF POPULATION, 1798

The time to buy is when blood is running in the streets.

—BARON NATHAN ROTHSCHILD,
WEALTHIEST MAN IN THE
NINETEENTH CENTURY

Spring, 1086
England

The ravens were the first sign.

As the horse-drawn wagon traveled down the rutted track between rolling fields of barley, a flock of ravens rose up in a black wash. They hurled themselves into the blue of the morning and swept high in a panicked rout, but this was more than the usual startled flight. The ravens wheeled and swooped, tumbled and flapped. Over the road, they crashed into each other and rained down out of the skies. Small bodies struck the road, breaking wing and beak. They twitched in the ruts. Wings fluttered weakly.

But most disturbing was the silence of it all.

No caws, no screams.

Just the frantic beat of wing—then the soft impact of feathered bodies on the hard dirt and broken stone.

The wagon's driver crossed himself and slowed the cart. His heavy-lidded eyes watched the skies. The horse tossed its head and huffed into the chill of the morning.

"Keep going," said the traveler sharing the wagon. Martin Borr was the youngest of the royal coroners, ordered here upon a secret edict from King William himself.

As Martin huddled deeper into his heavy cloak, he remembered the note secured by wax and imprinted by the great royal seal. Burdened by the cost of war, King William had sent scores of royal commissioners out into the countryside to amass a great accounting of the lands and properties of his kingdom. The immense tally was being recorded in a mammoth volume called the Domesday Book, collected together by a single scholar and written in a cryptic form of Latin. The accounting was all done as a means of measuring the proper tax owed to the crown.

Or so it was said.

Some grew to suspect there was another reason for such a grand survey of all the lands. They compared the book to the Bible's description of the Last Judgment, where God kept an accounting of all mankind's deeds in the Book of Life. Whispers and rumors began calling the result of this great survey the *Doomsday Book.*

These last were closer to the truth than anyone suspected.

Martin had read the wax-sealed letter. He'd observed that lone scribe painstakingly recording the results of the royal commissioners in the great book, and at the end, he'd watched the scholar scratch a single word in Latin, in red ink.

Vastare.

Wasted.

Many regions were marked with this word, indicating lands that had been laid waste by war or pillage. But two entries had been inscribed entirely in crimson ink. One described a desolate island that lay between the coast of Ireland and the English shore. Martin approached the other place now, ordered here to investigate at the behest of the king. He had been sworn to secrecy and given three men to assist him. They trailed behind the wagon on their own horses.

At Martin's side, the driver twitched the reins and encouraged the draft horse, a monstrously huge chestnut, to a faster clop. As they continued forward, the wheels of the wagon drove over the twitching bodies of the ravens, crushing bones and splattering blood.

Finally, the cart topped a rise and revealed the breadth of the rich valley beyond. A small village lay nestled below, flanked by a stone manor house at one end and a steepled church on the other. A score of thatched cottages and longhouses made up the rest of the hamlet, along with a smattering of wooden sheep-folds and small dovecotes.

" 'Tis a cursed place, milord," the driver said. "Mark my words. It were no pox that has blasted this place."

"That is what we've come to discern."

A league behind them, the steep road had been closed off by the king's army. None were allowed forward, but that did not stop rumors of the strange deaths from spreading to the neighboring villages and farmsteads.

"Cursed," the man mumbled again as he set his cart down the road toward the village. "I heard tell that these lands once belonged to the heathen Celts. Said to be sacred to their pagan ways. Their stones can still be found in the forests off in the highlands up yonder."

His withered arm pointed toward the woods fringing the high hills that climbed heavenward. Mists clung to those forests, turning the green wood into murky shades of gray and black.

"They've cursed this place, I tell you straight. Bringing doom upon those who bear the cross."

Martin Borr dismissed such superstitions. At thirty-two years of age, he had studied with master scholars from Rome to Britannia. He had come with experts to discover the truth here.

Shifting around, Martin waved the others ahead toward the small hamlet, and the trio set off at a canter. Each knew his duty. Martin followed more slowly, studying and assessing all he passed. Isolated in this small upland valley, the village went by the name Highglen and was known locally for its pottery, forged from mud and clay gathered out of the hot springs that contributed to the mists cloaking the higher forests. It was said that the town's method of kilning and the composition of the potter's clay were tightly guarded secrets known only to the guild here.

And now they were lost forever.

The wagon trundled down the road, passing more fields: rye, oats, beans, and rows of vegetables. Some of the fields showed signs of recent harvesting, while others showed evidence of being set to torch.

Had the villagers grown to suspect the truth?

As the wagon continued down into the valley, lines of sheep pens appeared, fringed by tall hedges that half hid the horror within. Woolly mounds, the bloated bodies of hundreds of sheep dotted the overgrown meadows. Closer to the village, pigs and goats also appeared, sprawled and sunken-eyed, dead where they'd dropped. Off in a field, a large-boned ox had collapsed, still tethered to its plow.

As the wagon reached the village green, the town remained silent. No bark of dog greeted them, no crow of rooster, no bray of donkey. The church bell didn't ring, and no one called out to the strangers entering the village.

A heavy silence pressed down over the place.

As they would discover, most of the dead still lay within their houses, too weak at the end to venture out. But one body sprawled facedown on the green, not far from the manor house's stone steps. He lay like he might have just fallen, perhaps tripped down the steps and broken his neck. But even from the height of the wagon, Martin noted the gaunt stretch of skin over bone, the hollow eyes sunken into the skull, the thinness of limbs.

It was the same wasting as in the beasts of the field. It was as if the entire village had been under siege and had been starved out.

The clatter of hooves approached. Reginald pulled beside the wagon. "Granaries are all full," he said, dusting off his palms on his pants. The tall, scarred man had overseen campaigns by King William in the north of France. "Found rats and mice in the bins, too."

Martin glanced over to him.

"As dead as everything else. Just like that cursed island."

"But now the wasting has reached our shores," Martin muttered. "Entered our lands."

It was the reason they'd all been sent here, why the village road was under guard, and why their group had been sworn to secrecy with binding oaths.

"Girard found you a good body," Reginald said. "Fresher than most. A boy. He's set 'im up in the smithy." His heavy arm pointed to a wooden barn with a stacked-stone chimney.

Martin nodded and climbed out of the wagon. He had to know for sure, and there was only one way to find out. As royal coroner, this was his duty, to discern the truth from the dead. Though at the moment, he'd leave the bloodiest work to the French butcher.

Martin crossed to the smithy's open door. Girard stood inside, hunched before the cold forge. The Frenchman had labored in King William's army, where he'd sawed off limbs and done his best to keep the soldiers alive.

Girard had cleared a table in the center of the smithy and already had the boy stripped and tied to the table. Martin stared at the pale, emaciated figure. His own son was about the same age, but the manner of this death had aged the poor lad here, made him seem wizened well beyond his eight or nine years.

As Girard prepared his knives, Martin examined the boy more closely. He pinched the skin and noted the lack of fat beneath. He examined the cracked lips, the flaky patches of hair loss, the swollen ankles and feet; but mostly he ran his hands over the protuberant bones, as if trying to read a map with his fingers: ribs, jaw, eye socket, pelvis.

What had happened?

Martin knew any real answers lay much deeper.

Girard crossed to the table with a long silver blade in his hand. "Shall we get to work, *monsieur*?"

Martin nodded.

A quarter hour later, the boy's corpse lay on the board like a gutted pig. The skin, splayed from groin to gullet, had been pulled and tacked to the wooden table. Intestines lay nestled and curled tight in the bloodied cavity, bloated and pink. From under the ribs, a brownish-yellow liver swelled outward, too large for one so small, for one so wasted to bone and gristle.

Girard reached into the belly of the boy. His hands vanished into the gelid depths.

On the far side, Martin touched his forehead and mouthed a silent prayer of forgiveness for this trespass. But it was too late for absolution from the boy.

All the lad's body could do was confirm their worst fears.

Girard hauled forth the boy's stomach, rubbery and white, from which hung a swollen purple spleen. With a few slices of his knife, the Frenchman freed the section of gut and dropped it on the table. Another whispery slip of blade and the stomach was laid open. A rich green mix of undigested bread and grain spilled over the board, like some foul horn of plenty.

A fetid smell rolled out, ripe and potent. Martin covered his mouth and nose—not against the stench, but against the horrible certainty.

"Starved to death, that is plain," Girard said. "But the boy starved with a full belly."

Martin stepped back, his limbs going cold. Here was his proof. They would have to examine others to be certain. But the deaths here seemed to be the same as those on the island, a place marked in red ink as "wasted" in the Domesday Book.

Martin stared at the gutted boy. Here was the secret reason the survey had been undertaken to begin with. To search for this blight on their homeland, to stamp it out before it spread. The deaths were the same as on that lonely island. The deceased appeared to eat and eat, yet they still starved to death, finding no nourishment, only a continual wasting.

Needing air, Martin turned from the table and stepped out of shadows and into sunshine. He stared across at the rolling hills, green and fertile. A wind swept down and combed through the fields of barley and oats, wheat and rye. He pictured a man adrift in the ocean, dying of thirst, with water all around him but unable to drink.

This was no different.

Martin shivered in the wan sunlight, wanting to be as far away from this valley as possible, but a shout drew his attention to the right, toward the other end of the village green. A figure dressed all in black stood before an open door. For a moment, Martin feared it was Death himself, but then the figure waved, shattering the illusion. It was Abbot Orren, the final member of their group, the head of the Abbey of Kells in Ireland. He stood at the entrance to the village church.

"Come see this!" the abbot shouted.

Martin stumbled toward him. It was more a reflex than a conscious effort. He did not want to return to the smithy. He would leave the boy to the care of the French butcher. Martin crossed the village green, climbed the steps, and joined the Catholic monk.

"What is it, Abbot Orren?"

The man turned and headed into the church. "Blasphemy," the Irish abbot spat out, "to defile the place in such a manner. No wonder they were all slain."

Martin hurried after the abbot. The man was skeletally thin and ghostly in his oversized traveling cloak. Of them all, he was the only one to have visited the island off the coast of Ireland, to have seen the wasting there, too.

"Did you find what you were seeking?" Martin asked.

The abbot did not answer and stepped back into the crude church. Martin had no choice but to follow. The interior was gloomy, a cheerless place with an earthen floor covered in rushes. There were no benches, and the roof was low and heavily raftered. The only light came from a pair of high thin windows at the back of the church. They cast dusty streaks of light upon the altar, which was a single slab of stone. An altar cloth must have once covered the raw stone, but it had been torn away and cast to the floor, most likely by the abbot in his search.

Abbot Orren crossed to the altar and pointed to the bare stone with a trembling arm. His shoulders shook with his anger. "Blasphemy," he repeated, "to carve these heathen symbols upon our Lord's house."

Martin closed the distance and leaned closer to the altar. The stone had been inscribed with sunbursts and spirals, with circles and strange knotted shapes, all clearly pagan.

"Why would these pious people commit such a sin?"

"I don't think it was the villagers of Highglen," Martin said.

He ran his hand over the altar. Under his fingertips, he sensed the age of the markings, the worn nature of the inscribed shapes. These were clearly old. Martin remembered his driver's assertion that this place was cursed, that it was hallowed ground to the ancient Celtic people, and that their giant stones could be found hidden in the misty highland forests.

Martin straightened. One of those stones must have been hauled to Highglen and used to form the altar of the village church.

"If it's not the people here who did it, then how do you explain this?" the abbot asked. He moved to the wall behind the altar and waved an arm to encompass the large marking there. It had been painted recently, and from the brownish-red color, possibly with blood. It depicted a circle with a cross cutting through it.

Martin had seen such markings on burial stones and ancient ruins. It was a sacred symbol of the Celtic priesthood.

"A pagan cross," Martin said.

"We found the same on the island, marked on all the doors."

"But what does it mean?"

The abbot fingered the silver cross at his own neck. "It is as the king feared. The snakes who plagued Ireland, who were driven off our island by Saint Patrick, have come to these shores."

Martin knew the abbot was not referring to true serpents of the field but to the pagan priests who carried staffs curled like snakes, to the Druid leaders of the ancient Celtic people. Saint Patrick had converted or driven off the pagans from Ireland's shores.

But that had been six centuries ago.

Martin turned to stare out of the church toward the dead village. Girard's words echoed in his head. *The boy starved with a full belly.*

None of it made any sense.

The abbot mumbled behind him. "It must all be burned. The soil sowed with salt."

Martin nodded, but a worry grew in his breast. Could any flame truly destroy what was wrought here?

He did not know for sure, but he was certain about one thing.

This was not over.

Present Day
October 8, 11:55 P.M.
Vatican City

Father Marco Giovanni hid in a dark forest of stone.

The massive marble pillars held up the roof of Saint Peter's Basilica and sectioned off the floor into chapels, vaults, and niches. Works of the masters filled the hallowed space: Michelangelo's *Pietà,* Bernini's Baldacchino, the bronze statue *Saint Peter Enthroned.*

Marco knew he wasn't alone in this stone forest. There was a hunter with him, lying in wait, most likely near the rear of the church.

Three hours ago he had received word from a fellow archaeologist who also served the Church, his former mentor at the Gregorian University in Rome. He'd been told to meet him here at midnight.

However, it had proved to be a trap.

With his back against a pillar, Marco held his right hand clamped under his left arm, stanching the bleeding along his left side. He'd been cut down to the ribs. Hot liquid flowed over his fingers. His left hand clutched the proof he needed, an ancient leather satchel no larger than a coin purse. He held tight to it.

As he shifted to peer down the nave, more blood flowed. It splattered to the marble floor. He could wait no longer, or he'd grow too weak. Saying a silent prayer, he pushed off the pillar and fled down the dark nave toward the papal altar. Each pounding step was a fresh stab in his side. But he hadn't been cut with any knife. The arrow had imbedded itself in the neighboring pew after slicing open his side. The weapon had been short, stubby, black. A steel crossbow bolt. From his hiding place, Marco had studied it. A small red diode had glowed at its base, like some fiery eye in the dark.

Not knowing what else to do, Marco simply fled, staying low. He knew he would most likely die, but the secret he held was more important than his own life. He had to survive long enough to reach the far exit, find one of the patrolling Swiss Guards, and get word to the Holy See.

Ignoring his pain and terror, he ran.

The papal altar lay directly ahead. The bronze canopy over it, designed by Bernini, rested on twisted columns. Marco flanked to the left of it, aiming for the transept on that side. He spotted the massive Monument to Alexander VII and the doorway sheltered beneath it.

It was the exit out onto Piazza Santa Marta.

If only—

A punch to his belly ended any hope. He fell back a step and glanced down. No fist had struck him. A steel shaft tipped by plastic feathers stuck out of his shirt. Pain came a breath later, shattering outward. Like the first arrow, this crossbow bolt also glowed with a fiery eye. The diode rested atop a square chamber at the base of the shaft.

Marco stumbled backward. A shift of shadows near the door revealed a figure dressed in the motley clothing of a Swiss Guard, surely a disguise. The assassin lowered his crossbow and stepped out from the sheltered doorway where he'd lain in wait.

Marco retreated to the altar and made ready to flee back down the nave. But he spotted another man garbed in a Swiss uniform. The man bent near a pew and yanked the imbedded bolt from the wood.

With terror overwhelming the pain in his belly, Marco turned toward the right transept, but again he was thwarted. A third figure stepped from the shadows of a confessional box, lifting another crossbow.

He was trapped.

The basilica was shaped like a crucifix, and three of its legs were now blocked by assassins. That left only one direction to flee. Toward the apse, the head of the cross. But it was a dead end.

Still, Marco hurried into the apse.

Ahead rose the Altar of the Chair of Peter, a massive gilt monument of saints and angels that housed the wooden seat of Saint Peter. Above it, an oval alabaster window revealed the Holy Spirit in the shape of a dove.

But the window was dark and offered no hope.

Marco turned his back on the window and searched around him. To his left sat the tomb of Urban VIII. A statue of the grim reaper in the form of a skeleton climbed from the pope's marble crypt, heralding the final fate of all men . . . and perhaps Marco's own doom.

Marco whispered in Latin, *"Lilium et Rosa."*

The Lily and the Rose.

Back in the twelfth century, an Irish saint named Malachy had a vision of all the popes from his century to the end of the world. According to his vision, there would be 112 popes in total. He described each with a short cryptic phrase. In the case of Urban VIII—who was born five centuries after Malachy's death—the pope was named "the lily and the rose." And like all such prophecies, the description proved accurate. Pope Urban VIII had been born in Florence, whose coat of arms was the red lily.

But what was most disturbing of all was that the current pope was next-to-last on Saint Malachy's list. According to the prophecy, the next leader of the Church would be the one to see the world end.

Marco had never believed such fancies before—but with his fingers clutched tight around the tiny leather satchel, he wondered how close they truly were to Armageddon.

Footsteps warned Marco. One of the assassins was closing in. He had only enough time for one move.

He acted quickly. Stanching his bleeding to leave no trace, he moved off to the side to hide what must be preserved. Once done, he returned to the center of the apse. With no other recourse, he dropped to his knees to await his death. The footsteps neared the altar. A figure moved into view. The man stopped and stared around.

It was not one of the assassins.

And not even a stranger.

Marco groaned with recognition, which drew the newcomer's attention. The man stiffened in surprise, then hurried over.

"Marco?"

Too weak to gain his feet, all Marco could do was stare, momentarily trapped between hope and suspicion. But as the man rushed toward him, his bearing was plainly full of concern. He was Marco's former teacher, the man who had set up this midnight rendezvous.

"Monsignor Verona . . .," Marco gasped, setting aside any suspicions, knowing in his heart that this man would never betray him. Marco lifted an arm and raised an empty hand. His other hand clutched the feathered end of the crossbow bolt still imbedded in his belly.

A single flicker of light drew Marco's attention downward. He watched the red diode on the crossbow bolt suddenly blink to green.

No . . .

The explosion blew Marco across the marble floor. He left a trail of blood, smoke, and a smear of entrails. His belly was left a gutted ruin as he fell to his side at the foot of the altar. His eyes rolled and settled on the towering gilt monument above him.

A name rose hazily to his mind.

Petrus Romanus.

Peter the Roman.

That was the final name on Saint Malachy's prophetic list, the man who would follow the current Holy Father and become the last pope on earth.

With Marco's failure this night, such a doom could not be stopped.

Marco's vision darkened. His ears grew deaf. He had no strength left to speak. Lying on his side, he stared across the apse to the tomb of Pope Urban, to the bronze skeleton climbing out of the pope's crypt.

From its bony finger, Marco had hung the tiny satchel that he'd protected for so long. He pictured the ancient mark burned into its leather.

It held the only hope for the world.

He prayed with his last breath that it would be enough.

FIRST

The Spiral and the Cross

Tuesday, May 9—For immediate release

VIATUS SETS SIGHTS ON WORLDWIDE FOOD SECURITY

OSLO, NORWAY (BUSINESS WIRE)—Viatus International, the world's market-leading petrochemical company, announced today the creation of its new Crop Biogenetics Research and Development Division.

"The mission of the new division is to develop technologies that will boost agricultural productivity to meet the rising global demand for food, feed, and fuel," said Ivar Karlsen, CEO of Viatus International.

"With the establishment of our company's Crop Biogenics division," Karlsen said, "we intend to meet this challenge with all our resources, establishing the equivalent of an agricultural Manhattan

Project. Failure is not an option—not for our company, not for the world."

In recent years, the company's patented hybridization and transgenic technologies have increased grain, corn, and rice yields by 35 percent. Karlsen said Viatus anticipates doubling its improved yield rate within the next five years.

Karlsen explained the necessity for such a new division during his keynote speech today at the World Food Summit in Buenos Aires. Citing the World Health Organization, he noted that one-third of the world is facing starvation. "We are in a global food crisis," he said. "Most of those suffering are in the Third World. Food riots are spreading worldwide and further destabilizing dangerous regions around the globe."

Food security, Karlsen said, has surpassed oil and water as one of the new millennium's greatest crises and challenges. "Both from a humanitarian standpoint and from a concern about global security, it is vital to hasten food production through innovation and biotechnology."

Leading the way in agricultural innovation: Viatus International is a Fortune 100 company based in Oslo, Norway. Founded in 1802, Viatus provides products in 180 countries around the globe, enhancing lives and life quality through research and innovation. It is publicly traded on the NYSE under the symbol VI. The name Viatus is based on the Latin *via,* the way, and *vita,* life.

1

Gunfire woke Jason Gorman from a bone-deep sleep. It took him an extra half breath to remember where he was. He'd been dreaming of swimming in the lake at his father's vacation house in upstate New York. But the mosquito netting that cocooned his cot and the pre-dawn chill of the desert jolted him back to the present.

Along with the screams.

His heart hammering, he kicked away the thin sheet and tore through the netting. Inside the Red Cross tent-cabin, it was pitch-dark, but through the tarp walls, a flickering red glow marked a fire somewhere on the east side of the refugee camp. More flames licked into existence, dancing across all four walls of the tent.

Oh, God . . .

Though panicked, Jason knew what was happening. He'd been briefed about this before heading to Africa. Over the past year, other refugee camps had been attacked by the Tuareg rebel forces and raided for food. With the price of rice and maize trebled across the Republic of Mali, the capital had been besieged by riots. Food was the new gold in the northern districts of the country. Three million people faced starvation.

It was why he had come here.

His father sponsored the experimental farm project that took up sixty acres on the north side of the camp, funded by the Viatus Corporation and overseen by crop biologists and geneticists from Cornell University. They had test fields of genetically modified corn growing out of the parched soils of the region. The first fields had been harvested just last week, grown with only a third of the water normally necessary for irrigation. Word must have spread to the wrong ears.

Jason burst out of his tent in his bare feet. He still wore the khaki shorts and loose shirt he'd had on when he fell into bed last night. In the predawn darkness, firelight was the only source of illumination.

The generators must've been taken down.

Automatic gunfire and screams echoed through the darkness. Shadowy figures dashed and pushed all around, refugees running in a panic. But the flow was turbulent, heading this way and that. With rifle blasts and the staccato of machine-gun fire arising from all sides, no one knew in which direction to flee.

Jason did.

Krista was still at the research facility. Three months ago he had met her back in the States during his state-side briefing. She had begun sharing Jason's mosquito-netted cocoon only last month. But last night she had stayed behind. She had planned to spend the entire night finishing some DNA assays on the newly har-vested corn.

He had to reach her.

Pushing against the tide, Jason headed toward the north side of the camp. As he feared, the gunfire and flames were the most intense there. The rebels in-tended to raid the harvest. As long as no one tried to stop them, no one had to die. Let them have the corn. Once they had it, they would vanish into the night as quickly as they'd come. The corn was going to be de-stroyed anyway. It wasn't even meant for human con-sumption until further studies were done.

Turning a corner, Jason fell over the first body, a teenage boy, sprawled in the alley between the ram-shackle hovels that passed for homes here. The teen-ager had been shot and trampled over. Jason crabbed away from his body and gained his feet. He fled away.

After another frantic hundred yards, he reached the northern edge of the camp. Bodies were sprawled everywhere, piled on one another, men, women, children. It was a slaughterhouse. Some bodies had been torn in half by machine-gun fire. Across the killing field, the research camp's Quonset huts stood like dark ships mired in the West African savannah. No lights shone there—only flames.

Krista . . .

Jason remained frozen in place. He wanted to continue onward, cursing his cowardice. But he couldn't move. Tears of frustration rose to his eyes.

Then a *thump-thump* rose behind him. He twisted around as a pair of helicopters flew low toward the besieged camp, hugging the terrain. It had to be government forces from the nearby base. The Viatus Corporation had scattered bushels of U.S. dollars to insure extra protection for the site.

A shuddering breath escaped Jason. The helicopters would surely chase off the rebels. More confident, he headed across the field. Still, he kept low as he ran. He aimed for the back of the closest Quonset hut, less than a hundred yards away. Deeper shadows would hide him there, and Krista's lab was in the next hut over. He prayed she'd kept herself hidden inside there.

As he reached the Quonset's rear wall, bright light flared behind him. A brilliant searchlight speared out of the lead helicopter and swept across the refugee camp below. Jason let out a rattling sigh.

That should scare off the rebels.

Then, from both sides of the helicopter, the chatter of machine-gun fire blasted out and ripped into the camp. Jason's blood iced. This was no surgical strike against invading rebel forces. This was a wholesale slaughter of the camp.

The second helicopter swung to the other side, circling outward along the periphery of the camp. From its rear hatch, barrels rolled out and exploded on impact, casting up gouts of flames into the sky. Screams erupted even louder. Jason spotted one man fleeing off into the desert, naked, but with his skin still on fire. The fire-bombing spread toward Jason's position.

He turned and ran past the Quonset hut.

The fields and granaries spread ahead of him, but no safety would be found there. Dark figures moved on the far side of the corn rows. Jason would have to risk a final dash across the open to reach Krista's research lab. The windows were dark, and the only door faced the open fields.

He paused to steady himself. One fast dash and he could be inside the hut. But before he could move, new jets of flame burst forth on the far side of the field. A line of men bearing flamethrowers set off down the rows of corn, burning the fields that had yet to be harvested.

What the hell's happening?

Off to the right, the single granary tower exploded in a fiery whirlwind that spiraled high into the air. Shocked, but using the distraction, Jason dashed to the Quonset hut's open door and dove through it.

In the glow of the fires, the room looked unmolested, almost tidy. The back half of the hut was full of all manner of scientific equipment used in genetic and biological research: microscopes, centrifuges, incubators, thermocyclers, gel electrophoresis units. To the right were cubicles with wireless laptops, satellite uplink equipment, even battery backup units.

A single laptop, still powered by the batteries, glowed with a screensaver. It rested in Krista's cubicle, but there was no sign of his girlfriend.

Jason hurried to the cubicle and brushed his thumb over the touchpad. The screensaver vanished, replaced with a view of an open e-mail account. Again it was Krista's.

Jason stared around the hut.

Krista must have fled, but where?

Jason quickly accessed his own e-mail account and toggled the address for his father's office on Capitol

Hill. Holding his breath, he typed rapidly as he described the attack in a few terse sentences. In case he didn't make it, he wanted some record. Just before he hit the Send button, he had a moment of insight. Krista's files were still up on the screen. He dragged them, attached them to his note, and hit Send. She would not want them lost.

The e-mail failed to immediately transmit. The attached file was huge and would take an extra minute to upload. He couldn't wait. Jason hoped the battery pack would last long enough for the e-mail to go through.

Fearful of waiting any longer, Jason swung toward the door. He had no way of knowing where Krista had gone. He hoped she had fled into the surrounding desert. That was what he was going to do. Out there were mazes of gullies and dry washes. He could hide for days if necessary.

As he hurried toward the exit, a dark figure appeared and blocked the doorway. Jason fell back with a gasp. The figure stepped into the hut and whispered in surprise.

"Jase?"

Relief flushed through him.

"Krista . . ."

He hurried to her, his arms wide to take her in. They could still both escape.

"Oh, Jason, thank God!"

His relief matched hers—until she lifted a pistol and fired three times into his chest. The shots felt like punches, knocking him backward to the floor. Fiery pain followed, turning the night even darker. Distantly he heard gunfire, explosions, and more screams.

Krista leaned over him. "Your tent was empty. We thought you'd escaped."

He coughed, unable to answer as blood filled his mouth.

Seemingly satisfied with his silence, she turned on a heel and headed back out into the nightmare of fire and death. She stopped, momentarily silhouetted against the flaming fields, then vanished into the night.

Jason struggled to comprehend.

Why?

As darkness folded over him, he would have no answer to his question, but he alone heard one last thing. The laptop in the neighboring cubicle chimed. His message had been sent.

2

October 10, 7:04 A.M.
Prince William Forest
Virginia

He needed more speed.

Hunched over the narrow handlebars of the motor-cycle, Commander Grayson Pierce flew the bike around a sharp corner. He leaned his six-foot frame into the curve, nearly shearing off his kneecap as he laid the bike low around the turn.

The engine roared as he opened the throttle and straightened his trajectory. His target raced fifty yards ahead of him, riding a smaller Honda crotch rocket. Gray pursued on an older-model Yamaha V-Max. Both bikes were powered by V-4 engines, but his motorcycle was larger and weighed more. If he was going to catch his target, he would need every bit of skill.

And maybe a bit of luck.

They'd reached a short straightaway through the parklands of Prince William Forest. A dense line of hardwoods framed the two-lane road. The mix of towering beech and aspen made for a handsome scenic drive, especially now, in October, when the leaves were changing. Unfortunately, a storm last night had blown most of those leaves into patches of slippery mire on the blacktop.

Gray snapped the throttle wider. Acceleration kicked him in the pants. With the slightest wobble, the bike rocketed down the straight stretch, turning the center line into a blur.

But his target was also taking advantage of the straight road. So far, most of Route 619 had been a roller-coaster ride of sudden turns, deadly switchbacks, and rolling hills. The hour-long chase had been brutal, but Gray could not let the other rider escape.

As his target slowed for the next turn, the distance between them narrowed. Gray refused to let up. Maybe it was foolhardy, but he knew his bike's capabilities. Since acquiring it, he'd had one of the robotics engineers from DARPA—the Defense Department's research and development branch—outfit the motorcycle with a few modifications.

They owed him a favor.

Gray's own outfit—designated Sigma—served as the muscle behind DARPA. The team consisted of former Special Forces soldiers who had been retrained in various scientific disciplines to act as its field operatives.

One of the modifications to the bike was a head's-up display built into his helmet. Across his face shield, data flickered on the left side, noting speed, RPM, gear, oil temperature. On the right side, a navigational map scrolled data that projected best possible gear ratios and speeds to match the terrain.

From the corner of his eye, Gray watched the tachometer slip into the red zone. The navigational array blinked a warning. He was coming at the corner too fast.

Ignoring the data, Gray kept hard on the throttle.

The distance between the two bikes narrowed further.

Thirty yards now separated them as they hit the curve.

Ahead, the rider tilted his bike and roared around the bend. Seconds later, Gray hit the same turn. He sought to eke out another yard by hugging tighter around the blind corner, skimming the center yellow line. Luckily, at this early hour the roads through here were empty of traffic.

Sadly, the same couldn't be said for the wildlife.

Around the corner, a black bear crouched at the shoulder of the road with a cub at her side. Both noses were buried in a McDonald's bag. The first motorcycle sped past the pair. The noise and sudden appearance startled the mother bear into rearing up, and the cub acted on pure instinct and fled—right into the road.

Gray could not get out of the way in time. With no choice, he swung the bike into a hard skid. His tires smoked across the blacktop. As he hit the soft loam of the opposite shoulder, he let the bike drop and kicked away. Momentum slid him across the moist leaves on his back for a good twenty feet. Behind him, the bike hit an oak with a resounding crash.

Coming to a stop in a wet gulley, Gray twisted around. He could see the hind end of the mother bear hightailing it into the woods, followed by her cub. Apparently they'd had enough fast food for one day.

A new noise intruded.

The roar of a motorcycle, coming up fast.

Gray sat straighter. Down the road, his target had swung around and was barreling back toward him.

Oh, great . . .

Gray ripped away the chinstraps and tugged off his helmet.

The other cycle rocketed up to his position and braked hard in front of him, lifting up on its front tire. The rider was short, but muscled like a pit bull. As the bike came to a stop, the rider pulled off his helmet, too, revealing a head shaved to the skin. He frowned down at Gray.

"Still in one piece?"

The rider was Monk Kokkalis, a fellow operative with Sigma and Gray's best friend. The man's stony features were carved into an expression of concern and worry.

"I'm fine. Hadn't expected a bear in the road."

"Who does?" Monk cracked a wide grin as he booted his kickstand into place and climbed off the bike. "But don't go thinkin' of welshing on our bet. You set no rules against natural obstacles. Dinner's on you after the conference. Porterhouses and the darkest ale they have at that steakhouse by the lake."

"Fine. But I want a rematch. You had an unfair advantage."

"Advantage? Me?" Monk stripped off one of his gloves to expose his prosthetic hand. "I'm missing my hand. Along with a fair amount of my long-term memory. *And* been on disability for a year. Some advantage!"

Still, the grin never wavered as Monk offered his DARPA-engineered prosthetic. Gray took the hand, feeling the cold plastic fasten firmly on him. Those same fingers could crush walnuts.

Monk pulled him to his feet.

As Gray brushed wet leaves from his Kevlar motor-cycle suit, his cell phone chimed from his breast pocket. He pulled it out and checked the Caller ID. His jaw tightened.

"It's HQ," he told Monk and lifted the phone to his ear. "Commander Pierce here."

"Pierce? About time you picked up. I've called you four times in the past hour. And may I ask what you are doing in the middle of a forest in Virginia?" It was Gray's boss, Painter Crowe, director of Sigma.

Fighting for some adequate explanation, Gray glanced back at his motorcycle. The bike's GPS must have betrayed his location. Gray struggled to explain, but he had no adequate excuse. He and Monk had been sent from Washington to Quantico to attend an FBI symposium on bioterrorism. Today was the second day, and Gray and Monk had decided to skip the morning lectures.

"Let me guess," Painter continued. "Out doing a little joyriding?"

"Sir . . ."

The sternness in the director's voice softened. "So did it help Monk?"

As usual, Painter had surmised the truth. The director had an uncanny ability to assess a situation. Even this one.

Gray looked over at his friend. Monk stood with his arms locked across his chest, his face worried. It had been a hard year for him. He had been brutalized in an enemy's research facility where a part of his brain had been cut out, destroying his memory. Though he had recovered what was left, gaps remained, and Gray knew it still haunted him.

Over the last two months, Monk had been slowly acclimating back to his duties with Sigma, restricted though they might be. He was on desk duty and offered only minor assignments here in the States. He was limited to gathering intel and evaluating data, often beside his wife, Captain Kat Bryant, who also worked at Sigma headquarters and had a background in Naval Intelligence.

Gray knew Monk was straining at the bit to do more, to gain back the life that had been stolen from him. Everyone treated him as if he were a fragile piece of porcelain, and he'd begun to bristle at all the sympathetic glances and whispered words of encouragement.

So Gray had suggested this cross-country race through the park that bordered the Quantico Marine Corps Reservation. It offered a chance to blow off some steam, to get a little grit in the face, to take some risk.

Gray covered the phone with his hand and mouthed to Monk, "Painter's pissed."

His friend's face broke into a broad grin.

Gray returned the phone to his ear.

"I heard that," his boss said. "And if you're both done having your bit of fun, I need you back at Sigma Command this afternoon. Both of you."

"Yes, sir. But can I ask what it's about?"

A long pause stretched as if the director was weighing what to say. When he spoke, his words were careful. "It's about the original owner of that motorcycle of yours."

Gray glanced at the crashed bike. *The original owner?* He flashed back to a night two years ago, remembering the roar of a motorcycle down a suburban street, running with no lights, bearing a deadly rider, an assassin of mixed loyalties.

Gray swallowed to gain his voice. "What about her?"

"I'll tell you when you get here."

1:00 P.M.
Washington, D.C.

Hours later, Gray had showered, changed into jeans and a sweatshirt, and sat in the satellite surveillance room of Sigma headquarters. He shared the space with Painter and Monk. On the screen shone a digital map. It traced a crooked red line from Thailand to Italy.

The path of the assassin ended in Venice.

Sigma had been tracking her for over a year. Her location was marked by a small red triangle on a computer monitor. It glowed in the middle of a satellite map of Venice. Buildings, crooked streets, and winding canals were depicted in precise gray-scale detail, down to the tiny gondolas frozen in place, capturing a moment in time. That time was shown in the corner of the computer monitor, along with the approximate longitude and latitude of the assassin's location:

10:52:45 GMT OCT 9
LAT 41°52'56.97"N
LONG 12°29'5.19"E

"How long has she been in Venice?" Gray asked.

"Over a month."

Painter ran a tired hand through his hair and narrowed his eyes in suspicion. He looked exhausted. It had been a difficult year for the director. Pale from spending much of the day in offices and meetings, Painter's mixed Native American heritage was only evident in the granite planes of his face and the streak of white through his black hair, like a tucked snowy feather.

Gray studied the map. "Do we know where she's staying?"

Painter shook his head. "Somewhere in the Santa Croce area. It's one of the oldest neighborhoods of Venice, not very touristy. A maze of bridges, alleys, and canals. An easy place to keep hidden."

Monk sat back from the other two, adjusting the connection of his prosthetic hand. "So why did Seichan pick that city of all the places in the world to hole up?"

Gray glanced to the corner of the monitor. It displayed a photo of the assassin, a woman in her late twenties. Her features were a mix of Vietnamese and European descent, possibly French, with her bronzed skin, slender features, and full lips. When Gray had first met her three years ago, she'd almost killed him, shooting him point-blank in the chest. Even now he pictured her in that same turtlenecked black bodysuit, recalling how it had hugged her lithe form, hinting at both the hardness and softness that lay beneath.

Gray also pictured their last association. She'd been captured and held prisoner by the U.S. military, badly bloodied and recovering from abdominal surgery. At the time, Gray had helped her escape custody, paying back a debt owed after she had saved his own life— but her freedom had not come without a price.

During the surgery, Gray's boss had a passive polymer tracker secretly planted in her belly. It was a condition for her release, extra insurance that they'd be able to monitor her location and movements. She was too important to let go, too intimately tied to a shadowy terrorist network known as the Guild. No one knew anything about the true puppetmasters of that organization—only that it was well entrenched and had tendrils and roots globally.

Seichan claimed to be a double agent assigned to infiltrate the Guild and discover who truly ran its operations. Yet she offered no proof except her word. Gray had pretended to allow her to escape, while at the same time he kept silent about the implanted tracker. The device offered U.S. intelligence services a chance to discover more about the Guild.

But Gray suspected her decision to go to ground in Venice had nothing to do with the Guild. He felt Painter Crowe's gaze on him, as if waiting for him to come up with an answer. His boss's face was impassive, stoic, but a flicker in those ice-blue eyes suggested that this was a test.

"She's returning to the scene of the crime," Gray said and sat straighter.

"What?" Monk asked.

Gray nodded to the map overlay. "The Santa Croce area also houses some of the oldest sections of the University of Venice. Two years ago, she murdered a museum curator in that city, one connected to the same university. Killed him in cold blood. She said it was necessary to protect the man's family. A wife and daughter."

Painter confirmed the same. "The child and mother do live in that area. We've got people on the ground trying to pinpoint her location. But the tracker is passive. We can't narrow her location to less than two square miles. In case she shows up, we do have the curator's family under surveillance. With so many eyes looking for her, she must be maintaining a low profile, possibly using a disguise."

Gray remembered the strain in Seichan's face when she had tried to justify the cold-blooded murder of the museum curator. Possibly guilt, rather than the Guild, had drawn her back to Venice. But to what end? And what if he was wrong? What if this was all an artful bit of trickery? Seichan was nothing if not brilliant, an excellent strategist.

He studied the screen.

Something felt wrong about all this.

"Why are you showing me this now?" Gray asked. Sigma had been tracking Seichan for over a year, so why the sudden urgency to call him back to central command?

"Word has filtered down from the NSA, passing through the new head of DARPA and down to us. With no real intelligence gained from Seichan's freedom this past year, the powers-that-be have lost patience with the operation and have ordered her immediate capture. She's to be brought in to a black ops interrogation center in Bosnia."

"But that's insane. She'll never talk. Our best chance of discovering anything concrete about the Guild is through this operation."

"I agree. Unfortunately, we're the only ones who hold that position. Now if Sean was still heading DARPA . . ."

Painter's words trailed off into a place of pain. Dr. Sean McKnight had been the founder of Sigma and the head of DARPA at the time. Last year he'd been killed during an assault on Sigma Command. The new head of DARPA, General Gregory Metcalf, was still fresh to his position, still dealing with the political fallout following the assault. He and Painter had been butting heads ever since. Gray suspected that only the president's support of Painter Crowe kept the director from being fired. But even that support had its limits.

"Metcalf refuses to ruffle any feathers among the various intelligence communities and has sided with the NSA on this matter."

"So they're going to bring her in."

Painter shrugged. "If they can. But they have no idea who they're dealing with."

"I'm between assignments. I could head out there. Offer my help."

"Help to do what? Help find her or help her get away?"

Gray remained silent, his feelings mixed. He finally spoke firmly. "I'll do whatever is asked of me," he said, staring pointedly at Painter.

The director shook his head. "If Seichan sees you or even suspects you're in Venice, then she'll know she's being tracked. We'll lose all advantage."

Gray frowned, knowing the director was right.

The phone rang, and Painter picked up the receiver. Gray was glad for the momentary distraction as he fought to settle his thoughts.

"What is it, Brant?" Painter said. As the director listened to his office assistant's reply, the crease between his eyes deepened. "Patch the call through."

After a moment, Painter held the phone receiver toward Gray. "It's Lieutenant Rachel Verona, calling from Rome."

Gray could not hide his surprise as he accepted the phone and placed it to his ear. He turned slightly away from the other two men.

"Rachel?"

He immediately heard the tears in her voice. There was no sobbing, but her normally crisp fluency was fractured into pieces, catching between words. "Gray . . . I need your help."

"Anything. What is it?"

He had not spoken to her in months. For over a year, he'd been romantically involved with the raven-haired lieutenant, even talking marriage, but in the end it had not worked out. She was too tied down to her job with the Italian carabinieri. Likewise, Gray had deep roots both professionally and personally here in the States. The distance proved too great.

"It's my uncle Vigor," she said. Her words rushed out as if hurrying ahead of a flood of tears. "Last night. There was an explosion at Saint Peter's. He's in a coma."

"My God, what happened?"

Rachel hurried on. "Another priest was killed, one of his former students. They suspect terrorists. But I don't . . . they won't let me . . . I didn't know who else to call."

"It's okay. I can be out there on the next flight." Gray glanced back to Painter. His boss nodded, needing no explanation.

Monsignor Vigor Verona had helped Sigma in two earlier operations. His knowledge of archaeology and ancient history had proved vital, along with his intimate connections within the Catholic Church. They owed the monsignor a huge debt.

"Thank you, Gray." She already sounded calmer. "I'll forward the investigative file. But there are some details kept out of the report. I'll fill you in once you're here."

As she spoke, Gray's attention settled on the computer monitor, specifically on the glowing red tracker in the center of Venice. The photo of Seichan stared back at him from the corner of the screen, her expression cold and angry. The assassin also had a past history with Rachel and her uncle.

And now she was back in Italy.

A sense of foreboding jangled through him.

Something was wrong with this whole situation. He sensed a storm brewing out there, but he didn't know which way the winds were blowing. He knew only one thing for certain.

"I'll be there as soon as I can," he promised Rachel.

3

October 10, 7:28 P.M.
Rome, Italy

As Lieutenant Rachel Verona stepped out of the hospital and into the dusky twilight of central Rome, she took a deep breath of the crisp autumn air, her anxiety easing a little. The sting of disinfectant had barely masked the odor of bodies languishing in beds. Hospitals always smelled like dread.

For the first time in years, she wished for a cigarette, anything to smoke out the sense of apprehension that had built inside her with every passing hour as her uncle remained in a coma. He was hooked to IV lines; electrodes led to machines that monitored his vital signs; a respirator moved his chest up and down. He looked a decade older, his eyes blackened and bruised, his head shaved and wrapped. The doctors had explained: subdural hemorrhage along with a small skull fracture. They were closely monitoring his intracranial pressure. MRI showed no brain damage, but he remained unconscious, which worried the doctors. According to the medical and police report, Vigor had arrived at the hospital in a semidelirious state. Before he slipped into a coma, he kept repeating one word in a frantic manner.

Morte.

Death.

But what did that mean? Had Vigor known what had happened to the other priest? Or was it just delirium?

No one could ask him. He remained unresponsive.

Still, it bothered her. She had held his hand most of the day, squeezing it occasionally, praying for some sign of recovery. But his fingers remained lax, his skin cold, as if something vital had escaped his body, leaving only this shell behind.

What especially tortured Rachel was that she couldn't help her uncle. Vigor had practically raised her, and he was the only real family she had left. So she had sat with him all day, only leaving her vigil to make the call to the United States.

Gray would be here by morning.

It was the only bit of good news in the past twenty-four hours. Though she couldn't help Vigor medically, she could use her resources to discover the truth behind the attack.

At the moment, the investigation into the explosion at Saint Peter's had turned into a multiagency quagmire, involving everyone from Italian intelligence services to Interpol and Europol. Everyone seemed to have come to the consensus that it was a terrorist attack. This assessment rose mainly from the postmortem mutilation of the dead priest's body. A strange mark had been burned into his forehead.

Someone had definitely left a message. But what was that message and who had sent it? As of yet, no group had claimed responsibility.

Rachel knew the quickest way to discover the truth was to instigate her own investigation, something with a narrower focus, more surgical than the current chaos generated by the various agencies.

So she had called Gray. Though such a plea for help was awkward on a personal level, she recognized she would need Sigma's global resources if she hoped to discover the truth. She also recognized that she couldn't do this alone. She needed someone she could fully trust. She needed Gray.

But was the call to him more than just professional?

She pushed that last thought aside as she crossed the hospital parking garage. Reaching her small blue Mini Cooper, she climbed inside and set off across Rome. She left the top down, and the freshening breeze helped clear her head, until a trundling tour bus swooped ahead of her, belching fumes.

Rachel swung off the main thoroughfare and wound through smaller streets framed by shops, cafés, and restaurants. She had been planning to head over to her apartment, to rest and collect her thoughts before tomorrow, but instead her path wound on its own toward the Tiber River. After a few turns, the shining dome of Saint Peter's rose into view on the far bank.

She continued to let traffic funnel her toward her goal. All of Vatican City had been closed to the public since the explosion. Even the pope had been shifted for security reasons to his summer residence at Castel Gandolfo. But all that failed to halt the flow of tourists and onlookers. If anything, curiosity had thickened the throngs.

Due to the congestion, it took Rachel an extra half hour to find a parking spot. By the time she reached the police barricade that cordoned off the famous square, full night had set in. Saint Peter's Square was usually crowded with the pious and the raucous, but at the moment, it was nearly deserted. Only a few uniformed men patrolled among the columns and in the open piazza. One stood post at the foot of the Egyptian obelisk that rose in the center of the square. They all bore rifles on their shoulders.

Rachel showed her credentials at the barricade.

The policeman frowned. He was middle-aged, thick around the belly, and stood slightly bowlegged. The city police and the militarized carabinieri were not always on the best of terms.

"Why are you here?" he asked brusquely. "Why does this attack concern the Carabinieri Tutela del Patrimonio Culturale?"

It was a fair question. Her agency oversaw the theft of art and the black market trade in antiquities. It had nothing to do with domestic terrorism. She had not been authorized to be here. In fact, due to her connection with one of the victims, she had been specifically warned to keep her distance.

But she had to see the crime scene for herself.

Rachel cleared her throat and pointed forward. "I'm here to catalog and document the site of the explosion, to verify that no art was stolen following the bombing."

"So, secretarial work." His voice rippled with disdain. He added under his breath, "No wonder they sent a woman."

Rachel refused to rise to the bait. She retrieved her credentials. "If you're done, it's late and I have much work to do."

He shrugged and stepped aside, but just barely. She had to brush against him to pass. He leaned into her, pressing, trying to intimidate her with his bulk and size. Rachel knew this game. In an organization that was mostly a male fraternity, she was treated as either a threat or something to be conquered.

Anger flared, momentarily burning through her anxiety and worry. She pushed past the brute, but not before making sure her heel found the man's instep. She ground down hard as she stepped past him.

He barked in surprise and hopped back.

"Scusi," she apologized coldly and continued into the square without looking back.

"Zoccola!" he swore at her.

She ignored him as she crossed the empty piazza. To either side, the encircling arms of Bernini's colonnades embraced her. She found her pace growing quicker as she passed the obelisk and fountains and continued toward the main doors to the basilica. Overhead, the breadth of Michelangelo's dome glowed against the night sky.

Passing between the giant statues of Saint Peter and Saint Paul that stood guard before the basilica, she glanced at the inscription below the sword-bearing apostle Paul. In Hebrew, it read, "I can do all things in Him who strengthens me." She couldn't read Hebrew, but it had been her uncle Vigor who had taught her the words as a young girl. She took strength from both that message and the memory of her uncle.

With renewed determination, she climbed the steps to the entrance to Saint Peter's. She found the doors unlocked. Crossing the church portico, she passed into the cavernous nave of the basilica. It stretched almost two hundred meters ahead of her. The church was dark except for a scatter of flickering votive candles, and at the far end of the nave the papal altar shone with the glow of portable sodium lamps. Even from here, Rachel made out the crisscross of crime tape.

The explosion took place in the apse, the area behind the main altar. She headed down the center aisle, ignoring the wealth of art, architecture, and history all around her. Her attention was focused on her goal.

Reaching the main altar, she stepped to the edge of the crime scene. At this hour, the area was deserted. Over the past two days, the investigators and experts had gone over the site with their evidence bags, brushes, swabs, tubes, and vials of chemicals. It was already known that the explosive charge was a dense form of heptanitrocubane, a new class of powerful energetics.

A shiver passed through Rachel as she stared down at the scorched marble. It was the only sign left of the actual attack. Even the blood had been cleaned off. But the floor was still marked with tape, displaying splatter patterns and estimating force trajectories of the blast. On the far side of the apse, a chalk outline marked where Father Marco Giovanni's body had come to rest. He was found at the foot of the Altar of the Chair of Saint Peter, beneath the alabaster window showing the dove of the Holy Spirit.

Rachel had read the report on the young priest. He'd been a student of her uncle, a fellow Vatican archaeologist. According to the file, he'd spent the past decade in Ireland, researching the roots of Celtic Christianity, studying the early fusion of pagan rituals with the Catholic faith. He concentrated specifically on the mythos surrounding the Black Madonna, a figure often epitomized as the fusion of the pagan Earth Mother with the Virgin Mary.

Why would such an archaeologist be targeted? Or was it random? Had her uncle and his student just been at the wrong place at the wrong time?

None of it made sense.

Rachel swallowed and turned. They'd found her uncle crumpled by the papal altar, blown by the blast wave, barely conscious.

Not wanting to contaminate the crime scene, Rachel circled around the outside of the taped-off area. She climbed the two steps to the left side of the apse. There was little room. She edged along the monument to Pope Paul III, with its statues of the virtues, Justice and Prudence, done in the likeness of the deceased pope's sister and mother.

Her feet slowed.

What am I doing here?

Rachel suddenly grew too conscious of the tomblike quiet of the basilica, of the weight of ages and death, of the stacks of tombs around and below her. It didn't help that across the apse, on the far side of the crime scene, stood the sepulcher of Pope Urban VIII. A bronze statue of the pope sat atop the monument, his hand raised in blessing. But below his feet rested his tomb, and rising from the top of the tomb was a bronze skeleton. An upraised bony hand was frozen as it wrote the name of the deceased pope on an open scroll.

Rachel shivered at the sight.

She was not normally so superstitious, but with Uncle Vigor so near death himself . . . What if she lost him?

She wanted to turn away, but she found her gaze lingering on the macabre statue, the symbol of death. Then she remembered. A cold wash swept through her, raising goose bumps over her arms.

Death.

She mumbled aloud the one word Vigor had kept repeating in his delirium. *"Morte."*

She studied the bronze statue crouched atop the tomb. What if Vigor had been trying to tell them something, something he knew?

Rachel hurried back around the taped-off crime scene to the other side of the apse. She tipped up on her toes to peer more closely at the statue, but though she examined it carefully, she still almost missed it. The brown leather cord was the same color as the aged bronze.

She pulled on a pair of latex gloves and climbed up on the edge of the tomb to reach it. Grasping the cord, she freed a tiny satchel that was half-hidden behind the bony palm of the Grim Reaper. She dropped back down with her prize. Was her discovery of any significance? Or was this some bit of decoration left by a supplicant or tourist?

She noted a mark burned into the leather. It held no significance. It was a crude spiral, like some magic charm.

Disappointed, she turned the small leather pouch over. Her breath caught in her throat as she saw what was burned into the leather on this side.

A circle stamped with a cross.

She had seen this mark before.

In the forensics report on the body of Father Marco Giovanni.

The same symbol had been branded into the forehead of the dead priest. It had to be significant, but what did it mean?

Rachel knew one place to look for an answer. She teased open the pouch and dumped the contents into her palm. She frowned down at the single object. It looked like a small blackened twig. She lifted it closer—and immediately realized her error.

The twig had a fingernail.

Horrified, she almost dropped it.

What she held wasn't a twig.

It was a *human finger.*

2:55 P.M.
Washington, D.C.

Painter sat at his desk in his windowless office and rolled a bottle of aspirin between his palms. A dull ache had taken root between his eyeballs, presaging a full-blown migraine. He shook the aspirin bottle and wished for something stronger, perhaps something chased by a tall single-malt Scotch.

Still, he would trade it all for one neck massage by his girlfriend. Unfortunately, Lisa was off on the West Coast, visiting her rock-climbing brother in Yosemite. She wouldn't be back for another week. On his own, he would have to settle for the comforts of Bayer Extra Strength.

For the past hour he'd been analyzing data and reports, most of which were still posted on the giant LCD wall monitors that surrounded his desk. As he glanced at one of the screens, he wished for the thousandth time that his office had an actual window. Maybe it was that part of him that was half Mashantucket Indian, but he needed some bit of connection to blue skies, trees, and the simple rhythms of an ordinary life.

But that was never going to happen.

His office, along with the rest of Sigma Command, was buried beneath the Smithsonian Castle on the National Mall. The covert facility occupied the Castle's old WWII-era bomb shelters. The location had been picked both for its convenient access to the halls of power and for its proximity to the Smithsonian Institution's many research facilities.

At the moment, Painter would've traded it all for one window. Still, this had been his home for the past few years, and he was very protective of it. After last year's assault on the facility, Sigma was still recovering. The damage had gone much deeper than just scorched walls and destroyed equipment. Washington politics was a complicated web of power, ambition, and bitter enmities. It was a place where the weak were torn apart by the strong. And fair or not, the assault had damaged Sigma's position among U.S. intelligence forces.

To make matters worse, Painter suspected that the true masterminds of the attack were still at large. The man who had led the assault, a division chief for the Defense Intelligence Agency, had been dismissed as a rogue agent, but Painter wasn't so sure. To pull off the assault, someone had to have been supporting him, someone buried even deeper within the web of Washington politics.

But who?

Painter shook his head and glanced at the clock. Such questions would have to wait. In a few minutes, he would be heading into another firestorm. He wasn't ready to butt heads again, but he had no choice in the matter. He'd already had a heated discussion two hours ago with Gray Pierce. Gray had wanted to bring Monk Kokkalis with him to Italy, but Painter wasn't convinced Monk was ready for a full operation. Medical and psych had not yet given Gray's partner a clean bill of health.

Besides, the details were still sketchy coming out of Rome. Painter was unsure which of Sigma's operatives were best suited for the mission, which scientific discipline would complement Gray's expertise in biophysics. Monk Kokkalis's specialty was forensics, and at the moment, such skills did not seem necessary. Recognizing this, Gray had finally acquiesced, but Painter hadn't sent him out alone. Until further details were gathered, all Gray needed was some muscle.

And that he got.

As Painter pondered taking another aspirin, the intercom chimed on his desk. Brant's voice followed. "Director, I have General Metcalf holding for you."

Painter had been expecting the teleconference call. He'd read the classified e-mail from the head of DARPA. With a heavy sigh, he tapped the connection and swung his chair around to face the wall monitor behind him.

The dark screen flickered into full color. The general was seated behind a desk. Gregory Metcalf was African

American, a graduate of West Point, and though in his midfifties, he remained as sturdy and hard as when he'd been a linebacker for the Point's football team. The only signs of his age were his salt-and-pepper hair and a pair of reading glasses held in his left hand. After Metcalf was assigned to head DARPA, Painter quickly learned not to underestimate the man's intelligence.

But there remained a wariness between the two.

The general shifted forward, and without any preamble asked, "Have you read the report I sent about the conflict in Africa?"

So much for simple courtesy.

Painter motioned to one of the wall monitors. "I have. Along with pulling NATO's report about the assault on the Red Cross camp. I also did a background check on the corporation running the test farm out there."

"Very good. Then I won't have to get you up to speed on the details."

Painter prickled at the condescension. "But I still don't understand what this has to do with Sigma."

"That's because I haven't told you yet, Director."

The ache between Painter's eyeballs grew sharper.

The general tapped at a keyboard in front of him. The wall screen split away to display a still photo next to the general. The picture showed a young white male, stripped to his boxers and strung up on a wooden cross in the middle of a charred and smoky field. The image was less like a crucifixion and more like a ghoulish scarecrow. In the background, Painter noted the dry African savannah.

"The young man's name is Jason Gorman," Metcalf said coldly.

Painter's brows pulled tightly together. "Gorman. As in Senator Gorman?"

The senator's name had come up during Painter's research into the Viatus Corporation. Sebastian Gorman was head of the Senate Committee on Agriculture, Nutrition, and Forestry. He was a powerful advocate for the advancement of genetically modified foods as a means to feed the starving world and supply new biofuel resources.

The general cleared his throat, drawing back Painter's stunned attention. "That is Senator Gorman's twenty-three-year-old son. The young man had a master's degree in plant molecular biology and was working toward his doctorate, but he went to Mali mostly to serve as the senator's eyes and ears on the project over there."

Painter began to understand why this crisis had risen to the levels it had in Washington. The powerful senator, surely distraught and wanting answers about the death of his son, must be shaking all of Capitol Hill.

But still Painter did not understand Sigma's role in the matter. From the NATO report, the attack had been perpetrated by Tuareg rebels, a brutal force who were constantly plaguing the West African republic.

Metcalf continued, "Senator Gorman received an e-mail message from his son on the morning of the attack. It described the assault in a few terse sentences. From the descriptions of helicopters and napalm bombing, the attack was both militarized and large scale in force and scope."

Painter sat straighter.

"Attached to the same e-mail was a set of research files. The senator did not understand why they'd been forwarded, nor could he decipher their scientific content. Not knowing what else to do, he sent them to his son's thesis professor at Princeton University, Dr. Henry Malloy."

"I'd like to see those files myself," Painter said, beginning to understand why Sigma had been called into the matter. The strange attack, the cryptic research, all fit the scope of Sigma. Painter's mind already began charting logistics and a plan of action. "I can have someone out in the field in Mali within twenty-four hours."

"No. Your role in this matter will be limited." Metcalf's voice deepened with an implied threat. "This mess is already escalating into a political shitstorm. Senator Gorman is on a witch-hunt, looking for any and all parties to blame."

"General—" Painter began.

"And Sigma's already on fragile ground. One misstep, and no one will be able to pick up the pieces."

Painter held back a stronger refrain, letting the implied lack of confidence in his group roll off his back. He had to pick and choose which fights to have with this man. This wasn't one of them.

"So what role do you see for Sigma?"

"To gather intelligence on those files, to determine if it warrants further investigation. And the first place to start is with Dr. Malloy. I want him interviewed, and the files reviewed."

"I can have a team over there by this afternoon."

"Very good. But there is one other thing. Something that I'd like you to undertake personally."

"What's that?"

"One piece of information has been kept quiet for now. I want your take on the matter." The general tapped at his keyboard, and the photo zoomed in to Jason Gorman's face. "Whoever strung the boy up mutilated his body."

Painter stood and moved closer to the wall monitor. A symbol had been burned into the young man's brow, as if someone had taken a branding iron to him. A circle and a cross.

"I want to know why they did this," Metcalf said. "And what it means."

Painter slowly nodded.

So did he.

9:35 P.M.
Rome, Italy

Rachel slid her Mini Cooper into the assigned parking place at her apartment complex. Seated behind the wheel, she took an extra moment to think about what she'd done. On the passenger seat was a small clear plastic bag holding the old leather pouch and its macabre contents.

She had left Saint Peter's without telling anyone about what she'd discovered.

It's late, she had justified in her head. *I can turn it over to the investigators in the morning. Give a full report then.*

But Rachel recognized the deeper truth behind her theft. It had been her uncle's words that had guided her to the hidden pouch. She had felt a certain possessiveness about that discovery. If she turned the pouch over to the authorities, not only would she be reprimanded for trespassing on a case that was beyond her jurisdiction, but she could be cut totally out of the loop. She might never find out the significance of the pouch. And lastly, she could not ignore a touch of pride about the matter. No one else had found the pouch. She trusted her own gut more than the muddle and chaos that was this international and interdepartmental investigation.

And her gut told her that she was out of her league. She needed help. She would wait until Gray arrived in the morning, get his take on all of this, and go from there.

Settled on a plan of action, Rachel grabbed the evidence bag and shoved it into her jacket. She climbed out of her car and headed for the stairs. Her apartment was on the third floor. Though small, she did have a nice view of the Coliseum from her balcony.

Reaching the third floor landing, she pushed through the stairwell door. As she headed down the hallway, she noted two things. Mrs. Rosselli was cooking with too much garlic again, and a glow shone out from under her own door.

Rachel stopped. She always turned off her lights before leaving her apartment. But then again, she had been upset this morning. Maybe she had forgotten.

Not taking any chances, she lifted a bit on her toes and crept silently down the hallway. This city was plagued by thieves and pickpockets, and break-ins were not uncommon in this area. Her eyes remained fixed on the bar of light under her door. As she drew closer, a shadow passed across the glow.

Rachel's skin went cold.

Someone was in her apartment.

Swearing under her breath, she backed away. She had no weapon. She considered knocking on Mrs. Rosselli's door, getting out of the hallway, but the garlic already stung her nose. Inside the old woman's cramped apartment, the fumes would be blinding. Instead, she reached into a pocket and pulled out her cell phone.

She retreated to the stairwell door and shoved through it, keeping an eye on her door. As she stepped onto the landing, something cold pressed against the bare nape of her neck.

She recognized the barrel of a pistol.

A hard voice confirmed the threat. "Don't move."

4

October 10, 3:28 P.M.
Rockville, Maryland

Monk bounced his baby girl on his knee. Penelope squealed, wearing a goofy smile that plainly came from her father. Luckily that's all she got from him. Her light auburn curls and delicate features were all from her mother.

"Monk, if you make her spit up . . .!"

Kat crossed out of the kitchen, drying her hands on a towel. She still wore her dress blues. She had come back from Capitol Hill an hour ago, where she'd been canvassing some former intelligence contacts on behalf of Sigma, helping Painter Crowe shore up some political breeches. Her only concession to being home was to unpin her hair and let its full cascade drape below her shoulders.

Monk remained in his sweatpants and T-shirt. Since dropping Gray off at the airport, he'd come straight back to their new home in the Maryland suburbs. What else was there to do? He knew Gray had gone to bat for him, tried to get him on board for the investigation in Italy. But that had been a wash.

He shifted the baby onto his lap.

"I have her bottle warmed up," Kat said, heading toward him with her arms out to take Penelope. She suddenly tripped, hopped a step, and caught her balance. She stared down at the floor. "Monk, how many times have I told you not to leave your hand just lying around?"

Monk rubbed the stub of his wrist. "The new prosthetic still chafes."

Kat sighed heavily and took Penelope. "Do you know how much one of those costs?"

Monk shrugged. The DARPA-designed prosthetic was a marvel of bioengineering, incorporating the latest in mechanics and actuators, allowing sensory feedback and surgically precise movements. Additionally, the stumped end of Monk's wrist was encased in a polysynthetic cuff, surgically attached and wired into nerve bundles and muscle tendons.

Monk manipulated the titanium contacts on his wrist sheath. On the floor, the disembodied hand lifted onto its fingertips, powered wirelessly from the controls in the sheath. The prosthetic hand might be the brawn, but the wrist cuff was its brain. Monk directed the hand back to the couch, picked it up, and reattached it to his wrist. He flexed his fingers.

"It still chafes," he mumbled.

Kat began to turn toward the kitchen, but Monk patted the seat next to him. Kat sighed again and joined him. Monk pulled her closer, catching a whiff of her hair and the scent of jasmine. She leaned into him. They sat quietly together. Penelope dozed off, a fist curled to her lips. It was nice to hold his entire family in a single embrace.

Kat finally spoke, softly and gently. "Sorry about Italy."

Monk rolled his eyes. He hadn't said a word about the matter to her. It was a touchy subject between them. But he should've known she would find out. With all her contacts in the intelligence communities, it was hard to keep any secrets from her.

She turned to face him. He recognized the play of mixed emotions in the soft concern of her eyes and the worried line of her lips. She knew how much he wanted to get back out into the field, but her fear for him was plain to read. He glanced down at his prosthetic hand. It wasn't a baseless fear.

Still, he loved his job and knew how important it was.

For the past year, while recuperating from his injuries—both mental and physical—he had grown to recognize this more fully. While he loved his family and acknowledged his responsibilities here, he also knew how vital Sigma was to keeping the world safe. He hated being sidelined.

"I heard you have another assignment today," Kat said.

"Just more paper-pushing," he groused. "I'm off to New Jersey to interview an egghead about some research files at Princeton. I'll be back by midnight."

Kat glanced down at her watch. "Then shouldn't you be getting ready?"

"I have time. Director Crowe is sending another agent to tag along. Someone with a background in genetics. A new recruit."

"John Creed."

Monk shifted and stared her in the face. "Is there anything you don't know?"

She smiled, leaned over, and kissed him. "I know that Penelope's bottle is getting cold."

Monk's prosthetic hand tightened on her shoulder, keeping her from getting up. "And I know her bottle can be warmed up again." His voice grew huskier. "And I still have another half hour."

"A whole half hour?" She arched an eyebrow. "You are growing ambitious."

Monk's face broke into a cockeyed grin. "Don't mock me, woman."

She kissed him again, lingering now, and whispered between his lips. "Never."

4:44 P.M.
Princeton, New Jersey

Alone in the basement laboratory, Dr. Henry Malloy ran the computer simulation for the third time. As he waited, he shook his head. It made no sense. He sat back and stretched. He'd been compiling the data sent from Senator Gorman's office for the past twenty-four hours. Due to the volume of raw data, he needed the lab's Affymetrix array station to analyze all the DNA studies and assays in the files.

A knock on the door drew his attention. The lab was kept locked to help protect its ozone-free status. The facility was only accessible with a proximity keycard.

With a few minutes still to go on the assay, he crossed to the door and opened it with a whispered hush of pressurized air. It was one of his doctoral students, Andrea Solderitch. Henry had hired the woman as his aide. She was attractive, with a shapely figure and auburn hair, but she was no twenty-something coed. She was in her midfifties, changing careers, formerly a registered nurse specializing in dialysis. And with the long hours spent together, he appreciated someone who occupied his same generation. They even liked the same music, which he often caught her humming under her breath.

At the moment, though, her expression was worried.

"What is it, Andrea?" he asked.

She lifted a sheaf of Post-it notes. "Senator Gorman's office has called three times, wanting to check on your progress."

Henry took the notes. He hated to have someone breathing down his neck, but he also understood the senator's agitation. While Jason Gorman had only been Henry's student, he still felt a stabbing pang of grief at the boy's untimely death, especially with the brutality behind it.

"I also came down here to remind you that you have that appointment with Dr. Kokkalis from Washington in another hour. Did you want me to fetch you something from the cafeteria before then?"

"I'm fine, but since you're here, I can use a fresh set of eyes on this data. Especially before I talk to Washington. See what you think."

Her expression widened, barely masking her delight.

"And I appreciate you coming in on your day off," he added as he led her toward the computer station. "I couldn't have gotten this all done without your help."

"No problem, Dr. Malloy."

The computer modeling had finally finished its third run. The screen displayed the chromosomal mapping for the corn sample planted in the test field out in Africa. All of the chromosomes were black, except for a single one highlighted in white.

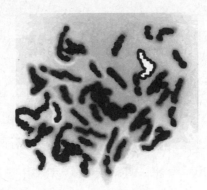

Henry tapped it on the screen. "Here you can see the radio-marked foreign DNA engineered into the genetically modified corn."

Andrea leaned closer. Curiosity crinkled her brow. "What's the source of the DNA? Bacterial?"

"Most likely. But I can't say for sure."

Still, Andrea's guess was on target. Most genetic modifications were engineered via bacterial recombination and gene splicing, taking beneficial traits of certain bacteria and incorporating them into the plant genome. One of the earliest successes was when genes from *Bacillus thuringiensis* were inserted into tobacco plants. They made the plants more insect resistant, requiring the use of less insecticide in the fields. The same method was now used in corn. Such biotechnology had grown so prevalent over the past ten years that currently one-third of all corn grown in the United States was genetically modified.

"If it's not bacterial DNA," Andrea asked, "then what?"

"I don't know. It's patented and classified by Viatus. It's only listed in the file as Dt222. The *Dt* stands for 'drought tolerant.' But that's not what I wanted to show you." Henry pointed at the screen. "This assay was sent to me by Jason Gorman two months ago."

"Two months ago?"

"I know. The boy was so excited to be involved in that African field study. He wasn't supposed to disseminate this information. It was a violation of his confidentiality agreement. I warned him to be more discreet and to keep quiet about it. I can only imagine his desperation on that last morning. Yet he still had the foresight to preserve whatever data he could."

Andrea nodded. "What did he send out that last morning?"

Henry tapped at the keyboard, bringing forth the latest data. "Let me show you. They had just harvested the first generation of corn from the seeds planted.

He sent the complete analysis of that harvest, including an entire DNA assay. Here are the results."

On the screen appeared a second batch of chromosomes. Again a majority of them were color coded in black, denoting normal corn DNA. But instead of a single chromosome in white, a second chromosome above it was stippled in white and black.

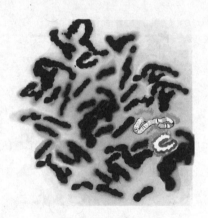

"I don't understand," Andrea said.

"Look closer."

Henry zoomed in on the picture of the transformed chromosome. It now showed a fine mapping of the individual genes, displaying a striping of black and white.

Henry explained, "The foreign DNA is incorporating itself into another chromosome, invading its neighbor."

"It's spreading?"

He sat back and stared over at Andrea. He allowed some excitement to enter his voice. "I can't say for sure. But I've compiled the data three times. Maybe the first sample that Jason sent was from a different hybrid. They could be testing more than one version of the corn out there. But if they're not, it would suggest that the genetic modification is unstable. It's changed from one generation to the next. The sample's become more *foreign* and less *corn*."

"What does that mean?"

He shrugged. "I have no idea. But someone needs to know about this. I've already passed on an inquiry to the Crop Biogenics division at Viatus. I'm sure they'll want this data. I may even be able to worm a new grant out of the corporation."

Andrea shifted to her feet. "Then maybe I can actually get that raise you keep hinting at." A shadow of a smile played over her face, catching a bit of his excitement.

"We'll see."

Andrea checked her watch. "If you don't need me, I should be getting home. My dogs have been cooped up all day. They're probably crossing their hind legs and dancing to get out."

Henry walked her to the door. "Thanks again for coming in on your day off."

Andrea paused at the door. "Are you sure I can't get you something to eat before I go?"

"No, I'm going to finalize the assay and upload it to the server. It shouldn't take long."

She waved as she exited. The door whooshed closed behind her.

Henry returned to his computer station. It would take him less than an hour to formalize his report. While the file Jason had sent from Africa cast little light on the young man's death, it did illustrate a brave heart, something his father could be proud of.

"You did good, Jason," Henry mumbled as he made a final review of all the files.

Over the next fifteen minutes, he typed a few notes and observations. He wanted to impress Viatus. Their Crop Biogenics division contracted with laboratories around the world to perform their assays, though mostly in India and Eastern Europe at the moment, where costs were cheaper. But Princeton's genomics laboratory was one of the best in the world. If he could persuade the corporation to toss a little business their way . . .

A slow smile spread as he worked.

A knock on the door interrupted him again. His smile widened. If he knew Andrea, she had not taken him at his word. She must have gone to the cafeteria to fetch him a bite to eat.

"Be right there!" he called out. He crossed the lab and swiped his proximity keycard to unlock the door.

5:30 p.m.

Monk climbed into the cab outside the train station. His partner was already in the backseat, giving directions to the driver.

"Carl Icahn Lab on the Princeton campus. It's on Washington Road."

Monk settled into the seat next to him, straightened his suit jacket, and leaned back. He rested a briefcase on his lap. He stared down at the custom-made Tanner Krolle case and ran a hand over its English bridle leather. It had been an anniversary gift from Kat two months ago, when he'd formally returned to duty, as limited as it might be. He understood the unspoken message behind the expensive purchase. Kat was more than happy to have him pushing papers and conducting routine debriefings and interviews. Anything to keep him out of harm's way.

He sighed, earning a glance from his new partner.

John Creed hunched a bit in his seat. Though wiry as a starved terrier, the man stood within a fingerbreadth of seven feet. He was one of Sigma's newest recruits, clean-shaven, with lanky red hair, freckled over most of his face. Despite his boyish features, his expression remained steadily dour.

Monk frowned and asked him a question that had been nagging him since they'd first met. "So, kid, how old are you? Fourteen? Fifteen?"

"Twenty-five."

Monk tried to hide his doubt. That seemed impossible. *Only seven years separated them?* Monk flexed his prosthetic hand, aware that a lot could happen over seven years. Still, he studied his companion more closely for the first time, trying to size him up.

On the train ride from Washington, Monk had read through the details about Dr. Henry Malloy, but he knew only the briefest bio on his traveling companion. Creed was from Ohio, had quit medical school after one year, and served two tours in Kabul as a grunt. Shrapnel from an IED had left him with a permanent limp. He tried for a third tour but ended up out of the service, though the details on that were less clear. Due to his test scores and background, he was recruited by Sigma and trained in genetics at Cornell.

Still, the kid looked like he could be in high school.

"So, Doogie," Monk continued, "how long have you been active?"

Creed just stared at Monk, plainly accustomed to ribbing about his baby-faced looks. "Finished Cornell three months ago," he said stiffly. "Been in D.C. for two months. Mostly getting settled in."

"So this is your first assignment?"

"If you call this an assignment . . .," he mumbled, and stared out the passenger window.

Though Monk felt the same way, he still bristled. "Nothing's trivial when it comes to fieldwork. Every detail matters. The right piece of information can make or break a case. It's something you need to learn, Doogie."

Creed glanced to him. His dour look turned a bit sheepish. "Okay. Point taken."

Monk folded his arms, hardly satisfied.

Kids. Think they know everything.

Shaking his head, Monk turned his attention outside as the cab crossed onto the Princeton campus. It was as if a verdant chunk of England had been dropped into the middle of New Jersey. Autumn leaves spread across rolling green lawns, ivy climbed walls of stately gothic stone buildings, even the dormitories looked like something out of Currier and Ives.

As they glided through this bucolic world, it did not take them long to reach their destination. The cab pulled to the curb, and they climbed out.

The Carl Icahn Laboratory occupied a corner of a wide green expanse. While many of Princeton's structures dated to the eighteenth and nineteenth centuries, the laboratory was only a few years old, a stunning example of modern architecture. Two rectangular buildings stood perpendicular to one another, housing the main labs. Joining them together was a two-story curved atrium, facing the parklands.

That's where they were to meet Dr. Henry Malloy.

"Ready?" Monk asked and checked his watch. They were five minutes late.

"Ready for what?"

"The interview."

"I thought you'd conduct the debriefing of the professor."

"Nope. It's all you, Doogie."

Creed sighed heavily through his nose. "Fine."

They entered the building and crossed into the atrium. A curving two-story wall of glass faced the park's lawn. Forty-foot-tall louvers sectioned the windows and were timed to move with the sun. They cast shadows deep into the atrium, dappling across chairs and tables. Spatters of students sat and chatted, their hands permanently glued to coffee cups.

Monk searched and spotted where he was supposed to meet Dr. Malloy. It was hard to miss. "This way," he said and led his companion across the atrium.

Off by a set of stairs rose a one-story sculpture. It looked like a half-melted conch shell. Even if not informed about it, Monk would have recognized the architectural design as Frank Gehry. The conch shell sheltered a small meeting place within its folds. A few people were already seated at a square conference table.

Monk crossed to join them. As he approached, he realized they were all too young. In his briefcase, Monk had a photograph of Dr. Malloy. The man was definitely not here.

Maybe the professor had come and gone already.

Monk stepped out of the conch and pulled out his cell phone. He dialed the man's office number. It rang and rang, then went to voice mail.

If he's already left, and I came all this way for nothing . . .

Monk dialed a second number. It was for the doctor's assistant.

A woman answered. Monk quickly explained about Dr. Malloy's absence.

"He's not there?" his assistant asked.

"No one here but a lot of kids who look like junior high students."

"I know," the woman said with a laugh. "Students just keep getting younger, don't they? And I'm sorry, but Dr. Malloy must still be in his lab. That's where I last saw him, and he never hears his cell phone. He can get so focused on what he's doing that he'll work right through a scheduled lecture. I feared as much today, so stuck around. He's very excited about what he's discovered."

Monk perked up with her last words. Had the professor figured something out, something that might help the case?

"Listen," the woman continued, "I'm just across the street in my office, finishing some work with my lab partner. There's an underground walkway that connects my building to yours. Ask one of the students. I'll borrow a keycard from the administrator and meet you down there. Dr. Malloy's lab is on the basement level. I imagine he'll want to show you the DNA assay himself."

"Okay. I'll meet you there." Monk pocketed his phone and waved his briefcase at Creed. "C'mon. We're heading directly to the guy's lab."

After getting directions from a coed in a very tight sweater, Monk led the way down to the basement level. The underground passageway was easy enough to find.

As they approached the tunnel entrance, a middle-aged woman waved to them from the other side. Monk waved back. She hurried over, out of breath, holding out her hand.

"Andrea Solderitch," she introduced herself.

After the introductions, she led them down a neighboring hallway. She talked almost nonstop, plainly nervous.

"There are only a few labs down here. So it's easy to get lost. Most everything else is storage rooms, mechanical spaces . . . oh, and the building's vivarium, where they house the lab animals. The genomics department keeps its microarray facility down here to keep it ozone free. It's right over here."

She lifted the keycard in her hand and approached a closed door.

"The department administrator tried calling the lab," she explained. "No answer. I'll just pop a look inside. I'm sure he wouldn't have left the campus."

She waved the card and pulled the handle. As the door whooshed open, Monk immediately smelled smoke, electrical from the tang to it—and beneath it, a stench, like burned hair. He grabbed for Andrea, but he was too slow. She saw what was inside. Her face dissolved into confusion, then horror. A hand rose to cover her mouth.

Monk pulled her to the side and passed her to Creed. "Keep her here."

He dropped his briefcase and reached to the shoulder holster inside his suit jacket. He pulled out his service pistol, a Heckler & Koch .45. The woman's eyes widened. She turned away, pushing her face into Creed's shoulder.

"Do you have a weapon?" Monk asked him.

"No . . . I thought this was just an interview."

Monk shook his head. "Let me guess, Doogie. You were never a Boy Scout."

Not waiting for an answer, Monk entered the lab, sweeping the blind spots. He was sure whoever had been here had come and gone, but he wasn't taking any chances. Dr. Henry Malloy was tied to a chair in the middle of the room. His head hung to his chest. Blood pooled under the chair.

A computer station behind him was a charred ruin.

Monk glanced around. They'd disabled the smoke detectors.

He crossed to the man and checked for a pulse. Nothing. But the body was still warm. The murderers hadn't been gone long. Monk noted the doctor's broken fingers. He'd been tortured. Most likely for information.

The killing blow had been a knife to the chest, one strike, expertly done. From the swift death, Malloy must have talked.

Monk sniffed. The burning stench was stronger by the body. He recognized the smell of charred flesh. With a finger, he gently lifted the man's chin. The head lolled back, revealing the source of the smell. In the center of the man's forehead, a raw burn, still blistering at the edges, marked his flesh, all the way down to the bone.

A circle and a cross.

A ringing chime drew his attention back to the doorway. It came from a cell phone. Not wanting to contaminate the scene any further, Monk retreated to the hall.

Andrea had her cell phone to her ear. Her eyes were damp, her nose running. She sniffed as she listened. "What?" she asked, less a question than an expression of shock. "No! Why?"

She fell against the wall and slumped to the floor. The phone tumbled from her fingers. Monk dropped to a knee beside her.

"What's wrong?"

She shook her head in disbelief. "Someone . . ." She pointed at the phone. "That was my neighbor. She heard my dogs barking, saw someone leaving my house. She went over. Door was open. They . . . they killed my dogs." She covered her face with her hands. "Why didn't I go straight home like I told Dr. Malloy?"

Monk glanced at Creed. His brows were pinched together, not understanding.

Monk did. He reached over and pulled the woman to her feet. "How long ago did your neighbor see the intruder?"

She shook her head, struggling for words. "I . . . I don't know. She didn't say. She called the police."

Monk glanced back to the body of Dr. Malloy. The professor had talked. Named names. Most likely including his assistant's. Dr. Malloy had thought Andrea had been headed home. He must have given the torturer her home address. They'd gone off to silence her.

And not finding her there . . .

It would take only a few inquiries, a few calls.

"We have to get out of here. Right now!"

Monk pointed back the way they'd come. As a group, they rushed down the hall toward the underground passageway. It crossed beneath the street to the neighboring university building, where Andrea had been working.

"You said you were at your office with your lab partner," Monk said as he hurried down the hall. "Did your partner know where you were headed?"

He got his answer as they reached the mouth of the tunnel. A tall man marched down the passageway toward them, dressed in a dark rain slicker—and it hadn't rained in days.

Their eyes met across the space.

Monk recognized a feral gleam. He pushed Andrea back and raised his pistol. At the same time, the man lifted his arm, parting his slicker to reveal a snub-nosed machine gun. He strafed the end of the passageway. The odd weapon made no more noise than a cake mixer, but rounds chewed into the corner behind which they'd vanished. Plaster and tile exploded and flew.

"The stairs!" Monk ordered and pointed back toward the atrium.

As they reached the bottom of the stairwell, footsteps echoed down from above.

Monk halted everyone. Looking up, he spotted a man hurrying down in boots and a black slicker, the same as the first. A second assassin. Retreating, he herded everyone back into the maze of hallways.

They had to find another way out.

As they fled into the dimly lit halls, a heavy metal door slammed somewhere on the opposite side of the basement.

Monk turned to Andrea.

"I think that came from the emergency exit," she whispered in bald terror.

Monk could guess what that meant.

A third assassin.

5

"The symbol's not in the database of any known terrorist group," Painter said. He stood before a conference table with a wall screen behind him. Glowing on the monitor was a blown-up rendering of the cross and circle.

Painter leaned on the table. The conference room was a new addition to Sigma Command, built after the firebombing. It held a circular table with computer stations before each chair. It could hold as many as a dozen people, but at the moment only three people were seated there.

Kat sat to Painter's immediate right, bringing her international intelligence experience to the table. On her right was Adam Proust, an expert in cryptology, and across the table, Georgina Rowe, a new Sigma recruit whose expertise was bioengineering.

"So we start at square one," Painter said and began to pace around the conference table. He had designed the room for just this purpose, to be able to move, to be able to observe those gathered around the table. "*What* does this symbol mean? *How* does it connect to the destruction of the Red Cross camp and the mutilation of the senator's son?"

Adam cleared his throat and half-lifted a hand toward the screen. He was in his midforties, casually dressed in jeans, a thin black sweater, and tweed sportcoat. "This mark has a long symbolic history, going back as far as early man. It's sometimes referred to as a quartered circle. The meaning is relatively uniform across cultures. The circle represents the earth. The cross, in turn, sections the world into four pieces. In Native American culture, those four pieces represent—"

"The four winds," Painter acknowledged. He had been taught something similar by his father.

"Precisely. And in other cultures, it represents the four elements—earth, wind, air, and fire. Sometimes they're represented thusly." He tapped at his computer station and the screen changed.

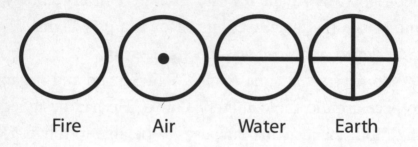

Fire   Air   Water   Earth

"As you can see, the quartered circle becomes the symbol for the earth itself, encompassing all four elements. This mark can be found around the globe. The historical etymology of the symbol is quite fascinating and goes back to pagan times. In several Nordic countries the mark can be found carved into slabs and standing stones. It's often accompanied by another petroglyph: the pagan spiral. The two are intimately related to one another."

"Related?" Painter asked. "How so?"

Adam lifted a hand, asking for a moment, and typed at his station. A new image appeared on the screen. "Here's a stylized pagan spiral. You can find variations of this around northern Europe."

Another tap at the screen placed the spiral over the quartered circle.

"See how the spiral starts at the center of the cross and expands outward to fill the circle. While the quartered circle represents the earth, the spiral is meant to symbolize life, specifically the journey of the soul, rising from life to death to rebirth."

Kat sighed. "This is all well and good, but I don't see how this relates to the atrocities committed in Africa. Aren't we getting off topic?"

"Maybe not," Georgina Rowe argued and shifted straighter in her seat. She was a stocky woman, her hair cut into a masculine bob. "I've reviewed the NATO report, and while details are still preliminary and far from definitive, I can't help but believe the attack had more to do with destroying the Viatus Corporation's farm there than with some rivalry between rebels and the Mali government."

"And I agree," Kat said. "The Tuareg rebels have never demonstrated this level of violence. Theirs have mostly been hit-and-run types of attacks. Not this wholesale slaughter."

"And trussing up that poor boy in the middle of a burned-out cornfield and branding him with that mark." Georgina shook her head sadly. "It had to be a warning against what that corporation was doing out there, its research into genetically modified foods. With my background in bioengineering, I'm well aware of the controversy surrounding GM foods. There's a growing movement against such manipulation of nature. And while it mostly stems from fear and misinformation, it's also compounded by the lax government supervision of this exploding industry. I can go into more detail . . ."

Painter stopped across from her. "For now, let's concentrate specifically on how it might relate to this case."

"That's easy enough. The anti-GM movement is especially strong in Africa. The countries of Zambia and Zimbabwe recently banned all food aid that contained GM foods, even though millions in both countries faced starvation. Basically it was a foolish policy of *better dead than fed*. Such lunacy is rampant and growing. I believe that the destruction of the Red Cross camp was meant as an attack on Viatus." She pointed to the symbol on the screen. "And I think Adam's description of the etymology of that symbol supports that."

Painter began to understand. "A symbol that represents the earth."

Georgina firmed her voice to match her conviction. "Whoever did this believes they're protecting the earth. I think we're dealing with a new and militant ecoterrorist group."

Kat's brows pinched together. "It does make a certain amount of sense. I'll have my sources concentrate on that angle. See if we can't figure out who these terrorists are and where they're based."

Painter turned back to Adam Proust, whose insight had offered a place to start. "We cut you off. Is there anything you wanted to add?"

"Just one more thing. About the quartered circle and the spiral. The two symbols were powerfully important and significant to the pagans of northern Europe. Especially the Druids. In fact, when the Nordic regions were converted to Christianity, the symbols became incorporated into the new faith. The Druid cross grew to become the Celtic cross used today."

Adam tapped a new image onto the screen, extending the vertical line of the pagan symbol to form a Christian cross.

"Likewise," Adam continued, "the spiral came to represent Christ, symbolizing his passage from life to death and finally his rebirth."

"And the significance of this?" Kat asked, impatient, plainly anxious to follow the bread crumbs left by Georgina's words.

But Painter recognized where Adam might be heading with this last assessment. He asked the cryptologist, "So you don't think this ecoterrorist group is based in Africa?"

He shook his head. "The quartered circle, while it can be found in some African cultures, mostly represents a sun symbol rather than the earth. I think we should be directing any inquiries toward northern Europe. Especially since the Viatus Corporation's headquarters are in Oslo, Norway."

Georgina smiled. "So in other words, we're looking for a bunch of pissed-off Druids."

Adam didn't return her smile, only shrugged. "There is a strong neopagan revival throughout Europe. And in fact, many of these groups are quite old. The Druid Circle of the Universal Bond. The Ancient Order of Druids. Both trace their organization back to the 1700s, while other groups claim an even longer heritage. Either way, the movement has been growing steadily of late, and a few sects are definitely militant in their beliefs and very anticorporation. I think that's where any investigation should concentrate. In northern Europe."

Kat nodded, if a bit stiffly, already planning in her head.

Painter circled back to the front of the conference room. "I think that gives us a good jumping-off point. If you'll all—"

His cell phone rang in his pocket, cutting him off. Painter lifted a hand, asking for a moment, took out his BlackBerry, and checked the ID. It was his assistant. Painter felt a twinge of misgiving. He had asked not to be disturbed unless it was an emergency.

"What is it, Brant?"

"Sir, operations just phoned in. There's been a flurry of 911 emergency calls coming out of Princeton. It seems a firefight has broken out at the Carl Icahn Laboratory."

Painter kept his face passive. The lab was where Monk Kokkalis and John Creed had been headed. The pair should've reached Princeton an hour or so ago. Painter deliberately kept his gaze away from Kat, Monk's wife.

"Get local authorities on the line and satellite feed up," Painter said, feigning more irritation than alarm. "I'll be right up there."

He lowered the phone and faced the room. "Okay, you all know your duties. Let's get to it."

Painter turned on his heel and headed toward the exit.

He sensed Kat's gaze fixed on his back. She was suspicious, but until he knew more about the situation, there was no need to alarm her.

Especially since she was pregnant again.

6:45 P.M.

Monk led the others through the basement, keeping his pistol pointed forward. He only had ten rounds . . . and at least three assailants. Not good odds, especially with the others carrying snub-nosed machine guns. He dared not waste a single shot. He'd left a second magazine back in his briefcase, but he'd dropped the case outside Malloy's lab.

"Is there another way out of here?" he asked Andrea.

"No . . . but . . ." She searched up and down the hall. John Creed kept a hold on her elbow to keep her moving.

"But what?" Monk pressed.

"The lab building was constructed to be modular. To make it easier to change room configurations," she said in a rush, then pointed up. "There's a large maintenance level between floors. With catwalks for work crews."

Monk glanced at the ceiling. That might work. "Where's the closest access point?"

She shook her head, still struggling with shock. "I don't know . . ."

Monk stopped and grabbed her shoulder with his prosthetic hand. "Andrea, take a breath, steady your—"

Machine-gun fire blasted. A figure rounded the far end of the hallway, his gun blazing. Rounds tore into the floor and walls. Monk shouldered into Andrea and fired blindly down the hall, wasting precious ammunition. The gunman ducked momentarily away. Monk shoved the woman through the closest door. Creed bowled through after them.

The door led to a small anteroom. A second set of double doors stood directly in front of them.

"Go!" Monk yelled.

They piled through into the next room. Lights flickered on automatically and revealed a large space divided by rows of stainless-steel cages. The smell of animal urine and musky bodies struck Monk immediately. He remembered Andrea's description of the basement level's layout. This must be the lab's vivarium, where its research animals were housed. A dog barked from one of the back rows. Closer at hand, smaller bodies stirred—and some not-so-small bodies.

Along the bottom row of larger cages, potbellied pigs snorted and nosed the air. Some squealed and spun in circles. They were young, each about the size of a football, bringing new meaning to the term *pigskin*.

Monk pushed the others down the row. They had no way to barricade the door, and the gunman would be on them any moment.

"Is there another exit from here?" Monk asked Andrea.

She nodded and pointed across the room.

"Hurry."

Monk heard clanking behind him. He turned to see Creed flipping open the lower cages as he chased after them. In his wake, small black-and-pink bodies tumbled out of their cages. They scurried and danced, squealed and screamed. More and more pigs joined the fray.

"What are you—?" Monk began.

"Obstacles," Creed said, yanking more cages open.

Monk nodded, understanding. Nothing like littering their trail with scores of squealing footballs. It should slow the gunman down.

They had almost reached the far end of the vivarium when Monk heard the double doors bang open behind them. A short spatter of gunfire followed, but it quickly ended with a startled bark, followed by the clattering fall of a body to the floor.

Chalk one up for the pigskins.

Monk pushed Andrea to the end of the hall and through another set of double doors. Moments later they were back in a basement hallway.

"Those access points into the maintenance spaces," Monk pressed. "Is there one nearby?"

"The only one I know about for sure is back at Dr. Malloy's lab."

Monk studied the crisscrossing hallways and maze of rooms. He was lost. "Can you get us back there?"

"Yes. It's this way."

Andrea headed off, less shocked, more determined. Monk kept to her side. Creed followed. Monk noted him clutching his upper thigh. His pant leg was damp.

Creed met his gaze and waved him on. "Took a ricochet. Just grazed. Keep going."

They had no choice. After another turn, Monk suddenly recognized the hallway. They'd come full circle back to Dr. Malloy's lab. Confirming this, Monk spotted his briefcase resting in the hall outside the open door.

They headed toward it at a full run.

Down the opposite end of the hall, another gunman appeared with a swirl of his black rain slicker. The open lab door still lay another ten yards away.

Monk kept his arm level and fired at the assailant. "Keep going!" he yelled as Andrea and Creed slowed. "Make for the lab!"

While it might be crazy to run *toward* a man wielding a machine gun, the room offered the only hope of escape.

Monk fired another two rounds. He was almost out, but the shots kept the assailant off balance. Unfortunately, the brief firefight had not gone unnoticed. Behind them, a new barrage erupted. Another gunman. The attackers were trying to trap them in a crossfire.

But by now, they'd reached the lab.

Andrea and Creed dashed inside. Monk bent down as the whine of a round ripped past the crown of his head. He snatched his abandoned briefcase and rolled sideways into the laboratory.

As soon as he was through, Creed slammed the door behind him.

"Locks automatically," Andrea said, hugging her arms around her chest. She kept well clear of the chair where Dr. Malloy's body was still tied.

Monk gained his feet, holding his pistol in one hand and his Tanner Krolle briefcase in the other. "That maintenance access?"

Andrea turned and pointed toward the ceiling above a lab table. A square panel was marked by an electrical hazard symbol.

Monk turned to Creed. "Get her up there. Keep moving."

"What about you?"

"Don't worry about me. I'll be right behind you. Now move it!"

As Creed lifted Andrea onto the table, Monk dropped to one knee. He needed to buy the others as much time as possible to get away. Monk knew it was vital to get the woman to safety. Dr. Malloy must have told her something, something worth killing her over. Whatever that was, Monk wanted to know.

Creed already had the maintenance hatch open and used both arms to shove Andrea through it.

Sheltering behind the dead body in the chair, Monk snapped his briefcase and let it drop open on the floor. All the while, he kept an eye on the door. Locked or not, he knew the door would offer no more protection than a piece of tissue paper. Especially with the firepower behind these bastards.

And Monk was down to the last two rounds in his pistol. He needed the fresh magazine in his briefcase.

As he reached for the spare, the doorknob exploded into the room, along with a good section of the jamb. The door swung open from the impact.

Monk caught a fluttering glimpse of a black slicker and fired at it. Twice. His pistol slide locked open as he ran out of ammunition.

The gunman spun out of view.

Monk snatched for the new magazine while ejecting the spent one. From the corner of his eye, he spotted an arm wave beyond the doorway. A black metal object the size of a baseball flew into the room.

Oh, crap . . .

Grenade.

Monk dropped both pistol and spare cartridge. Still on one knee, he lifted his open briefcase, caught the grenade inside, and snapped the case shut between his palms. Standing and swinging his arm around, he underhanded the briefcase back through the open doorway.

Even before it passed the threshold, Monk was moving. He turned, leaped to the tabletop, then bounded straight for the open ceiling hatch. Creed's boots had just vanished ahead of him.

"Go!"

Too late.

The explosion deafened and flashed brilliantly. The blast wave shoved Monk up into the crawl space between floors. He struck some HVAC ductwork with his head and collapsed on top of Creed. They struggled for a bit to untangle themselves. Monk took an elbow to an eye.

Cursing and dazed, Monk waved the others onward. He doubted the gunmen would follow them, but until they were somewhere safe and sound, somewhere with lots of guns, he wasn't going to let his guard down.

They stumbled onward, half deaf, half blind.

As Andrea had said, the maintenance space was equipped with catwalks to assist the work crews. Using the walkways, it didn't take long to climb out of the bowels of the building and into the chaos above. Police had already converged on the place. Squad cars, SWAT vans, and a gathering media circus greeted them in the fields outside the building.

As they stumbled into the open, police surrounded them immediately. Even before Monk could begin to explain, a hand grabbed him, pulled him aside, and showed him a badge.

"Homeland Security," the mountain of a man declared. "Dr. Kokkalis, we have orders from Washington to get you all to safety."

Monk didn't protest. He liked those orders just fine. But as they were led off, he glanced forlornly back at the building.

Kat was going to kill him.

That briefcase was damn expensive.

6

Where was she?

Gray crossed out of the terminal of Rome's main airport and headed toward the taxi queue. Horns blared and tour buses rumbled. Even this early in the morning, the airport was snarled with traffic and congested with travelers coming and going.

Gray kept his phone pressed to his ear as he hustled through the crowds. His way was made easier by the lumbering giant who forged a path ahead of him, like a water buffalo fording a flooded river. Gray followed behind in his bodyguard's wake. Joe Kowalski was not a happy traveler. The former seaman clearly preferred the high seas to commercial air travel. He continued to grouse as they headed toward the taxi line.

"Could those seats have been any tighter?" The hulking man cracked his neck and wore a sour expression. "My knees were practically rubbing my ears. Like that airline wanted to perform a damn prostate exam on me. And I wouldn't have minded that if we'd had one woman stewardess." Kowalski glanced back at Gray. "And that gal with a mustache doesn't count."

"You didn't have to volunteer to come," Gray answered as he waited on hold on the phone.

"Volunteer?" Kowalski scowled. "At time-and-a-half pay? That was like putting a gun against my back. I've got a girlfriend to support."

Gray still failed to understand the relationship between the former seaman and the university professor, but at least she had him showering more frequently. Even the black stubble atop Kowalski's head was trimmed into cleaner lines.

Gray waved an arm to keep them moving. He remained on hold with the office of the Comando Carabinieri Tutela del Patrimonio Culturale, where Rachel worked. Before leaving Washington, the plan had been to rendezvous with her outside the international terminal, but she was not anywhere among the throngs of travelers. He had tried calling her apartment and her cell phone, but there was no answer. Thinking she was stuck in traffic, Gray had waited in the terminal for an extra half hour.

During that delay, he had used the time to check in with Sigma. It was a little past midnight back home. The director had filled him in on the details of the operation that had blown up in New Jersey. Monk had been involved in a firefight. It all involved a possible ecoterrorist group, but details were still sketchy.

Hearing that, Gray had an urge to hop on the plane and head back home, but Painter insisted that they had matters locked down for the moment. A key person-of-interest had been secured and was being questioned. Gray was ordered to maintain his current status.

Finally a woman's stern voice spoke in Gray's ear, speaking rapidly in Italian. After dating Rachel for over a year, Gray had acquired some fluency with the language.

"Lieutenant Verona is not in the TCP today. According to the roster, she's on leave. Perhaps another officer might assist you—"

"No, thank you. *Grazie.*"

Gray hung up and pocketed his phone. He knew Rachel had been planning to take time off, but he'd hoped she was at the station for some reason. He grew worried. Where could she be?

Kowalski hailed a taxi, and they climbed inside.

His partner glanced at him. "How about that hospital?" he said. "The one where her uncle is being treated?"

"Right." Gray nodded. He should've thought of that. Maybe her uncle had taken a turn for the worse. Such an emergency would've pulled Rachel away. Distraught, she could easily have forgotten about the time.

Gray dialed information and got connected to the hospital operator. An attempt to reach Vigor's room failed. He did reach a floor nurse.

"Monsignor Verona remains in intensive care," the woman informed him. "Any further inquiries must be made through his family or through the *polizia*."

"I just wanted to know if his niece might be there visiting. Lieutenant Rachel Verona."

The woman's voice warmed up. "Ah, his *nipote* Rachel. *Bellissima ragazza*. She spent many hours here. But she left last night and has not come in this morning."

"If she does show up, can you let her know I called?" Gray left his number.

Pocketing his cell phone, he sagged in his seat. He stared at the passing scenery as the taxi sped along the interstate toward downtown Rome. Rachel had arranged a room at a small Italian bed-and-breakfast. Gray had stayed there before. Back when they were dating.

He struggled to think of any other reason why Rachel would not have shown up. Where could she be?

Worry edged toward panic. He willed the taxi to go faster.

He would check for any messages at the hotel, then head directly over to her apartment. It was only a handful of blocks from the hotel.

Still, it would take time to get there.

Too much time.

With each passing mile, his heart pounded harder, his left hand tightened on his knee. As they finally passed through one of the ancient city gates and headed into central Rome, the taxi's passage became a crawl. The streets grew narrower and narrower. Pedestrians scooted sideways; a bicycle zigzagged between the cars.

At last the taxi pulled into a side street and came to a stop in front of the small hostelry. Gray hopped out, grabbed his bag, and left Kowalski to pay the driver.

The hotel appeared nondescript from the street. A small brass plaque on a wall, no larger than Gray's palm, read Casa di Cartina. The hotel had been converted out of three adjoining buildings, all dating from the eighteenth century. A half flight of stairs led down to a small lobby.

Gray headed below. The reason for the hotel's name became apparent as soon as the brush of the hanging bell announced Gray's entrance. All four walls of the room were covered with ancient maps and bits of cartography. The hostelry's owners came from a long line of world travelers and mariners, stretching back to before Christopher Columbus.

A wizened old man in a buttoned vest met Gray behind a small wooden front desk. His face cracked into a warm smile. "It has been a long time, Signor Pierce," the proprietor said warmly in English, recognizing Gray.

"It has, Franco."

Gray exchanged a few pleasantries, long enough for Kowalski to come striding into the space. The larger man's eyes swept the walls. With a background in the navy, he nodded his approval at the choice of decor.

"Franco, I was wondering if you had heard any word from Rachel." Gray forced his voice not to sound strained. "I was hoping she'd left a message."

The man's face crinkled in confusion. "A message?"

Gray felt a sinking in his chest. Clearly there had been no message. Maybe she was back at her—

"Signor Pierce, why would la signorina Verona leave a message? She is already up in your room, waiting for you."

Gray's relief felt like a rush of cold water. "Upstairs?"

Franco reached into a cubby behind his desk, removed a key, and passed it to Gray. "Fourth floor.

I gave you a nice balcony room. The view of the Coliseum is very nice from that room."

Gray nodded and took the key. *"Grazie."*

"Can I have someone bring up your bags?"

Kowalski scooped Gray's duffel from the floor. "I got it." He bumped Gray in the rear with his bag to get him moving.

Gray thanked Franco again and headed to the stairs. It was a narrow, winding way, more ladder than stairwell. They had to go single file. Kowalski eyed it doubtfully.

"Where's the elevator?"

"No elevator." Gray set off up the stairs.

Kowalski followed. "You've got to be goddamn kidding me." He wrestled to get himself and the bags up. After two flights, his face had turned a deep red and a string of curses flowed in a continual stream.

Reaching the fourth floor, Gray followed the wall signs to find their room. The layout was a convoluted maze of sharp corners and sudden dead ends.

He finally reached the correct door. Though it was his room, he still knocked before using the key. He pushed open the door, anxious to see Rachel, surprised at the depth of his desire. It had been a long time . . . maybe too long.

"Rachel? It's Gray."

She was seated on the bed, framed against the window, bathed in the morning sunlight. She stood up as he quickly entered the room.

"Why didn't you call?" Gray asked.

Before she could speak, another woman answered, "Because I asked her not to."

Only now did Gray notice the handcuff that bound Rachel's right arm to the headboard. Gray turned.

A slim figure, wrapped in a robe, stepped from the bathroom. Her black hair was wet, freshly combed straight past her shoulders. Almond eyes the color of cold jade stared back at him. Her legs, bare to mid-thigh, crossed casually as she leaned on the bathroom door frame.

In her free hand, she leveled a pistol at him.

"Seichan . . ."

1:15 A.M.
Washington, D.C.

"We're not going to get anything more out of her," Monk told Painter as he sank into the seat across the desk. "She's exhausted and still in a state of shock."

Painter studied Monk. The man looked just as exhausted. "Did Creed finish his assessment of the genetic data?"

"Hours ago. He still wants to crunch the data past a statistician to be sure, but for the moment, he confirms Andrea Solderitch's story. Or at least as much as we can verify."

Painter had kept current with the status reports. Dr. Malloy's assistant had described a conversation with the professor just an hour before he was murdered. The professor had been compiling the genetic assay that made up the bulk of the file that Jason Gorman had e-mailed his father. It had revealed a genetic map of the corn harvested in Africa. Radioactive markers showed which genes were foreign to the corn.

Two chromosomes.

"And what about that original file?" Painter asked. "The one Jason Gorman sent to the professor two months ago. The one that contained the genetic data from the seeds *originally* planted in that field?"

Monk ran a hand over his bald scalp. "The techs at Princeton are still trying to recover the data. They've checked all the servers. The professor must have kept the file isolated to his own computer. The one torched by the assassins. All evidence of it is gone."

Painter sighed. They kept hitting dead ends. Even the gunmen had vanished. No bodies had been found. The assassins must have escaped the blast and slipped past the cordon around the laboratory.

"Though we don't have hard proof, I believe Andrea's story," Monk continued. "According to her, the professor found only *one* chromosome of foreign

DNA in the original seed. He believed the two files showed that genetic modification was unstable in the harvest.

"But without that first file," Painter said, "we can't prove it."

"Still, it had to be why the professor was tortured and murdered. The assassins must have had orders to destroy all evidence of that first file . . . and everyone who knew about it. And they almost succeeded."

Painter frowned. "Still, all we have is Ms. Solderitch's word. And according to her, even the professor wasn't entirely certain about that instability. The samples could have come from two different genetic hybrids. They might be unrelated to one another."

"So what do we do next?"

"I think it's time we go to the source of all this."

Monk stared at the seed-shaped logo printed atop the file on Painter's desk. "Viatus."

"It all seems to come back to that Norwegian corporation. You've read the intelligence report on that symbol burned into the boy and the professor."

Monk's face tightened with distaste. "The quartered circle. Some pagan cross."

"Initial conjecture is that it might represent an eco-terrorist group. And maybe it does. Maybe some lunatics have a personal vendetta against Viatus. And that first file held some clue about it all." Painter sighed and stretched. "Either way, it's high time we had a talk with Ivar Karlsen, CEO of Viatus International."

"What if he won't talk?"

"Two murders on two continents—he'd better talk. Bad press can sink stock values faster than any sour earnings report."

"When do you want to—"

A hurried knock on the door cut Monk off. Both men turned as the door swung open. Kat rushed into the room and crossed to the desk. Monk lifted an arm, offering a hand, but he was ignored.

Painter sat straighter. This can't be good . . .

Kat's eyes were narrow with concern, her cheeks flushed as if she'd run all the way down here. "We've got trouble."

"What?" Painter asked.

"I should've gotten this sooner." Her voice was brittle with frustration. "Interpol's inquiry and ours must have crossed somewhere over the Atlantic, got mixed up. Neither side realized we were talking about two separate incidents. Stupid. Like dogs chasing their tails."

"What?" Painter asked again.

Monk took his wife's hand. "Slow down, hon. Take a breath."

The suggestion only made her angrier, but she kept her grip on his hand. "Another murder. Another body marked with the cross and circle."

"Where?"

"Rome," Kat said. "The Vatican."

She didn't have to explain more.

7:30 A.M.
Rome, Italy

"Let's all just stay calm," Seichan said, keeping her pistol steady as a rock.

Behind Gray, Kowalski dropped both bags and raised his hands. His voice soured. "I hate traveling with you, Gray. I really do."

Gray ignored him and faced the former Guild assassin . . . that is, if she was *former.* "Seichan, what are you doing?"

His words encompassed multiple questions. *What was she doing in Rome? Why was she holding Rachel hostage? What was she doing pointing a gun at him? How could she even be here?*

The satellite feed from her implant had her placed in Venice. Painter would have called Gray immediately if she had moved from there to here.

She ignored his question and asked one of her own. "Are you armed?" She nodded to encompass Kowalski.

"No."

Seichan eyed Gray, as if weighing the truth of his words. And it was the truth. They had traveled by commercial airline and had no time to acquire weapons.

Seichan finally shrugged, pocketed her pistol, and entered the room. She moved with a leonine grace, all legs and hidden strength. Gray didn't doubt she could have her pistol back out in the blink of an eye.

"Then we can all talk like friends," she said mockingly and tossed Gray a tiny key. It plainly fit Rachel's handcuff.

He caught the key, stepped over to the bed, and leaned down to unlock the cuff.

"Are you okay?" he whispered in Rachel's ear as he worked the key, his cheek near hers. The nape of her neck smelled familiar, stirring old feelings, warming embers that Gray thought had long gone cold. As he straightened, he noted that she'd let her hair grow out longer, past her shoulders. She had also thinned down, making her high cheekbones more prominent, increasing her resemblance to a young Audrey Hepburn.

Freed, she rubbed her wrist. Her voice was hard with fury and brisk with embarrassment. "I'm fine. In fact, you might want to hear what she has to say." Her voice lowered. "But be careful. She's drawn tight as a bowstring."

Gray turned to face Seichan. She strolled to the window, staring out across the rooftops of Rome. The curve of the Coliseum stood against the horizon.

"Where do you want to start, Pierce?" She didn't bother to glance at him. "Not expecting me in Rome?"

She dropped a hand to her lower left side. It wasn't done casually, but accusingly. The tracker had been implanted during abdominal surgery last year. Just in that spot.

She confirmed what Gray feared. "It was suspicious enough that I escaped so easily from Bangkok. But when there was no hard pursuit, I knew something was wrong." She turned and cocked an eyebrow at Gray. "A Guild agent escapes custody, but there is no more than a cursory search?"

"You found the implant."

"I'll give you all credit. It was difficult to find. Even a full-body MRI in Saint Petersburg failed to reveal it. Five months ago, I had a doctor perform exploratory surgery, starting with where you all operated on me."

Here was the flaw in Painter's original plan. They'd underestimated the level of paranoia in their target.

"The surgery took three hours," she continued with a growing edge to her voice. "I watched it all in a mirror. They found the implant buried in my healed wound—a wound I sustained saving *your* life, Pierce."

Anger hardened her face, but he didn't fail to note a slight wounding in her eyes.

"So you removed our tracker." Gray pictured the crooked path on the surveillance monitor. "But you still kept it with you."

"I found it useful. It allowed me to hide in plain sight. I could park the tracker somewhere for a while, then move off on my own."

"Like you did in Venice."

She shrugged.

"The city where the curator you murdered lived. Where his family still lives."

Gray let the accusation hang. Seichan shook her head very slightly and glanced away. He had a difficult time reading the play of emotions that flickered past.

"The girl had a cat," she said more quietly. "An orange tabby with a studded collar."

Gray knew the *girl* must be the curator's daughter. So Seichan had indeed gone to check on the family, moved in close enough to observe the simple routine of their lives, a family shattered by the death of a husband and a father. She must have planted her tracker on the cat's collar. It was a smart move. The cat's wandering through the neighborhood streets and rooftops would make the tracker seem active. It was no wonder the agents on the ground could find no trace of her in the

Venetian neighborhood. With the hounds following the false trail, the real cat had escaped.

Gray wanted more answers from this woman. One question was foremost in his mind, a conversation they'd never completed. "What about your claim that you're a double—"

Seichan glanced sharply back at him. Her expression didn't change, but her eyes turned rock hard, warning him to back off. He had been about to question her assertion that she was a mole planted in the Guild, a double agent put there by Western forces, but plainly this was a conversation she didn't want in public. Or maybe he misread her expression. Maybe the bitterness in those eyes merely scoffed at his gullibility. He remembered her last words in Bangkok.

Trust me, Gray. If only a little.

Staring at her now, he let the question drop.

For now.

"Then why are you here in Rome? Why meet like this?" Gray gestured toward Rachel.

"Because I need a bargaining chip."

"Something to leverage against me?" Gray glanced at Rachel.

"No. Something to offer the Guild. After events in Cambodia, suspicions have run high concerning my loyalty. As well as I can tell, the Guild has been sniffing around the recent bombing at Saint Peter's. Something has piqued their interest. Then I heard that Monsignor Verona was involved in this incident—"

"Incident?" Rachel burst out. "He's in a coma."

Seichan ignored her. "So I came here. I believed I could benefit from this situation. If I could acquire some key piece of information about this bombing, I could buy my way back into the full trust of the Guild echelon."

Gray studied Seichan. Despite the callous nature of her words, the reasoning matched her claim two years ago. She had supposedly been sent into the Guild to root out its leaders. The only way to keep rising in the shadowy hierarchy—up the bloody food chain—was to produce results.

"I'd hoped to interrogate Rachel," she explained. "But when I got here, I found someone ransacking her apartment."

Gray turned to Rachel, who nodded confirmation, but there remained an angry glint in her eyes.

"The Guild determined that the assassins were after something the murdered priest had in his possession, something they wanted desperately. The assassins probably searched the man's body, but the explosion left them time for little else. Like searching the monsignor."

"So someone assumed Vigor must have had it," Gray realized and turned to Rachel. "And that his niece might have ended up with it after acquiring his possessions from the hospital."

Seichan nodded. "They went to look for it."

A wince of dread tightened in his gut. If they'd found Rachel, they would have carried out a brutal interrogation, then killed her. And after failing to find anything at her apartment, they were probably hunting for her right now, setting up surveillance at likely locations: apartment, place of work, even the hospital.

There was only one way to protect Rachel.

"We have to find out what they're looking for," Gray concluded aloud.

Rachel and Seichan shared a glance.

"I have it," Rachel said.

Gray could not hide his shock.

"But we have no idea of its significance," Seichan said. "Show him."

Rachel reached into a pocket of her jacket and pulled out a tiny leather satchel, no larger than a coin purse. She briefly described her discovery, how she found the object hanging from a bronze skeleton's finger in Saint Peter's Basilica.

"Uncle Vigor led me to it," she finished and handed over the satchel. "But Seichan and I haven't been able to determine anything else. Especially about what's inside."

Seichan and I . . .?

From the casualness of her statement, it almost sounded like the two were partners, not kidnapper and victim. Gray glanced toward the bathroom. While Rachel had talked, Seichan had stepped out of view, leaving her towel on the floor. He heard her shuffling in there, and he was equally sure she was listening to them. Any attempt to make for the door and she'd be on them.

"Are you truly all right?" Gray whispered to Rachel, catching her eye.

She nodded. "She only handcuffed me when she took a shower. Not exactly the trusting type."

At the moment, Gray appreciated Seichan's caution. Rachel was headstrong like him. Given the chance, she'd have bolted for her freedom. That might have ended badly. If the other hunters had caught her, they would not have been so gentle.

Kowalski stepped closer now that Seichan was out of sight. He pointed at the satchel. "What's in that thing?"

Gray had already teased open the leather strings. Now he emptied the contents into his palm. He sensed the weight of Rachel's gaze on him, waiting for his assessment.

"Is that—?" Kowalski had leaned over Gray's shoulder. He pulled away. "Oh, man, that's sick."

Gray didn't disagree, scowling his distaste. "It's a human finger."

"A mummified finger," Rachel added.

Kowalski's expression soured. "And knowing us, it's probably cursed."

"Where did it come from?" Gray asked.

"I don't know, but Father Giovanni was working in the mountains of northern England. At an excavation there. There were no more details in the police report."

Gray rolled the leathery digit back into the purse. As he did so, he noted the crude spiral burned into the leather. Curious, he turned the satchel over and spotted another mark on the other side. *A circle and a cross.* He immediately recognized it from Painter's description of events back in D.C. There had been two other murders on two continents, both bodies bearing this same mark.

Gray faced Rachel. "This symbol. You said you knew the satchel had to be connected to the bombing. Why were you so certain?"

He got the answer he was expecting.

"The attackers branded Father Giovanni"—she touched her forehead—"with the same mark. It was a detail left out of the press. Interpol was investigating its significance."

Gray stared down at the pouch in his palm.

Make that *three* murders on *three* continents.

But how were all these deaths connected?

Rachel must have read something in his face. "What is it, Gray?"

Before he could answer, the hotel phone on the nightstand rang. Everyone froze for a moment. Seichan stepped back into the room, dressed in black slacks and a burgundy blouse. She pulled on a battered black leather jacket.

"Is anyone going to get that?" Kowalski asked as the phone rang again.

Gray stepped to the table and picked up the receiver. "Hello?"

It was Franco, the hotel owner. "Ah, Signor Pierce, I just wanted to let you know your three visitors are headed up to your room."

Gray struggled for a moment to understand. It was a common custom in Europe to announce visitors, in case their guests might be indisposed. And Franco knew Rachel and Gray were ex-lovers. He wouldn't want them caught with their pants down, so to speak.

But Gray wasn't expecting anyone. He knew what that meant. He mumbled out a hurried *"Grazie,"* then faced the others. "We've got company on the way up."

"Company?" Kowalski asked.

Seichan immediately understood. "Were you followed?"

Gray thought back. He'd been so concerned about Rachel's absence he'd failed to pay strict attention to the surrounding traffic. He also remembered his earlier concern about the hunters, how they might be setting up surveillance on anyone and everyone connected to Rachel. Gray had placed several calls.

His concern must have reached the wrong ears.

Seichan read the growing certainty in his face and swung for the door. She pulled out her pistol from the small of her back.

"Time for an early checkout, boys."

7

October 11, 8:04 A.M.
Oslo, Norway

Ivar Karlsen watched the storm building across the fjord. He loved hard weather and welcomed autumn's rough descent into winter. Icy rain and snow flurries were already sweeping the colder nights. Frost greeted most mornings. Even now, he felt the chill on his cheeks as he leaned his knuckles on the ancient stones and stared out the arched window.

He kept guard at the top of Munk Tower. It was the highest point of Akershus Fortress, one of Oslo's most prominent landmarks. The imposing stone structure was first built on the eastern harborside by King Haakon V during the thirteenth century to defend the city. Over time it had been reinforced with additional moats, ramparts, and battlements. Munk Tower, where he stood now, had been constructed in the middle of the sixteenth century, when cannons had been added to the defense of the fortress and castle.

Ivar straightened and rested a hand on one of the ancient cannons. The cold iron reminded him of his duty, of his responsibility to defend not only this country, but the world. It was why he had picked the ancient fortress to host this year's UNESCO World Food Summit. It was a fitting bastion against the troubling times that were upon them all. One billion people were facing food shortages worldwide, and he knew that was only the beginning. The summit was critical for the world and for his company, Viatus International.

He would not let anything thwart his goals—not what had happened in Africa, not even what was going on in Washington, D.C. His objectives were vital to world security, not to mention his own family legacy.

Back in 1802, when Oslo was still called Christiania, the brothers Knut and Artur Karlsen combined a logging company with a gunpowder mill to found an empire. Their wealth became legendary, elevating them to true barons of industry. But even back then, the pair tempered their good fortune with good deeds. They founded schools, built hospitals, improved the national infrastructure, and, most important, sponsored innovation in the rapidly growing country. It was why they had named their company *Viatus*, from the Latin *via*, which meant "path," and *vita*, which meant "life." To the Karlsen brothers, Viatus was the *Path of Life*. It epitomized their belief that the ultimate goal of industry was to improve the world, that wealth should be tempered by responsibility.

And Ivar intended to carry on that legacy, one that stretched to the founding of Norway itself. Stories circulated that the Karlsen family tree had its beginnings as far back as the first Viking settlers, that its roots were even tangled with those of Yggdrasil, the world tree of Norse mythology. But Ivar knew such claims were just colorful tales told by his old *bestefar* and *bestemor*, stories passed from one generation to another.

Either way, Ivar remained proud of his family's history and of Norway's rich Viking lore. He welcomed the comparison. It had been the Vikings who truly forged the northern world, sweeping in their dragon-prowed longships across Europe and Russia, even to America.

So why shouldn't Ivar Karlsen be proud?

From his vantage high atop Munk Tower, he watched the storm clouds stack across the skies. It would be pouring rain by midmorning, freezing sleet by the afternoon, possibly the first true snowfall by evening. Snow had come early this year, another sign of the shifting weather patterns as nature roiled against the damage done by man, lashing back against the choking toxins and rising carbon levels. Let others question mankind's hand in this global meltdown. Ivar lived in a land of glaciers. He knew the truth. Snowpack and permafrost were melting at record paces. In 2006 Norwegian glaciers had retreated faster than ever recorded.

The world was changing, melting before his eyes. Someone had to take a stand to protect mankind.

Even if it had to be a bloody Viking, he thought with a grim smile.

He shook his head at such foolishness. Especially at his age. It was strange how history weighed more heavily upon one's heart as one grew older. Ivar was fast approaching his sixty-fifth birthday. And though his red hair had long since gone snowy, he wore it shaggy to his shoulders. He also kept fit with a vigorous exercise routine, laboring both in steam lodges and out in freezing temperatures, as in his long cold climb this morning to reach this high perch. Over the years, the routine had left his body hard, his face weathered to a ruddy leather.

He checked his watch. Though the UNESCO summit was not due to start until tomorrow officially, he had several organizational meetings still to attend.

As the storm rolled up the fjord, Ivar headed back down the tower. He caught glimpses of the preparations below in the courtyard. Despite the threat of rain, booths and tables were being set up. Luckily, most of the talks and lectures would occur in the grand upper rooms and banquet halls of Akershus Castle. Even the medieval fortress church would host a series of evening concerts, encompassing choral groups from around the world. In addition, the military museums associated with the fortress—the Norwegian Resistance Museum and the Armed Forces Museum—were being readied for the visiting groups, as were the lower sections of the castle itself, where guides would lead tours into the ancient dungeons and dark passages, sharing the stories of ghosts and witches that had always haunted the gloomy fortress.

Of course, the reality of Akershus was just as gruesome. During WWII, the fortress had been occupied by the Germans. Many Norwegian citizens were tortured and murdered within these walls. And afterward, war trials were conducted and executions performed, including those of the famous traitor and Nazi collaborator Vidkun Quisling.

Reaching the bottom of the tower, Ivar passed into the courtyard. With one foot in the present and the other in the past, he failed to note the round-bellied man blocking his way until he was almost atop him. Ivar recognized Antonio Gravel immediately. The current secretary-general for the Club of Rome did not look pleased.

And Ivar knew why. He had hoped to put the man off for another few hours, but clearly it could not wait. The two men had been butting heads ever since Ivar joined the ranks of his organization.

The Club of Rome was an international think tank comprised of industrialists, scientists, world leaders, and even royalty. Since its inception in 1968, it had grown into an organization encompassing thirty countries across five continents. The main goal of the organization was to raise awareness of critical global crises that threatened the future. Ivar's father had been one of the founding members.

After his father died, Ivar assumed his position and discovered the Club of Rome suited both his personality and his needs. Over the passing years, he thrived in the organization, rising to take a leadership position. As a result, Antonio Gravel felt threatened and had spent the past months growing into an ever larger thorn in Ivar's side.

Still, Ivar kept his expression warm and inviting. "Ah, Antonio, I don't have much time. So why don't you walk with me?"

Antonio followed him as he set off across the court-yard. "You'll have to find the time, Ivar. I allowed this year's conference to be hosted here in Oslo. The least you can do is to properly address my concerns."

Ivar kept his face passive. Gravel had *allowed* nothing, but fought Ivar every step of the way. The man had wanted this year's summit to take place in Zurich, home of the club's new international secretariat. But Ivar had outmanipulated the secretary-general, coaxing the summit to Oslo, mostly because of a special excursion Ivar had arranged, scheduled for the last day of the conference, a trip limited to the top tier involved in the summit organization.

"As secretary-general of the Club of Rome," Antonio pressed, "I think it's only fitting that I accompany the VIPs who are heading to Spitsbergen."

"I understand, but I'm afraid that's not possible, Antonio. You understand the sensitive nature of where we're headed. If it were just me, I'd of course welcome your company, but it was the Norwegian government that limited the number of visitors to Svalbard."

"But . . ." As Antonio struggled to find a suitable argument, the raw desire shone from his face.

Ivar let him stew. It had cost Viatus a mint to arrange a fleet of corporate jets to fly the elite of the conference to the remote Norwegian island of Spitsbergen in the Arctic Ocean. The goal of the trip was a private tour of the Svalbard Global Seed Vault. The vast underground seed bank had been established to store and preserve the seeds of the world, specifically crop seeds. It had been buried in that perpetually frozen and inhospitable place in case of a global disaster—natural or otherwise. If such an event should ever transpire, the frozen and buried seeds would be preserved for a future world.

It was why Svalbard had earned the nickname the Doomsday Vault.

"But . . . I think on such a trip," Antonio continued, "the executive board of the Club of Rome should show a united front. Food security is so vital today."

Ivar forced his eyes not to roll. He knew that Antonio Gravel's desire had nothing to do with food security, but everything to do with his aspiration to rub elbows with the next generation's world leaders.

"You're right about food security," Ivar conceded. "In fact, that very topic will be the focus of my keynote speech."

Ivar intended to use his keynote to swing the Club of Rome's resources in a new direction. It was a time for true action. Still, he read Antonio's darkening expression. Anger had replaced the man's coddling tones.

"Speaking of your speech," Antonio said bitterly, "I obtained an early draft and read it."

Ivar stopped and turned to the man. "You read my speech?" No one was supposed to know its content. "Where did you get it?"

Antonio dismissed the question with a wave of his hand. "It doesn't matter. What matters is that you can't give such a speech and still expect to represent the Club of Rome. I've brought the matter up with Copresident Boutha. And he concurs. Now is not the time to broadcast warnings of imminent world collapse. It's . . . it's irresponsible."

Blood burned the chill from Ivar's face. "Then when *is* that time?" he asked, working his tight jaw. "When the world has slid into chaos and ninety percent of its population is dead?"

Antonio shook his head. "That's what I'm talking about. You'll make the club look like madmen and doomsayers. We won't tolerate it."

"Tolerate it? The core of my speech comes from the Club of Rome's own published report."

"Yes, I know. *The Limits to Growth.* You cite it often enough in your speech. That was written back in 1972."

"And it's even more timely today. The report outlines in great detail the collapse that the world is currently barreling straight for."

Ivar had studied *The Limits to Growth* in great detail, mapping out its charts and data. The report modeled the future of the world, where population continued to grow exponentially while food production only grew arithmetically. Eventually the population would outstrip its ability to produce food to sustain itself. It would hit such a point like a locomotive and overshoot it. Once that happened, chaos, starvation, and war would ensue, with the end result being the annihilation of mankind. Even the most conservative models showed that 90 percent of the world population would die as a result. The studies had been repeated elsewhere with the same dire results.

Antonio shrugged, dismissing the entire matter. Ivar balled a fist and came close to breaking the man's nose.

"That speech," Antonio said, oblivious to the danger. "What you're advocating is radical population control. It will never be stomached."

"It must be," Ivar argued. "There's no way we can dodge what's coming. The world has gone from four billion to six billion in only two decades. And it shows no signs of slowing. We'll be at nine billion in another twenty years. And even now, the world is running out of arable farmland, global warming is wreaking havoc, and our oceans are dying. We will hit that overshoot point sooner than anyone is expecting."

Ivar grabbed Antonio's arm, letting his passion show. "But we can mitigate its impact by planning now. There is only *one* way to avoid complete worldwide collapse—and that's to slowly and steadily lower the human biomass of this planet *before* we hit that overshoot point. The future of mankind depends on it."

"We'll manage just fine," Antonio said. "Or don't you have faith in your own research? Aren't the GM foods your corporation is patenting supposed to open new lands, produce greater yields?"

"But even that will only buy us a small window of time."

Antonio glanced at his watch. "Speaking of time, I must be going. I've delivered Boutha's message. You'll have to adjust your speech accordingly if you wish to deliver the keynote."

Ivar watched the man stride off toward the drawbridge that spanned the Kirkegata entrance.

Standing in the courtyard, Ivar remained as rain began to drizzle out of the sky, the first portent of a greater deluge. He let the icy drops cool the pounding of his heart. He would address these matters with the copresident of the club later. Perhaps he should temper his rhetoric. Maybe it was better to use a more gentle hand on the rudder that steered the world's fate.

Calmed again and resolute, he headed across the courtyard toward the bulk of Akershus Church with its large rosette window. He was already late for the meeting. Within the Club of Rome, Ivar had gathered like-minded men and women, those willing to make hard choices, to stand by their convictions. While Antonio and the two copresidents might be the figureheads of the Club of Rome, Ivar Karlsen and his inner cabal kept their own pact, a club within the club—a heart of iron, beating with the hope of the planet.

Crossing into the church, Ivar saw that the others had already gathered within the small brick-walled nave. Chairs had been pushed to one side, and a choral stage had been set up to the left of the altar. Arched windows let in murky light, while a brightly lit gilt chandelier sought to add a meager bit of cheer.

Faces turned as Ivar entered.

Twelve in all.

They were the true powers behind the club: leaders of industry, Nobel Prize–winning scientists, government representatives from major nations, even a Hollywood celebrity whose high-profile advocacy had drawn both attention and money to their group's causes.

Each served a specific purpose.

Even the man who approached Ivar now. He was dressed in a black suit and wore a haunted expression.

"Good morning, Ivar," the man said and offered his hand.

"Senator Gorman, please accept my condolences for your loss. What has happened in Mali . . . I should have spent more to secure the camp."

"Do not blame yourself." The senator gripped Ivar's shoulder. "Jason knew the dangers. And he was proud to be involved in such an important project."

Despite the reassurance, the senator was plainly uncomfortable with the topic, still raw from the death of his son. From a distance, the two men could almost be brothers. Sebastian Gorman stood as tall and weathered as Ivar, but he kept his white hair neatly trimmed, his suit pressed to a razor edge.

Ivar was surprised to find the senator here, but perhaps he shouldn't have been. In the past, Gorman had proven to be unwavering in his determination. The U.S. senator had been instrumental in expanding biofuel research and development throughout the Western world. The summit here was important to his issue. And with an election coming up, the senator would find time to mourn for his son later.

Still, Ivar understood the man's pain. He'd lost a wife and son in childbirth when he was in his early thirties. The tragedy had come close to destroying him back then. He had never remarried.

"Are we ready to get started?" the senator asked, stepping away.

"Yes. We should begin. We have much ground to cover."

"Good."

As the senator gathered everyone toward the bank of waiting chairs, Ivar stared at his back. He felt no twinge of guilt. Viatus meant the *path of life*. And sometimes that path was hard, requiring sacrifices to be made.

Like the death of Jason Gorman.

Upon Ivar's orders, the young man had been murdered.

A tragic loss, but he could afford no regrets.

8

October 11, 8:14 A.M.
Rome, Italy

They had less than a minute. The unexpected *guests* that the innkeeper had warned about were headed up. Gray didn't want to be there when they arrived.

He led everyone in a rush down the hall toward the hotel's fire escape. It was just around the corner from his room. Reaching the window, he tugged it open and stepped aside for Rachel.

"Head down," he ordered. "Get out of sight."

Rachel clambered through the window and onto the iron ladder.

Gray pointed to Kowalski, poking him in the chest. "Stay with her."

"Don't have to tell me twice," he answered and followed.

Seichan stood two steps away in the hallway, her legs wide, her arms out, her hands cradling a black Sig Sauer pistol. She kept it pointed down the hall.

"Do you have another weapon?" he asked.

"I've got it covered. Get moving."

Muffled voices arose down the hall, along with the creak of wooden floorboards. The assassins had reached their floor and were headed toward their room. The hotel's convoluted layout had probably saved their lives, bought them just enough time to slip the ambush.

But not much more than that.

Gray backed to the window and ducked through. Seichan came next. Without even turning, she back-stepped cleanly through the open window, never dropping her guard of the hallway.

Rachel and Kowalski were already headed down. They were a floor below when shots suddenly fired up at them. Gray didn't hear the blasts, but he did recognize the *ping*s of ricochets and the puffs of brick dust from the wall.

Kowalski cursed, pulled Rachel behind him, and began a fast retreat back up the fire escape.

Gray spotted the shooter, half-hidden by a Dumpster. The bastards already had the alley exit covered. Seichan fired back. The gunman ducked away, but her pistol had no silencer. The blasts stung Gray's ears and were surely loud enough to be heard by the assassins inside.

"Make for the roof!" he ordered.

The shooter below took potshots as they fled, but Seichan kept him pinned down, and the iron cage of the fire escape helped shelter them. Luckily, they didn't have far to go. The hotel was only five stories high.

Reaching the top, Gray herded everyone away from the roof's edge. He stared across the expanse of pigeon droppings, vent pipes, and graffiti-sprayed heating and cooling equipment. They needed another way down. Even now he heard boots landing hard on the fire escape's iron railings. The others were headed up after them.

Gray pointed to the far side of the hotel. Another building abutted it. It was one story shorter. They had to get out of sight, or at least out of the direct line of fire.

They sprinted for the low wall that separated the two buildings. Gray reached it first and leaned over. A whitewashed metal ladder was bolted to the side of the hotel and led down to the lower building's roof.

"Go!"

Rachel rolled over the edge and scrambled down the rungs. Kowalski didn't bother to wait his turn. He grabbed the edge of the wall, hung by his fingers, and merely dropped. He landed on his backside on the tar-papered roof below.

A gunshot drew Gray's attention around.

A black-masked head ducked below the fire escape on the far side.

"Now or never, Pierce!" Seichan warned.

She fired twice more, discouraging anyone else from showing themselves. Taking advantage of the cover, Gray flipped over the edge of the roof, grabbed the ladder, and ignored the rungs. Like a fireman on a pole, he slid down its length.

More shots echoed above.

As his heels hit the tar paper, he stared up. Seichan flew over the wall and snatched one-armed for the ladder. Her other hand still clenched her smoking pistol. In her haste, she missed her grip on the topmost rung and began a headlong tumble. She tried for a second hold, dropping her gun and reaching out. Fingertips caught for half a breath. Her pistol tumbled and struck near Gray's toes. Her momentary grip ripped away.

She fell.

Gray lunged out and got under her. She landed heavily in his arms. The impact took him down to one knee, but he caught her. Momentarily stunned, she breathed hard, a hand clutched on Gray's wrist.

Kowalski retrieved her gun, then helped them back to their feet.

Seichan shoved roughly out of Gray's arms, took an unsteady step, then gained her balance. Turning, she cleanly plucked her pistol out of Kowalski's fingers before he could react.

"Hey . . ." Kowalski stared at his empty hand as if the appendage had betrayed him.

"There's another fire escape over here," Rachel called to them. Her eyes momentarily flickered between Gray and Seichan.

They all hurried over. The top of the fire escape was sheltered behind a bulky ventilation unit. They began a rapid descent, leaping from landing to landing. This fire escape dumped into a different alley. It would buy them an extra half breath, but Gray knew that whatever net had been cast around the hotel was surely being extended. They had to escape before it fully closed around them.

At the end of the alleyway, a street opened. They headed toward it. With no way to identify the assassins, they were still in grave danger. They could stumble right into one of them and not even know it. They had to get well away from the area, out of the city.

Gray's questioning glance slid from Rachel to Seichan. "Anyone have a car?"

"I do," Rachel answered. "But it's parked around the corner from the hotel."

He shook his head. It was too dangerous to go back. And considering that the streets had already turned into a parking lot due to the morning gridlock, a car might not even serve them.

A growl on his left warned him of the danger. Gray leaped back as a motorcyclist sped through the stalled traffic, riding almost up on the narrow sidewalk. Kowalski was a second slower. The cyclist nearly clipped him, which only pissed the big man off.

"Screw you, Knievel!"

Kowalski shoved with both arms as the man passed.

The rider flew out of his seat. The cycle struck a parked car and toppled on its side. A second motorcyclist who hadn't seen the altercation and was following the same winding path could not get out of the way in time. He was forced to drop his bike and skid along the street gutter.

Seichan stared at Gray and lifted an eyebrow.

Good enough, he answered her silently.

Seichan went for the first bike; Gray headed to the second.

They needed transportation.

Seichan's pistol discouraged any complaints from the first rider. Catching on quickly, Rachel followed Gray.

She flipped out her carabinieri ID and held it high, yelling in Italian, full of command. The second rider backed away from his fallen motorcycle.

Gray righted the bike and hitched his leg over it. Rachel climbed on behind him, hugging one arm around his waist.

Seichan had already mounted the other. Kowalski stood in place, not sure what to do. Siechan patted the leather seat behind her.

"You gotta be kidding me," he said. "I don't ride bitch behind anyone."

Seichan still had her Sig Sauer in hand. She flipped it around and offered the butt end toward Kowalski. She couldn't maneuver and fire at the same time.

It was like offering a bone to a dog.

Kowalski could not resist. He took the gun and climbed on behind her. "That's more like it."

They set off as police sirens sounded in the distance. Gray took the lead. Swerving back and forth through traffic, he skirted the creeping cars and dodged bicycles. Rachel shouted directions in his ear, guiding them toward the wider thoroughfares where the congestion wasn't so tight. They slowly gained speed.

But they didn't get far.

A squeal of brakes drew Gray's attention around.

Behind them, a black Lamborghini peeled out of a side street, tires smoking, and aimed straight for

Seichan and Kowalski. A black-jacketed figure leaned out the passenger window of the sports car and lifted a thick-barreled weapon to his shoulder. He aimed at the trailing motorcycle.

Gray recognized an M32 grenade launcher.

So did Seichan.

She tucked lower in her seat and gunned her engine, but in the tight traffic, there was nowhere to run.

With his target trapped, the gunman fired.

2:22 A.M.
Washington, D.C.

Monk waited with Kat in her office within Sigma Command. They shared her leather sofa, sprawled together. Monk cradled Kat, appreciating the warmth of her body, the softness of her touch. While Sigma Command had a series of bunk rooms, neither of them would be able to sleep until they finally got word about Gray.

"I should be there with him," Monk mumbled.

"He has Kowalski."

Monk stared down at her.

"Okay," she agreed. "That might make matters worse. But we don't know for sure anything is even wrong."

"He's not answering his phone."

Kat curled tighter to him. "He *was* meeting Rachel," she said and cocked an eyebrow, leaving the implication hanging.

Monk wasn't buying that explanation.

A long stretch of silence followed, with each lost in their own thoughts. Painter was continuing to pull strings to find out what was happening in Rome. Kat had also made further inquiries into the bombing at the Vatican. She was waiting for a comprehensive report from Interpol to come through. This moment of quiet was just the eye of the storm. Still, Monk took what he could.

He reached and placed a palm over her belly. Her hand rose to cover his. Their fingers entwined.

"Is it wrong to hope for a boy?" he asked.

She used her other hand to punch him halfheartedly in the leg. "Yes . . ."

Monk tightened his arms around her and teased. "But a boy . . . someone I can play catch with, shoot hoops with, go fishing . . ."

Kat wriggled, then sighed and leaned into him. "You can do all those things with a daughter, you sexist pig."

"Did you call me a sexy pig?"

"*Sexist* . . . oh, never mind."

He leaned down and kissed her lips. "I like *sexy* better."

She mumbled between their lips. Monk could not make out her words, but after a moment more, a contented silence followed. A knock on the door interrupted them. They broke their embrace and sat up. Kat stood and crossed to the door, running a hand down her suit. She glared back at Monk, as if it were all his fault.

Kat opened the door to find Painter standing outside. "Director—"

Painter cut her off and pointed down the hall. "I was on my way down to satellite com. We've got trouble in Rome."

Monk gained his feet. "Gray?"

"Who else?" Painter set off down the hall.

8:21 A.M.
Rome, Italy
The Lamborghini drove straight at the trailing motorcycle. There was nothing Gray could do.

At the same moment the gunman fired his weapon, Kowalski blasted wildly with his pistol back at the car. The windshield spider-webbed. The car shimmied slightly—enough to throw off the aim of the gunman as he pulled the trigger.

From the grenade launcher, a spiraling trail of smoke rocketed out, passed over Kowalski's head, and shot down the street. It struck the corner of a building at the next intersection.

Smoke, fire, and bricks blasted outward.

Panicked pedestrians fled in all directions. Cars rammed one another in the intersection. In the lead, Gray reached the crossroads first. He fought through the mess, jerking and swerving through the chaos and smoke, seeking every crack to make his escape.

Seichan and Kowalski closed the distance.

Behind them, the Lamborghini, blocked by the traffic, swerved onto the sidewalk. It accelerated, heedless of the pedestrians in the way.

Once past the intersection, the road cleared. Gray opened the throttle and shot down the street. Seichan kept to his right flank.

"Gray!" Rachel yelled in his ear. She unwrapped one arm from around his waist to point ahead.

Down the street, a second black Lamborghini fishtailed around a corner and sped straight at them. The first car closed from behind.

Rachel pointed to the left. "Stairs!"

Gray spotted an arched pedestrian walkway between two buildings. He turned sharply, braking and skidding on both tires for a full yard, then righted the bike. With a twist of the throttle, he shot toward the stone stairway. Seichan followed, skirting wider but keeping pace.

Gray heard a string of curses flowing from Kowalski, punctuated by *pops* from his pistol as he fired at the two sports cars.

Reaching the stairs, Gray downshifted and gunned the engine. Lifting up on his back tire, he hit the stairs and used momentum, balance, and a low gear to ratchet up the steps. Thankfully there was only one flight and the walkway flattened out. Still, the path was narrow and crooked.

Gray shot down the walkway. He didn't slow. He trusted the guttural growl of the two motorcycles to clear the path of any pedestrians. Still, he risked a glance back. He had no view of the street, but he was sure a gunman or two had been dropped off to give chase. The cars were probably circling around to meet them at the other end.

But where did this walkway end?

Gray had his answer as the path suddenly emptied into a wide plaza. A roadway circled its outer edge. As he shot into the open, Gray gaped at the massive ancient structure that filled the center of the space ahead of him. It climbed high into the sky.

The Coliseum.

But he had no time to sightsee.

"Got company!" Kowalski bellowed and pointed to the right.

Gray turned. The two Lamborghinis swung into the circling street.

"Gray!" Rachel said and pointed to the left.

A third Lamborghini, as sleek and black as the others, shot into view. Somebody had plenty of money to spare.

With no choice, Gray shot straight across the street, cutting through all lanes of traffic and out onto the pedestrian plaza that circled the Coliseum. It was a park of cement walkways, grassy lawns, and stretches of blacktop. Nimbleness was their only hope of escape. And speed.

Unfortunately, the same described a Lamborghini.

All three sports cars left the roadway, angled into the plaza, and closed toward them from both sides.

Gray had no choice.

If it was a race they wanted . . .

2:23 A.M.
Washington, D.C.
Ensconced before the bank of monitors, Painter stared at the satellite feed from the National Reconnaissance Office. It showed a view of an open plaza in the center of Rome. An ancient amphitheater filled the center. The Coliseum looked like a giant stone eye staring back at him.

"Zoom in closer," Painter ordered the technician.

"Are you sure that's Gray?" Monk asked. He and Kat flanked Painter on either side of the monitor.

"The explosion was a block from his hotel. Reports from the police describe a chase under way outside the Coliseum."

The image on the screen swelled and swept down upon the plaza. Details grew less distinct. But two black cars clearly raced around the periphery of the stone amphitheater. Ahead, a pair of motorcycles sped down walkways and across grassy lawns. One of the bikes shot off the top of a stairway, landed on its back tire, and sped away.

"Yeah," Monk said with appreciation. "That's got to be Gray."

The two cars were rapidly closing the distance.

"There!" Kat said and pointed at the screen.

A third car, coming from the opposite direction, aimed straight for the two bikes. A small explosion erupted near one of the motorcycles, sending a trash can and a section of brick wall high into the air.

"Grenade," Painter muttered.

What was going on?

Pinned on three sides, the two bikes turned and fled along the only path open to them.

Kat's voice turned incredulous. "They aren't . . . they can't think . . ."

Monk leaned closer. "Oh, yeah, that's *definitely* Gray."

9

Gray leaned hard over the handlebars. Rachel hugged tight to him. He aimed straight for the massive stone structure. It rose fifteen stories at its highest point, climbing in towering levels of immense arches and colossal columns. At the lowest level, each archway entrance was sealed by a tall steel gate, but directly ahead was the main entrance, where tourists normally lined up.

Gray shot straight toward it.

The Coliseum was not yet open to the public at this early hour, but the gates were open, and the crowds had already begun to gather in anticipation. The gunfire and blasts had chased most of them clear. Still, clutches of people took refuge wherever they could. A pair of men dressed as gladiators had even climbed one of the plaza's trees.

The presence of tourists and bystanders also kept the armed police who guarded the site wary and cautious, discouraging them from shooting out of hand. The guards had cleared the entrance site.

With the way conveniently open, Gray shot toward the main gate.

A single guard stepped into view, ready to defend the site. He leveled his weapon and yelled a warning at them. Rachel screamed back at him. She waved her arm, holding her carabinieri credentials high.

The man hesitated, his face clouded by confusion.

It was enough.

Gray shot past him as he leaped to the side. Seichan followed. They blasted into the outer passageway that circled the central arena. Lined by archways and held up by columns, the enclosed shadowy space was cavernous. The roar of the cycles echoed off the walls, growing into a deafening crescendo.

A chatter of gunfire drew his attention to the left. One of the Lamborghinis kept pace out in the sunlit plaza. A gunman fired an assault rifle out the passenger window. But the stone walls and steel gates shielded them. Sparks spat off the steel.

A loud splintering crash sounded behind them.

Gray glanced over his shoulder. A second Lamborghini rammed through the gateway and gave chase inside the space. It was unfortunately vast enough to accommodate the small sports car.

A fiery explosion drew Gray's attention back around. One of the steel gates, bent and smoking, blasted into the passageway ahead. The third Lamborghini shot through the wreckage and skidded to a stop, blocking the way.

A dark figure leaned out the window, leveling his smoking weapon straight at them.

"Go right!" Rachel yelled and pointed to a nearby stone ramp.

Obeying, he made a hard turn, leaning out with his knee. The bike skidded, tilted precariously, *too* precariously. He burned his kneecap across the stone as the bike began to fall. Gritting his teeth, he willed the bike back up.

In the end, the angle saved his life. A loud boom deafened, and a spiraling contrail of smoke shot past the tilted bike, missing Gray by inches. He felt the burn of its passage across his cheek.

The grenade rocketed away and slammed straight into the windshield of the other Lamborghini. A flaming blast blew out its windows and flipped the car over on its side.

As searing heat washed outward, Gray gunned for the ramp. Seichan and Kowalski had already skirted around one of the massive support columns and converged toward them. The two bikes reached the ramp together and shot down a short shadowy passageway and back into sunlight.

At the end of the ramp, the full extent of the stadium opened. It climbed in four massive levels, covering six acres. Though the amphitheater had been damaged over the centuries by vandals, fires, earthquakes, and war, it still held an ageless grandeur, a testament to time and history. Directly ahead stretched the arena itself, where great battles had been fought and death was a sport. Long ago, the original wooden floor had rotted away and exposed the underground maze of stone passages and cells that once housed animals, slaves, and gladiators.

A modern elevated boardwalk now crossed over the open pit and ended at a flat stage on the far side. Gray took advantage of it. Without slowing, he led the way across it, speeding straight down the center of the narrow boardwalk. The roar of the pair of cycles echoed across the space, dredging up the ghosts of ancient spectators as they clapped and bellowed for blood.

And the ghosts would not be disappointed today.

A fresh barrage of gunfire erupted behind them. In his rearview mirror, Gray spotted a pair of gunmen taking up positions at the end of the boardwalk. They had combat assault rifles at their shoulders. After the first wild hail of bullets, Seichan was forced to drop her motorcycle, her rear tire blown. The bike skidded on its side. Seichan and Kowalski rolled across the planks, tangled together.

Kowalski tried to get up on his knees, but Seichan tackled him before he took a bullet to the head. Together, they tumbled off the boardwalk and vanished into the pit below.

It was the only option.

Exposed and out in the open, Gray and Rachel would never make it to the far side. Once the assassins secured their positions and steadied their aim, their prey would be picked off. Gray braked to a hard stop. He knew he had less than a second. He twisted, grabbed Rachel around the waist, and rolled her off the bike to the boardwalk.

Bullets chewed across the planks straight at them.

Gray held tight and continued to roll. He took them over the edge of the boardwalk and down into the darkness of the pit.

2:35 A.M.
Washington, D.C.

Painter leaned in closer to the monitor. "Can you zoom in any tighter?"

The satellite technician shook his head and sat back. "This is the best resolution I can manage from this satellite. I can run the current data through a high-res filter, but compiling it will take hours."

Painter turned to Kat. She was on the phone. He met her eyes.

"Italian military is responding," Kat said. "They're ten minutes out. Local police have the area locked down."

Painter stared back at the screen. They had lost sight of the motorcycles as the pair shot into the Coliseum. But seconds later they reappeared, racing across the center of the arena. The detail was poor, little more than a vague representation. But as they watched, one bike suddenly spun and skidded to a stop. Seconds later the other braked and stopped. Movement blurred around the spots, then all seemed to go dead still.

The resolution was not fine enough to tell if there were any bodies on the ramp.

Monk leaned over the technician's shoulder. "Sir . . ." He pointed and drew Painter's attention back to the screen. "I think I see something again. On the bridge."

The technician nodded. "Looks like two figures. Maybe three."

His finger traced the barest flicker of pixels on the screen. They flowed toward the downed motorcycles.

Even with such low resolution, Painter recognized the stalking pattern of true hunters.

He mumbled to the screen, half plea, half prayer. "Get the hell out of there, Gray . . ."

8:36 A.M.
Rome, Italy

Rachel leaned on Gray's shoulder. Each step sent a jolt of pain up her right leg. She had wrenched her knee tumbling into the subterranean region of the Coliseum. As she hopped alongside him, she searched around the space.

With the sun still low, deep shadows covered them. She had learned from Uncle Vigor that these lower levels were called the *hypogeum*, which simply meant "underground." It was here that all manner of beasts had been housed—lions, elephants, tigers, giraffes— along with slaves and gladiators. Crude elevators raised and lowered cages or elaborate set pieces.

But all that was left of the spectacle were the crumbling ruins of walls, blind cubbies, and tiny cells. Lacking any roofs, the upper level was left exposed to the sun and rain. Grass and weeds covered the floor, while thick moss matted the walls. Due to the fragile nature of the ancient structures and the danger of sudden collapses, the level was out of bounds for tourists—but not for archaeologists. Uncle Vigor had once sneaked Rachel down here when she was a teenager.

If I could just get my bearings . . .

Gray suddenly stopped. Furtive movement sounded behind them: the scuff of stone, the heavy rush of breath. They ducked back into one of the cells. Two figures appeared.

Rachel felt Gray sag with relief. "Seichan . . ."

The woman hissed at him and lifted a finger to her lips. Kowalski trailed her. Blood covered half his face, running thickly from a jagged cut above his eye. He also lifted a hand to warn them to be quiet.

Rachel then heard it, too.

The tramp of boots on the boardwalk overhead.

The gunmen had not fled as Rachel had hoped. They still hunted their prey.

Seichan pointed up, then shoved her arm out. Her pantomime was clear. If they stayed directly under the boardwalk, they'd be less likely to be spotted. But that meant moving as silently as possible.

Gray nodded and began to head toward the far side of the hypogeum. Rachel tightened her grip and stopped him. He stared back at her questioningly. She knew the layout of these levels. If they followed the boardwalk, they'd just hit a solid wall. Only a few ways still led out of the hypogeum.

She pointed along their path, made a chopping motion on her arm, and shook her head. It was military sign language for *dead end.* Turning, she pointed toward an exit few people knew about. Her uncle had shown it to her long ago. But to reach that spot, they'd have to abandon the shelter of the boardwalk and head out into the exposed maze.

Gray studied her with his face tight, his eyes hard pieces of blue ice.

Are you sure?

Rachel nodded. His fingers tightened on her shoulder, thanking her, reassuring her. For just a flash, she wanted those arms around her, holding her just as tightly. But he let go and crouched with Kowalski. They whispered too low to hear.

Seichan drew next to her. She also kept her attention on the two Americans. Rachel didn't doubt the woman could read their lips. Rachel glanced sidelong at her. A purplish bruise was forming on Seichan's cheek. Rachel also noted how much weight she'd lost since they'd first met years ago. Her face was more gaunt, hollow and haunted around the eyes. It left her looking like something carved out of stone, hard and unyielding. Still, there remained a cold fire in her dark green gaze.

Gray slid back and drew them all into a crouch under the boardwalk. He glanced up, listening as one of the hunters passed overhead. The gunmen were watching both halves of the hypogeum. Any flicker of movement, and both would be on them. From their high vantage, it would be like shooting fish in a barrel.

As the assassin moved past, Gray whispered, "We'll need a distraction. Kowalski's got one round left in his pistol. It's not much but—"

The cautious tromp of boots suddenly changed cadence. The slow step turned into a heavy-footed run. Boots pounded toward their position.

Gray's whispering must have been heard.

Kowalski lifted his pistol, ready to shoot, but Seichan placed a cautioning hand on his shoulder.

The pounding passed their position and continued down the boardwalk, heading toward the far side. They were running off. Something had spooked them.

"The police . . ." Gray guessed aloud.

" 'Bout time," Kowalski said.

Seichan did not share their relief. Her expression soured. She was on several terrorist watch lists, including Interpol's.

Before they could make any decision, a new noise intruded. It came suddenly. The *thump-thump* of a helicopter. Gray stepped out from under the boardwalk and stared up. Rachel joined him.

A wasp-bodied black helicopter swept over the rim of the coliseum.

"That's not the *polizia*," Rachel said.

In fact, there were no markings on the craft.

As it banked over the stadium, a side door cranked open in the helicopter.

Gray grabbed Rachel's shoulder. "Run!"

It was clear now why the gunmen had fled. Not from the police, but from a new level of assault. Why shoot fish in a barrel when depth charges worked so much better?

"This way!" Rachel yelled.

She ran, ignoring the protest from her knee, adrenaline burning away pain. She headed along a curving wall lined by stone cells. The others followed.

"What's going on?" Kowalski bellowed.

Rachel took the first right passage, then the next left. She ended up at a dead end. "Back!"

They scrambled around. Rachel kept hold of Gray's shoulder, limping. While she knew where the exit was located, she did not have this rat maze memorized. Backpedaling, she found the correct turn this time. Ahead, a straight passage ended at a narrow archway. That was it! The arch marked a staircase down to a lower level of the hypogeum.

She had started toward it when Gray grabbed her from behind and shouldered her back into one of the side cells. The others piled in, too. Gray covered her as a thunderous *whump* sounded that shook the walls and stones underfoot. A moment later, a wash of flames billowed past overhead, rolling smoke and reeking of poisonous chemicals.

Gray shoved her back out of the shelter. She stumbled, deaf, eyes watering. Overhead, the helicopter swept past, swirling smoke and flames. A black steel barrel was rolled to the lip of the open hatch.

Oh, no . . .

Panicked, knowing what was coming, Rachel sprinted down the passageway, gasping in pain as she hurdled rocks and sections of tumbled wall. The arched opening gaped ten yards away. Focused on her goal, her heel landed on a moss-encrusted stone. Her foot slipped, and her leg twisted. She stumbled—but never hit the ground.

Gray scooped her around the waist and carried her the last few steps. They dove together through the archway. Bodies shoved into them from behind. They fell as a group, tripping, tumbling down the flight of stone steps.

They landed in a pile at the bottom as the world exploded above them.

The blast, striking near the opening, immediately deafened them. Pressure slammed Rachel's ears and felt like it cracked her skull. Rocks tumbled and bounced. Flames gusted down the throat of the stairwell, washing across the roof overhead. Her skin burned. Her lungs could draw no air.

Then in a rush, the pressure popped. The flames were sucked away, back out of the tunnel. Cool air drafted up from the lower levels and washed over them.

Hands shoved and dragged. They crawled away from the stairs down into the murky lower passages. After a few yards, they all slowly gained their feet. Rachel used the walls to haul herself up. She panted, felt like vomiting, fought the rising gorge. She took great gulps of cool air.

"Keep going," Gray urged.

Rachel leaned on the wall as they stumbled away. They had to keep moving. The concussions and fires could drop the upper level on top of them. They had to get clear.

"Can you find that exit?"

She coughed. "I think . . . maybe . . ."

Gray grabbed her elbow. "Rachel."

She nodded, regaining her balance, both inside and outside. "Yes. This way." She pulled out her cell phone and flipped it open. The meager glow didn't cast much light, but it was better than nothing.

Holding on to Gray's shoulder, she set off. It wasn't far, but this level was a rabbit warren of cells, passages, and cave-ins. She headed out, lost in the past as much as the present.

She remembered Uncle Vigor taking her down here, tantalizing her with tales of heroes and monsters, of strange beasts and great pageantry. He had also told her about one of the grandest of shows, a rare event held at the Coliseum. A spectacle called a *naumachiae*.

She spoke aloud as she led the others. "Before these underground levels were built, early in the Roman empire, they used to flood this area, creating a great lake in the middle of the Coliseum. Famous sea battles were reenacted here, along with demonstrations of swimming horses and bulls."

Kowalski trailed behind them, dusty, bloody, and burned. "Right now, a swim sounds pretty damn good to me."

"What did they do with all the water after the show?" Gray asked.

"You'll see," Rachel said.

Another two turns and they ended up at a wall. An iron grate sealed a narrow, low passageway. Even in the meager light, it plainly led down at a steep angle.

"They cleared this just last year, confirming what Uncle Vigor already knew." Rachel unlatched the gate and pulled it open.

Before she could explain more, a loud rumbling crash echoed across the space. Rock dust wafted in a thick cloud and rolled over them.

"The bombs are triggering a cave-in," Rachel said.

Closer at hand, a marble block fell from the roof a yard away and crashed heavily to the floor. More groans and rumbles followed. Like the first tip of a domino, the entire level was beginning to collapse on top of them.

"This way," Rachel said. "Hurry."

She ducked into the steep passage and led the way down. Behind her the others followed single file. They hadn't taken more than a half-dozen steps when the floor shook, accompanied by an ominous rumble of thunder. More dust filled the air, choking and blinding them.

Rachel hurried onward, covering her mouth with her arm. She felt blindly ahead of her. The steep floor grew even steeper. Rachel used one hand to brace herself and held forth her glowing cell phone in the other.

"How much farther?" Gray gasped out.

She didn't answer. She didn't know.

After a long silent minute, a trickling echo reached her. She rushed onward. In her haste, she lost her footing on the floor, landed on her backside, and slid, losing her cell phone. It skittered ahead of her—then vanished.

Unable to stop, she followed it. For a gut-wrenching moment the world dropped under her. She fell through open air. A small scream escaped her, but she landed in a shallow stream of frigid water. The fall had only been a meter or so.

"Watch out!" Gray called.

Rachel rolled clear as the others slid, skidded, and dropped into the water with her. Rachel retrieved her cell phone from the edge of the stream. It still glowed. She held it up.

They were in a long stone tube, clearly man-made from the crudely hewn slabs. A wan stream flowed across its bottom.

"Where are we?" Gray asked.

"Old city sewers," Rachel answered and began to follow the flow. "It was how the ancient Romans drained the flooded stadium."

The others splashed behind her.

Kowalski sighed heavily. "I should've known. A tour of Rome with Pierce had to end up in the damn sewers."

10

Painter readied for the battle to come. He sat at his desk. He was as prepared as could be expected. After the long night, he'd taken a short nap, showered, and changed into a fresh set of clothes.

Hours ago he'd learned that Gray and Kowalski were safe and headed out of Rome. Commander Pierce had already given a sketchy report of events in Italy, but he needed to keep moving. A full debriefing would follow once he was settled in a secure location outside the city.

The office intercom buzzed. Brant spoke crisply. "Sir, I have General Metcalf for you."

Painter had already been alerted that the head of DARPA was arriving at Sigma Command. It was a rare visit. And not normally a good sign.

Painter pressed the intercom button. "Brant, send the general straight in."

Seconds later the door swung open. Painter stood as General Gregory Metcalf stalked into his office. He entered with his hat under his arm and his face locked into deep furrows.

Painter stepped around the desk to shake the man's hand, but Metcalf headed straight to a chair, tossed his cap on the desk, and waved Painter back to his own chair.

"Do you have any idea of the political shitstorm blowing out of Italy?" Metcalf said as introduction.

Crossing back behind his desk, Painter sank into his chair after Metcalf took his seat. "I'm aware of the situation, General. We're monitoring all the chatter across various intelligence channels."

"First, a firefight at a hotel, then a street chase with a trail of carnage left behind it, and to top it all off, one of the world's Seven Wonders is left firebombed. And you inform me that one of our . . . *your* operatives was at the heart of it all?"

Painter breathed through his nose. He kept the tips of his fingers resting on the edge of his desk. "Yes, sir. One of our best field agents."

"Best?" Metcalf said with sharp sarcasm. "I'd hate to see your worst."

Painter let some bite enter his own voice. "He was ambushed. He was doing what was necessary to protect an asset. To keep them all alive."

"At what cost? As I understand it, he was pursuing a matter that was a domestic Italian concern. That their own intelligence services, along with Interpol, had things well in hand. If your agent's involvement exposed or damaged—"

Painter cut him off. "General, the case has implications far beyond Italy. It was why I asked to have this face-to-face meeting. So far no one knows Sigma is involved, and I wish to keep it that way."

Metcalf studied Painter, waiting for more details. Painter let him stew. He imagined that lesser men broke under that steely gaze. Painter didn't blink.

Metcalf finally huffed out his exasperation and leaned back. "So then tell me what happened."

Painter allowed his shoulders to relax. He reached to his desk, opened a file, and slid a photo toward the general. "Here is a forensic photo of the victim killed at the Vatican."

Metcalf took the picture and examined it. His eyebrows pinched together, his equivalent of raw shock. "It's the same mark," he said. "Branded into the forehead, like Senator Gorman's son."

"And the Princeton professor," Painter agreed. He knew Metcalf had already read the report on the events at the university.

"But what does this priest have to do with what happened in Africa? I understand Jason's connection to the university professor, but this?" He slid the photo back to Painter. "It makes no sense."

"The field agent in Italy—Commander Gray Pierce—has recovered and protected a vital piece to that puzzle. A piece that someone was willing to destroy the Roman Coliseum to acquire."

"And we have it."

Painter nodded.

"What is it?"

"We're still trying to figure that out. It's an old artifact with possible ties to an excavation site in England. I'd rather keep the details quiet for now. Limited to a need-to-know basis."

"And you don't think I need to know?"

Painter stared at him. "Do you really want to know?"

Metcalf's eyes had at first narrowed angrily, then edged toward some dark amusement. "Good point. After what happened in Rome, maybe not. Plausible deniability might be the best course for now."

"I appreciate that," Painter said. And he meant it. It was the widest degree of latitude he'd ever gotten from the man.

And yet he needed more.

"Whatever is going on stretches far beyond the borders of Italy," Painter continued. "And the best way to root out the truth is to keep our involvement quiet."

Metcalf nodded, agreeing.

"Before events transpired in Italy, I had come to the conclusion that we needed more information about the genetic project being conducted at the Red Cross camp."

"The farm run by the Viatus Corporation."

"So far the deaths of the two Americans—Jason and his professor—are tied to that project. How and why we don't know. But that's where we need to extend the investigation. We need more details. Information that can only be found in one place."

"You're talking about Viatus itself."

"There's a conference starting tomorrow in Oslo. The World Food Summit. The CEO of Viatus, Ivar Karlsen, is speaking at the conference. Someone needs to corner him, get him to talk, to open up about the true nature of the research that was under way in Africa."

"I've heard about Karlsen's reputation. He's no pushover. Strong-arming him will get you nowhere."

"I understand."

"He also has powerful friends—including here in the U.S."

"I'm well aware of that."

Painter had a complete dossier on the man and his company. Viatus had made vast inroads into the United States: financing a biofuel consortium in the Midwest, partnering with a major petrochemical company that produced fertilizers and herbicides, and of course sharing several lucrative patents with Monsanto for genetically modified seed strains.

Metcalf continued. "In fact, I already know about the summit in Oslo. A mutual friend of ours will be attending. Someone who's been riding DARPA for answers to his son's murder."

"Senator Gorman?" That surprised Painter.

"He's already in Oslo. Despite the circumstances surrounding his son's death, he remains a close associate of Ivar Karlsen. You don't want to make either man angry. Any interrogation of Karlsen will have to be done with the greatest discretion."

"I understand. Then that further supports the second reason I asked for this meeting."

"And what's that?"

"Due to the delicate nature of the matter and the threat of international ramifications, I'd like to conduct Karlsen's interview myself."

Metcalf hadn't expected that. He took a moment to digest the request. "You want to go out into the field? To Oslo?"

"Yes, sir."

"Who will oversee Sigma while you're gone?"

"Kathryn Bryant. She's been acting as my second-in-command. She has a background in Naval Intelligence with ties throughout the international communities. She'll be perfectly suited to maintain command and co-ordinate any field op."

Metcalf leaned back as he pondered this plan.

Painter knew the man had a firm code about personal accountability. It was why he had climbed so swiftly up the ranks in the Armed Forces. Painter pressed that very issue now.

"You've already explained how thin the ice is under Sigma," he said with conviction. "Give us this chance to prove ourselves. And if this blows up, let it be by my own hand. I'll take full responsibility."

Metcalf remained silent. He again fixed Painter with that steely gaze. Painter matched it, as firm and un-yielding.

A slight nod and the man stood up. He held out his hand this time. Painter shook it across his desk.

Before Metcalf let go, he squeezed a notch harder. "Tread lightly over there, Director Crowe. And speak just as softly."

"Don't worry. It's what my ancestors are known for. We're very light-footed."

This earned a small crooked smile as Metcalf let go and headed toward the door. "Perhaps. But in this case, I was referring to Teddy Roosevelt."

As the general left, Painter remained standing. He had to give the guy credit. He was right about Teddy. The motto was fitting for any agent heading out into the field.

Speak softly—but carry a big stick.

4:10 P.M.

"And those were the words Director Crowe used?" Kat asked.

Monk stood in front of her. She was seated on the sofa in her office. "His *exact* words. He needs a big stick."

"But do *you* have to be that big stick?"

Monk crossed to her and dropped to one knee, getting eye-to-eye with his wife. He knew this was going to be a hard sell. He had spoken to Painter thirty minutes ago. The director had offered Monk a field position, to accompany the big man himself to Oslo, Norway. Still, it had taken until now to get up enough courage to broach the subject with Kat.

"It's really nothing more than a glorified interview," Monk promised. "Like I've been doing here in the States these last months. This assignment's only a little farther away."

She wouldn't meet his eye. She stared down at her hands, which were clenched together in her lap. Her voice was low. "Yeah, and look how easy your last assignment ended up being."

Monk scooted closer and pushed between her knees. "We all made it out safely."

In fact, he had just checked on Andrea Solderitch. She'd already been moved to a guarded location, protected by Homeland, personally watched over by Scot Harvath, an agent Monk fully trusted to keep her safe.

"That's not the point," Kat said.

Monk recognized that. He reached forward, slid his hands under the bottom of her blouse, and gently palmed her bare belly. Her skin was hot under his palms. She trembled at his touch.

"I know the point," Monk said huskily. "My memory might be a little like Swiss cheese, but I don't forget what's truly important, not for one second of any day. And that's why I'm going to make sure nothing happens."

"You can't control everything."

Monk stared up at her. "Neither can you, Kat."

Her eyes remained wounded. He knew how hard she had fought to watch over him during his recovery, how she hated being apart. Even now. Her protectiveness was born out of raw fear. For months she had believed Monk was dead. He could only imagine what that must have been like. So, though it wasn't healthy for either of them, he didn't press the matter.

Even now, he refused to force her hand.

If she didn't want him to go, he wouldn't.

"I hate the idea of you out in the field," Kat said. She pulled his hands out of her shirt and clutched them tightly between hers. "But I'd hate myself more for telling you not to."

"You don't have to tell me," he said quietly, suddenly feeling selfish. "You know that. I get it. There will be other missions. When we're both ready."

Kat stared hard at him. Then she sagged slightly, rolled her eyes, and reached out to grab the back of his head. She pulled him forward. Her lips hovered over his. "Always the martyr, aren't you, Kokkalis?"

"What—?"

She silenced him with her lips, pressing hard, parting her mouth, tasting him. Then she pulled back, leaving him gasping, leaning forward for more.

"Just make sure you come back with all your parts intact this time," she said, poking his prosthetic with a finger.

Always the slower of the two, Monk struggled to catch up with her thoughts. "Are you saying—?"

"Oh, dear God, Monk. Yes, you can go."

Joy, along with a large measure of relief, swept through him. He cracked a huge smile, but it just as suddenly slipped into something more lascivious.

Kat read his thoughts and pressed a finger over his mouth. "No, not even one joke about you being a big stick."

"Oh, c'mon, babe . . . would I do that?"

She removed her finger, leaned down, and kissed him again. He slid his hands under her rear and dragged her onto his lap.

He whispered as he pulled her fully to him, "Why say it, when I can prove it?"

10:15 P.M.
Terni, Italy

Gray stood guard before the window, staring out at the dark garden behind the old country farmhouse. He also had a view of the parking lot and the nearby Via Tiberina road. They had traveled eighty miles to reach the small town in the Umbria region, noted for its ancient Roman ruins and baths.

Rachel had suggested the location. The two-story farmhouse had been converted into a hotel, but still retained much of its original charm, with chestnut beams, bricked archways, and iron chandeliers. It was also remote and off the beaten path.

Still, Gray refused to let his guard down. After events in Rome, he wasn't taking any chances. And he wasn't the only one.

Down in the garden, he noted a flicker of red ash. He hadn't known Seichan smoked—but then again, he knew almost nothing about her. She was an unknown quantity and a needless risk. He knew the standing orders out of Washington: capture her at any cost.

Still, she'd guarded their backs today, saved his life in the past.

As he watched her patrol the grounds, he heard the water shut off in the neighboring bathroom with a heavy *thunk* of the pipes. Rachel had finished her shower. After an hour in the sewers, they'd all needed some time with soap and very hot water.

They also needed a moment to regroup, to decide on a course of action. Moments later, Rachel exited the steaming bathroom, barefooted, wrapped only in a towel, her hair still dripping.

"Shower's free," she said, then glanced around the room. "Where's your partner?"

"Kowalski's gone downstairs. Fetching a late dinner from the kitchen."

"Oh." She remained standing in the doorway, her arms around her chest, suddenly awkward. She wouldn't meet his eyes. They hadn't been truly alone together since crashing back into each other's lives. He knew he should turn away, allow her a moment of privacy, but he couldn't.

She slowly stepped over to the bed, still favoring her left leg. Tylenol and a brace had helped her wrenched knee, but she needed at least a day of rest. On the bed was a stack of new clothes, still tagged and wrapped in tissue: for her, jeans, a midnight blue blouse, and a calf-length coat.

As she walked, she clung to her towel like a shield. There was no need. Gray knew intimately what lay under that towel. What his hands hadn't explored, his lips had. But it wasn't just the flesh that stirred him now. It was the memory of warmth, of soft words in the night, of promises that were never fulfilled.

He finally had to turn back to the window—driven away not by shyness, nor even out of politeness, but from an overwhelming sense of loss for what might have been.

He heard her shuffle by the bed, listened to the rustle of tissue paper. She didn't return to the bathroom to change. She shed her towel and dressed behind him. He sensed no seduction in her boldness, more an act of defiance, challenging him, knowing it both pained him and shamed him.

Then again, maybe it was all his imagination.

Once dressed, she joined him at the window and stood at his shoulder. "Still keeping watch, I see," she said softly.

He didn't answer.

She stood with him for a quiet moment. Down in the gardens, the sudden flare of a match illuminated Seichan's form as she lit another cigarette. Gray felt Rachel stiffen beside him. She glanced at him, then turned swiftly away and crossed back toward the bed.

Before either could speak, a rap on the door drew their attention. Kowalski entered, burdened by a wide wooden tray and two bottles of wine under one arm.

"Room service," he said.

As he stepped inside, he quickly noted the discarded towel in the middle of the floor. His eyes flickered between Rachel and Gray, then rolled slightly. He carried his burden to the room's table, whistling under his breath.

He left the tray on the table, but kept hold of both bottles of wine. "If you need me, I'm going to take a long hot bath. And I do mean long. I may be in there for at least an hour."

He glanced significantly at Gray in what passed as subtlety for the big man.

Rachel's face turned to a pale shade of crimson.

Gray was saved from further embarrassment by the ringing of his cell phone on the bedside table. He

checked his watch. That had to be Painter. He collected the phone and moved back to the window.

"Pierce here," he said as the secure connection
clicked through.

"So are you settled?" the director asked.

"For the moment."

Gray appreciated focusing back on the matter at
hand. Kowalski headed into the bathroom with his two
bottles of wine. Rachel sat on the bed and listened to
his end of the conversation. Over the next fifteen minutes, Gray and Painter compared notes: three murders
on three continents, the violence perpetrated to cover
up what was going on, the significance of the pagan
symbol that seemed to link everything together.

Painter described his plan to travel to Norway to investigate Viatus and its CEO.

"And Monk is going with you?" Gray asked, both
surprised and glad for his friend.

"Along with John Creed, our new resident geneticist. He was the one who decrypted the data from Jason
Gorman's e-mail." Painter's voice firmed to a more
serious tone. "Which brings us to what Lieutenant
Verona discovered, what someone apparently wanted
destroyed."

"The mummified finger."

Gray glanced at Rachel. They'd had a long discussion on the train ride out of Rome. Father Marco

Giovanni had been working at an excavation site in northern England, somewhere in the mountainous and remote region that bordered Scotland. They still had no more details about the excavation. All they knew was that Vigor's former student had been researching the roots of Celtic Christianity, when pagan worship merged with Catholicism.

Gray had already related some details to Painter. But he hadn't expanded on what Rachel had divulged on the train.

"Director, maybe you'd better hear this from Lieutenant Verona herself. I'm not sure of the significance, but it's worth noting if only for thoroughness."

"Very well. Put her on."

Gray crossed back to the bed and passed her the cell phone. "I thought you should tell Painter what you learned."

She nodded. He remained standing near the bedpost. After a few pleasantries, Rachel cut to the strange matter of the priest's obsession.

"Before everything went to hell in Rome," Rachel explained, "I had acquired a list of published papers and treatises written by Father Giovanni, some going back to when he was a student. It was plain he was fixated on a specific mythology of the Catholic faith, an incarnation of the Virgin Mary known as the Black Madonna."

Gray listened with half an ear as she explained. He was familiar with the subject. He had studied comparative religions before joining Sigma and knew the history and mysteries surrounding the cult of the Black Madonna. Over the centuries, going back to the very start of Christianity, statues and paintings had appeared that depicted the Mother of Christ with dark or black skin. These came to be revered and treasured. Over four hundred of the images still existed in Europe, a few dating all the way back to the eleventh century. And a large number of them were still worshiped and venerated: the Black Madonna of Częstochowa in Poland, the Madonna of Hermits in Switzerland, the Virgin of Guadalupe in Mexico. The list went on and on.

Despite this ongoing veneration, controversy continued to surround these unique Madonnas. While some claimed miraculous properties associated with them, others declared the dark skin was due to nothing more than accumulated candle soot or the natural darkening of wooden statues or old marble. The Catholic Church avoided acknowledging any significance or spiritual powers for these incarnations.

Rachel continued with Father Giovanni's fixation. "Marco was convinced that Celtic Christianity built its foundations upon the Black Madonna, that this image represented the fusion of the old pagan Earth Mother with the new worship of the Virgin Mary. He spent his career searching for this connection, the true source behind the mythology."

Rachel paused, plainly listening to a question from Painter, then answered, "I don't know if he ever found that source. But he found something, something worth dying over."

Rachel stopped again to listen, then said, "Right. I agree. I'll pass you back to Commander Pierce."

Gray accepted the phone, lifted it to his ear, and returned to the window. "Sir?"

"Considering Rachel's story, it seems plain what your next step must be."

Gray had no doubt of the correct answer. "Investigate the excavation site in England."

"Precisely. I don't know how the murders in Africa and Princeton tie to Father Giovanni's research. But there must be some connection. I'll follow up in Oslo concerning the genetic research—you see what that mummified finger points to."

"Yes, sir."

"Do you need any additional personnel for this mission? Or can you manage with Joseph Kowalski and Lieutenant Verona?"

"I think the leaner we move, the better."

Despite his best effort, a strained edge tightened his voice. There remained one detail he had never divulged to Painter Crowe. Gray stared down into the garden, to the crimson glow of a cigarette. He hated to lie to the director, even if it was only a sin of omission, but if Gray told Sigma Command about their new ally here, Painter would have no choice but to send a team to collect her, to cart her off to an interrogation camp.

Gray could not allow that.

Still, he hesitated.

Was he making the right choice? Or was he needlessly putting the entire mission in jeopardy?

Gray turned from the window to discover Rachel staring at him. In her eyes, he recognized that his decision threatened more than just his own life. Still, he also remembered a pained plea two years ago, one full of need and hope.

Trust me, Gray. If only a little.

Facing the dark window again, Gray stared at his reflection. After a long steadying breath, he spoke into the phone.

"We'll be fine on our own."

11

Ivar Karlsen pulled on the heavy oak door, its planks strapped with hammered iron. Snow swirled through the moonless night and whipped in sudden gusts into the narrow arched entry. Cold pinched his exposed cheeks, while the iron handle was so frozen it burned his fingers as he hauled open the door. The day's storm had indeed turned into the first true snowfall by evening.

The harsh weather stirred Ivar, got his heart pounding, his breath blowing strongly. Perhaps he did indeed have Viking blood running through his veins as his old *bestemor* claimed.

Ducking through the door, he stamped his boots to dislodge the caked snow. A dark stairway lay ahead, leading down into the depths below Akershus Castle. Ivar threw back the hood of his fleece-lined sherling coat and pulled a flashlight from his pocket. Clicking it on, he headed down the stairs.

The stone steps had been laid when the fortress was first built, dating back to the medieval period. His steps echoed off the low walls. He had to duck to keep from brushing the ceiling. Reaching the lower level, the stairs ended at an old guardroom with the original iron wall hooks and torch brackets still intact. Heavy beams held up the ceiling.

On the far side, a brick archway opened on a hall of tiny cells where downtrodden nobles and all manner of high criminals had been kept in squalid and miserable conditions. It was here that the Nazis had tortured Ivar's countrymen, those who resisted the German occupation. Ivar had even lost a granduncle down here. Honoring that sacrifice, Viatus continued to donate large sums to the preservation and upkeep of Akershus.

Ivar swept his flashlight down the throat of the gloomy dungeon passageway. This section was closed to the usual castle tours. Few even knew of its existence . . . or its darker history. It was here that those who committed high treason to the crown and country were held. The Nazi collaborator Viktor Quisling had been kept locked down here before he was executed.

Many others had met their deaths, going back centuries.

Ivar's fingers closed over an old coin in his coat pocket. He kept it with him at all times. It was a 1725 Frederick IV four-mark, minted by Henrik Christofer Meyer. Meyer had also died down here, whipped and bloodied, for replacing silver with copper in the king's coinage and pocketing the savings.

King Frederick IV—considered at the time to be a benevolent and merciful leader—still held to a strict code of honor. It was rumored that he had Viking blood in his lineage. And following the Viking code, betrayal of any manner had to be dealt with harshly.

Upon the king's order, Meyer was not only ordered whipped at the post and sentenced to life imprisonment, he was also marked permanently as a traitor to the crown. Meyers was branded with a hot iron poker in the center of his forehead. The king used one of the mint master's own substandard coins for the branding, burning the image into the man's flesh.

The coin in Ivar's pocket was one of those very coins. It had been in his family for centuries, the story passed from one generation to the next. It grew to represent the Karlsen family code: to balance mercy and generosity, yet never tolerate treachery in any form.

Ivar heard the door above open and slam closed, cutting off his reverie. Footsteps echoed as someone hurried down the steps.

A slim, long-legged woman entered the guardroom. She carried a bit of the winter chill with her. Snow frosted her fiery hair; her gold eyes reflected his flashlight. She wore a long gray coat over dark clothes.

"I'm sorry I'm late, Ivar," she said. She tossed her hair, scattering snow like some ancient goddess of winter.

Though only in her late twenties, Krista Magnussen had become the chief geneticist for his corporation's Crop Biogenics division. She had risen quickly, demonstrating both brilliance and a seemingly supernatural resourcefulness. It was only last year that Ivar had learned the true basis of her resourcefulness. The revelation had come at a time when things had begun to go awry with his careful plans. The house of cards he'd been meticulously building had begun to lean. It had needed shoring up.

Krista again proved her value; Ivar had been shocked to discover that she was not entirely who she appeared to be. Corporate espionage was commonplace throughout the industry, but he'd never suspected such a young, brilliant woman. And he never suspected the reach of her connections. She worked for a shadowy network that went by many names. They offered their mercenary services in exchange for access and a percentage of future profits. Over the past year, they had proved to be invaluable at shoring up his plans, even accelerating them.

And it had been Krista herself who dealt with the delicate and unfortunate matter of the senator's son.

She moved closer, gave Ivar a firm hug, and brushed his cheek in a chaste kiss. Her lips were still cold from the storm.

"I'm also sorry," she said, "that I had to summon you so suddenly at this hour."

"If it's important . . ."

"It is." Krista shook her long coat, shivering off snow and melting droplets. "I've just heard that our targets in Rome survived."

"They're alive? I thought you said they were dead."

"We underestimated them," Krista said with a shrug. She made no effort to justify, obfuscate, or avoid responsibility. As always, Ivar respected her candor.

"Do they still possess the artifact?"

"Yes."

"How do you know all this?" he asked with a frown.

Krista smiled, still coldly. "It seems our attack got someone's attention, someone with something to prove.

After events in Rome, we were contacted. Offered a deal. We now have someone on the inside."

"Can they be trusted?"

"I don't leave such matters to mere trust, Ivar. Our organization will be staying close to them, keeping a fire lit under them."

"I don't understand. If you have someone on the inside, why not have them secure the artifact or destroy it?"

"That may not be the wisest choice." Her eyes sparkled in the darkness, shining with a brilliance that dazzled.

"What do you mean?"

"Father Giovanni betrayed you. Took your money, allowed you to finance his research. Yet when he found the artifact, he stole it. Fled with it."

Ivar's fingers tightened on the coin. *The priest was made to pay for his crime.* Shortly after learning of Krista's connections, Ivar had told her the bloody story of Henrik Meyer, as both a lesson and a warning to her. Instead, she took the story to heart and suggested the mutilations, to help disguise the murders, to make them look more like the work of ecoterrorists. Ivar also found a certain satisfaction in the punishment, a return to an older form of justice, where those who betrayed the world were marked for all to see.

Krista continued. "But with the artifact secure again, now is our chance to hunt for what remains missing. To discover what Giovanni sought."

Ivar's attention focused fully back on her. He could not keep the desire out of his voice. "The Doomsday key . . ."

Such a discovery would not only secure his plan, it could make history. The key had the potential to unlock a mystery stretching back millennia.

Krista explained her plan. "Those who now hold the artifact have proved to be resourceful in the past. With the proper motivation, they might succeed where Father Giovanni failed."

Ivar reined in his raw desire and maintained his practicality. "And you're certain you can handle such an undertaking?"

"Not just me." Krista smiled, this time warm and full of assurance. "As I promised from the beginning, you'll have the full support of the Guild."

She crossed to him. "We will not fail you. I will not fail you."

Moving into his arms, she kissed him again. Not chastely this time, but full on the lips. Her hair brushed his neck, icy and damp, sending chills through him, but her lips, mouth, and tongue burned like liquid fire.

Ivar forgot about the coin in his pocket and reached to the small of her back. He pulled her closer. He recognized that she was seducing him, and he suspected that she knew he wasn't fooled. But neither of them pulled away.

They both knew what was at risk, what waited to be won.

The future of mankind.

And the power to control that fate.

SECOND

Fire and Ice

12

October 12, 10:12 A.M.
Hawkshead, England

It seemed impossible that murder could be traced back to such an idyllic countryside.

Gray drove down the winding road framed by rolling hills. With each passing mile the lane grew narrower until it was barely wide enough to accommodate the rented Land Rover. A patch of hardwood forest overhung the road, creating a tangled tunnel of woven branches. Once clear of the woods, the vistas opened again and revealed the rounded peaks of the surrounding fells, or what passed for mountains here in England. Snow already covered the crags in a white blanket since an early winter storm had blown across the district the night before.

Closer at hand, meadows and hedge-lined farm tracts cut the landscape into a quilt of brown grasses and fallow fields. Streams and creeks sparkled among mirror-smooth lakes and smaller highland tarns. Ice rimed the edges of all the waterways, and windblown snow frosted the entire landscape.

The natural beauty struck one to silence.

Or almost everyone.

"You're lost, aren't you?" Kowalski accused from the backseat.

"I'm not lost," Gray lied.

Rachel rattled her road map and eyed Gray doubtfully.

Okay, maybe they were a little off course . . .

They had left Liverpool two hours ago and followed the directions easily enough up into the Lake District of northern England. The highways were well marked, but once Gray exited the major thoroughfares, he ended up in a countryside of meandering lanes, unmarked roads, and a broken landscape of hills, forests, and lakes.

Even GPS proved to be no help. None of the roads matched its software. They might as well have been driving through open country.

Their destination was the town of Hawkshead, one of the many honeypot villages that nestled within the natural wonderland of the English Lake District. They were to meet a colleague of Father Giovanni, a historian from the University of Edinburgh named Dr. Wallace Boyle. Boyle had organized the dig out in a remote section of the central fells and still oversaw the site. He had agreed to meet them at a hotel pub in Hawkshead.

But first Gray had to find the place.

Rachel studied the map and searched out the window for any landmarks. Behind Rachel, Seichan sat next to Kowalski and stared sullenly out at the rolling hills and dales. She had barely spoken a word since leaving Italy and continued to hover at the edge of their group, maintaining a wary distance.

"If we don't get somewhere pretty damn quick," Kowalski continued, "you're going to have to stop at the next tree or bush. My back molars are floating."

Gray sped up the next hill. "If you hadn't downed those four pints of beer back in Liverpool—"

"Not my fault. All those cockamamie names. Blackwater Brewery's Buccaneer. Cains Double Bock. Boddington's Bitters. Tetley's Cask. Guy can't tell what he's getting 'til he tastes it. Took a while to find a good one."

"But you drank them all down."

"Of course I did. It would've been rude not to."

Rachel folded her map and gave up. "It can't be much farther," she said with little conviction. "Maybe we should stop and ask for directions."

Moments later, it proved unnecessary. With a final rattling push, the Land Rover topped the next rise, and a small village appeared, spread across the valley ahead.

Gray looked over at Rachel. The relief on her face answered his question. It had to be Hawkshead. Cobblestone lanes crisscrossed past fenced gardens and squat timbered homes. Snow mantled the village's slate roofs, and thin trails of smoke rose from the chimneys. Across the way, an old stone church crouched atop a hill and overlooked the village, like a grim gray deacon scowling down at the town below.

As they wound down toward the village, stacked-stone walls rose alongside the road. The Land Rover rumbled over an arched granite bridge to enter the outskirts of town. The buildings and homes were of wattle-and-daub construction with exposed timbers, traditional for an English Tudor town. Small front gardens and window boxes hinted at the splendor that must be spring and summer here, but after the storm last night, snow piled atop boxes and across yards, creating a wintry Christmas scene.

Gray slowed the Land Rover to a crawl as his tires crunched over icy cobbles. He headed toward the main square, where their meeting place—the Kings Arms Hotel—was located. They were already twenty minutes late. Reaching the square, Gray slid the SUV into a small parking lot.

As they exited the vehicle, the cold bit into any exposed skin. The dampness of Liverpool and the long heated drive had not prepared them for the icy chill of the Lakeland elevations. Wood smoke scented each cold breath. Bundling tighter into their thick coats, they set off.

The Kings Arms Hotel lay on the far side of the main square. The squat, slate-roofed building had greeted travelers for five hundred years, stretching back to the Elizabethan era. A low stone wall cordoned off a beer garden in front, its tables and chairs currently covered in a thin coat of fresh snow, but the fiery glow from the inn's lower windows promised steaming warmth and hot drinks. They hurried toward it.

Kowalski trailed them. "Hey, lookit all the bears . . ." His voice had a wistful note to it, a tone as incongruous as a bull suddenly singing an aria.

Gray glanced back at him. Kowalski's gaze was fixed on a shop window. Beyond the frosted glass, amber light revealed a display of teddy bears of every size and shape. The sign above the door read Sixpenny Bears.

"There's one dressed like a boxer!" Kowalski began to detour toward the window.

Gray directed him back. "We're already late."

Kowalski's shoulders slumped. With a final longing glance back at the shop, he continued after them.

Rachel stared at the big man with a bewildered expression.

"What?" Kowalski said grumpily. "It was for Liz, my girlfriend. She . . . she's the one who collects bears."

Rachel stared a moment longer, her expression doubtful.

Kowalski grumbled under his breath and tromped heavily toward the inn.

Seichan stepped next to Gray and touched his elbow. "You go inside. Meet with that historian. I'll keep watch out here."

Gray stared over at her. That hadn't been the plan. Though her face remained calm and disinterested, her eyes continued to roam the square, most likely analyzing the area for sniper roosts, escape routes, and the best places to duck for cover. Or maybe she just refused to meet his eye. Was she truly seeking to guard them or maintaining a cold distance?

"Is something wrong?" he asked, his legs slowing.

"No." Her eyes flashed toward him, almost angrily. "And I mean to keep it that way."

Gray didn't feel like arguing. After all that had happened in Italy, perhaps it would be best to keep a guard outside. He headed after Kowalski and Rachel as Seichan dropped back.

Joining the others, he crossed through the frozen beer garden and reached the front door. He noted a sign near the entryway that read "Good dogs and children welcome." That probably excluded Kowalski. Gray considered ordering his partner to stay outside with Seichan, but that would only make the woman angrier.

Gray pulled the door open. A heady warmth flowed out, accompanied by the smell of malt and hops. The pub was straight off the hotel lobby. A few voices echoed out to them, along with a booming laugh. Gray followed Kowalski into the pub. His partner aimed straight for the restroom with a quickness to his step.

Gray remained at the entrance and searched the room. The pub of the Kings Arms was small, a scatter of wooden tables and booths built around a stacked-stone fireplace. A roaring fire had been stoked against the cold. Next to the hearth stood a life-sized wooden model of a crowned king, likely the namesake of the hotel.

Another thundering burst of laughter drew Gray's attention to a corner booth near the fire. A pair of locals, dressed in hunting clothes and knee-high boots, stood before the table and its lone occupant.

"Fell right in the bog, you say, Wallace!" One of the hunters chuckled, wiping at an eye with one hand while hoisting a tall glass of dark ale in the other.

"Arse over kettle! Straight in," the man in the booth agreed, a Scottish brogue thickening his tongue.

"Wish'un I could've seen that, right enough."

"Ah, but the stench afterward, lads. That you wouldn'ta want to be near. Not at all." Another hearty laugh followed from the man seated in the booth.

Gray recognized Dr. Wallace Boyle from his picture on the University of Edinburgh website. But the professor in the photo had been clean-shaven and dressed in a formal jacket. The man here had a grizzly dusting of gray beard and was outfitted like his fellow hunters in a frayed herringbone jacket over a quilted waistcoat. On the table rested a moss-green tweed cap, fingerless gloves, and a thick scarf. Next to him, propped upright on the bench seat, was a shotgun zippered into a gunslip.

Dr. Boyle noted Gray's attention and approach. "Tavish, Duff, looks like those reporters I was setting to meet have arrived."

That had been their cover story: a pair of international journalists covering the bombing at the Vatican, following up on the death of Father Giovanni. Kowalski acted as their photographer.

The two hunters glanced Gray's way. Their faces went hard with the usual suspicion of locals for outsiders, but they nodded in wary greeting. With a final heft of their drinks, they left the table.

"Cheers, Wallace," one said as he departed. "We best be going anyway. It's already getting to be brass monkeys out there."

"And it'll get colder," Wallace agreed, then waved Gray and Rachel over toward his table.

Kowalski had returned from the restroom, but he never made it past the bar. His eyes were fixed to the chalkboard over the fireplace that listed the local brews. "Copper Dragon's Golden Pippin? Is that a beer or some sort of fruity drink? I don't want anything that has fruit in it. Unless you call an olive a fruit . . ."

Gray tuned out his partner as he headed over to Wallace's table. The professor stood, unfolding his six-foot-plus frame. Though in his midsixties, the man remained robust and broad-chested, like a younger Sean Connery. He shook their hands, his gaze lingering a little longer on Rachel. The man's eyes pinched for a moment, then relaxed, hiding whatever had momentarily perplexed him.

Rachel began to slide into the booth first, then suddenly froze. Her side of the bench was occupied. A wiry furred head lifted into view and rested a chin on the wooden table, not far from a half-eaten platter of bangers and mash.

"Rufus, get down from there," Wallace scolded, but without much heat. "Make room for our guests."

The black-and-tan terrier huffed through its nose in exasperation, then ducked away and came strolling out from under the table. He moved closer to the fire, circled twice, then collapsed down with an equally loud sigh.

"My hunting dog," the professor explained. "A mite spoiled, he is. But at his age, he's earned it. Best fox flusher in the isles. And why shouldn't he be? Born and bred right here. A true Lakeland Terrier."

Pride rang in the man's voice. This was not a professor headed toward early retirement, nor even one resting on his laurels, which were many, according to the man's bio. Dr. Wallace Boyle was considered to be a leading expert on the history of the British Isles, specifically the Neolithic age through the Roman occupation.

They all settled into the booth. Gray placed a small digital recorder on the table, maintaining their cover as journalists. After a few pleasantries about the weather and their drive, Wallace quickly turned to the matter at hand.

"So, you've come all this way to see what we discovered up in the fells," Wallace said. His brogue grew less heavy, his speech more formal, tailoring it to his audience. "Since the death of Father Giovanni, I've been fielding questions and inquiries nonstop for the past two days. Yet no one's seen fit to come out here in person. Then again, the good father himself hadn't been out here in months."

"What do you mean?" Rachel asked.

"Father Giovanni left at the end of summer. Headed to the coast, then off to Ireland, last I heard from him." Wallace shook his head sadly and tapped his glass of beer with a fingernail in some semblance of a toast to the dead. "Marco was a brilliant chap. Truly a great loss. His research and fieldwork on the roots of Celtic Christianity could have changed the way we view history."

"Why did he come here to begin with?" Gray asked. "To the Lake District."

"He would've ended up here eventually, I suppose. Even if I hadn't summoned him following my discovery up in the mountains."

"Why's that?"

"Marco's passion—or more like his obsession—had him scouring any and all areas where paganism and Christianity overlapped." Wallace lifted an arm to encompass the region in general. "And the history of this district is a story of that very conflict written in stones and ruins. It was the Norse who first came to this area, sailing over from Ireland to farm here in the ninth century, bringing all their traditions. Even the word *fell* comes from the Norse word for 'hill.' In fact, the village of Hawkshead was founded by a Norseman named Haukr, whose name still lives on in this place. That should give you some idea of the long history of this region."

Wallace nodded out the window toward the church that overlooked the town. "But times change. During the twelfth century, the entire area came under the ownership of the monks of Furness Abbey, the ruins of which can be found not far from here. The monks cultivated the region, traded in wool and sheep, and ruled the superstitious villagers with an iron fist. Tensions dragged on for centuries between the ancient pagan ways and the new religion. The old rituals continued to be performed in secret, often at the prehistoric sites that litter the countryside."

"What do you mean by *prehistoric* sites?" Rachel asked.

"Places dating back to the Neolithic period. Five thousand years ago." Wallace ticked them off on his fingers. "Ancient stone circles, henges, barrows, dolmens, hill forts. While Stonehenge might be the most famous, it's only one among several hundred such sites spread across the British Isles."

"But what interested Father Giovanni about your specific excavation?" Gray asked, seeking to draw the professor closer to the core of their investigation.

Wallace cocked one brow. "Ah, well, that you will have to see for yourself. But I can tell you what led *me* to this region."

"And what was that?"

"A single entry in an old book. An eleventh-century text nicknamed the Doomsday Book."

Kowalski stepped to their table. He carried a tall glass of pilsner in each hand, drinking from both. He paused in midsip upon hearing Wallace's words. "Doomsday," he said. "Great. Like we don't have enough problems already."

11:05 A.M.
Seichan walked the full length of the square. In her mind, a map formed of the local area. Every detail, brick by brick, every street, alley, building, and parked car. All became fixed in her head.

She noted two men dressed in hunting gear as they left the pub. She stalked them as they ambled over to a truck in the parking lot. She made sure they drove away.

Afterward, she found a good vantage point from which to observe the Kings Arms Hotel. It was the doorway of a closed gift shop. The alcove allowed her to shelter against the occasional stiff gust and to keep out of direct sight. On her right, the shop's window displayed a pastel-colored diorama of small ceramic animals dressed in little outfits: pigs, cows, ducks, and, of course, tiny bunnies . . . lots and lots of bunnies. The Lake District was the home of Beatrix Potter and her creation Peter Rabbit.

Despite her need to watch the hotel, Seichan's attention drifted to the shop window. She remembered very little about her childhood, and what she did remember she wished she could forget. She had never known her parents and was raised in an orphanage outside of Seoul, South Korea. It had been a squalid place with few comforts. But there had been a few books, including Beatrix Potter's, brought years ago by a Catholic missionary. Those books and others were her true childhood, a place to escape the hunger, abuse, and neglect. As a young girl, she had even made a toy bunny out of a scrap of burlap stuffed with dry rice. To keep it from being stolen, she had kept it hidden behind a loose board in the wall, but eventually a rat found it and ate out the stuffing. She had cried for a solid day, until one of the matrons beat her, reminding her that even sorrow was a luxury.

In the doorway, Seichan turned her back to the window display, shutting out those memories. Still, it wasn't just the past that pained her. Through the window, she watched Gray converse with an older man in tweed garb. It had to be Dr. Wallace Boyle. Seichan studied Gray. His black hair was longer, lankier across his forehead. His face had also grown harder, making his cheekbones stand out. Even his ice-blue eyes had a few more crinkles at the edges—not from laughter, but from the passing of a hard couple of years.

Standing in the cold, dusted with snow, Seichan remembered his lips. In a single moment of weakness, she had kissed him. There had been no tenderness behind it, only desperation and need. Still, she had not forgotten the heat, the roughness of his stubble, the hardness of his hold on her. Yet in the end it had been meaningless to both of them.

The hand in her coat pocket touched the scar on her belly.

They had just been dancing a game of betrayal.

Like now.

A vibration in her pocket alerted her to a call.

Finally.

It was the real reason she had stayed out in the cold. She removed the phone and flipped it open.

"Speak," she said.

"Do they still have the package?" The voice on the phone was calm and assured but crisp at the edges, with an American accent. It was her sole point of contact, a woman named Krista Magnussen.

Seichan bridled at having to take orders from anyone, but she had no choice. She had to prove herself. "Yes. The artifact is secure. They're meeting with the contact right now."

"Very good. We'll make our move once they're at the excavation site in the mountains. The team set the charges in place last night. The fresh snowfall should cover up any evidence."

"And the objective?"

"Remains the same. To light a fire under them. In this case, literally. The archaeological site is now more of a liability than an asset. But its destruction must appear natural."

"And you have that covered."

"We do. Leaving you free to focus fully on your objective."

Seichan read the threat behind the words. There would be no excuse for failure. Not if she wanted to live.

As she listened to the mission specifics, she continued to watch the hotel window. Not focusing on Gray any longer, she stared at the Italian woman seated beside him. Rachel smiled at something the professor said, her eyes sparking warmly even across the cold distance.

Seichan held nothing against Rachel Verona—but that would not stop her from poisoning the woman.

11:11 A.M.

Rachel listened as the conversation continued. While the professor's history lesson was intriguing, she sensed something deeper going on here—in regard to the story of Father Giovanni and something else, something yet unspoken. The man's gaze kept lingering on her, not lasciviously, but more like he was sizing her up. She had a hard time maintaining eye contact with him.

What was going on?

"I still don't understand," Gray said beside her. "What does this Doomsday Book have to do with your discovery up in the mountains?"

Wallace held up a hand, asking for patience. "First of all, the book's true name wasn't Doomsday, but rather *Domesday.* After the old English root *dom,* which meant 'reckoning' or 'accounting.' The book was commissioned by King William as a means to assess the value of his newly conquered lands, a way to assign tax and tithing. It mapped out all of England, down to every town, village, and manor house, and took a census of the local resources, from the number of animals and plows in the fields to the number of fish in its lakes and streams. To this day, the book remains one of the best glimpses of life during that time."

"That's all fine," Gray pressed, plainly wanting to hurry him along. "But you mentioned that a *single* entry led to your current excavation. What were you talking about?"

"Ah, now there's the rub! You see, the Domesday Book was written in a cryptic form of Latin, compiled by a single scribe. There remains some mystery as to why this level of security was necessary. Some historians have wondered if there might not have been a secondary purpose to this great compilation, some secret accounting. Especially as a few of the places listed in the book are ominously marked with a single word in Latin that meant 'wasted.' Most of those locations are concentrated in the northwest region of England, where the borders were constantly changing."

"By the northwest," Rachel asked, "you mean like here, the Lake District?"

"Exactly. The county of Cumbria was rife with border wars. And many of the spots listed as *wasted* were sites where the king's army had destroyed a town or village. They were noted because you couldn't tax what no longer existed."

"Really?" Kowalski asked, scowling at his two glasses of ale. "Then you never heard of the death tax?"

Wallace glanced from Kowalski to Gray.

"Just ignore him," Gray recommended.

Wallace cleared his throat. "Closer study of the Domesday Book revealed a bit of a mystery. Not all of the *wasted* sites were the result of conquest. A scattering of references had no explanation. These few were marked in red ink, as though someone had been tracking something significant. I sought some explanation and spent close to ten years on one of those entries, a reference to a small village up in the highland fells that no longer exists. I searched for records to this place, but it was as if they'd been expunged. I almost gave up until I found an odd mention in the diary of a royal coroner named Martin Borr. I found his book up at Saint Michael's."

He waved toward the hilltop church at the edge of town. "The book was discovered in a bricked-off cellar during a renovation. Borr was buried up in the cemetery at Saint Michael's, his possessions given over to the church. While his journals wouldn't say exactly what had happened to that village, the man did hint at something horrible, suggesting that *doomsday* might indeed be a more accurate name for that book. He even marked his diary with a pagan symbol, which is what drew me to the tome to begin with."

"A pagan symbol?" Rachel's hand strayed toward her coat pocket, where she kept the leather satchel with its macabre contents.

Gray placed his palm over her fingers and squeezed gently, his intent plain. Until he knew more about this man, he didn't want Rachel showing him what she'd found. Rachel swallowed, too aware of the heat of Gray's palm on her skin. She slipped her hand away and placed it on top of the table.

Wallace failed to notice their quiet communication. "The symbol was definitely pagan. Here, let me show you." He dipped a finger in his glass of ale and drew on the wooden table, with a few deft strokes, a circle and a cross. A familiar symbol.

"A quartered circle," Gray said.

Wallace's brows rose, and he stared a bit harder at Gray. "Exactly. You'll find this symbol carved into many ancient sites. But to find a Christian diary marked with it caught my attention."

Rachel sensed they were drawing near to the heart of the mystery. "And this diary helped you to find that lost village up in the mountains?"

"Actually, no." Wallace smiled. "What I found was even more exciting."

"What do you mean?" she asked.

Wallace sat back, folded his arms, and swept his gaze over the lot of them. "Before I answer that, how about you telling me first what's really going on? Like what you're all doing here?"

"I don't understand," Gray said, feigning confusion, attempting to maintain their cover story as journalists.

"Don't take me for a fool. If you're reporters, I'm a steamin' bampot." Wallace's gaze settled fully on Rachel. "Besides, right off, I recognized you, my young lassie. You're Monsignor Verona's niece."

Shocked, Rachel stared over at Gray. He looked like he'd been punched in the stomach. Kowalski merely rolled his eyes, picked up his glass, and downed the remaining contents in one gulp.

Rachel saw no reason to continue the subterfuge. She faced the professor. She now understood why the man had been staring at her so oddly. "You know my uncle?"

"Aye. Not well, but I do. And I'm sorry to hear he's still in a coma. We met at a symposium years ago and began an ongoing correspondence. Your uncle was very proud of you—a carabiniere in charge of antiquities theft. He sent photos, and at my age, I don't forget a pretty young face like yours."

Rachel shared a glance with Gray, looking apologetic. She hadn't known of this personal connection.

Wallace continued. "I don't understand the reason for this bit of subterfuge, but before we go any further, I want some explanation."

Before anyone could speak, the professor's terrier began a low growl at the back of its throat. The dog climbed to its legs beside the fire and stared toward the entryway of the hotel. As the door swung open, the growl deepened.

A figure stepped into the hotel, knocking snow from her boots.

It was only Seichan.

13

October 12, 1:36 P.M.
Oslo, Norway

The luncheon ended with a warning.

"Mankind can no longer wait to respond to this crisis," Ivar Karlsen said, standing at a podium at the far end of the dining hall. "A global collapse faces this generation or the next."

Painter shared the table at the back of the hall with Monk and John Creed. They had arrived in Oslo only an hour ago and barely made it to the opening luncheon of the World Food Summit.

The dining room of Akershus Castle was straight out of a medieval storybook. Hand-hewn wooden beams held up the ceiling, while underfoot, an oak floor was laid out in a herringbone pattern. Overhead, chandeliers sparkled down upon long tables draped in linens.

The meal had included five courses, an irony for a summit that had gathered to discuss world hunger. The lunch had been a study in Norwegian cuisine, including medallions of reindeer in a mushroom sauce and a pungent dish of lutefisk, a Norwegian whitefish specialty. Monk was still dragging his spoon around his dessert bowl, chasing the last cloudberry out of the whipped cream. Creed merely cradled a cup of coffee in his hands and listened to the keynote speaker attentively.

With the speaker's podium at the far end of the hall, Painter had a hard time getting much of a read on Ivar Karlsen, but even across the distance, the man's passion and earnestness were plain.

"World governments will be too slow to respond," Ivar continued. "Only the private sector has the fluidity to act with the necessary speed and innovation to turn aside this crisis."

Painter had to admit that the scenario presented by Karlsen was frightening. All the models he presented ended the same way. When unchecked population growth hit the point of stagnating food supply, the resulting chaos would kill over 90 percent of the world population. There seemed only one solution, a final solution not unlike Hitler's.

"Population control must be started immediately. The time to act is now, or even better, *yesterday*. The only way to avoid this catastrophe is to slow the rate of population growth, to apply the brakes before we hit the wall. Yet do not be fooled. We *will* hit the wall. It is inevitable. The only question is do we kill all the passengers or do we walk away with only a few scratches. For the sake of humanity, for the sake of our future, we must act now."

With those final words, Karlsen lifted a hand to a smattering of applause. It was far from enthusiastic. For the opening to the summit, it certainly cast a pall of gloom.

One of the men seated at the front table stood and took the microphone next. Painter recognized the dour-faced South African economist. Dr. Reynard Boutha, copresident of the Club of Rome. Though Boutha nodded to Karlsen as he assumed the podium, Painter read the tension and irritation in the copresident's expression. He was not happy with the tone of the keynote.

Painter barely heard Boutha's words. They were mostly conciliatory, more optimistic, an acknowledgment of the great strides already made in feeding the world's hungry. Painter kept his focus on Karlsen. The man's face was passive, but he gripped his water glass tightly, and deliberately kept his eyes away from Boutha, refusing to acknowledge the other's message of hope.

Monk came up with the same evaluation. "Guy looks like he's ready to punch his fist through something."

The concluding farewell by Boutha ended the luncheon. Painter immediately shot to his feet. He turned to Monk and Creed. "Head back to the hotel. I'm going to have a few words with Karlsen, then meet you there."

John Creed stood. "I thought our appointment wasn't until tomorrow morning."

"It's not," Painter said. "But it never hurts to say hello."

He pushed against the tide of people leaving the luncheon. A small clutch of admirers surrounded Karlsen, congratulating, questioning, shaking his hand. Painter edged nearer. Off to the side, he overheard Boutha speaking to a hawk-nosed man in a poorly fitting suit.

"Antonio, I thought you warned Mr. Karlsen against such an inflammatory speech."

"I did," the other answered, his face red and blotchy. "Does he ever listen? But at least he toned down the worst of it. His original keynote called for mandatory birth control in third world countries. Can you imagine how that would've been received?"

Boutha sighed and headed away with the other man. "At least he'll be away from the conference starting tomorrow."

"Small blessing there. He'll be in Svalbard with some of our biggest donors and sponsors. I can only imagine what he'll say when he has them alone. Perhaps if I went along, too . . ."

"You know the scheduled flights are full, Antonio. Besides, I'll be along on that trip to put out any fires."

They passed Painter without a glance, leaving the way open to Karlsen. Painter stepped forward and took the CEO's arm in a double-handed shake, one hand on his palm, the other on his wrist.

"Mr. Karlsen, I thought I should take a moment to introduce myself. I'm Captain Neal Wright from the U.S Office of the Inspector General."

The man extracted his hand, but his warm smile never faltered. "Ah, the investigator from the Department of Defense. Let me assure you that you'll have my full cooperation concerning the tragedy in Mali."

"Of course. And I know our interview isn't scheduled until tomorrow. But I just wanted to say I found your talk fascinating." Painter played off what he had just heard. "Though I wonder if you were perhaps pulling your punches."

"How so?" The casual interest in his face sharpened.

"It seems drastic methods will be necessary to curb population growth. I had hoped you would have gone into more specific details rather than mere generalities."

"You may be right, but it's a controversial subject, one best handled delicately. Too often, people blur the line between population control and eugenics."

"As in who are allowed to breed children and who are not?"

"Precisely. It's not a subject for those bound by political expediency or popular opinion. That's why governments of the world will never solve this problem. It's a matter of will and timing." Karlsen checked his watch. "And speaking of the latter, I'm unfortunately running late for another appointment. But I'd be happy to chat more about this when we meet tomorrow at my office."

"Very good. And thank you again for the illuminating talk."

The man nodded as he stepped away, his mind already shifting to the next task at hand.

Painter watched him leave. As Karlsen neared the hall entrance, Painter palmed the cell phone in his pocket and pressed the button on its side. A narrow radio frequency burst from the phone and activated the polysynthetic receiver implanted inside his ear.

A chatter of voices, along with the clink of dishes being cleared from the tables, immediately burst in his ear. The sounds were amplified from the bug he had just planted inside the jacket sleeve of Ivar Karlsen as they shook hands. The electronic surveillance device was no larger than a grain of rice. It had been DARPA engineered, based on one of Painter's own designs. He might be director of Sigma now, but he'd started as a field operative. His specialty was microengineering and surveillance.

Painter watched Karlsen come to a sudden stop outside the banquet hall. He clasped hands with a silver-haired man who matched him in height. Painter recognized Senator Gorman. Straining to listen in on their conversation, Painter weeded out the background noise and concentrated on Karlsen's voice.

"—you, Senator. Were you able to catch the keynote?"

"Just the end of it. But I'm well aware of your views. How was it received?"

Karlsen shrugged. "Fell on deaf ears, I'm afraid."

"That will change."

"Unfortunately true," Karlsen said a little sadly. He then clapped Senator Gorman on the shoulder. "By the way, I should let you know I just met that investigator from D.C. He strikes me as a very capable fellow."

Painter allowed a slight smile to form. *Nothing like making a good first impression . . .*

The senator's gaze swept the ballroom. Painter kept his face turned away and slipped smoothly among a clutch of people. The senator's security clearance was not high enough to know anything about Sigma. As far as the senator knew, Painter was merely a DoD investigator. Still, he preferred anonymity. General Metcalf had warned against ruffling the man's feathers. The senator had a quick temper and little patience, which he amply demonstrated now.

"It's a stupid waste of resources to send someone all the way here," Gorman complained. "The investigation should be concentrating its resources in Mali."

"I'm sure they're just being thorough. It's not an inconvenience."

"You're too generous."

With those words, the two men left together.

Painter kept the microreceiver live in his ear and strode toward the exit. He continued to eavesdrop on the conversation.

It was good to have the upper hand, for once.

In a room off the banquet hall, Krista Magnussen sat before an open laptop. She studied the image of the man frozen on the screen with mild interest. He was strikingly handsome with his whip-hard body, black hair, and flashing blue eyes. During the luncheon, she had observed everyone who made contact with Ivar Karlsen. A small wireless camera was situated in a corner of the room, focused on the front of the hall. There had been no audio, but the surveillance allowed her to run each image through face-recognition software and cross-reference it against a Guild database.

As she waited, the man's face digitized into a hundred reference points and uploaded. Moments later, the screen flashed in red with a single word, along with an operative code beneath it.

The word made her go cold.

Sigma.

The operative code she knew equally well.

Terminate upon sight.

Krista returned the camera feed to live. She leaned close to the monitor. The man was gone.

Antonio Gravel was having a bad day.

Standing out in the hallway, he had meant to waylay Ivar Karlsen after the luncheon, to try one last time to convince the bastard to let him join the trip to Svalbard. He was even willing to offer some concession, to ingratiate himself if necessary. Instead, Ivar had run into the U.S. senator. Antonio waited in the wings to be introduced, but as usual, the bastard deliberately ignored him. The two men departed, deep in conversation.

Antonio could barely breathe after the insult. Anger grew to a blinding white fury. He swung away savagely and smacked squarely into a woman hurrying out a side door. She was dressed in a long fur coat, her hair done up in a scarf. He struck her so hard that a large pair of Versace sunglasses slipped from her face. She deftly caught them and perched them back on her nose.

"Entschuldigen Sie bitte," Antonio apologized. He'd been so startled and mortified that he slipped into his native Swiss German—especially as a confounding flicker of recognition fluttered through him.

Who . . . ?

Ignoring him, she shoved past, glanced into the banquet room—then rushed down the hallway with a flare of her ankle-length coat. She was plainly late for some engagement.

He watched her disappear down the closest stairwell. Irritated, he shook his head and started to leave the other way.

Then he suddenly remembered.

He jolted and swung back around.

Impossible.

He had to be mistaken. He had only met the geneticist once, at an organizational meeting regarding the Viatus research project in Africa. He didn't recall her name, but he was certain it was the same woman. He had spent most of that dull meeting staring at her and undressing her with his eyes, imagining what it would be like to force himself on her.

It had to be her.

But she was supposed to be dead, a victim of the Mali massacre. There had been no survivors.

Antonio continued to stare toward the stairwell. What was she doing here, alive and unharmed? And why was she keeping herself hidden, her features under wraps?

Antonio's eyes narrowed as a slow realization warmed through him. Something was up, something no one was supposed to know about, something tied to Viatus. For years, he'd been seeking some dirt on Ivar, a way to rein the bastard to his will.

At long last, here might be his chance.

But how to best turn it to his advantage?

Antonio swung away, already plotting his game. He knew which card to play first. A man who'd lost a son during that massacre. Senator Gorman. What would the U.S. senator think if he learned there had been a survivor of the attack, someone Ivar was keeping secret?

With a grim smile, he headed off.

The day had suddenly gotten much brighter.

3:15 P.M.

Painter headed under the brick archway that passed through the fortress wall of Akershus. Even though it was only a little after three in the afternoon, the sun was already low in the sky at this near-Arctic latitude. Beyond the archway, the fjord's harbor opened. Snow still frosted the verdigris-stained cannons that lined the walkway and pointed out to sea, ready to protect the town against warships. Though at the moment, there was only a Cunard cruise ship parked dockside.

As seagulls swooped and screamed through the diesel-fouled air, Painter continued along the cruise ship's towering bulk and aimed for the city proper. Over the past hour, he'd kept tabs on Ivar Karlsen, eavesdropping on his conversations. With the bug, he'd had a good chance to discover more details about the CEO, insights that might prove invaluable for tomorrow's interview.

The conversations had mostly been of mundane matters, but still, it was clear the man was deeply committed to facing issues of hunger and overpopulation. Karlsen was all about real-world solutions and practicality. It was plainly the man's mission in life.

Painter also caught an intriguing bit of conversation about the drought-resistant corn strains being developed by Viatus, a version of which had been tested at the Mali research farm. As of last week, mass seed shipments were already under way to places around the world, triggering a spike in stock prices for Viatus. And still Ivar was not satisfied. He promised that his company's Crop Biogenics division was continuing to craft new strains with desirable features: insect-resistant wheat, frost-tolerant citrus, weed-killing soybeans. The list went on and on, including a rapeseed strain that could produce oil essential to the manufacture of biodegradable plastic.

But the conversation had ended on a darker note. Karlsen had brought up a quote from Henry Kissinger. It had been in response to a question about his company's shift in focus from petrochemicals to engineered seeds. He had said, paraphrasing Kissinger, "Control oil and you control nations, but control *food* and you control all the people of the world."

Did Karlsen truly believe that?

A few minutes after that, the man had climbed into a corporate limo and left for his research complex outside of Oslo. The hidden microtransceiver had a limited range, so Painter had to abandon his spying for now. And just as well. Karlsen's talk about the Crops

Biogenics division had lit a fire under Painter. He barely felt the cold as he crossed into the shadow of the towering cruise ship and navigated through the passengers hovering at the gangplank.

He had to prepare for another facet of the investigation, one that would require a bit more stealth this evening.

As he moved through the passengers, a burly figure in a parka bumped against him. Spotting the impact a fraction of a second before, Painter instinctively moved to sidestep him. A fiery lance of pain stabbed into his side.

He spun away from it, catching a flash of silver off a knife held low in the man's grip. If he hadn't dodged at the last moment, the blade would've struck him square in the stomach. He couldn't count twice on such a lucky break. The man came at him again.

So far, no one else had noted the attack.

Painter snatched a camera from around one of the oblivious tourists' necks. Gripping the shoulder strap, he swung the heavy Nikon SLR and struck the attacker square in the ear. As the man fell to the side, Painter leaped in closer, snagged the leather strap around the man's wrist, and used the grip to wrench his struggling form over his hip and hard to the pavement.

The man's face struck the cement. A bone snapped in his trapped arm. The knife tumbled across the ground.

As yells erupted all around, Painter vaulted over the prone body, going after the loose weapon. Before he could reach it, the knife suddenly jolted, emitting a sharp hissing, and skittered like a loose rocket across the icy ground. Painter hesitated, recognizing the lethal weapon.

A WASP injector knife.

The dagger's handle held a bulb of compressed gas, making the blade doubly dangerous. Once stabbed into a victim, the press of a button blasted a basketball-sized volume of cold air through the impaled blade and into the victim's gut, snap-freezing and pulverizing all internal organs. It could kill a brown bear with one jab.

Propelled by the blast of gas, the knife rocketed into the tangle of boots and legs. The waterfront had erupted in chaos. Some people fled from the fight; others crowded closer. Someone shouted, "That guy stole my camera!"

A slew of ship security personnel pounded down the gangway. More forced their way through the crowd.

Painter clutched a hand to his side and dove into the chaos of the churning crowd. The heavy coat and last-minute dodge had saved his life. Still, hot blood welled through his fingers. Fire flamed his side. He could not get caught. Still, it wasn't only security he had to worry about. As he ran, he kept watch on the crowd around him.

Had the attacker come alone?

Not likely.

As Painter stumbled through the passengers and tourists, he searched faces around him and watched hands. How many others were disguised like the first one, planted in the crowd and guarding this exit out of Akershus?

He knew one thing for certain. This had been no random mugging. Not with the attacker wielding a WASP injector. Somehow his cover had been blown. A net had been set up around the fortress grounds.

He had to get clear of the docks, put some distance between himself and the ambush. The crowds grew less tight around him as he hopped into the parklands that bordered the dock. Icy snow covered the ground and crunched under his boots. Bright red drops splattered into the snow. He was leaving an easy trail to follow.

Fifty yards away, another man in a parka hopped the border fence and came tromping toward him. So much for the subtle approach now. Not knowing if the man had a gun, Painter turned and fled for the patch of pine trees that filled the back half of the park. He had to get under cover.

The assassin followed the fresh trail of prints in the snow. He ran in a low crouch, his blade clutched in his left hand. He hit the tree line and kept one eye on the trail and the other on his surroundings. Under the trees the way became shadowy but not so dim that he lost sight of the trail. No one had been through here since the last snowfall. Only one set of prints marred the virgin snow.

Along with a dribbling track of blood.

The path zigzagged through the trees. Clearly the target feared a gun and took up a defensive pattern. It was a waste of effort. The assassin cut a straight path through the forest, paralleling the crooked flight.

Ahead, the glade opened. The trail of prints fled straight across. His prey had abandoned caution and was trying to reach the city streets beyond the park. Tightening his grip on the knife, he raced to close the distance.

As he reached the glade's edge, a low branch of a neighboring pine whipped around. It struck him across the shins with the force of a battering ram. His legs were knocked from under him. He flipped face-forward into the snow. Before he could move, a heavy weight landed on his back and crushed the remaining air out of him.

He realized his mistake. The man had backtracked, hidden behind the pine, and ambushed him, hauling back the branch that had cracked across his shins.

It was his last mistake.

A hand shot down and gripped his chin. The other pinned his neck to the ground. A sharp yank. His neck snapped. Pain flared as if the top of his skull had blown away—then darkness.

5:34 P.M.

"Hold still," Monk scolded. "I only have one more suture."

Painter sat on the edge of the tub in his boxers. He felt the needle pierce his flesh. The spray anesthetic only dulled the sharpest edge of the pain. At least Monk worked swiftly. He'd already debrided and cleaned the wound, shot him full of prophylactic antibiotics, and with a final deft twist of his needle forceps, he closed the four-inch laceration under the left side of Painter's rib cage.

Monk dropped everything into a sterile Surgipack on the bathroom floor, picked up a roll of gauze and adhesive tape, and set about wrapping Painter's chest.

"What now?" Monk asked. "Do we stick to our schedule?"

After the attack, Painter had fled into the city, taking an extra few minutes to make sure he wasn't followed. Then he'd called Monk. As a precaution, he ordered them to change hotels and rebook under another alias. Painter joined them there.

"I see no reason to change," Painter said.

Monk nodded toward the wound. "I see about four inches of reason."

Painter shook his head. "They were sloppy. Whoever set up the attack must have done so hastily. Somehow I was made, but I don't think we're more exposed than that."

"Still, that's pretty damn exposed."

"It just means extra precautions will be necessary from here. I'll have to avoid the summit. Keep out of sight. That means leaning more heavily on you and Creed."

"So we're still going to recon that research facility tonight?"

Painter nodded. "I'll monitor via radio. Nothing fancy. Slip in, tap into the servers, and get the hell out of there."

It was a simple operation. Courtesy of Kat Bryant's sources, they had identification cards, electronic keys, and a full schematic of the Viatus facility. They would go in after midnight when the place was mostly deserted.

John Creed hurried into the bathroom. He wore a lab coat with the Viatus logo on the pocket. He must have been trying on his disguise. "Sir, your phone. It's buzzing."

Painter held out a hand and took the cell. He read the Caller ID and frowned. It was General Metcalf's number. Why was he calling? Painter had avoided briefing Washington on what had happened until he knew more. To have the operation closed down before it even started would not sit well with anyone.

Especially Painter.

He flipped the phone open and answered. "General Metcalf?"

"Director Crowe. I suspect you're still settling in over there, so I'll be brief. I just received a call from Senator Gorman. He was very agitated."

Painter struggled to understand. He'd done nothing to provoke the senator.

"Gorman received a cryptic call half an hour ago. Someone claiming to have information on the attack in Africa. The caller said he knew of a survivor to the attack."

"A survivor?" Painter could not hide his own surprise.

"The caller wants to meet at the bar of the senator's hotel. To give further details. He'll only meet with Gorman alone."

"I don't think that's wise."

"Neither do we. That's why you're going to be at that bar. The senator knows that a DoD investigator is already in Oslo. He personally requested you be there. You're to maintain a low profile, to intervene only if necessary."

"When's the meet?" Painter asked.

"Tonight at midnight."

Of course, it would be.

Painter finished the call and tossed the phone back to Creed.

"What?" Monk asked.

Painter explained, which only deepened Monk's frown.

Creed spoke a fear they all shared. "It might be a trap. Meant to draw you out into the open again."

"We should call off the operation at Viatus," Monk suggested. "Go with you as backup."

Painter considered that option. Monk had been out of the field for some time, and Creed had barely gotten his feet wet. It would be risky to send them over to the research facility by themselves. Painter studied Monk, weighing the variables.

Monk guessed the intent of his attention. "We can still do this, sir, if that's what you're thinking. The kid might be green, but we'll get it done."

Painter heard the certainty in the man's voice. With a sigh, he stopped overanalyzing the situation. He wasn't at his desk in Washington anymore. This was field-work. He had to trust his gut. And his gut was telling him that events were rapidly escalating out of control.

Delay was not an option.

"We stick to the schedule," he said forcefully, brooking no argument. "We need access to that server. From today's attack, it's clear someone is getting both bolder and more agitated. A bad combination. We can't let them lock us out. So we'll just have to split up to-night."

Creed looked concerned, but not for himself. "Sir, what if you're attacked again?"

"Don't worry. They had their one free shot at me." Painter reached the sink and picked up the WASP dagger that he'd confiscated from the assassin in the park. "Tonight, I'll be the one doing the hunting."

6:01 P.M.

Bundled in a fox-fur–lined coat and hood, Krista strode down the central path of Frogner Park in the west-end borough of Oslo. She had an apartment that overlooked the snowy park, but she could not stand to wait indoors any longer. She carried her phone with her.

The sun had set, and the temperature had plummeted.

She had the park to herself.

She continued along the path through the sculpture garden. Her warm breath frosted the air. She needed to keep moving, but tension kept her stiff.

Spread around her were more than two hundred sculptures created by Gustav Vigeland, a Norwegian national treasure. Most of the sculptures involved nude stone figures frozen in various combinations and twisted poses. Presently the sculptures were covered with snow, as if wrapped in tattered white cloaks.

Ahead rose the towering central sculpture. It sat on the highest point of the park and was lit up for the night. It was named the Monolith. It always reminded Krista of something out of Dante's *Inferno*, especially at night. Maybe that's why she was drawn to it now.

The sculpture was a circular tower four stories high carved out of a single block of granite. Its entire surface was a writhing mass of human figures, tangled, twisted, entwined, a dark orgy in stone. It was supposed to represent the eternal cycle of mankind, but to her, it looked like a mass grave.

She stared up at it, knowing what was coming.

What we are about to unleash . . .

She shuddered inside her coat and clasped her fur-lined hood tighter to her throat. It was not remorse that kept her trembling, but the sheer enormity of what was unfolding. It was already under way, had been for over a decade, but in the next days, there would be no turning back. The world was about to change, and she had played a primary role in it all.

But she had not acted alone.

Her phone, still clutched in her pocket, vibrated. She took a deep breath and exhaled a stream of white mist. She had failed today. What would be her punishment? Her eyes scanned the dark parklands around her. Were they already closing in on her? Death did not frighten her. What terrified her was being taken out of the game now, at this last moment. In her haste and desire, she had acted rashly. She should have contacted her superiors before attempting to take down the Sigma operative on her own.

She lifted the phone and tucked it into her hood.

"Yes?" she answered.

Alone in the park, she did not have to worry about anyone eavesdropping. The satellite phone was also encrypted. She readied herself for whatever would come.

Still, she was not prepared for the voice on the line. All warmth drained out of her. She might as well have been naked in the cold park.

"He lives," the voice said flatly. "You should have known better."

With her breath trapped in her chest, she could not speak. She had only heard this voice once before in her life. It had been after her recruitment, after a brutal initiation, when she'd carried out an assassination, killing an entire family, including a newborn baby. The Venezuelan politician had been supporting an investigation into a French pharmaceutical company, an investigation that needed to be stopped. She had also taken a bullet through her leg from the man's security team, but she still escaped without leaving a trace behind. Not even a drop of her own blood.

During her recovery, she had received a call, congratulating her.

From the man on the phone now.

It was said he was one of the Guild leaders, those who were only referred to as "Echelon."

She finally found her voice. "Sir, I take full responsibility for the failure."

"And I imagine you've learned from this mistake." The tone remained flat. She could not tell if the speaker was angry or not.

"Yes, sir."

"From here, leave the matter to us. Steps are being taken. But a new threat has arisen, more immediate than Sigma sniffing at our door. Something you'd best handle on the ground there."

"Sir?"

"Someone knows there was a survivor of the Mali massacre. They are meeting with Senator Gorman tonight."

Krista's fingers tightened on her phone. How could that be? She'd been so careful. Her mind raced through the last few days. She'd kept herself well hidden. Anger warmed through her terror.

"That meeting must not happen," the speaker warned and told her the details of the midnight rendezvous.

"And the senator?"

"Expendable. If word reaches him before you can shut this down, take him out. No evidence must be left behind."

She knew it wasn't necessary to acknowledge that.

"As to the operation in England," the man continued, "all is in place there?"

"Yes, sir."

"You know how important it is that we find the key to the Doomsday Book."

She did. She stared up at the Monolith's writhing tower of bodies. The key could either save them or damn them.

"Do you trust your contact over there?" he asked.

"Of course not. Trust is never necessary. Only power and control."

For once, a hint of amusement tinged his words. "You were taught well." The phone connection ended. But not before a last few cryptic words. "Echelon has its eyes on you."

Krista remained standing before the Monolith. With the phone still at her ear, she shuddered again—with relief, with terror, but mostly with one certainty.

She must not fail.

14

October 12, 4:16 P.M.
Lake District, England

Gray eyed his transportation doubtfully.

His transportation stared back at him, equally unsure, stamping a hoof for emphasis.

"The Fell Pony," Dr. Wallace Boyle said as he worked among the assembled horseflesh. "You'll not find a heartier pony on God's green earth. Perfect for mountain trekking. Sure-footed and strong as an ox."

"You call these guys *ponies*?" Kowalski asked.

Gray understood his partner's consternation. The dusty-black stallion being saddled for Gray had to stand over fourteen hands, almost five feet tall at the withers. It chuffed into the cold air and scraped a hoof into the half-frozen mud.

"Ack, be still already, Pip," a ranch hand said as he gave the saddle cinch another tug.

The group had left Hawkshead by car an hour ago. Wallace had guided them to this horse farm deep in the mountains. Apparently the only way to reach the excavation site from here was either on foot or by horseback. Wallace had called ahead and arranged for their four-legged transportation.

"The Fell Pony has a long tradition in the region," he continued as their mounts were tacked. "The wild Picts used them against the Romans. Viking farmers used them as plow horses. And the Normans who came later made pack animals out of them to haul lead and coal."

Wallace rubbed the neck of his brown gelding and climbed up into his saddle. His terrier, Rufus, trotted through the assembled horses and lifted his leg on a fence post. The dog's initial distrust of Seichan seemed to have settled into a wary truce. He gave her a wide berth as she slipped a toe through a stirrup and leaped smoothly atop a sturdy-looking bay mare.

" 'Fraid you're going to have to excuse ol' Rufus," Wallace had explained back at the pub. "Set in his ways, he is. And I'm embarrassed to say he's a bit of a bigot. Took a bite out of a Pakistani grad student last spring."

Rachel had looked aghast.

Seichan had not reacted at all. She merely stared at the dog until its tail sank, and it retreated into its master's shadow. Afterward she joined them at the table.

Rachel, having been recognized, had come clean about their true intentions with Wallace, though she kept some details sketchy. She didn't mention the mummified finger.

The professor had listened soberly, then shrugged. "No worries, lass. Your secret is safe with me. If I can help you catch the boggins who killed Marco and sent your uncle to the hospital, then all's the better, I say."

So they had set off.

But even now, they still had a long way to go.

Gray mounted his stallion, Pip, and after a bit of a shuffle, they left the farm and headed overland. Dr. Boyle led the way atop his gelding. They followed single file up a winding trail.

Gray had not been on horseback in ages. It took him a good mile to feel comfortable, to fall into an easy rhythm with his mount. Around him, the English fells climbed higher and gathered closer. Off in the distance, the snowy crown of England's highest mountain, Scafell Pike, shone in a last blaze of fire as the sun sank away.

As they trekked, a wintry silence blanketed the highlands. All that was heard was the crunch of snow under their ponies' hooves. Gray had to admit that Wallace's estimation of their mounts was not all bluster. Pip seemed to know where to place each hoof, even through the snow. Going downhill, the stallion never lost his footing and kept a steady balance.

Another two miles, and the way opened enough for Gray to sidle his mount next to Rachel and Seichan. The two had been whispering together.

As Gray joined them, Rachel struggled to free her plastic canteen. Seichan noted her difficulty and dropped her reins. Guiding her horse with her legs, she freed a thermos and unscrewed the top.

"Hot tea," Seichan said and held a cup out to Rachel.

"Thank you." Rachel took a sip, the steam bathing her face. "Ah, that's good. It warms right through you."

"It's a special herbal blend of mine."

Rachel nodded her thanks again as she finished her tea and passed back the cup.

Ahead, Kowalski slouched in his saddle, half-asleep, his head nodding, trusting his pony to follow behind Wallace's.

They rode through a sparse forest of alder and oak, over ferny bracken in a landscape of snow-covered turf and icy trickles of streams. Gray was glad to be on horseback, not trekking on foot. Unlike Rufus, who didn't seem to mind as he trotted alongside them, hopping from hillock to hillock through the damper areas. The air grew colder as the sun sank away.

"How much farther, do you think?" Rachel asked. She kept her voice hushed. The cold silence of the place had that effect.

Gray shook his head. Wallace had refused to give any more detail than "far up in the wilds of the fell." Still, Gray didn't worry about finding their way back. Before he set off, he had activated a handheld GPS unit in his pocket. It monitored their trail, leaving little digital bread crumbs to follow.

Rachel huddled deeper into her heavy jacket. Her breath puffed into the cold air. "Maybe we should have waited until morning."

Seichan spoke hollowly. "No. If there are any answers out here, the quicker we find them and move on, the better."

Gray agreed, but right now a roaring fire sounded pretty damn good. Still, he noted a strained set to Seichan's lips. She kept her eyes fixed straight ahead of her.

Dropping back, Gray used the moment to truly observe the two women. They were studies in contrasts. Rachel rode easily, swaying in a relaxed but ready manner, adapting to her new environment. She spent much of the time looking around her, taking it all in. Whereas Seichan rode as if into battle. She was plainly a skilled rider, but he noted how she corrected even the slightest misstep by her pony. As if everything had to bend to her will. Like Rachel, she also took in her surroundings, but her gaze darted about, pinched with calculation.

Yet despite their differences, the two women bore some striking similarities. Each was strong-willed, confident, challenging. And at times, they could take his breath away with a single glance.

Gray forced his attention away as he realized there was one other trait both women shared. He had no future with either one of them. He had closed that chapter with Rachel long ago, and it was a book best never opened with Seichan.

Lost in private thoughts, the group continued silently through the mountains. Over the next hour, the trek became a blur of rocky escarpments, snowy cliffs, and patches of black forest. At last they crested a rise and a deep valley appeared ahead. The way down was staggeringly steep.

Wallace drew them to a halt. "Almost there," he said.

Under a crisp starry sky, they'd had little difficulty riding in the dark, but below lay true night. A dark wood filled the valley.

But that wasn't all.

Against that black canvas, a few ruddy glows dotted the forest, like tiny campfires. They would've been easy to miss during the day.

"What are those glows down there?" Gray asked.

"Peat fires," Wallace said, blowing into his gloved palms to warm the ice from his beard. "A goodly part of the fells is covered in peat. Mostly blanket mires."

"And that would be *what* in English?" Kowalski asked.

Wallace explained, but Gray was familiar enough with peat. It was an accumulation of decayed vegetable matter: trees, leaves, mosses, fungi. Piles of it formed in damp areas. Deposits were common in places where glaciers had retreated and carved out a mountainous landscape, like here in the Lake District.

Wallace pointed down into the valley. "Below is a forest growing out of one of the deepest peat bogs in the region. It stretches thousands of acres from here. Most of the peat deposits in the region only go down ten feet or so. The valley here has spots that are ten times as deep. It's a very old bog."

"And the fires?" Rachel asked.

"Aye, that's one good thing about peat," Wallace said. "It burns. Peat has been harvested as a fuel source for as long as man has been around. For cooking, for heating. I suspect such natural fires as those below are what gave ancient man the idea to start burning the bloody muck to begin with."

"How long have these valley fires been burning?" Gray asked.

Wallace shrugged. "No saying. They were smoldering when I first came here three years ago. Creeping slowly underground, they're all but impossible to smother. They just burn and burn, fed by a bottomless well of fuel. Some peat fires have been known to burn for centuries."

"Are they dangerous?" Rachel asked.

"Aye, lassie. You have to be careful where you step. Ground may look solid, even covered in snow, but a few feet below could be a fiery hell. Flaming pockets of peat and rivers of fire."

Wallace tapped his mount with his heels and began his descent into the valley. "But no worries. I know the safe paths. Don't go straying off on your own. Stick to my heels."

No one argued. Even Rufus moved closer to his master's side. Gray pulled out his GPS unit, making sure it was still tracking their route. On the small screen was a topographical map. A line of small red dots traced their trail back out of the fells. Satisfied, Gray returned the device to his coat pocket.

He noted Seichan staring at him. She glanced away, a bit quickly, when caught.

Wallace led them down a switchbacking path into the valley. Loose scree and crumbling turf made for a treacherous descent, but Wallace proved true to his word. He got them safely to the valley floor.

"Keep to the trail from here," Wallace warned and set off.

"What trail?" Kowalski mumbled.

Gray understood his partner's confusion. Ahead lay a flat stretch of snowy open ground. The only features were a few mounds of heather and a handful of lichen-covered boulders that looked like huddled stone giants. To the far left, a rosy glow shone from a patch of black turf outlined by green sphagnum moss. Smoke smudged upward against the snowy backdrop. The cold air smelled like a burned ham.

Wallace took a deep breath. "Reminds me of home," he said gustily as he exhaled, his brogue thickening. "Nothing like the scent of burning peat to accompany a nice dram of Scotch whiskey."

"Really?" Kowalski perked up, his nose in the air.

Wallace led them in a winding route among the tall boulders. Despite his warnings, he seemed little concerned. Most of the fires were at the edges of the valley. A few were even up in the higher hills. Gray knew that such hot spots were usually started by wildfires that burned down into the subsurface, then smoldered there for years. The edges of the peat deposits were the most vulnerable to such penetration.

Beyond the open stretch, the wall of dark forest opened. Snow-laden boughs reflected the starlight, but below the bower, the way was pitch-black. Wallace had prepared for that. Leaning down, he clicked on a lantern tied to his saddle. As in a cave, the single lamp had a long reach.

They headed into the forest, still keeping to single file. The air grew less smoky. The forest was a mix of myrtle, birch, and pine, along with massive oaks that looked centuries old. Their trunks were gnarled, their branches still encrusted with dry brown leaves. Acorns littered the snowy ground, which accounted for the number of squirrels that chattered and fled from their path.

Gray saw something larger scurry off, low to the ground.

Rufus made an aborted lunge toward it, but Wallace yelled, "Leave it be! That badger will skin your nose straight off your face."

Kowalski eyed the dark forest with open suspicion. "What about bears? Do you have any in England?"

"Of course," Wallace said.

Kowalski stepped his pony closer to the man with the shotgun.

"We have plenty of bears in our zoos," Wallace continued with a smile. "But none in the wild since the Middle Ages."

Kowalski scowled at the man for scaring him, but he didn't move away.

They continued through the old forest for another half hour. Traveling in the dark, Gray became thoroughly lost. The dense forest hid any landmarks.

Finally, the trees fell away and another field opened. Starlight bathed a wide shallow hollow almost an acre in size. Grasses and bracken poked from the fresh snow that covered the hollow, along with stumps of trees that had been felled to open the area.

It was otherwise unmarked—but it was not empty.

To one side stood two dark tent-cabins. Heavy fabric stretched on steel frames. Beside them, squares of excavated peat were piled into tiny pyramids, ready to burn as heat for the cabins. But no one was here. During the winter months the site was abandoned due to the threat of heavy snow.

Still, it wasn't the dark campsite that drew everyone's attention. Gray stared into the center of the hollow. The excavation site was marked off with yellow survey strings that crisscrossed the area in a large grid. As if trapped in this string web, giant stones rose from the ground in a crude ring. Each one towered twice Gray's height. Atop one pair of stones lay a massive slab, forming a crude doorway into the circle.

Gray remembered Wallace's description of the Neolithic sites that dotted the region. Apparently he had found a new one, one lost for ages in this bog forest.

"Looks like a little Stonehenge," Kowalski said.

Wallace slid from his saddle and took his pony's lead in hand. "Only this site is older than Stonehenge. Much older."

They all dismounted. A rough sheltered paddock stood near the cabins, where they walked their ponies and set about unloading saddles and rubbing down their mounts. Kowalski fetched water from a nearby stream.

Wallace explained about the discovery, how clues found in the Domesday Book had led him here, to a place marked in Latin as "wasted." "I found no trace of the town itself. It must have been razed to the ground. But while hunting, I came upon this stone circle. It was half-buried in peat. An untrained eye could easily have mistaken it for ordinary boulders, especially as they were covered in lichen and moss. But the rocks were a type of bluestone not native to the fells."

His excitement grew as he talked. With the ponies settled, Wallace led them over to the stone ring. He carried his lantern. Gray also removed a flashlight from his saddlebag. As a group, they climbed over the survey strings and crunched through the ankle-deep snow. The stone ring sat in a square of excavated soil. Over the years, teams of archaeologists had been slowly digging the rocks free of the layers of peat.

"The stones were half-buried when I first stumbled here. Their monstrous weight sank them into the muck over the passing millennia."

"Millennia?" Rachel asked. "How old is the place?"

"I've dated it to two thousand years older than Stonehenge. That corresponds to the time of the first settlers to occupy the British Isles. To give you some perspective, that's a thousand years *before* the Great Pyramids were built."

As they reached the dark ring, Gray flashed his light toward the nearest stone. Cleared of moss and lichen, there was no doubt it was man-made. Crude petroglyphs had been etched into the side facing Gray. The carvings covered the entire exposed surface—but it was all the same motif.

"Spirals," Gray mumbled, drawing Rachel's attention.

She joined him, as did Wallace.

"A very common pagan symbol," the professor said. "Representing the soul's journey. This example is almost an exact replica of stone markings found at Newgrange, a pre-Celtic tomb complex in Ireland. Newgrange was dated to around 3200 B.C., about the same age as this ring, suggesting they were likely built by the same tribe of people."

"The Druids?" Kowalski asked.

Wallace scowled. "Och, where did you learn your history, young man? Druids were Celtic tribal priests. They didn't come onto the stage for another three thousand years." He waved an arm to encompass the Neolithic stone ring. "This is the handiwork of the earliest tribe to settle the British Isles, a people who were here long before the Celts and Druids."

Kowalski merely shrugged, taking no offense at this slight to his knowledge.

Wallace sighed. "But I guess I understand how most people make that mistake. The Celts revered this lost people, believed them to be gods, even incorporated that culture into their own. They worshiped at these old sites, folded them into their mythology, believing the ancient stones to be the home of their gods.

In fact, what's considered to be high Celtic art today is based on these old pagan carvings. Ultimately, everything traces back to here." Wallace pointed to the towering henge stones. "But the bigger question remains, *who* were these ancient ring-builders?"

Gray sensed Wallace's excitement stoking higher. It looked like he had more to say, something that he was still holding back, ever the showman. But before he could continue, Rachel interrupted.

"You better see this."

She had circled to the far side of the stone and stood within the ring. Her arm pointed to the surface of the stone on that side.

Gray and the others stepped over the survey strings to join her. He lifted his flashlight. There was only a single symbol carved into the rock on that side. Turning, he shone his light across to the other standing stones—twelve in total, he noted. Each was marked with the same symbol.

"The quartered circle," Gray said.

Wallace nodded. "Now you know why I was so sure that the diary of that medieval scholar, Martin Borr, pointed straight here. The mark was drawn on his journal."

Gray turned in a slow circle.

What did it all mean?

Facing the first stone again, Gray contemplated its significance. Spirals on one side, a pagan cross on the other. He realized it was the same pattern as the two symbols burned into the leather satchel: *a spiral on one side, a cross on the other.*

Gray faced Rachel. He read the same understanding in her eyes. He also knew what she was thinking. If they wanted answers, it was high time they came clean with Dr. Wallace Boyle.

8:42 P.M.

Wallace studied the artifact. He sat at a card table in one of the tent-cabins, the lantern at his elbow. Rachel sat next to him. She warmed her hands on a cup of tea. It was the last from Seichan's thermos. She sipped it, appreciating the heat if not the slight bitterness. She would have preferred a dollop of cream with it, but the tea went a long way to chasing the last of the chill from her body.

The team had spent two hours out in the cold, taking pictures and measurements, recording everything here. But to what end?

Rachel stared across the table at Gray. As they had worked, Gray had grown more introspective. She knew him well enough to recognize when he was troubled, when he sensed he was missing something. She could read the calculations going on in his head, knew the primary question plaguing him.

What was so important about this site?

Seichan sat next to Gray. She had contributed little to the day's work, as if she were leaving it up to them to solve this puzzle. Now they all waited for the professor's assessment. A pair of bunkbeds filled the back half of the space. Kowalski lay sprawled on one of the bunks with an arm over his eyes, shielding them against the lamplight. Since his snores weren't rattling the tent fabric, he must still be awake.

"I don't know what to make of it," Wallace finally said with a shake of his head. He held the leather satchel. He'd already examined the mummified finger. "I don't know where Marco found this, nor why anyone would kill for it."

"Then let's go back to the beginning," Gray said. "Why Father Giovanni first came here. What he hoped to gain from visiting this site."

"It was the bodies," Wallace mumbled, still fingering the satchel.

Rachel sat straighter. "Bodies? What bodies?"

Wallace finally placed the satchel down and leaned back in his chair. "What you have to understand is that for ages, peat bogs were revered by the ancient Celts and their Druids. They would bury or sink objects of worship into the bogs. Such places have proved to be archaeological treasure troves. Swords, crowns, jewels, pottery, even entire chariots. But human remains were also found here."

The professor let that sink in as he stood and stepped over to a small camp stove, where he warmed his hands over a burning briquette of peat. He nodded down at the stove. "Peat was the source of life, so it had to be honored. And that honoring often came in the form of human sacrifice. The Celts would kill their victims and toss their bodies into the peat bogs to appease the gods." He turned to face the table again. "And what goes into the peat ends up being preserved for the ages."

"I don't understand," Rachel said.

Gray explained. "The acidic nature and lack of oxygen in the peat keep things from rotting."

"Aye. Pots of butter have been found in bogs, a hundred years old. And the butter is still fresh and edible."

Kowalski groaned in disgust and rolled to his side. "Remind me not to have toast at your house."

Wallace ignored him. "In the same way, those sacrificed bodies were preserved. They're known as 'bog mummies.' The most famous being Tollund Man, found in Denmark. He's so well preserved that he looks as if he fell into the bog yesterday. Intact skin, organs, hair, eyelashes. Even his fingerprints can still be discerned. Examination revealed that he'd been ritually garroted. The knotted rope was still around his neck. And we know it was the Druids who killed him, as the man's stomach was filled with mistletoe, a plant sacred to the Celtic priests."

"And you found a bog mummy here?" Gray asked.

"Two, actually. A woman and a child. We discovered them as we were excavating the stone ring. They were found in the center, curled together in death."

Seichan asked her first question. Her eyes flickered to Rachel, then away again. "Were they sacrificed?"

Wallace perked up at her question. "That's exactly what we wondered. It's now well accepted that stone rings were solar calendars, but they also served as burial sites. And this site here must have been especially holy. A stone ring within a sacred bog. We had to know if this was a natural burial or a murder."

This last was said with a twinge of guilt.

"We were under instructions to leave the bodies intact, to send them to the university whole, but we had to know. There was no rope around the necks of the bodies, but there was another way to discover if this was a ritual sacrifice."

Rachel understood. "Mistletoe in the stomach."

Wallace nodded. "We performed a small examination. Well documented, I might add." He moved to his pack, undid the ties, and removed a file. He shrugged as he returned to the table. "I wasn't supposed to keep a hard copy."

He sifted through the file and pulled out a set of photos. One showed the woman and child curled in black soil. The woman cradled the child in her arms. They were tucked together as if asleep. The bodies were gaunt and emaciated, but the woman's black hair still draped her face. The next photo showed the woman naked on the table. A hand was in view, holding a dissecting scalpel.

"Before we sent the body on to the university, we wanted to see if there was any mistletoe pollen in her stomach. It was a minor violation."

"Did you find any?" Rachel asked, suddenly not feeling so well.

"No. But we found something else rather disturbing. If you have a weak stomach, you might want to turn away."

Rachel forced herself to keep looking.

The next photo showed a Y-shaped incision across the abdomen. The belly was peeled open, revealing the mass of internal organs. But something was clearly wrong. Wallace flipped to another photo, showing a close-up of a yellow liver. Growths protruded from its surface, covering it like a grisly field.

Wallace explained. "We found them growing throughout her abdominal cavity."

Rachel covered her mouth. "Is that what I think it is?"

Wallace nodded. "They're mushrooms."

Shocked and disgusted, Gray sat back. He struggled to understand what was going on, what had been discovered here. He needed someplace to ground his inquiry, so he returned to where he first started.

"Back to Father Giovanni," Gray said. "You said the bodies drew him here."

"Aye." Wallace returned to his seat and straddled his chair. "Marco heard about our discovery. In a place where Christianity and the pagan ways were still in conflict."

"Still, that conflict didn't truly draw him," Gray said and stared down at the first photo of the woman with the child. There was no mistaking that tableau. Like a Madonna and child. And not just any Madonna.

The tannins from the peat had dyed the woman's skin a deep brownish-black.

"I sent him a photo of the mummies. He came the next day. He was interested in any manifestation or reference to his Black Madonna. To find such a set of bodies in a sacred pagan burial site, in a land where Christianity and ancient ways still mixed, he had to discover for himself if there was any connection to the mythology of his dark goddess."

"And was there?" Rachel asked.

"That's what Marco spent the past years investigating. It had him shuffling all over the British Isles. In the last month, though, I could tell that something had him especially agitated. He would never say what it was."

"And what's your take on the mummies?" Gray asked.

"Like I said, we didn't find any mistletoe. I think the bodies were dead when they were buried in the bog. But who buried them and why? And why did Martin Borr mark his book with this pagan symbol? That's what I wanted to know."

"And?" Gray pressed the man. He was annoyingly oblique with his answers, teasing them out for greater effect.

"I have my own hypothesis," Wallace admitted. "It goes back to where I started my investigation. The

Domesday Book. Something laid waste to the nearby village or town. Something horrible enough to raze the place to the ground, to wipe all records off the maps. All records, that is, except for the cryptic reference in the great book and the mention in Martin Borr's diary. So what happened to warrant such a reaction? I would wager it was some sort of plague or disease. Not wanting it to spread, to keep it secret, the place was destroyed."

"But what about the bodies here?" Rachel nodded down to the photos.

"Just close your eyes and put yourself back in that town. A place isolated and under siege by some great illness. A town mixed between devout Christians and those who practiced the ancient ways in secret, who certainly must have known about this stone ring near their town, who perhaps still worshiped here. Once doom fell upon this valley, each side most likely beseeched their gods for salvation. And some probably hedged their bets, mixing the two faiths. They took a mother and a baby boy, representative of the Madonna and her child, and buried them in this ancient pagan site. I believe these two are the only bodies that escaped the fiery purge, the only two left from that old plague."

Wallace touched the dissection photo with a finger. "Whatever struck that village was strange indeed.

I don't know of anything like this that has ever been reported in the annals of medicine or forensics. The bodies are still under investigation, and that's being kept a guarded secret. They won't even tell me what they found."

"But shouldn't you be kept informed?" Gray asked. "Aren't you a tenured professor at the University of Edinburgh?"

Wallace's brow crinkled in confusion, then relaxed. "Oh, no, you misunderstood me. When I said the *university* took the bodies, I didn't mean Edinburgh. My grant came from abroad. It's not an uncommon practice. For field studies, you take funds wherever you can find them."

"So who took the bodies?"

"They were sent to the University of Oslo for initial examination."

Gray felt kicked in the gut. It took him an extra moment to respond. *Oslo.* Here was the first solid connection between events here and what Painter Crowe was investigating in Norway.

While Gray grappled with the implications, Wallace continued. "I guess ultimately it all goes back to extremophiles."

The oddity of the non sequitur snapped Gray's focus back. "What are you talking about?"

"My funding," Wallace said in a tone that made it sound as if it should be obvious. "Like I said. In this business, you get money where you can."

"And how do extremophiles fit in with all that?"

Gray was well aware of the term. *Extremophiles* were organisms that lived under extreme conditions, ones that were considered too harsh to support life. They were mostly bacteria, found living in toxic environments like boiling deep-sea rifts or volcanic craters. Such unique organisms offered potential new compounds to the world.

And the world's industries had certainly taken note, generating a new business called *bioprospecting*. But instead of prospecting for gold, they were after something just as valuable: new patents. And it turned out to be a booming business. Already extremophiles were being used to patent new industrial-strength detergents, cleansers, medicines, even an enzyme used widely by crime labs for DNA fingerprinting.

But what did all that have to do with bog mummies in England?

Wallace tried to explain. "It goes back to my initial hypothesis, one I pitched to my potential sponsors. A hypothesis about the Doomsday Book."

Gray noted that he called it Doomsday, rather than Domesday, this time. He imagined that the professor, with his usual flair for the dramatic, had sought funding using the book's more colorful name.

"As I mentioned, those few places in the book marked in Latin as 'wasted,' seemed to have been wiped off the map—literally and figuratively. What would make those old census takers do that unless something dangerous had struck these towns?"

"Like a disease or plague," Gray said.

Wallace nodded. "And potentially it was something never seen before. These were isolated places. Who knew what might have risen out of the bogs? Peat bogs are soups of strange organisms. Bacteria, fungi, slime molds."

"So they hired you as both an archaeologist and a bioprospector."

Wallace shrugged. "I'm not the only one. Major industries are turning to field archaeologists. We're delving into ancient places, sites long closed up. Just this past year, a major U.S. chemical company discovered an extremophile in a newly opened Egyptian tomb. It's all the rage, you see."

"And for this dig, the University of Oslo funded you."

"No. Oslo is just as strapped as any university. Nowadays most grants are generated from corporate sponsors."

"And which corporation hired you?"

"A biotech company, one working with genetically modified organisms. Crops and whatnot."

Gray gripped the table's edge. *Of course.* Biotechnology companies were major players in the hunt for extremophiles. Bioprospecting was their life's blood. They cast feelers out in all directions, across all fields of study. Including, it seemed, archaeology.

Gray had no doubt *who* sponsored Wallace's research.

He spoke that name aloud. "Viatus."

Wallace's eyes grew larger. "How did you know?"

11:44 P.M.

Seichan stood outside her cabin. She held a cigarette in her hand, unlit and forgotten. The stars were as crisp as cut glass in the night sky. Streams of icy fog crept through the trees. She inhaled a deep breath, smelling the peat smoke, both from their camp stoves and from the smoldering fires underground.

The ring of stones, rimed in ice, looked like chunks of silver.

She pictured the two bodies buried in the center. For some reason, she thought back to the curator she had slain in Venice—or rather, to his wife and child. She pictured the two of them buried here instead. Knowing it was born out of guilt, she shook her head against such foolish sentimentality. She had a mission to complete.

But tonight her guilt had sharpened to an uncomfortable edge.

She stared down at her other hand. She held a steel thermos. It had kept her tea warm. The warmth also kept her biotoxin incubated. The group had talked at length about extremophiles after the revelation about the source of Dr. Boyle's funding. The source of the toxin supplied to her was a bacteria discovered in a volcanic vent in Chile. Frost sensitive, it had to be kept warm.

No one noticed that only Rachel drank the tea.

Seichan only pretended to sip at it.

Pocketing her cigarette, she crossed to a windblown bank of snow and set about filling the thermos with handfuls of snow. The cold would sterilize the thermos, killing any remaining bacteria. Once it was packed full, she screwed the top back on. Her fingers trembled. She wanted to blame it on the cold. She threaded the top on wrong, and it jammed. She fought it for a breath as anger flared hotly through her. Frustrated, she yanked her arm back and hurled the thermos into the forest.

For half a minute, she breathed heavily, steaming the air.

She didn't cry—and for some reason that helped center her.

A door cracked open in the other cabin. She shared her cabin with Rachel; the men shared the other. She stepped into the open to see who else was still up.

The large frame and lumbering gait identified the man readily enough. Kowalski spotted her and lifted an arm. He pointed a thumb toward the paddock.

"Going to see a man about a horse," he said and disappeared around the corner.

It took her a moment to realize he wasn't actually meeting someone by the ponies. She was *that* out of sorts. She heard him whistling back there as he relieved himself.

She checked her watch. It was a few minutes before midnight. The timetable was set. There was no going back. They'd had sufficient time to examine the site. The Guild would only allow so much latitude for Gray's team to track Father Giovanni's path, to discover the key before anyone else. She had argued for more time but had been slapped down. So be it. They would have to keep moving.

She glanced toward the other cabin. Kowalski had better not be too long. He wasn't. After a minute, he came lumbering back, still whistling under his breath.

"Can't sleep?" he asked as he joined her.

She fingered her cigarette out and lifted it as explanation enough.

"Those things'll kill you." He reached into a pocket, pulled out a stub of a cigar, and matched her gesture. "So you might as well get it over with quickly."

He clenched the chewed end between his molars, pulled out an old-fashioned box of wooden matchsticks, and deftly scratched two sticks across the fabric of the tent. Twin flames lit up. He passed one to her. He'd plainly done this before.

He spoke around the end of his cigar. "Gray just hit the sack. Spent like two hours trying to get more out of that old professor. I had to get the hell out of there, get some fresh air. That dog kept stinking up the place. And no wonder. Did you see what he feeds that damn mutt? Sausages and onions. What sort of dog chow is that?"

Seichan lit her cigarette. She let the guy ramble, grateful for the mindless chatter. Unfortunately, his chatter was apparently leading up to something—and not all that smoothly.

"So," he said, "what's up with you and Gray?"

Seichan choked as she inhaled.

"I mean, he's always eyeballing you. And you just stare right through him as if he were a ghost. Like two schoolkids with the hots for each other."

Seichan balked at the innuendo, ready to deny, uncomfortable with how close the man was to the truth. Luckily she was saved from responding.

As midnight struck, the valley exploded.

Throughout the forest, geysers of flame shot skyward, one after the other. They were accompanied by soft concussions, easy to miss unless you were listening for them. The incendiary charges, coupled with a rubidium thermal catalyst that turned water into an accelerant, had been planted deep into wet peat, timed to blow at midnight. The entire valley was meant to burn.

Closer at hand, three more explosions erupted from the center of the ring of stones. Fiery spirals twisted high into the sky.

Even across the distance, the heat burned her face.

People came running out of the cabins behind them. Kowalski cursed hotly next to her.

She didn't turn, hypnotized by the flames. Her heart pounded. The conflagration began to spread outward—quickly, *too* quickly—both here and out in the forest. The ignited charges were only supposed to chase Gray's team off—to light a fire under them literally and figuratively—while destroying all evidence in their wake.

She watched the flames grow.

Someone had miscalculated, underestimated the combustibility of the peat. For a moment, an oily flicker of distrust flashed. Had she been betrayed? Were they meant to die here?

Going coldly logical, she mentally snuffed out those doubts. There was no gain in their deaths. At least not at this time. It had to be an error of execution. The old fires, smoldering for years, must have weakened the stability of the peat beds, turning the entire valley into tinder for the right torch.

Still, the end result was the same.

As she stared, the fires closed in a circle around them.

They would never get out of here alive.

15

Monk strode briskly across the research park. Under his heavy coat, he wore a Viatus security uniform. At his side, John Creed was equally bundled against the cold, but he had a lab jacket folded over one arm.

They had no trouble driving through the main gates of the Viatus campus, flashing their false ID cards. They had parked their car in the employee parking lot and headed on foot across the grounds. Viatus had facilities around the world, but Oslo was home to their main facility. The place was spread over a hundred acres, with various divisions and office buildings dotting a parklike setting. All the structures were sleek and modern, plainly influenced by Scandinavian minimalism.

In the center of the campus rose a meeting hall, made entirely of glass. It shone like a diamond. Through the walls could be seen the sweeping hull of a Viking ship. It was not a model, but an authentic piece of history. The ship had been discovered frozen in ice somewhere up in the Arctic region of Norway. It had cost millions to salvage and preserve it, all financed by Ivar Karlsen.

It must be good to be so rich.

Monk continued across the campus. The Crop Biogenics Research Lab was in a remote corner, a long walk from the parking lot.

Monk pulled the hood of his parka farther over his head. "So, Doogie," he said, trying to distract himself from the cold, "what exactly did you do to wash out of the Corps and end up in Sigma, anyway?"

Creed made a dismissive noise and mumbled, "Don't ask." Plainly he didn't want to talk about it. And he was edgy.

Plus calling him Doogie probably didn't help.

Creed was not exactly the talkative type, but Monk had to admit the man was sharp. He had already acquired a smattering of Norwegian, even honing a decent accent. Monk knew only one person who was that quick. He pictured her smile, the curve of her backside, and the barely perceptible bump of her growing belly. Thinking of Kat helped keep him warm long enough to reach their destination.

The Crop Biogenics lab looked like a silver egg standing on end. It was all mirrored glass and reflected the grounds, giving the facility a surreal appearance, as if the building were in the process of warping into another dimension.

The lab building was a relatively new construction, completed only five years ago. It had been engineered with a sophisticated security system that required only a skeletal staff at night.

Not an obstacle for someone outfitted with DARPA's latest toys.

Monk carried a backpack over one shoulder and a Taser XREP pistol tucked under the other. The weapon discharged a small electrified dart that could knock out a target for five minutes. It was a precaution that he hoped they would not have to employ.

Creed moved to the main entrance.

Monk touched his throat. He had a microphone taped over his larynx and an earpiece in place. "Sir, we're heading into the building now."

Painter responded immediately in his ear, "Any problems?"

"Not so far."

"Good. Keep me updated."

"Yes, sir."

Creed stepped to the electronic key reader. He slipped a card into its slot. A thin wire ran from the keycard to a device fastened around his wrist. It was a hacking device that used quantum algorithms to pick any lock, basically the equivalent of a digital skeleton key. The lock released, and Creed pulled the door open.

They headed inside.

The entry was dimly lit, and the receptionist's desk was empty. Monk knew that a security guard manned a monitoring station on the floor above. As long as they set off no alarms, they should have no trouble reaching the computer servers on the basement levels. Their mission was to open a back door into the research mainframes. With any luck, they'd be out of there in under ten minutes.

As Monk crossed the lobby, he kept his face averted from the cameras. As did Creed. They had memorized the cameras' positions from the schematics provided by Kat.

Together they headed toward the bank of elevators. Creed walked a bit quickly. Monk touched his arm and forced him to slow down, to not act so panicked.

They reached the elevator bay, where the push of a button opened a set of doors. They moved inside. Another key reader glowed red. The elevator would not move without the proper code.

Monk hovered a finger over the B2 button—Basement Level 2—where the servers were housed.

Creed waited to swipe his skeleton key. Monk hesitated before he pressed the button.

"What?" Creed mouthed, fearful of speaking English in case the elevator was monitored.

Monk pointed to the buttons below his finger. They ran from B2 to B5. According to the schematics provided, there were not supposed to be any levels below B2.

So what was on those levels?

Monk knew they had a mission, but there was a subtext to this night's operation: to find out what was really going on at Viatus. It was a long shot that the corporation kept anything incriminating on its servers. Any real dirt was most likely buried much deeper.

Like underground.

Monk shifted his finger down and pressed B5. Creed glared at him, plainly questioning what he was doing.

Just a little improvisation, he answered silently. Sigma wasn't about following orders blindly but about thinking on your feet.

Creed needed to learn that.

Monk pointed toward the key reader and motioned for Creed to swipe his electronic card. The detour would only take an extra minute. He would simply take a peek below. If it was just a maintenance level or some sort of employee swimming pool, they could quickly hop back up to B2, tag the servers, and get out of there.

With an exasperated sigh, Creed shoved in his card. After a half second, the light flashed green.

The elevator began to descend.

No alarms sounded.

The levels ticked downward, and the elevator opened into a closed lobby. A sealed door stood directly across from them. Monk paused, suddenly having second thoughts.

What would Gray do here?

Monk mentally shook his head. Since when was following Gray's example a good thing? The man had an uncanny knack for trouble.

As the elevator began to close, Monk grabbed Creed by the elbow and leaped into the lobby.

"Are you nuts?" Creed hissed under his breath, shaking loose Monk's grip.

Probably.

Monk moved closer to examine the door. It had no key reader. Only a glowing panel that was plainly meant to read a palm.

"What now?" Creed whispered.

Undaunted, Monk placed his prosthetic hand atop the reader. Pressure sensitive, the pad grew brighter.

A bar of light scanned up and down. He held his breath—then heard the lock's tumblers release.

A name flashed above the reader.

IVAR KARLSEN

Creed frowned as he read the name, then glared over at Monk, angry that he'd not been informed about this extra precaution.

It had been Kat's idea. She had obtained the CEO's full records, including a palm print. It had taken only a moment to digitize the data and feed it into the equivalent of a laser printer. The device had then burned a copy of the print across Monk's synthetic palm, scoring the blank skin into a perfect match.

If anyone had full access to this facility, it was certainly its CEO.

Monk moved to the unlocked door.

Let's see what Ivar's hiding down here.

11:46 P.M.

Painter kept watch across the street from the Grand Hotel Oslo. He sat on a bench with a wide view of the entrance. It was no wonder Senator Gorman had chosen this place as his residence. Built in an extravagant Louis XVI revival style, the hotel climbed eight stories and took up an entire city block, with a central clock tower looming over its entrance. It was also conveniently located directly across from Norway's parliament buildings.

A perfect choice for a visiting U.S. senator.

And an unlikely spot for an ambush.

Still, Painter wanted to be thorough. He had been here for an hour, wearing a heavy coat, hat, and scarf. He also moved with a bit of a hunch that was only half faked. His knife wound had begun to ache as the pain relievers wore off. For the past hour, he had canvassed all the public areas of the hotel, including the Limelight Bar, where Gorman was supposed to meet their mysterious contact. As an extra precaution, Painter had the stolen WASP dagger tucked into the back of his belt and a small 9mm Beretta in a shoulder holster.

But so far, everything appeared quiet.

Painter glanced up at the clock tower. It was a few minutes before midnight. *Time for this spy to come in out of the cold.*

Standing up, he headed across the street, as prepared as he could be.

Monk had already checked in, and earlier in the evening Painter had had a short but intense conversation via satellite phone with Gray. He had learned that the Viatus Corporation had funded the dig in England. They had been bioprospecting for new organisms to exploit for their genetic research. Had they found something? Gray had described the gruesome discovery, at a Neolithic stone ring, of bodies buried and preserved in a bog, bodies riddled with some sort of fungus.

Was that significant?

Painter recalled that the murdered Princeton geneticist had believed the new genes inserted into the Viatus corn samples were not of bacterial origin. Could they have been *fungal,* genes extracted from those mushrooms? And if so, why all the secrecy and bloodshed to hide the fact?

Painter shoved the questions aside for now. He needed to focus on the immediate task at hand. He entered the lobby and circumspectly observed his surroundings. He compared the faces of the hotel employees with those in his earlier canvass and made sure there were no strangers among them.

Satisfied, he strode over to the hotel bar. The Limelight was dark and richly paneled, illuminated only by the glow of wall lanterns. Red leather club chairs and sofas divided the space. It smelled vaguely of cigars.

At this hour the establishment was sparsely populated. It wasn't hard to spot Senator Gorman over by the bar. Especially with the burly man sitting next to him, wearing a suit too small for his bulk. He might as well have *bodyguard* stenciled across his forehead.

The guard sat with his back to the bar and, with no subtlety, scanned the patrons for any threats.

Painter observed them from the corner of his eye. He passed among the chairs and took a seat at a booth near the entrance. A barmaid took his order.

Now to see who, if anyone, showed up.

He didn't have long to wait.

A man appeared, wearing a heavy ankle-length overcoat. He searched the bar, then his gaze fixed on the senator. Painter was startled to realize he'd seen this man before, back when the luncheon had broken up. He'd been complaining to the Club of Rome's co-president.

Painter struggled to remember his name.

Something like Anthony.

He played back the conversation in his head.

No . . . Antonio.

A satisfied smile flickered over the man's features as he spotted the senator. This had to be their guy. From the earlier conversation, the man clearly had no love for Karlsen. Antonio's smile faded as he finally noted the bodyguard, too. The instructions had been for the senator to come alone. Antonio hesitated near the entrance.

Time to move.

Painter slid smoothly out of his seat and crossed in front of Antonio. He grabbed the man's elbow in one hand and poked his Beretta in the man's ribs. He kept a smile on his face.

"Let's talk," Painter said and guided him away from the bar.

It was his intention to interrogate the man in private. The less Senator Gorman was involved in all this, the better for all.

Antonio allowed himself to be led away at gunpoint, his face a mask of terror.

"I work for the U.S. government," Painter said pointedly. "We're going to have a short conversation before you meet with the senator."

The terror faded from his eyes, but not completely. Painter guided him toward a settee in an empty area of the lobby. It was partially shielded by a low wall and a potted fern.

They never made it.

Antonio suddenly tripped and fell to one knee. He gurgled and gagged. His hands fluttered to his neck. Protruding from his throat was the pointed barb of an arrow bolt. Blood splattered the marble tile floor as Antonio dropped to his hands and knees.

Painter noted a small blinking light at the back of the man's neck, nestled in the plastic feathers of the bolt. Painter's body reacted before the thought even formed.

Bomb.

He leaped forward and dove over the low wall. He'd landed behind it when the charge exploded. It was as loud as a thunderclap in a cave. Pain squeezed his head. He went momentarily deaf—then sound returned.

Screams, shouts, cries.

It all sounded hollow.

He rolled back up, keeping sheltered behind the nearby wall. Smoke choked the lobby, lit by puddles of fire. The explosion had blackened a large section of the floor. Antonio's body had been obliterated into bits of flaming ruin. The superheated air burned with a chemical sting.

Thermite and white phosphorus.

Painter coughed and searched the lobby. From Antonio's position, the arrow had to have come from inside the hotel, off to the left. From that direction, two masked figures ran through the smoke from the staircase. Another slammed through the front door.

They pounded toward the Limelight Bar.

They were going after the senator.

12:04 A.M.

Monk stood at the open door. Beyond the threshold stretched a long hall. Lights turned on, one after the other, illuminating the way ahead.

"We'll take a fast look," Monk whispered. "Then get the hell out of here."

Creed waited for Monk to take the lead, then followed. The kid barely breathed, and he definitely didn't blink.

Halfway down the passage, double doors opened to the right and left. Monk headed toward them. The place smelled of disinfectant, like a hospital. The smooth linoleum floor and featureless walls added to the sense of sterility.

He also noted that there were no cameras in this hall. Apparently the company placed its full trust in the extra layer of electronic security down here.

Monk reached the doors. They were palm-locked like the other. Monk pressed his hand against it. Surely there were no areas off-limits to Karlsen.

He was right.

The lock *snick*ed open.

Monk headed through and found himself in an enclosed entryway facing another set of doors. The antechamber was glass. Beyond the doors opened a huge room. Lights flickered on, but they were muted a soft amber.

He tried the next set of doors. Unlocked. The doors were clearly not intended to keep anyone *out*, so much as to keep the room's occupants *in*.

As Monk pushed into the next room, he gaped at the walls to either side. Extending the length of the long room were floor-to-ceiling windows. A low tonal buzzing filled the room, like a radio tuned between stations.

Creed followed at his heels. "Are those—?"

Monk nodded. "Beehives."

Behind the glass, a solid mass of bees writhed and churned in a hypnotic pattern, wings flickering, bodies dancing. Racks and tiers of honeycombs rose in stacks to the roof. The hives were divided into sections along the length of the room. Each apiary was marked with a cryptic code. Studying them, Monk noted that each number was prefixed with the same three letters: IMD.

He didn't understand the significance, but plainly the bees were used in some sort of research.

Or maybe Ivar just had a real hard-on for fresh honey.

Monk moved with Creed to the closest bank. The buzzing grew louder, the agitation more frenzied. The lights, though muted, must have stirred them.

"I think they're Africanized bees," Creed said. "Look at how aggressive they are."

"I don't care where they came from. What is Viatus doing with them?"

And why all this security?

Creed reached toward a small drawer in the hive window.

"Careful," Monk warned.

Creed pinched his brows and pulled open the drawer. "Don't worry. I've worked with bees before at my family's farm back in Ohio."

The drawer came out to reveal a sealed box with a meshed end. A single large bee rested inside.

"The queen," Creed said.

The bees became even more frenzied within the cage.

Monk noted that the box was stamped with the same cryptic code as the cage. As Creed returned the drawer to its slot, Monk freed a small pen camera. Pressing a button, he took a short digital video. He recorded the banks of bees and the numbers above each hive.

It could be important.

For now, the best they could do was document it all and get the hell out. Once finished recording, Monk checked his watch. He still wanted to check the room across the hall before they headed to the servers and finished their primary mission.

"C'mon," Monk said and led his partner back out into the hallway.

Stepping across the hall, Monk pressed his palm against the other door's reader. As the door unlocked, he headed inside. It opened into an anteroom similar to the other lab. But here respirator masks hung on wall pegs to one side. Ahead, lights flickered on as before. The room beyond the door was the same size as the other.

But there were no bees.

The room held four long raised beds running the length of the room. Even from here, Monk recognized the little fleshy umbrellas growing out of the beds in riotous exuberance.

"Mushrooms," Creed said.

Monk passed into the next room. The door opened with the small pop of an air seal. The room was negatively pressurized to keep the air inside. Monk immediately understood why.

Creed covered his mouth and nose.

The stench struck like a slap to the face. The air was muggy, hot, and smelled like a mix of brine, dead fish, and rotted meat. Monk wanted to turn tail and run out, but Painter had related his discussion with Gray.

About mushrooms.

It couldn't be a coincidence.

Monk freed his camera, ready to document it. Creed joined him. He handed over a respirator from the anteroom. Monk pulled it over his face gratefully.

At least someone's thinking . . .

The respirator's filters took the edge off the stink. Able to breathe, he headed to the closest bed. The mushrooms were growing out of watery black mulch that looked oily.

Creed slipped on a pair of latex gloves and joined him. He shook open another glove. "We should get a sample of the fungus."

Monk nodded and set about recording it all.

Creed reached toward one of the mushrooms. He delicately grabbed it by the base and pulled it up. It lifted freely—but with it came a fleshy chunk of something attached to it. Creed shuddered and dropped it in disgust. It splashed into the wet mulch, shivering the surface like a soup of loose gelatin.

Only then did Monk recognize the growth medium for the mushrooms.

Clotted blood.

"Did you see . . .?" Creed stammered. "Was that . . .?"

Monk had noted what Creed's mushroom had been attached to. It was a kidney. And from the size of it, possibly human.

Monk waved Creed back to the gruesome task. "Get a sample."

With his camera recording, Monk moved down the long bed of mushrooms. The smallest were closest to the door. They were white as bone. But the mush-rooms grew larger along the row, gaining a richer hue of crimson.

Monk noted a couple of brown stalks poking out of the blood. He lowered his camera for a closer look. They were not stalks. With a cold chill, he realized they were human fingers.

He reached and pinched one of the fingers with his prosthetic hand. He pulled the finger up, dragging a hand out of the muck. As he raised it higher, he saw it was attached to a forearm. Mushrooms grew out of the flesh.

Gritting his teeth, he slowly lowered the limb back into the tank. He didn't need to see any more. Entire bodies lay buried in the blood, fertilizer for the mush-rooms.

He also noted the dark brown skin of the arm, an uncommon sight in snow-white Norway. Monk re-called the farm site in Africa, the one destroyed in a night of bloodshed and fire.

Had more than *corn* been harvested from there?

Monk found himself breathing harder. He moved quickly to the end of the row. Here the mushrooms had matured into thick stems topped by ribbed pods. They looked fleshy and fibrous.

With his prosthesis, Monk nudged one of the pods. As he touched it, the bulb contracted in a single squeeze.

From its top, a dense powdery smoke puffed outward and spread quickly through the air.

Fungal spores.

Monk danced back, thankful for the respirators. He did not want to breathe in those spores.

As if signaled by the first pod, others began to erupt. Monk retreated, chased by swirling clouds of spores.

"We have to get out of here!" Monk yelled across the room, his words muffled by the respirator.

Creed had just collected a sample of the mushroom and tied it into his loose latex glove. He glanced at Monk, not understanding. But his eyes widened as more of the puffballs exploded into the air.

They had to get back out into the hall.

Suddenly, overhead vents opened in the ceiling, perhaps triggered by a biological sensor. Foam jetted out of the ceiling in a massive flush. It spread over the floor and piled up quickly. Monk ran under one of the vents and almost got knocked down by the force of it. He slipped and slid.

By the time he reached Creed, the foam was waist deep.

"Go!" Monk hollered and pointed toward the door.

Together they slammed through the first door and into the anteroom. It was also full of foam, all the way to the ceiling. They had to paw their way through it blind.

Monk hit the hallway door first.

He shoved the handle and shouldered into the door. It refused to budge. He shoved again and again, but he knew the truth.

They were locked inside.

12:08 A.M.

As smoke choked the lobby, Painter vaulted over the low wall. Fires still burned on the floor. Blood made the marble slippery. He had his pistol out and skidded straight into the masked gunman who had barreled through the front door. Focused on the bar, the assailant failed to see Painter in time. Painter fired point-blank into his chest.

The impact spun the attacker away, blood flying.

One down.

People screamed and fled out into the street or hid behind furniture. Painter sprinted straight across the open lobby.

Ahead, at the entrance to the Limelight Bar, the senator's bodyguard appeared in a shooter's stance, arms out, cradling his service weapon. He had taken cover behind a potted plant. It wasn't enough shelter. The other two gunmen already had their sights fixed on the entrance.

Fern leaves shredded under a barrage of machine-gun fire. The man was knocked flat on his back. Painter never slowed. He leaped to a chair outside the bar and flew headlong into the space. He landed on one of the leather sofas and shoulder-rolled to his feet.

He had only seconds.

A cascade of gunfire tore into the room. It arced across the wall behind the bar, shattering bottles and mirrors.

Painter took in the room with one glance.

The senator was not in sight.

The bodyguard would not have left him in the open. There was only one door leading out of this place. The restroom at the back. Painter ran for it and slammed through the door. A bullet burned past his ear. The shot had come from inside the bathroom.

Senator Gorman stood with his back to a row of sinks, a pistol in his hand, pointed at Painter.

Painter raised his arms. "Senator Gorman!" he called out firmly. "I'm General Metcalf's man!"

"The DoD investigator?" Gorman lowered his pistol, his face collapsing with relief.

Painter rushed forward. "We have to get out of here."

"What about Samuels?" The senator glanced back at the door.

Painter guessed that was the bodyguard. "Dead, sir." He motioned the senator toward the stained-glass window at the back of the restroom.

"It's barred shut. I looked."

Painter shoved the window sash open. An ornate set of iron bars did block the way. He punched his palm into them, and the grate popped free and swung open on its hinges. During his earlier canvass of the meeting place, he had removed the bolts.

Never hurt to secure a back door.

"Out!" Painter commanded and offered the senator a knee to climb up.

Gorman took the help and hauled himself into the window.

As Painter pushed the senator, he heard a *thunk* behind him. A glance revealed a black arrowhead sticking out of the restroom's plank door.

Oh, crap . . .

Painter sent the senator sailing out the window and followed on the man's heels. Literally—he took an Italian loafer to the left eye. But it was small damage, considering the explosion that followed.

Flames and smoke blasted out the open window.

The heat rolled over them.

Painter shoved off the senator. As the blast of flames died, Painter dashed to the window, tugged the lower sash down, and swung the iron bars back in place.

Let them wonder how they'd escaped a locked room.

The confusion might buy them an extra few minutes as their pursuers continued to search the hotel.

Painter returned to Gorman's side. "I have a car stashed two blocks away."

They hurried off together.

Gorman puffed at his side, cradling a jammed shoulder. After a block, he stared over at Painter and asked an existential question. "Who the hell are you?"

"Just your everyday civil servant," Painter muttered while concentrating on another task. He resecured the throat mike to his neck and activated it. "Monk, how are you doing over there?"

Monk heard a few frazzled words in his ear, but after knocking loose his respirator, he fought a mouthful of foam. He shoved against the door, hoping it would miraculously open. It must have locked down once the foam had been triggered.

Maybe there was another way out.

Before he could move, hot water blasted from above. The foam immediately melted from the top down. The sheer volume of it collapsed in on itself. It took less then thirty seconds.

Monk glanced over at Creed. He stood there like a skinny wet dog waiting to shake. The man's eyes were bright with shock.

"Biohazard foam," Monk explained. "Used as a knockdown agent for airborne pathogens. We should be okay."

Proving that, the lock clicked open at Monk's elbow. It must have been timed to the sterilization cycle. He twisted the handle and exited into the hall.

As he stepped free, voices echoed down the hall. He had a clear view to the elevator lobby. The door stood half open as someone argued in Norwegian out in the lobby. Monk recognized the uniformed arm of a security guard.

The automated safety protocol had summoned security.

Monk froze. He couldn't retreat back into the mushroom lab. That would surely be the first place they'd check. He had only one other option. Stepping into plain view, he hurried across the hall and placed his palm on the reader beside the other door. He held his breath as it scanned, watching the far door, praying that no one turned around.

Finally, the lock freed. With a silent sigh of thanks, he shoved the door open. He and Creed rushed inside.

Monk kept the door cracked open enough to watch the hallway.

A team of security guards, four in total, were led by a technician in a lab coat. The man looked like he had just woken up. Apparently access here required a certain level of clearance.

Monk allowed the door to slip closed, though he remained crouched where he could listen. The other lab door opened and closed. Men remained out in the hall. Monk heard them talking in low voices. He didn't know how many. At least three, he guessed.

Now what?

"Make some room," Creed said behind him.

Monk turned. His partner had shed his parka and donned his lab coat. He'd also dried his hair and finger-combed it roughly in place. Creed stepped into the anteroom. While Monk had been manning the door, his partner had gone into the larger room with the glass-walled apiaries.

"What are you doing?" Monk asked, eyeing him up and down.

Creed moved aside. Beyond the closed inner door, a stir of movement drew Monk's eye. In the outer room, a thin cloud of bees swirled and gathered.

"What did you do?" Monk asked.

Creed lifted an arm. In his hand, he held a meshed drawer. "I stole the queen." Creed pointed to the left. "And I broke the hive seal."

Monk frowned. From one of the apiaries, a thick column of bees boiled out where the drawer used to be.

THE DOOMSDAY KEY · 313

"But why?" Monk asked.

Beyond the door, the bees gathered into a growing swarm.

"They're definitely Africanized," Creed said as he eyeballed his captured queen. "Very aggressive."

"That's great, but again—*why?*"

"To get us out of here." Creed pointed to the anteroom's inner door. "Open it when I say *now.* But keep behind the door."

Monk began to understand. He switched places with Creed and moved to the anteroom's inner door. Creed took his post by the hallway door and watched the gathering swarm of bees.

The cloud now hugged against the anteroom's glass door and walls, drawn by their queen's trail. Buzzing grew so loud it made Monk's skin crawl.

Creed continued to wait. He placed the drawer with the queen on the floor. In the other room the swarm grew so thick that it blocked the light.

"Be ready," Creed said as he straightened back up.

Monk grabbed the handle of his door.

With a final swipe through his hair, Creed faced the door and pulled it open. Monk was blocked from view, but he heard the startled outbursts of the security guards out in the hallway.

Creed put on an air of irritation and snapped at them in Norwegian.

As the guards struggled to decide if the new technician was a threat or not, Creed kicked the drawer across the floor toward the guards.

"Now!" he yelled.

Monk yanked his door open and crowded behind it.

The swarm immediately swept into the anteroom like an angry fist.

Creed dropped back and dragged his door fully open. With the way clear to their queen, the hive shot into the hall in a thick cloud. Panicked, one of the guards fired a wild shot.

A mistake.

Monk knew enough about Africanized bees to know they were sensitive to loud noises.

Screams followed, which only made matters worse.

Creed lunged over and grabbed the sleeve of Monk's jacket. Time to go. Monk followed Creed out the door. There was no need for stealth. Four guards writhed in the center of the swarm, covered thickly in a stinging mass. The bees filled mouths and crawled up noses.

Monk and Creed sprinted down the hall.

A few ambitious bees gave chase. Monk got stung several times, but the swarm remained close to their queen. With his long legs, Creed reached the door to the elevator lobby first. He pounded through. Monk slammed the door closed behind him.

Creed called the elevator, and the doors glided apart immediately. The cage was still on this level. They hurried inside. With no time to reach the servers, Monk abandoned their primary mission and pressed the lobby button. It was time to get out of here. Creed didn't argue.

Monk stared over at him as the elevator climbed.

"You did good, Doogie."

"Really?" He scowled sourly. "I'm still Doogie?"

Monk shrugged as they exited the elevator and hurried across the front foyer. He didn't want the kid's success to go to his head. As they headed back out into the night, a voice suddenly whispered in his ear, angry and urgent.

"Monk, report in." It was Painter.

Monk thumbed his throat mike. "Sir, we're heading out now."

A heavy sigh of relief followed. "And the mission?"

"We ran into a little trouble with bees."

"Bees?"

"I'll explain later. Should we rendezvous back at the hotel?"

"No. I'm headed your way now. I've got company with me."

Company?

"There's been a change in plans," Painter said. "Things have gotten a little too hot here in Oslo. So we're pulling up stakes and moving somewhere a little colder."

Still soaking wet from the foamy shower, Monk felt the ice-cold night cut down to his bones. *Colder than this?*

As Monk headed across the corporate campus, he pictured Gray nestled in a warm cabin, a fire blazing in a camp stove.

Lucky bastard.

16

As the forest burned, Gray clutched the lead rope of his stallion. He and the others had quickly saddled the ponies. They didn't have a moment to spare.

After the initial firestorm, the flames had died down to hellish glows all around them. A pall of thick smoke covered the valley, dimming the stars. A single blaze marked a section of the woods that had caught fire. Likely an old deadfall, dry and ready to burn. The rest of the snowy forest had resisted the flames so far.

But they were far from safe.

"Mount up!" he called to the others.

They had to move now. Every second counted as a more insidious danger closed around them. Peat fires traveled underground, spreading outward in smoldering channels and deeper fiery pits. Though the woods were dark, they hid a raging conflagration below.

Wallace had estimated that the entire valley would be consumed in less than an hour. No rescue could reach them in time. Gray had used his satellite phone to contact Painter, to briefly explain their situation and pass on their GPS coordinates, but even the director had agreed that air support could not be mobilized in time to reach them.

They were on their own.

As Gray climbed into the saddle, one of the massive stones in the ring toppled over as the peat beneath it burned and gave way. As it struck, a spate of flames erupted from the dark soil. Other stones had already fallen, some vanished completely into fiery pits.

This was no natural peat fire.

Someone had torched the place, plainly meaning to destroy the excavation site—and anyone here.

Rachel walked her pony next to Gray, keeping a firm grip on her reins. Her mount's eyes rolled white, on the edge of panic. Rachel looked no less scared.

They all knew the danger.

As the fires had erupted, one of the ponies had broken out of the paddock. Wild and tossing its head, it had fled into the forest. Moments later, they heard a crash, a fresh blaze of flames erupted, and a horrible screaming followed.

Gray glanced over at the toppled stone as it slowly sank into the fiery mire, reminding him of the danger beneath their feet. Any misstep and they'd end up like the panicked pony.

Seichan hurried over to Gray's stallion's side. It was her mount that had fled and died. Gray leaned down, grabbed her forearm, and hauled her up into the saddle behind him.

"Let's go!" He pointed toward the darkest section of the forest, where there were no glows at the moment. They had to break through the ring of fire and get up into the hills.

Gray led the way with Wallace at his side.

Ahead of them trotted the terrier, Rufus.

"He'll find us a safe route," the professor said, his face ashen. "Peat burns most ripe. His nose may pick up what we can't see."

Gray hoped he was right, but the entire valley reeked of burning peat. It was a slim chance the dog could nose out the subtle seep of smoke from the subterranean fires. But what other course did they have?

And maybe the dog did sense something. As they headed out, the terrier's path switchbacked through the woods, with sudden stops and turns.

Gray kept their pace to a slow trot, balancing speed and caution. The dog bounded through the snow and across an icy stream. It seemed impossible that on a night so cold, with the ground mantled in snow and ice, there could be a hellish inferno below.

But they were reminded of just that danger as a red deer leaped past their trail, frightened by the fires. It flew sure-footedly through the trees, then bounded into a snow-filled gully. The ground gave way beneath it. Its hindquarters dropped into a fiery pit, casting up a swirl of flames and burning ash. Its neck stretched in a silent posture of agony, then its body went limp and fell the rest of the way out of sight. Smoke roiled upward. A wash of heat chased back the chill of the night.

It was a sobering lesson.

"Christ on a spit," Kowalski mumbled atop his pony.

Seichan's arms tightened around Gray's waist.

As they continued through the smoky woods, new blazes grew throughout the forest as the spreading inferno lit dead trees into torches. They gave one such tree a wide berth. It was an old oak, brittle and lightning-struck. The flames danced through its white branches, a warning of the danger flowing under its roots.

Even Rufus began to slow. He would stop often, his head swiveling, nose in the air, whining, plainly less sure. But he kept them moving, sometimes having to backtrack, dancing straight through the legs of their skittish mounts.

Finally, though, he came to a complete standstill. It was at an old dry riverbed, a shallow declivity that wound across the way ahead. There didn't appear to be any threat, but the dog sidled back and forth across the nearest bank. He made one tentative move down into the channel, then thought better of it and retreated. Something was spooking him. He returned to the head of their stalled line of ponies. His low whine turned into a fearful whimper.

Shifting in his saddle, Gray stared into the woods. All around them the wildfire below had begun to crest to the surface, showing its true fiery face. Not far off, a large pine toppled into the forest, taking smaller trees with it. It crashed with a spiraling wash of flames. More and more of the woods was suffering the same fate. Whole sections were now collapsing into the burning bog, either knocked to the ground as their roots were burned away or felled by their sheer weight as the ground itself turned to fiery ash.

They had to keep moving. The longer they waited, the worse their circumstances. They needed to reach the hills.

"C'mon, you old cur," Wallace urged his dog in a gentle admonishment. "You can do it, Rufus. C'mon, boy. Find us a way home."

The dog stared up at his master, then down at the gully. With a tremble, he sat down. He continued to shake, but his judgment was firm. There was no safe way forward.

Gray slid out of his saddle and passed his reins to Seichan. "Stay here."

"What are you doing?" Rachel asked.

Gray crossed to a mossy stone beside their trail. He had to know for sure. Bending at the knees, he hauled the rock free and lumbered to the edge of the snowy riverbed. With a swing of his arms, he heaved the stone in a low arc over the bank. It landed in the middle of the gully—and crashed through to the fiery bog below. Flames spat up. Snow melted around the edges and boiled back up with a hiss of steam.

The hole immediately grew larger, sending out blazing tendrils. Other spots erupted along the channel. Tossing the boulder had been like throwing a stone in a pond. Fiery ripples spread outward in a cascading effect as fresh oxygen reached the buried inferno. Flames spat, and more steam rose. It spread outward, following the course of the old riverbed.

"You had to do that," Kowalski said. "Couldn't leave well enough alone."

Gray ignored him and stepped to another stone. He dragged it up, and using his entire body, he swung and tossed the rock to the other bank. It was less than eight yards across. The stone struck the far bank and landed with a dull thud. It sat imbedded in turf and snow.

"It's still solid over there. If we can reach the other side . . ." Gray turned to Wallace. "How good are these Fell Ponies at jumping?"

The professor eyed the fiery course. "They're good," he said hesitantly. "But that's still a bloody long leap."

Kowalski added his assessment. "Not like we have much choice."

Another tree crashed deeper in the woods behind them.

"Aye, that's true," Wallace said.

"I'll go first." Gray hurried back to his mount. He raised an arm toward Seichan to help her down.

"I'm going with you," she said.

"No. Our weight will only make it harder to—"

"Do you see any free horses running around here?" Seichan snapped back, cutting him off. "I have to ride double with someone. And your stallion's the biggest."

Gray realized she was right.

He pulled up into the saddle. The others cleared to the side as he backed the horse a good distance away from the bank.

"Hold tight," Gray said.

She obeyed, hugging her arms and pressing her cheek against his back. "Go," she whispered.

Tilting forward in the saddle, he kicked back and gave the reins a crack. The stallion, already bunched, as if knowing what its rider wanted, shot forward with a thunder of hooves. It accelerated into a full gallop within only a few strides.

Gray felt the power of the stallion through the saddle. Its heaving breath streamed white behind them. Its neck stretched as it gained even more speed—then hit the bank.

With a surge of muscle, it leaped high. Gray went weightless, lifting from the saddle with Seichan strapped tightly to him. They crested the fires. He felt the wash of heat from below.

Then they struck the far bank.

Gray slammed back into the saddle, catching his weight with both stirrup and skill. The stallion trotted a few paces to wean away momentum. Gray pulled on the reins and quickly turned his mount.

Seichan still clung hard against him.

He returned to the fiery riverbed and heaved out a sigh of relief. He waved an arm for the others to follow, not yet trusting his voice. A shudder passed through him, but Seichan's arms held tightly.

"We made it," she mumbled to his back.

The others quickly followed. Wallace came flying over with Rufus clutched in his lap. Gray had to give the old guy credit. He could definitely ride.

Rachel came next. She backed her horse and made a smooth run for the river. Gray might have the largest pony, but Rachel had the fastest. It hit the bank, but something went wrong.

One hoof slipped as the edge crumpled beneath it.

Gray knew immediately there was trouble. The jump was too low, the pony's body turned to the side.

They would never make the far side.

Rachel fought to keep her seat. As the mare leaped, she immediately felt the center of gravity shift under her. She clenched her legs to keep in her saddle. She pulled the reins close to her chest and leaned hard over the saddle's pommel.

Twisted askew, she stared straight down into the fiery heart of the wildfire. She wasn't going to make it. The pony was already dropping. Searing heat bathed her.

She heard cries of alarm.

Then they hit the ground. The front hooves struck solid turf, reaching the far bank, but the mare's hind end crashed into the smoldering edge of the river of fire.

The impact threw Rachel flat on her stomach atop the pony. With the wind knocked out of her, she lost the reins and her footing and slid backward toward the fire.

Beneath her, the poor mare screamed in agony and fought to kick herself free, which only stirred the flames higher.

As she slid, Rachel caught the edge of the saddle. Fire burned the soles of her boots. The bucking mare, frenzied by agony, threatened to throw her off. Worse, the mare began to roll.

"Hold on!" a voice screamed.

She glanced up. It was Seichan. The woman dove forward and grabbed the mare's lead. Gray came up on the other side and tried to get hold of the halter's crownpiece.

Together, they fought to keep the mare from rolling.

Seichan wrapped the lead in her arms, dropped to her backside, and dug in her heels. Gray lost hold of the halter as the mare thrashed its head and screamed. He made another lunge for it.

"Just get her!" Seichan yelled as she was dragged toward the river herself.

It took all of Rachel's strength to keep her grip. She felt her legs burning, pictured her pants on fire. Then fingers clamped on her wrist. Gray was suddenly there, sprawled across the mare's withers. He yanked her forward with one arm, his other braced on the saddle's pommel. He hauled her up to his chest, his face red and strained.

"Climb over me!" he ordered her, staring straight at her.

The iron resolve of those steel-blue eyes hardened through her.

Gasping, she reached up and clutched a fistful of his coat. She pulled herself atop him, reached to his belt with her other hand, and crawled over him. At last she cleared the river's edge and rolled off him to land on her hands and knees in the snow.

Gray scrambled back, dropped next to her, then scooped her under one arm and half-carried her up the bank. They collapsed together into the snow. She hugged him, suddenly sobbing.

Behind her, a gunshot blasted.

Jerking around, she saw Seichan standing below, her back to them. She held a smoking pistol. The screams of the mare ended as its body collapsed to the ground and slid farther into the fire.

Seichan sank to the snowy bank, cradling her pistol.

Great.

Still on the other side of the fiery river, Kowalski had watched Rachel's mare stumble. Her pony still burned at the river's edge. How was he going to make it across?

His mount, a gelding, was not as tall as Gray's stallion and not half as fast as Rachel's mare. Plus his pony had no balls, which already made him edgy.

Kowalski held a hand to his stomach. He really should have gone on that diet Liz was pushing.

Gray called from the other side. "What are you waiting for?"

Kowalski lifted one of his fingers at Gray. He patted his pony's neck. "You can do this . . . right?"

His pony tossed its head and rolled a scared eyeball at him.

Right there with you, bud.

He backed his pony, going a little farther, giving himself more of a running start. Still, he hesitated. The pony did, too. It refused to set, dancing its hooves nervously. They both had as much to lose.

We just have to calm ourselves, take a moment to collect—

A pine exploded directly behind them. It went off like a Roman candle. Flaming debris blew high, pelted the back of his coat, and struck the pony's rump.

Given a fiery kick, the gelding took off with a surge of adrenaline-driven muscle. Kowalski came close to falling but quickly regained his balance, riding high in the stirrups. The pony thundered under him, hit the bank, and went airborne.

If Kowalski were braver, he would have *whoop*ed. Or if he had a cowboy hat, he might've waved it. Instead, he leaned down and clung tightly to his gelding with both arms.

Below, as if knowing the last of them were escaping, the entire creekbed collapsed into an inferno of fire. Flames shot upward around them.

Kowalski squeezed his eyes shut, bathed in searing heat.

Then they hit the far side with a crash of hooves on solid ground. The impact threw him over his pony's head. He went flying and landed in a snowbank. He lay on his back for a stunned breath and took inventory.

Still alive . . .

He pushed up to his elbows and gained his feet. He staggered over to his mount, both their legs still trembling. Once at the gelding's side, he threw his arms around its neck and hugged tightly.

"Freakin' love you, you ball-less wonder."

Twenty minutes later, the exhausted team climbed a rocky path out of the valley. Flames danced their shadows across the slope. Below, the entire valley smoldered and burned.

Seichan, aching and bone-tired, rode behind Kowalski. She stared over at Gray and Rachel. They rode together atop his stallion. Rachel had her arms around Gray's waist, her head on his shoulder. After the near-fatal fall, she had stayed close to Gray, drawing off his solidity and strength.

Seichan tried not to sneer at her vulnerability.

But she could not so easily dismiss another pang.

She took note of how quickly the two melded together, how easily they became one. While riding double with him earlier, she had also held Gray, smelled the musk of his sweat, felt the heat of his body. But she had felt nothing more from him. She might as well have been a saddlebag.

Yet even now, as she watched them, Gray rubbed a palm along Rachel's arm. It was a comforting gesture, done reflexively, as he continued to keep an eye on their rocky trail.

Seichan turned away, anger building. Not at Gray, but at her own foolishness. She remembered Kowalski's words to her before the forest exploded. *Two schoolkids with the hots for each other.* She had thought she'd kept her feelings hidden better than that. But what about the man's assessment of his partner? Could he be right about Gray?

She allowed herself a moment to believe it to be true. But only a moment. She stared over at him and recognized there could be no future between them. The gulf was too deep and too wide.

And it would only grow deeper and wider.

Especially with what must happen next.

Free of the woods, it was time she moved her plan to the next level.

2:07 A.M.

Gray called for a halt so they could rest and water the horses. They had reached an ice-blue tarn, one of many that dotted the region like droplets of quicksilver.

He also wanted to check on Rachel's burns. He had packed her lower legs with snow immediately after her mishap to draw off any residual heat. Her skin had been bright pink and a couple of spots might shallowly blister, but he wanted to double-check.

The group slipped off their ponies. They were all saddle-sore and burned crisp around the edges. Even after clearing the fiery river, it had been a close call.

If it hadn't been for Rufus leading us the rest of the way out . . .

Gray watched the professor fish out a piece of dried sausage and feed it to his terrier. Rufus deserved heaping platters of sausages. Still, the terrier was more than happy to get a good scratch for a job well done.

Wallace leaned down and scrubbed his fingers along the dog's side. "Good boy, you mangy mutt."

His tail wagged furiously.

Even Seichan tossed Rufus a crumble of cheese as she stretched her legs. The terrier caught it deftly. He seemed to have gotten over his initial distrust of her. She wandered down to the icy tarn and stood limned by the moonlight reflecting off the water.

Gray studied her.

Back when Rachel had come close to falling into the flames, Seichan had been the first out of the saddle, racing to her aid. Even Gray was a half step behind her. He had never properly thanked her for her help.

But first he had some details to attend to.

Kowalski had started a small fire with some twigs and matches. Despite all that had happened, the night was cold and a fire was still welcome. Everyone headed toward it like weary moths to a flame.

Gray took a moment to warm his hands. Then, with a sigh, he shrugged off his pack and dropped to his haunches. He unzippered a flap and slipped out his satellite phone.

"Calling home?" Kowalski asked.

"Have to update Painter. Let him know we escaped that hellhole."

As Gray lifted the phone, Seichan spoke behind him. "I don't think so."

He turned to find her pointing a gun at his face.

"What are you doing?" he asked.

"Toss me your phone."

"Seichan . . ."

"Do it."

Gray realized the futility of resisting. He knew how well this woman could shoot. He flipped the phone over to her. She caught it smoothly, her pistol never wavering, then lobbed the phone underhanded into the lake.

"Time for all of us to drop off the grid," she said.

Gray could guess what she meant. If he never reported in, Painter would think they'd never made it out of the burning forest. It would take searchers weeks to sift through the ashes.

But what Gray still couldn't understand was *why*.

The question must have been plain to read.

Seichan explained. "Our goal is to find the key Father Giovanni was hunting. In the past, you've proved quite capable, Pierce." She lifted an eyebrow toward Gray. "The Guild has full confidence in you."

Gray shook his head, kicking himself. He had suspected she might use these events to her advantage, to help her return to the good graces of her former masters—whether truly or as a double agent. Either way, he had thought she'd make her move later. He had let his guard down. But in truth, it was more than that. Fury built in him. A part of him had trusted her.

He let some of that anger show. "How are you going to get us to cooperate? You can't hold a gun against us the whole time."

"That's true." She holstered her pistol.

The move made Gray even more worried. Her next words confirmed his fear.

"That's why I poisoned Rachel."

Shock silenced Gray.

Rachel stepped forward. "What?"

"In the tea." Seichan didn't even look at her. She kept her focus on Gray. "A designer biotoxin. Kills in three days. Unfortunately, symptoms will progress. Nausea, headaches, eventually the bleeding will start."

Rachel stammered for a moment, clearly fighting her disbelief. "But you saved my life. Out in the woods."

Gray understood. "She needed you alive."

Seichan shrugged. "There is an antidote. An enzyme specifically designed for this toxin. A lock and key, you might say. There is no other cure. And just to be clear, I don't know what the antidote is, where it might be found, or how to obtain it. You'll be given the antidote only when you hand over the key."

"I don't understand. What *key* are you even talking about?"

"The item Father Giovanni was truly searching for. The key to the Doomsday Book."

Wallace jolted with her words. "That's just a myth."

"For Rachel's sake, you'd better hope it's not. We have three days to find it."

"And what guarantee do we have that you'll keep your end of the bargain?" Gray asked.

She rolled her eyes at his question. "Do I really have to answer that?"

Gray scowled back at her. She was right. She didn't. There was no guarantee, and no need to offer one. With Rachel's life in the balance, they had no choice.

Kowalski folded his arms and glared over at Gray. "Next time, Pierce, listen to the dog."

17

October 13, 3:23 A.M.
Oslo, Norway

Krista had not slept.

It had been a long night, with events seeming to go from bad to worse. But in the final hour, perhaps all ended well. She would know in a few minutes.

She stood before a roaring fire, dressed in an Italian cashmere robe. The hearth was tall enough to walk into without stooping. Her bare toes curled into the sable rug on the floor. A bank of gothic windows, framed in iron, looked out into the snowy courtyard of Akershus Castle. Moonlight cast the world in silver, yet mirrored the fire's flames.

And her reflection stood between them.

Between ice and fire.

A bit of poetry from Robert Frost ran through her head as she waited. She remembered memorizing it at the Catholic girls' school outside of Boston, back when her father used to visit her at night while her mother was drunk.

Some say the world will end in fire,
Some say in ice.

Krista did not care which it was, as long as she was on the winning side. She returned to studying the flames, but pictured another fire. One that had almost ruined everything. She had received an update shortly after midnight from a spotter in the English fells. He had reported on the success of the implanted incendiary charges. But the fire had quickly raged out of control, threatening all. She was forced to wait another two hours before she got the confirmation that the others had escaped the woods. That the operation continued as planned.

If I had failed there . . .

A chill swept through her.

It would have been a disaster, especially with the way matters fared at the Grand Hotel. It had taken her too long to discover that it had been Antonio Gravel who contacted the senator, and he ended up being a more cunning target than she had anticipated. After contacting the senator, the man had vanished. He wasn't at his hotel or at the summit. Only too late did she learn of his predilection for young hookers, those who didn't mind a bit of rough play. Unable to find him quickly enough, she had been forced to set up an ambush at the hotel. It was more brazen than she would have liked, but she had little time for subtlety. She had also hoped to take out two birds with one shot. She had ordered her men to kill Antonio as soon as he entered the hotel, then to use the chaos and confusion to assassinate the senator.

Senator Gorman's death had not been specifically ordered. He was only supposed to be killed if Antonio spoke to him, but Krista did not like loose ends. Especially loose ends that could recognize her. Jason Gorman, love-struck over his new girlfriend, had sent pictures to his father.

Such exposure worried her.

And she didn't like to worry.

In the end, the senator had escaped, and not through any fault of her own. She had been explicitly instructed *not* to pursue the dark-haired Sigma operative. It was not her fault he had shown up.

Still, anxiety kept her tense and cold. She stayed close to the fire, the belt of her robe snugged tightly.

At last, her phone vibrated. She immediately brought it to her ear.

"I'm here," she said.

"I understand the operation in England continues as planned."

"It does." She let a little pride shine through.

"And Senator Gorman escaped."

Her vision narrowed, shadowed at the corners. All her earlier confidence evaporated upon hearing the tone of the man's voice.

"Yes," she forced out.

Silence stretched. Krista's heart pounded in her throat.

"Then we can proceed with the second tier of our plan."

Krista hid a long sigh of relief, but she was also confused. "Second tier?"

"To begin cleaning house in preparation for the endgame."

"Sir?"

"Echelon has met and reevaluated the coming scenarios. In the end, there seems little need for a continuing relationship with Viatus. We find Ivar Karlsen growing quickly into more of a liability. Especially after some strange events this past night at his research facility. His best use now is as a scapegoat, someone to draw fire away from us."

Krista let her mind go cold, recalibrating her role.

The man continued. "We have all the pertinent research. What Ivar Karlsen has set in motion cannot be reversed and will serve us in the end, with or without him."

"What am I to do?"

"You'll accompany him to Svalbard as planned and await further orders. I understand he's opted to leave earlier than expected."

"Another storm is rolling in faster than predicted. He wants to make sure it doesn't interrupt his plans."

"Very wise. Because a storm is definitely brewing out there." The man's voice faded. "You have your orders."

The line went dead.

Krista lowered the phone and clutched it between her palms. She shifted closer to the fire but found no warmth. She stood there unmoving, losing track of time. Her breathing grew harder.

Finally, a voice spoke behind her.

"Are you coming to bed, Krista?"

She glanced over her shoulder. Ivar Karlsen stood naked in the doorway to his bedroom. At his age, he remained solid, his belly flat, his legs strong and muscular. And more important, he needed no pill to perform.

"Is everything all right?" he asked.

"Couldn't be better."

She turned fully to face him. Dropping her phone into a pocket, she undid the sash of her robe and let the garment slither off her shoulders to pile atop the fur rug. She stood with her back to the flames, all too aware of the fire, all too aware of the icy chill of the castle room.

She stood where she belonged.

Between ice and fire.

THIRD

Seeds of Destruction

18

October 13, 8:43 A.M.
Airborne over the Norwegian Sea

The sun remained low in the sky as the private jet soared over the Arctic Circle. During the late autumn months, there was little daylight where they were headed. The archipelago of Svalbard lay halfway between the northern coast of Norway and the North Pole. With over half of its landmass buried under glaciers, it was home to little besides reindeer and polar bears.

Even Saint Nick would have a hard time calling this place home.

But for the moment, Painter enjoyed the leather and mahogany cabin of the private jet, a Citation Sovereign wangled by Kat. She also had their flight manifest altered to show that they were executives of a coal consortium. It was a decent cover. The major industry of the archipelago was coal mining.

The jet's cabin sat seven, so there was plenty of room for the four of them to stretch out. They had all managed to get a little sleep, needing it after the long night, but they'd be landing in less than an hour at Longyearbyen, the largest settlement on the Svalbard islands.

Painter leaned back in his leather captain's chair. He sat across a table from Senator Gorman. Monk and Creed shared a neighboring couch. It was time to lay all their respective cards on the table, to firm up the tentative game plan for the coming confrontation.

Painter knew they would have to move fast, to jump as soon as their tires hit the tarmac. They had fled Oslo knowing two things. First, that with Painter's cover blown and the senator being hunted, the place had grown too hot. Second, that their major suspect had already abandoned the city and was headed to the same frozen islands. It was their best chance to corner Karlsen and get some real answers.

The CEO of Viatus was leading a group of summit leaders to view the famous Svalbard Global Seed Vault. It was the Noah's Ark for seeds, meant to protect its precious cargo—over three hundred thousand seed species—against wars, pestilence, nuclear attack, earthquakes, even drastic climate changes. Designed to last for twenty thousand years, this Doomsday Vault was buried five hundred feet under a mountain, in what was considered to be the most remotely populated place on earth.

If they wanted a private conversation with Karlsen, far from prying eyes, this was the place for it. But such a meeting wasn't without significant risk.

"Senator," Painter pressed one last time, "I still think it might be best if you stayed in Longyearbyen. If we need you, we can pull you into the investigation."

Painter continued to maintain the ruse that the three of them were from the office of the Inspector General, working for the Defense Criminal Investigative Service. They even had the badges to prove it.

"I'm going with you," Senator Gorman said, nursing a cup of coffee.

Painter had noted that he'd spiked it with some brandy from the stocked bar. Not that Painter blamed the guy. Gorman had taken a series of hard blows in the past few hours. He had been a close associate, bordering on friends, with Karlsen.

Gorman's voice hardened. "If Ivar truly had a hand in the death of my son . . ."

"We still don't know how much ties directly back to him," Painter offered thinly.

The senator wasn't buying it.

"He fucking shook my hand." Gorman slammed a fist on the table, rattling the coffee cups and saucers. He glared across the table. Plainly the senator would not be swayed from coming. Painter could only imagine the pain of his loss, followed by such a betrayal, but at the moment Painter didn't need someone flying off half-cocked.

Still, the man had one solid argument and stated it again. "You'll need me to get close to Ivar."

Painter folded his hands in his lap, recognizing the truth. Karlsen had left an hour before them, racing ahead of a storm blowing in from the pole. He would likely already be at the seed vault by the time they landed. And security there was tight, especially with the arriving dignitaries from the summit.

Senator Gorman continued. "To get inside, you'll need both me and my ID pass. Even your badges won't get you past security. With my invitation, I can get at least one of you into the vault."

It had already been decided that Painter would be that *one*. Monk and Creed would maintain a defensive perimeter outside and offer backup.

Painter had also reviewed the security at the seed vault. The place was sealed behind steel-reinforced doors, monitored by a sophisticated video-surveillance system, not to mention patrolled by the couple of thousand polar bears that roamed the island. Additionally, for this event, a contingent of the Norwegian army would be on hand to bolster security.

So crashing this party without the senator would be as hard as cracking into Fort Knox.

Recognizing all this, Painter finally relented. He straightened in his chair and eyed everyone. "Then before we land, let's figure out what we know—and, just as important, what we don't. Once we hit the ground, we'll need to jump."

Monk nodded. "Where do we start?"

"With our primary target, Ivar Karlsen." Painter focused on Gorman. "You've worked with him for years. What can you tell us about him?"

The senator leaned back, clearly trying to rein in his anger, but his expression remained black. "If you'd asked me that yesterday, I would've said he was a rugged, stand-up sort of guy, someone who knows how to make a buck, but also knows the responsibility behind such wealth. Sort of Rockefeller crossed with FDR."

"And how did you first meet?"

"Through the Club of Rome. I joined simply to make political and business connections. What better way to firm up my career than to hobnob with an international group of industrialists, politicians, and celebrities." He shrugged, shameless about his ambition. "But then I met Ivar. His passion was electric, his rhetoric compelling. He firmly and wholeheartedly believes in preserving the world, safeguarding mankind's future. Sure, some of his suggestions for managing population growth may be extreme. Mandatory birth control, sterilization, paying families not to have children. But someone has to make those hard choices. It's what drew me to him to begin with. His no-nonsense manner and sensibility. But I wasn't the only one in his inner circle."

Painter's interest sharpened. "What do you mean?"

"Within the Club of Rome, Ivar gathered like-minded people, those who also believed tough choices were needed. We were sort of a club within the club. Each of us worked on special projects for him. Mine, like I said, was to use my political clout to expand biofuel development. But there were other projects overseen by various members of the circle."

"Like with bees?" Monk asked, referring to the test hives he had seen in the subterranean lab. He rubbed at a stinging welt on his cheek.

The senator shrugged. "I wouldn't know. We each ran our separate projects."

"Then let's talk about the project that started this whole mess," Painter said. "Where all the bloodshed seemed to originate. It all flows back to the genetic research done at Viatus, specifically the testing of its drought-resistant corn. We know Viatus funded the research into extremophiles and that they discovered some fungal organism in the mummies preserved in the English peat." Painter nodded to Monk. "And we know that research continues today and that those bodies found at the mushroom lab were likely from the test farm in Africa."

Painter had already set in motion an order to search those underground labs. But Viatus was one of the largest corporations in Norway, with massive global and financial ties. By the time some judge okayed a search, Painter suspected that the corporation would have purged those labs, leaving behind only sterilized, empty rooms.

"So I think it's safe to conclude," Painter finished, "that the mysterious genes noted in the corn seeds by Professor Malloy at Princeton were from that fungal source. And that apparently those genes are unstable. Possibly making the corn dangerous to consume."

Gorman shook his head. "But why massacre the village? The corn wasn't even meant for human consumption."

Painter had one explanation. "It was a refugee camp. Food was scarce. Hungry people get desperate. I wager some locals sneaked into the fields at night and stole an ear or two of corn for their families. And maybe those who were running the farm turned a blind eye to such trespasses. It would offer the corporation the perfect chance to conduct real-world human studies without needing to acknowledge it."

"Only no one anticipated the gene altering itself," Monk said with a grimace. "After learning that, they had to wipe the slate clean, but not before collecting a few test subjects along the way. Who would miss a refugee or two, especially in a firebombed camp?"

Painter noted that the senator had grown pale, that his gaze had slipped into a thousand-yard stare. Grief shadowed his eyes. But it was more than that.

"Viatus is already shipping their new drought-resistant corn seed," Gorman said. "They have been for the past week. Fields are already being planted for the season across much of the southern hemisphere and equatorial latitudes. Millions of acres."

Painter sensed something worse coming. Gorman had gone pale. It suddenly struck Painter. To mass-produce the seed for global distribution, Viatus had to have already grown it somewhere and harvested it.

But where?

"The production fields for this new corn seed," Painter asked. "Where are they?"

Gorman would not meet his eye. "I helped broker the deal for Viatus. GM seed production is a billion-dollar-a-year industry. It's like pouring money into cash-strapped areas." His voice went dull with shock. "I spread the money out. Throughout the U.S. corn belt—Iowa, Illinois, Nebraska, Indiana, Michigan . . . thousands and thousands of acres, in a patchwork across the Midwest."

"And this is the same corn that they were testing in Africa?" Monk asked.

"Not exactly, but it was in the same genetic line."

"And probably just as unstable," Painter added. "No wonder they burned down that test farm in Africa. The cat was already out of the bag."

"But I don't understand," Monk said. "How could that seed already be planted? What about safety studies?"

Gorman shook his head. "Safety studies on genetically modified foods are a joke. Food *additives* get more testing. GM foods have no formal risk assessment guidelines and rely mostly on self-regulation. Approvals are based on filtered or outright fraudulent reports by the industry. To give you some idea, of the forty GM crops approved last year, only eight have published safety studies. And in the case of the seeds being shipped by Viatus, they are not meant for human consumption, so they're even less on any agency's radar. And besides . . . I helped push it through."

The senator closed his eyes and shook his head.

No wonder Karlsen needed him, Painter thought.

"Still, if the corn's not meant for human consumption," Monk said, "maybe the danger can be contained."

Creed finally spoke up and quickly quashed this hope. "It will still get into the human food supply."

All eyes turned to him.

The newest member of Sigma seemed to shrink a little under their combined attention, but he held up. "After what happened in Princeton, I looked a little deeper into GM crops. In 2000, a GM corn called StarLink, a corn not approved for human consumption like the Viatus strain, ended up contaminating food products across the country. More than three hundred brands. It was suspected of triggering allergic reactions and resulted in a massive recall. The Kellogg Company had to close its production line for two weeks just to clean out the contamination."

The senator nodded. "I remember. The government had to buy up Kellogg stock to keep the industry afloat. Cost us billions."

"And that was only one of many such reports of foreign GM products ending up in the human food supply." Creed glanced over at Painter. "There remains a much larger concern about all this."

"What's that?"

"Pollen migration and genetic contamination."

Frowning, Painter waved for him to explain in more depth.

"There is no way to contain pollen movement of a GM crop. It blows in the wind, gets washed into neighboring fields. Some seeds have been found growing as far away as thirty miles from a planting. So don't be fooled. Wherever fields are planted with the Viatus corn, it will spread from there."

"And genetic contamination?"

"Even more concerning. There have been cases of genetic modifications passing from engineered species into wild ones, spreading the contamination at the genetic level into the biosphere. And with the instability noted by Dr. Malloy in the Viatus corn sample, I think that likelihood is even greater."

"So what you're saying is that the whole Midwest could be contaminated?" Monk asked.

"It's too soon to say that," Painter said. "Not until we have more answers."

Still, Painter remembered what Gray had discovered in England. The mummies in the peat bog had been riddled with mushrooms, just like the bodies found at the lab. Had Karlsen unwittingly unleashed that organism back into the world?

Worse, what if it wasn't an accident?

Karlsen had clearly manipulated the senator to his own ends. But what was his goal in all of this?

Only one man could answer that.

The pilot interrupted. "We've begun our descent into Longyearbyen. Please secure your seats for landing."

Painter glanced out the window as the sun finally began to rise. It was high time he had a conversation with that man. Still, he checked his watch. He had one other concern as the jet dipped toward the frozen archipelago, one that grew more worrisome with each passing hour.

11:01 A.M.
Spitsbergen, Norway

"Still no word from Gray?" Monk asked as he stood in the icy parking lot. He wore a snowsuit, boots, gloves, goggles, and carried a helmet under one arm.

Painter shook his head, clutching his satellite phone. "I had hoped by sunrise to have heard something from him. Or from the patrols. They had choppers up at first light, searching the highlands. Fire crews report the entire valley is a smoldering ruin. I also checked with Kat. He's not checked in with Sigma Command either."

Monk read the pain in the director's face. "He had to make it out of there. Maybe there's a reason he's gone silent."

From his expression, Painter took little consolation from Monk's words. If Gray had gone silent, it was because he was in some sort of trouble. The director stared off into the distance.

The sun still hung low on the horizon, reflecting painfully off the ice and snow that covered the island of Spitsbergen. In another month the archipelago would sink into a permanent Arctic night that would last four months. Even at midday the temperature had climbed to only a single degree Fahrenheit above zero. It was a barren place, treeless and broken into sharp peaks and crevices. The name of this island of the Svalbard archipelago—*Spitsbergen*—translated from the Dutch meant "jagged mountain."

It was not a landscape that inspired hope.

Especially with the dark skies rolling in from the north.

"There's nothing more we can do at our end," Painter finally said, his voice firming again. "I have Kat continuing to monitor reports from both the fire crews and the search-and-rescue teams. She'll do what she can to coordinate a wider search. Until then, we have our own objective here."

Painter stood next to the Volvo SUV he had driven from the airport. Monk had followed in a second vehicle, hauling a trailer behind it. Creed was back there now freeing the two snowmobiles. They'd rented the pair of Lynx V-800 snow machines from a travel service that offered winter safaris into the wilds of the archipelago. The travel agency's logos were painted brightly on their sides.

Inside the Volvo, Senator Gorman sat in the passenger seat. The plan was for the senator and Painter to head directly to the Svalbard seed vault. Monk and Creed would take a more circuitous route overland by snowmobile. The pair would get as close as possible to the vault without raising suspicions, which was the primary reason for the rentals.

According to the tour operator, his company regularly led overnight tours into the mountains to view the wildlife that inhabited the place. But since the construction of the Doomsday Vault, the well-publicized site had become a frequent tourist stop. Their presence should not warrant a second look. Monk and Creed would be ready in case further firepower was needed or a fast evacuation was necessary.

"A back door out of the bank vault," as Painter described it.

The roar of an engine erupted from behind their tow vehicle.

"Let's get moving," Painter ordered. He clapped Monk's forearm in a warm grip. "Stay safe."

"You, too."

The two men headed in opposite directions. Painter climbed back into his SUV; Monk joined his partner by the two snowmobiles. Creed sat atop one, outfitted like Monk in a snowsuit and helmet.

Monk crossed to his machine and hiked a leg over it.

As Painter spun out of the parking lot, Monk checked the assault rifle secured beside his seat. Creed had a matching weapon. They didn't bother hiding the guns. Here in Spitsbergen, where polar bears outnumbered humans, such firepower was a requirement. Even the glossy tourist brochure Monk had picked up at the rental agency had stated, "Always carry a weapon when traveling outside the settlements."

And Monk was not about to break Norwegian law.

"Ready?" he yelled, lifting an arm toward Creed.

His partner revved his engine as answer.

Donning his helmet, Monk twisted his ignition key. The beast roared to life beneath him. Throttling up, Monk edged his snowmobile toward the snowy valley beyond the lot. His machine's rear track bit into the ice with a sure grip. The pair of skis glided smoothly as he dipped over the edge and sped down into powder.

Creed followed in his tracks.

Ahead rose the mountain of Plataberget, home to the Doomsday Vault. Its jagged peak scratched into a lowering sky. Behind it, the world was nothing but dark clouds.

Definitely an ominous place.

Especially as Monk recalled the final warning printed in that tourist brochure. It pretty much summarized this harsh land.

Shoot to kill.

11:48 A.M.

Painter parked his vehicle in the designated slot. They had to pass through two barricades manned by Norwegian military guardsmen on the only road up the mountainside. Other trucks and a large bus already occupied the small parking lot, likely the transportation used by the World Food Summit contingent.

As Painter climbed out of the heated SUV into the icy cold, he also noted a minibus-sized snow vehicle resting on massive treads like a tank. It was a Hagglunds, the official vehicle for exploring Antarctica, painted with the Norwegian flag and army insignia. A couple of soldiers stood near the vehicle, smoking. There was also a smaller two-man Sno-Cat, similarly marked, patrolling the perimeter. Though at the moment, judging by the way it careened and wheeled around out there, someone was doing a little joyriding with it.

Senator Gorman, bundled in a parka, joined Painter and they headed toward the entrance to the seed vault. The only section of the installation that was aboveground was a concrete bunker. It stuck out of the snow at an angle, like the prow of a ship encased in ice. And maybe in some ways it was. Buried below was the Noah's Ark for seeds.

The entrance towered thirty feet, a flat concrete surface decorated at the top with a windowlike plate of mirrors and prisms lit by turquoise fiber optics. It glowed in the darkening day. Already the storm clouds were rolling over the mountain, pressing the sky down on them. A gust of wind kicked up a whirlwind of ice crystals and stinging snow.

Hunched against the cold and wind, they hurried toward the entrance.

Crossing a small bridge, they reached the outer blast doors that sealed the facility. Another pair of armed guards checked the senator's pass and logged in their identification.

"You are very late," one of the guards said in halting English.

"Trouble with our flight," Gorman answered. He grinned good-naturedly at the young guard and shivered against the cold. "Even way up here, airlines still somehow lose your bags. And the cold . . . *brr* . . . I don't know how you can stand it out here. You're made of heartier stuff than me."

The soldier matched Gorman's big grin, as did his partner, who probably didn't even speak English. The senator just had that way about him. Painter had to hand it to him—the guy had charisma. He could turn it on or off like a flashlight. It was no wonder he was so successful in Washington.

The door was hauled open for them. Painter knew that three massive locks secured the vault. As an additional safeguard against malicious attacks, no single person on the planet had all three keys.

Once they were through the doors, the winds cut off, which was welcome, but the air inside was no warmer. Kept at a near constant zero degrees Fahrenheit, it was like stepping into a walk-in freezer.

Down a short ramp, a long circular tunnel stretched, large enough to accommodate a subway train. Underfoot lay cement slabs; overhead ran rows of fluorescent lights and an open lattice of pipes and utility conduits. The walls—steel-reinforced concrete blown with fiberglass—were roughly textured, giving the place a cavelike appearance.

Painter had studied the schematics for the facility. The layout was simple. The tunnel descended five hundred feet and ended at three massive seed vaults, each sealed by its own air lock. The only other feature was a set of office rooms down by the vaults.

Voices echoed up to them. Brighter lights glowed far ahead.

As they walked down the tunnel, Senator Gorman spoke softly and waved an arm at the walls. "Ivar was one of the major financiers for the vault here. He firmly believed in preserving the natural biodiversity of the world and judged all other such seed banks to be inadequate or half-assed."

"I get that about him. Man likes to be in control."

"But in this case, he's probably right. There are over a thousand seed vaults scattered around the world, but a majority of them are threatened. The national seed bank in Iraq was looted and destroyed. In Afghanistan, it was the same. The Taliban broke into their storehouse, not for the seeds, but to steal the plastic containers. And other seed banks are just as fragile. Poor management, suffering economies, failing equipment, all threaten these depositories. But most of all it was a lack of vision."

"And Karlsen stepped in?"

"The vault was the brainchild of the Global Crop Diversity Trust. But when Ivar heard about the project, he added his full support—both financially and vocally." The senator rubbed his temples with his gloved fingertips. "I still can't balance that man with the monster he seems to be. It makes no sense."

They continued in silence. Painter had heard the trace of doubt in Gorman's voice. After the initial shock of betrayal, skepticism had begun to creep back. It was human nature. No one wanted to believe the worst of their best friend or to face their own gullibility and blindness.

Ahead, a group of people massed near the end of the tunnel. The gathering rang with a party atmosphere. Along one wall stood a row of ice sculptures, lit from below to a stunning brilliance: a polar bear, a walrus, a model of the mountain, even the symbol for Viatus. On the other side stood a cold buffet and a steaming coffee bar.

Gorman plucked a champagne flute from a passing hostess. She was dressed in mukluks and a heavy coat. At this event, the parka was the equivalent of a black tie. Two dozen bundled guests crowded the tunnel, but from the number of servers and piles of untouched food, attendance was lower than expected.

Painter knew that the attack at the Grand Hotel—blamed on terrorists—had scared away several of the attendees.

Still, for a party just a hop, skip, and jump from the North Pole, it was a smashing success. At a microphone, a familiar figure was in midspeech. Reynard Boutha, copresident of the Club of Rome, spoke at length about the importance of preserving biodiversity.

"We are in the midst of a genetic Chernobyl. A hundred years ago, the number of varieties of apples cultivated in the United States stood at over seven thousand. Today, it's down to three hundred. Beans numbered almost seven hundred. Now it's down to thirty. Seventy-five percent of the world's biodiversity has vanished in just one century. And every day another species goes extinct. We must act now to preserve what we can before it's lost forever. That's why the Svalbard Global Seed Vault is so important, why we must continue to raise money and awareness . . ."

As Boutha continued, Painter spotted Karlsen across the crowd. He was flanked by two women. One was svelte and tall with long blond hair, her face mostly hidden within the hood of her parka. The other woman was older and bent Karlsen's ear as Boutha spoke.

"Who's that?" Painter asked, indicating the woman speaking to Karlsen.

"She's the former president of Rockefeller's Population Council and another member of Ivar's inner circle. They've been friends for years."

Painter knew about the Population Council. They were major advocates for population control through family planning and birth control, and if you believed some of the wilder rumors and rhetoric, some of their methods bordered on eugenics.

No wonder Karlsen was such good friends with her.

Gorman pointed out a few other figures in the crowd who were members of the inner cabal. "That large fellow with the beer gut over there represents a major German chemical and pharmaceutical company. Viatus has been researching how to incorporate one of their insecticides into a new generation of GM crops. If he's successful, it would severely lessen the pesticide load needed in fields, making crops cheaper to grow and increasing yields."

Painter nodded as Gorman listed others. It seemed Karlsen's circle consisted of those who were either seeking ways to address the overpopulation crisis or researching ways to increase food supplies. The senator was right. The man did seem to have the world's welfare at heart.

So how *did* that balance with a man who ordered the massacre of a village and who pushed forward the wholesale release of a genetic threat that could contaminate and corrupt the biosphere?

The senator's earlier assessment was right.

It didn't make sense.

Painter drew his attention back to Karlsen. Before he confronted the man, he wanted to know all the key players. "What about that other woman," he asked, "the blonde practically hanging off Karlsen's arm?"

Gorman squinted. "I don't know. She looks vaguely familiar, but she's not a member of his inner circle. Maybe just a *friend*."

Satisfied, Painter nudged Gorman and headed through the crowd. In such a gathering, it was doubtful Karlsen would do anything directly to threaten them. Where could he run?

Shifting through the partygoers, Painter soon stood before Karlsen. The man was momentarily alone, having finished his conversation with the Population Council president. Even the woman hanging on his arm had wandered off toward the buffet table.

Karlsen failed to recognize Painter. His gaze skipped over and fixed on Senator Gorman instead. The Norwegian's face immediately brightened with delight as he thrust out an arm.

Reflexively, Gorman shook it.

"Dear God, Sebastian," Karlsen said. "When did you get here? *How* did you get here? I tried calling your hotel when you didn't show up at the airport. With all the commotion after that attack last night, I couldn't get through. I thought maybe you'd flown home."

"No. Security just moved me to a new hotel," Gorman explained smoothly. "I couldn't make it to the airport in time, and I didn't want to hold everyone up. So I booked my own flight."

"You didn't have to do that. I insist that Viatus cover your expenses."

Painter watched the two interact. Though the senator put on a good show, he was plainly out of sorts, clearly on edge and unsettled.

Karlsen, on the other hand, looked genuinely pleased to see the senator. His expression was sincere. Painter could read no evidence that the man standing here had ordered the senator's assassination the night before. Either Karlsen truly wasn't involved or he was one frighteningly cool customer.

Gorman glanced over at Painter. The senator's expression radiated growing doubt. He stammered for a moment, then lifted a hand toward Painter. "I think you've already met the investigator from the office of the Inspector General."

The Norwegian's weighty gaze dropped on Painter. A moment of confusion settled back to recognition. "Of course, I'm sorry. We spoke briefly yesterday. You'll have to forgive me. It's been an insane twenty-four hours."

Tell me about it, Painter thought.

As he shook Karlsen's hand, he continued to study the man's face, looking for cracks in his demeanor.

If the man knew Painter was more than just a DCIS agent, he wasn't showing it.

"The senator was kind enough to allow me to join him," Painter said. "I had hoped we might still conduct our interview. I only have a few questions, to tie up some loose ends. I promise it won't take long. Maybe there's a private place we could chat."

Karlsen looked put out, but he glanced over at Gorman. Maybe for just an instant, Painter spotted a flicker of guilt. It had been the senator's son who had been killed in the massacre in Africa. How could he say no in front of a grieving father?

Karlsen checked his watch, then nodded toward a doorway off to the right. "There are some offices back there. Catering has taken up the front half, but there's a small conference room that should be unoccupied."

"That will do fine."

They headed off together.

From across the crowd, Painter noted the blond woman staring at them. Though her expression was deadpan, it was also colder than the Arctic temperature in the vault. Caught looking, she glanced away.

Abandoned at the party, she did not look happy.

Krista watched the trio enter the vault's administration office. That couldn't be good.

Moments ago, she had almost choked on the olive floating in her vodka tonic, shocked to see the black-haired Sigma operative appear out of nowhere. With Senator Gorman in tow. She had barely gotten out of the way in time.

She stared at the office door as it closed. How could they be here? She thought she'd left them far behind in Oslo.

Suddenly feeling as if eyes were upon her from all directions, she adjusted the hood of her parka so its mink-lined edge better shadowed her face. She was glad she had taken the extra precaution to don a blond wig for the excursion here. She didn't want any more trouble like with Antonio Gravel.

She retreated down the tunnel. It ended at a cross passage that branched into the three seed vaults, each secured by air locks. With everyone still listening to speeches, she had the place to herself for the moment and a chance to regroup.

Leaning her back against one of the seed vault doors, she clutched the phone in her pocket. She had not heard any word from her superior. What was she supposed to do? He had told her that he'd take care of the Sigma operative, but here the man was with the senator. Should she act on her own? Wait for orders? At her level in the organization, she was expected to think on her feet, to improvise as needed.

She took several deep breaths and let a plan crystal-
lize. If she had to act, she would. For now, she'd just
see how matters unfolded here. Still, that didn't mean
she shouldn't take precautions.

She slipped out her phone. So far underground she
had no hope of getting a cell signal. But after arriving here she had excused herself from Ivar's side and
found an outside line in the office computer room. She
had wired a booster into the line so she could use her
phone here.

She dialed one-handed. She had men standing ready
at Longyearbyen. It was time to call them in. As the
line was picked up, she spoke tersely and ordered them
to secure all roads off the mountain. She wanted no
surprises.

Once done, she clicked off the line and felt more
settled. It was the waiting that had worn on her more
than anything. It felt good to act, in even this small
way. She adjusted a stray blond hair back in place. She
should head to the restroom and recheck her makeup.

But before she could take a step, the phone vibrated
in her hand. Her entire body went cold and trembled in
sync with her cell. She lifted it to her ear.

"Yes?" she answered.

A familiar voice responded and finally passed on her
orders. They were simple and direct.

"If you want to live, get out of there now."

19

October 13, 10:13 A.M.
Aberdaron, Wales

Gray rolled their SUV down the long hill toward the church by the sea. They had driven all night, taking turns at the wheel, napping in between. Everyone looked exhausted.

In the rearview mirror, Gray saw Rachel staring out the window. She had not slept at all. Her eyes looked hollow. She often kept a palm pressed to her belly, plainly scared about what was brewing inside her, a biotoxin that could kill her in three days.

On the other side of the vehicle, the woman who had poisoned her seemed unconcerned. Seichan had slept most of the night. She wasn't worried that they might escape. They couldn't even risk calling for help. If Seichan was taken into custody, Rachel was dead.

"Professor," Gray said loudly enough to stir Wallace as he drowsed between the two women. Rufus, roused from the rear compartment, stretched his neck.

"We there?" Wallace asked grumpily.

"Almost."

"About bloody time."

It had been a long night. They had left the Lake District by pony, going by paths known to Dr. Boyle. Well before sunrise, they had ended up in the highland village of Satterthwaite, where they abandoned their ponies in a farmer's field. Gray had hot-wired an old Land Rover for their use.

But before that, during the long horseback ride, Gray had questioned the professor at length about the object they'd been ordered to find: *the key to the Doomsday Book*. According to Wallace, a myth surrounding the book claimed that hidden in its cryptic Latin text was a map to a great treasure.

"It's all rubbish, I tell you," Wallace had finished dismissively, glaring pointedly at Seichan.

She had shrugged. She had her orders, too.

Needing some lead to follow, Gray had pressed Wallace about the travels of Father Giovanni, specifically where the Vatican archaeologist had gone after visiting the stone ring in the peat bog. Wallace knew few details, as Father Giovanni had become more and more secretive over time. The professor offered only one bread crumb they could follow.

"After what we found in the Lake District, Marco went off to explore another spot marked as 'wasted' in the Domesday Book, the oldest of those entries."

Wallace had gone on to explain how an island in the Irish Sea was the first to be described in the Domesday Book in that strange manner. Bardsey Island lay off the coast of Wales. According to Wallace, Father Giovanni had gone to speak to a priest who knew the history of that island very well.

That's where they were headed now. After leaving the Lake District, they had driven south all night, returning to Liverpool again, then continuing into Wales. Their destination lay at the tip of a Welsh peninsula, a finger of land pointed straight at Ireland.

Bardsey Island lay a couple of miles farther out to sea. Gray spotted its gray-green hump against the darkening sky. It was a small isle, only two miles wide. A flush of rain brushed that hilltop and headed slowly toward shore.

Luckily, at the moment their immediate goal lay much closer. The church of Saint Hywyn sat above the beach, facing wind and waves. It was here that Father Giovanni had started his quest.

Gray pulled into the parking lot.

The church was all gray stones and tile roof. Large gothic windows stared out into a grim-looking cemetery. It overlooked a fishing village of colorful stone houses and crooked streets.

They all piled out of the car, stretching legs and hunching against the cold stiff breeze blowing off the sea. Waves rolled heavily against the beach. The air smelled of seaweed and salt.

"I'll stay by the car," Seichan said. "Don't want someone stealing it again."

Gray didn't even bother to acknowledge her. He buried a flicker of fury—not to avoid provoking her, but because she didn't deserve any response from him.

Glad to be free of her, Gray led them around the side of the church toward the rectory. On the trip down to Wales, he had used Seichan's phone to call ahead to Saint Hywyn's and arrange a meeting with Father Timothy Rye. The priest had been pleased about his interest, until he learned the reason behind the visit.

"Marco's dead?" Father Rye had said. "I can hardly believe it. I just saw him a few months ago."

Gray hoped the priest had information they could use.

Before they even reached the rectory door, it popped open. The priest was older than he sounded on the phone. He was as thin as a stick, with only wisps of white hair atop his head. Bundled in an overlarge wool sweater, he tottered to greet them on a gnarled cane, but he wore a warm, welcoming smile.

"Get yourselves out of the wind before it kicks you in the teeth already." Father Rye waved a bony arm to urge them through his door. "I have a pot on the stove, and Ol' Maggie dropped off a plate of her cranberry scones. Best in all of Wales."

They were ushered into a wood-floored room with rafters so low Kowalski had to duck. The walls were the same stone as the church, and a hearty fire danced in a small hearth. A long table had been set for a late morning tea.

Gray's stomach growled at the floury smell of freshly baked scones, but he wanted to keep the visit short. Time squeezed his chest. He checked on Rachel. The old priest had already taken a shine to her, practically taking her by the hand to the table.

"You sit here. By me."

Father Rye shuffled a bit. Wallace still hung at the door with Rufus, plainly not sure whether to leave his dog out in the cold.

"What are you waiting there for?" the priest scolded. "Get yourselves out of the cold."

The invitation was for both. Rufus headed inside even before Wallace moved. The terrier made straight for the fire, curled up, and dropped with a sigh.

Once the rest of them settled, Gray started in. "Father Rye, can you tell us why Father Giovanni—"

"Poor boy." The priest cut him off and crossed himself. "May he rest in peace." He turned and patted Rachel on the hand. "And I'll say a prayer for your uncle in Rome, too. I know he was a good friend of Marco's."

"He was and thank you."

The priest turned back to Gray. "Marco . . . now let me think. He first came here to the church some three years ago."

"That would be just after he first visited my excavation," Wallace added.

"He came quite often after that, traipsing all over Wales. We talked about all manner of sorts, we did. Then last June, he returned quite agitated from Bardsey Island. Like he'd been spooked to the bone. He prayed all night in the church. I heard him, I'm afraid—not that I was eavesdropping, mind you—asking over and over again for forgiveness. When I woke the next morning, he was gone."

Gray returned to that first visit. "Did Father Giovanni say why he first came here?"

"Aye. He was on a holy pilgrimage to Bardsey Island. Like many people before him. To pay homage to the dead."

Gray tried to sort through what he was hearing. Clearly the good father hadn't been totally honest with the elderly priest. But a few words made sense. "What dead are you talking about?"

"The twenty thousand saints buried on Bardsey." The old man pointed an arm toward the small window, which looked out to sea. The island was all but lost to sight as rain poured heavily over it. "Marco wanted to know all about the history of the dead."

Gray did, too. "What did you tell him?"

"What I tell all pilgrims. That Bardsey Island is a sacred place. Its history is a long one, going back to the peoples who first came to these fair lands. The ones who stood the stones on end and built the ancient cairns."

Wallace perked up here. "You're talking about the Neolithic tribe who first inhabited the British Isles."

"Aye. You can still find their hut circles up on Bardsey. It was a sacred place even back then. Home of royalty. Do you know the Celtic tales of the Fomorians?"

Gray shook his head. Wallace's eyes pinched. He plainly understood but wanted to hear what the old priest had to say.

"What are Fomorians?" Rachel asked.

"Not *what,* but who. According to Irish legends, when the Celts first came to these islands, they found them occupied by an ancient race, quite monstrous. Supposedly they were descendants of Ham, who had been cursed by Noah. The Celts and Fomorians fought over Ireland and its islands for centuries. Though not as skilled with swords, the Fomorians were known to be able to cast plagues upon their invaders."

"Plagues?" Gray asked.

"Aye. To quote one Irish ode, they cast out a 'great withering death' upon their enemies."

Gray glanced at Rachel and Wallace. Could this be the same as what wiped out the highland village?

"Other stories abound over the centuries," Father Rye continued, "of great wars and wary peace between these two peoples. The Irish storytellers do admit it was the Fomorians who passed on knowledge of agriculture to the Celts. But at the end, one last great battle was fought on Tory Island, and it resulted in the death of the Fomorian king."

"But what does all this have to do with Bardsey Island?" Wallace asked.

The priest lifted one brow. "As it is said, Bardsey was home to ancient royalty. According to local stories, it was on Bardsey that the Fomorian queen made her home. She was a great goddess who had the power to heal the sick, even cure the plagues."

Wallace mumbled under his breath, "No wonder Marco kept coming back."

Gray wanted to ask Wallace what he meant, but Father Rye was on a roll.

"And so the Celts took possession of all the lands. But even their priests, the Druids, recognized how sacred this region was. They made their center of learning on nearby Anglesey Island. Students gathered from all over Europe to study there. Can you imagine? But it was Bardsey Island that the Druids considered to be the most holy. Only the most elevated of the Druids were allowed to be buried there. Including the most famous Druid of all time."

Wallace must have known this legend. "Merlin."

Seichan stood on the leeward side of the Land Rover, keeping out of the wind. She opened and closed a folding knife while keeping watch on the rectory door. She didn't fear anyone trying to escape, nor even using the rectory phone. Though to ensure the latter, she had slipped over and cut the telephone wires.

She could have simply gone inside with them, but piecing together bits of history was not her specialty. She looked down at the knife in her hand. She knew where her talents lay. And she didn't need Gray distracted. She felt the fury radiating from him, stoking higher the closer she came. So she stayed away. She needed him focused.

For all their sakes.

She had watched the Audi sedan slip into the nearby town soon after they arrived. They were being watched from afar. Her handler, Magnussen, was keeping her on a short leash, tracking them out of the mountains. The hunters skillfully swapped out vehicles. She counted at least three tails. Unless you knew to look for them, they would have been impossible to pick out.

But not for her.

With a flip of her wrist, she snapped the folding blade closed and slipped it into her pocket. Sensing eyes on her even now, she needed to move. She abandoned the vehicle and strode toward the door to the old church. Its stone face was cold and imposing, as hard as the people who eked out a living off the sea here. The weight of centuries was palpable. Even its door was massive, scarred, and old. She tried the handle and discovered the church had been left open.

It always surprised her to find a door unlocked.

It felt somehow wrong, an unnatural state of being.

Before she thought better of it, she pulled open the door. The wind was kicking up. No telling how long the others would be. She entered the church and passed through the entry to the nave. Expecting a gloomy, somber interior, she was surprised to discover an airy and high-raftered space. The walls had been painted a creamy white that captured and held the meager daylight flowing through the arched windows. Polished wooden pews flanked either side, and a bright blue carpet led down the center aisle.

The church was empty, but she found herself unable to move any deeper into the nave. Suddenly tired, Seichan slipped into the closest pew and sat down. She stared over at the cross. She was not religious, but she recognized the pain in the crucified image of Christ.

She knew that agony.

Her breathing grew heavier as she stared. Her vision suddenly blurred. The tears came suddenly, welling up from somewhere deep inside. She covered her face as if trying to stop them, hide them, deny them.

For a long moment, she remained bent in the pew, unable to move. A pressure built inside her chest. It grew to an excruciating point, something large trying to squeeze out a small hole. She waited for it to pass, prayed for it to end—and eventually it did, leaving her both hollow and strangely disappointed. A shudder shot through her body, just once. She then took a long trembling breath, wiped her eyes, and stood up.

She turned her back on the cross and headed out of the nave and out of the church. The cold wind struck her and slammed the door behind her. It reminded her of an important lesson.

People should keep their doors locked.

Gray tried not to scoff. "You're saying Merlin is buried on Bardsey Island?"

Father Rye smiled and sipped his tea. "Of course, we all like to tell that story around these parts. It's said he's buried in a glass tomb on the island. It's surely fanciful, but it makes for a fine story, don't you think?" He winked at Rachel. "Though many do believe, including a few historians, that the Arthurian legends of Avalon arise from Bardsey."

Kowalski spoke around a mouthful of scone. "What's Avalon?"

Gray nudged him under the table. They didn't need the old priest rambling off the subject. They had to find out more about Father Giovanni.

But he was too late.

"Ah, according to Celtic legend," Father Rye explained, "Avalon was an earthly paradise. It was where King Arthur's sword, Excalibur, was forged. Where the enchantress Morgan Le Fay ruled. It was an island of rare apple trees, granting the place its name, from the Welsh word *afal*. Avalon was considered a place of great healing and longevity. And at the end of the Arthurian cycle, it was where King Arthur was taken to be healed by Morgan Le Fay after the Battle of Camlann. And of course, like I said, it was where the magician Merlin was buried."

Wallace's face grew more sour with the telling. "Bollocks," he finally burst out. "Everyone thinks Avalon or Camelot is in their own backyard."

Father Rye took no offense at the professor's outburst. "As I said, it's only legend. But like Avalon, Bardsey Island has long been considered a place of great healing. Even a travel book from 1188 attests to this claim. The writer described the people of Bardsey as being uncommonly free of disease and 'scarcely any die except of extreme old age.' And then, of course, we must not forget our magical apples."

"Apples?" Kowalski asked.

"Maybe we should move past myths," Gray commented, trying to redirect the conversation back to Father Giovanni.

"They're not myths." Father Rye stood up, crossed to a bowl on a counter, snatched up an apple, and tossed it toward Gray. "Does that feel like a myth to you, young man? Maggie's son picked that from a tree growing on the island just last week."

Gray frowned down at the fist-sized fruit.

"There is no other apple like it on earth," Father Rye said proudly. "A few years back, some apples from that tree were taken to the National Fruit Collection in Kent. They tested the Bardsey apple and determined two things. First, that the tree was a new variety never seen before. And second, that the apple was unusually free of any rot or disease. They tested the gnarled old tree itself and found it to be in the same health. Arborists believe the tree may be the lone surviving specimen from an orchard that the monks of Saint Mary's once planted on the island a thousand years ago."

Gray stared at the small apple in his hand, sensing the passage of time and history it represented. No matter what one might believe, there did seem to be a long, strange history of healing tied to this island: first the Fomorian queen, then the Celtic legends of Avalon, and now in his hand, something that had been scientifically proved to be unusually healthy.

He looked out the window at the hump of green land.

What was so special about that island?

Apparently Father Rye wasn't done with his history lesson.

"Moving forward through time, all things must come to an end," he said. "And the Celts were no exception. The Romans eventually vanquished them, but only after years of fierce fighting. During this time, the Romans claimed that the Druids cast curses upon their troops, just as the Fomorians had done to the Celts long ago. And after the Druids were gone, the Church came here and settled these pagan lands. They set up an abbey on the island in the thirteenth century. The ruins of its tower can still be found there."

Wallace drew their conversation full around. "But what about the twenty thousand saints you mentioned at the beginning?"

Father Rye sipped his tea, nodding at the same time, but somehow never spilling a drop. "Bardsey is known as the Isle of Twenty Thousand Saints. A name marking the number of persecuted Christians buried there."

"So many?" Wallaced pressed. "Surely there's no archaeological evidence for such a mass burial?"

"You are right. I imagine the legend is more allegorical than literal. Though local folklore does whisper of a great death that fell on Bardsey, a withering sickness that slew most of the villagers and monks. Their bodies were burned to ashes and cast out to sea."

Gray recognized the pattern of that story. Just like the highland village. All evidence burned and swept away, leaving only rumor and a cryptic entry in the Domesday Book.

"Either way, the island has been considered holy ground since the Church first came here. Bardsey grew to become a place of pilgrimage, from ancient times to today. The Vatican declared that three trips to Bardsey were equivalent to one trip to Rome. Not a bad deal, if you ask me. And many others thought the same."

Father Rye pointed in the direction of his church. "The oldest part of Saint Hywyn's dates back to 1137. Through its doors, thousands and thousands of pilgrims have flowed on their way to Bardsey. Including most of the Irish and English saints of that time."

As if summoned by the priest's words, the rectory door burst open and a tall boy pounded into the room with all the verve that only a thirteen-year-old could muster. The boy quickly pulled off his cap to reveal hair so red it looked ready to set fire to the room.

"There you are, Lyle," Father Rye said and stood up. "Does your da have his ferry ready for our guests?"

Lyle eyed the crowd. "He does, Father. He ran me up to fetch 'em. Though they'd better be quick. The blow's kicking up fierce already."

Father Rye placed his palms on his hips, looking forlorn at losing his guests. "You best be going. You don't want to be caught midcrossing when that storm hits."

Gray nodded. "Let's go." He got everyone moving toward the door.

"Can my dog stay with you?" Wallace asked the priest. "There's one thing Rufus can't stomach and that's boats."

Father Rye's smile returned. "I'd like that. You can nab him up on your way back."

Rufus looked happy enough with that decision. He lowered his head back to his paws as he lay by the fire.

As Gray headed to the door, Father Rye called out, "Lyle, when you get to the island, make sure you show them the Hermit's Cave."

Gray glanced back.

Father Rye winked at him. "Where Merlin is buried."

11:22 A.M.

Rachel eyed the ferry doubtfully. The small boat looked sound enough. It was a double-hulled catamaran, with a covered pilot's cabin in front and an open deck in the stern. She had been on such boats before when diving in the Mediterranean. They were notoriously stable and reliable.

Still, as she watched it roll and tilt in the chop, Rachel grew concerned. With one hand clutching her coat closed at her neck, she stared into the stiff wind. She could smell the rain. Though dry here, a heavy downpour swept toward the coast.

Her expression must have been easy to read.

"The *Benlli*'s a good boat," the ferryman attested. Decked out in a heavy sweater and yellow slicker, he was Lyle's father, Owen Bryce. His boy bounced over the rolling deck with the agility of a red-haired monkey. His father watched him proudly. "Don't you fret, miss. We'll get you there safe. She runs low with a steep deadrise."

Rachel didn't know what he meant, but she took confidence in his vocabulary. He seemed to know what he was talking about.

Lyle appeared and offered her his hand. She took it as she hopped from jetty to boat. Gray and Wallace were already aboard, with their heads together. Kowalski followed behind with Seichan.

Rachel kept away from Seichan and took a seat next to Gray. Still, she sensed the woman's presence—not because she was staring at Rachel, but because she purposefully wasn't. It made her angry. She felt she deserved at least to be acknowledged.

To take her mind off Seichan and the rocking boat, she focused back on Gray. He had to speak loudly as the catamaran's twin outboard engines gurgled to a roar.

"Back at the rectory," Gray said, "I heard you mumble something about not being surprised Father Giovanni kept coming back here."

Rachel had heard the same. It had been when Father Rye had been talking about the pagan queen.

Wallace nodded. "Aye. As a historian of Neolithic Britain, I'm quite familiar with the Irish tales of the monstrous Fomorians who supposedly first inhabited the lands here. It was said they were giants who ate people alive. But it was the vicar's description of them as *descendants of Ham,* a figure straight out of the Bible, that must have pinched Marco's nose and kept him focused here."

"How so?" Gray asked.

"To start with, Celtic tales were all told orally. Spread by word of mouth. The only reason we even have them today is because of the Irish monks who survived the ravages of the Dark Ages in seclusion, who spent their days meticulously decorating and illuminating manuscripts. They preserved the core of Western civilization through the Middle Ages. Including preserving Irish legends and sagas by writing them down for the first time. But what you must understand is that the monks were still Christians, so in their retelling, many of these stories took on a biblical slant."

"Like the Fomorians being described as descendants of Ham," Gray said.

"Precisely. The Bible never actually denotes a race for these cursed descendants of Ham, but early Jewish and Christian scholars interpreted the curse to mean that Ham's descendants were black-skinned. It was the way that slavery was once justified."

Gray sat back, understanding dawning in his face. "So what you're saying is that the Celts described the Fomorian queen as being *black,* so the monks made her a descendant of Ham."

Wallace agreed. "A dark-skinned queen who could cure the sick."

"And to Marco, she was possibly an early pagan incarnation of the Black Madonna." Gray looked out toward the island as the boat churned into the choppier open waters. "Perhaps even the legends of the sorceress Morgan Le Fay and Avalon tie back to that same mythology. Another woman bearing magical healing powers."

Rachel's eyes widened. "No wonder Father Giovanni became obsessed with this place."

"For that reason, and also the key." Wallace folded his arms and easily rolled with the boat's motion.

"The key to the Doomsday Book?" Rachel asked. "I thought you said that was rubbish."

"I may have thought it was rubbish, but Marco didn't. All the legends of the key suggest that it unlocked a vast treasure, a treasure that could save the world. Marco believed I was on the right course in studying the places marked as 'wasted.' And I'm growing to think he's right."

"Why's that?" Gray asked.

"Father Rye's stories. He spoke of how the Fomorians battled the invading Celts by casting plagues on them. It was said the Druids did the same when the Romans invaded. So it makes me wonder if the Celts learned something from the conquered Fomorians, something more than just agriculture. A new means of warfare, a new weapon. Maybe there was a core of truth behind these stories. A truth buried in the Domesday Book."

Rachel began to get a glimmer of where he was headed, but Gray got there first.

"You think that ability to cast plagues survived into the eleventh century. Maybe an early form of biowarfare."

Rachel pictured the condition of the mummies. Emaciated, with mushrooms growing internally.

"Could someone have poisoned these villages with some sort of fungal parasite?" Gray asked. "And if so, who?"

"As I said before, all the villages noted in the Domesday Book were located in places of friction between Christians and pagans. And I think it's especially telling that the first place struck was Bardsey Island. Hallowed ground for the Druids. They could not have liked the monks and Christians being here."

"So you think some secret sect of Druids wiped them out?"

"And after that, they took their war to the main-land of England. I suspect they began casting these plagues in the borderlands in hopes the conflict would spread throughout England."

Wallace had to catch himself as the ferry hit a huge wave. Once reseated, he continued. "Perhaps the hidden purpose of the Domesday Book was to map these incursions, to keep track of them. The census takers who compiled the book were sent out to all corners of Britain, collecting information from villagers and townspeople alike, surely doubling as spies."

"Did it work?" Rachel asked, caught up in the story.

"Well, those hot spots never did spread," Wallace said with a shrug. "Someone must have found a way to thwart the attacks. Then buried it safely away."

"The key to the Doomsday Book," Gray said. "You believe it's some sort of cure."

Wallace touched the tip of his nose, acknowledging the same.

"And we're on the right track?" Gray asked, glancing significantly at Rachel. They didn't have much room for error.

His hand slipped over hers, squeezed her fingers, then let go. She wished he had kept on holding. His skin had been hot, his grip reassuring.

Wallace answered Gray's question. "Marco certainly believed in the key. And judging from that gruesome little keepsake of his, he discovered something. And we know he started here at Bardsey."

The professor nodded toward the growing bulk of the dark island. It was buried in the storm. And a moment later, so were they. The winds kicked up, blowing freezing slaps of water across the boat. Then rain suddenly pounded the boat, as if trying to drive them under the sea. Visibility dropped to yards.

"Hang tight!" Kowalski bellowed from the pilothouse, where he stood with the captain. "Swells dead ahead!"

The bow of the boat rose high, pointed at the sky— then dropped like a rock. After that, motion became a blur. The ferry lurched and heaved, rocked and pitched.

Without warning, Rachel's stomach did the same. A queasy heat swept through her. Her hands went clammy and cold. She didn't have time to make it to the ship's water closet. She swung around in her seat, bent over the rail, and emptied her stomach in a single large wrack of her body. It left her so drained she had a hard time keeping a grip on the wet rail.

Below her face, the sea surged up and down, looking ready at any moment to wash up and over her. Her hands slid. She felt herself tipping.

Then strong arms closed around her, holding her firmly but gently.

"I've got you," Gray said.

She leaned against him, her stomach still rolling with the waves. The rest of the trip was no smoother, but he never left her side.

After what seemed like hours, land filled the world ahead. The storm grew less fierce. Rain receded to a drizzle. A long concrete slipway stuck out into the small harbor, next to it a stone jetty. The ferryman slid his boat skillfully beside the dock as Lyle ran and tossed bolsters between the jetty and the boat. Moments later, they were tied up.

Rachel clambered happily off the rocking boat. The solid crunch of stones under her feet had never felt so good.

"Are you okay?" Gray asked.

She had to take some personal inventory before slowly nodding. "I think so. Just glad to be away from the waves."

Gray touched her arm. Concern shone in his eyes. "Are you sure it was just the waves?"

Rachel wanted to nod again. But she placed a hand on her belly, remembering what Seichan had said about the poison. One of the first symptoms was nausea.

She glanced back to the boat.

What if it wasn't the waves?

12:05 P.M.
Bardsey Island, Wales

The tractor climbed up the hill from the harbor. It dragged a hay trailer behind it, and its straw-strewn bed held a collection of sodden people. A tarpaulin staked over the trailer shielded against spats of rain, but it offered no protection against the cutting wind.

Gray huddled below the sides of the trailer, trying his best to hide from the more stubborn gusts. The worst of the storm had abated for the moment, but the sky to the west only grew darker, threatening a worse gale to come.

As they climbed the hill, a panoramic view of the small island opened up. Behind the trailer, out at the tip of the island, rose a tall red-and-white-striped lighthouse. It blinked into the storm with a steady turn of its lamp. Between the lighthouse and the hill was farmland. There were only a dozen or so full-time residences on Bardsey Island, mostly farmers and those who rented cottages to visiting hikers, bird-watchers, and pilgrims.

The only roads were dirt. The only vehicles were tractors.

They'd definitely stepped into another era.

As they neared the crest of the hill, the tractor slowed to a halt. The boy Lyle hopped from the back of the tractor to the bed. He was their official driver and tour guide. He crouched in the middle of the bed as a roll of thunder echoed over the hilltop.

Lyle waited for it to fade, then spoke. "Father Rye said you might be wanting to visit the old Hermit's Cave. It's off a wee bit on foot. I can show you."

Kowalski patted his pockets, looking for a cigar. "Not really feeling like paying the hermit a visit."

Gray ignored Kowalski and joined Lyle. "You said you helped Father Giovanni before and that he spent most of his time at the ruins of the old abbey. Did he spend any time up at the cave?"

"Not really. Just once at the beginning. Don't think he went back after that."

Gray knew he had better take a look to be thorough. "Show me."

"I'll go with you," Wallace volunteered. "Be a shame to come all this way and not pay my respects to the dearly departed Merlin."

The sarcasm ran thick in his voice.

Gray glanced at Rachel. She shook her head. She still looked a little queasy, but he wasn't sure if it was from motion sickness, toxicity, or something in between.

He hopped out of the bed and was surprised to see Seichan jump out after him. Without a word, she headed after Wallace and the boy.

Gray suspected that Seichan's interest lay less in the hermit's cave than in a desire not to be left alone with Rachel. Shouldering his pack, he followed after the others up a side trail.

Seichan slowed enough to come even with him. "We need to talk," she said, not looking at him.

"We have nothing to talk about."

"Quit being an ass. Despite what you think, I don't want to be in this position any more than you do. It wasn't my choice to poison Rachel. You know that, right?"

She finally looked at him.

He wasn't buying it.

"The end result is the same," he said. "You get what you want, and others pay the price." He let his spite show. "So how *was* your visit with the Venetian curator's family?"

Her eyes narrowed. Wounded, angry, she swung away. Her voice grew more brittle.

"Whatever is going on here has the Guild stirred up, from its top brass on down. They're dispensing a huge amount of resources to find this lost key. I've only seen them this mobilized once before. Back when we were searching for the Magi's bones."

"Why's that?" Gray hated to get involved with her, but if she had insight, he dared not dismiss it.

"I don't know. But whatever is happening over at Viatus, it's only the head of the beast. I suspect the Guild has been manipulating and exploiting the corporation merely as a resource. It's what they do best. They're like a parasite that invades a body, sucks it dry, then moves on."

"But what is their end goal?"

"To find that key. But the bigger question is *why is the key so important to the Guild?* Discover that and you may be one step closer to finding it."

She stopped speaking, letting that sink in. Gray had to admit she was right. Maybe he did have to look at the problem from the other way around, work backward.

She finally continued. "We know that Viatus took those mummies and experimented on them. But the bodies were discovered three years ago. So for years now the project has been running below anyone's radar. I certainly wasn't aware of it. Yet just as Father Giovanni makes a run for the Vatican, the Guild rises up. Anyone with an ear to the ground like mine could hear it. In the last twenty-four hours, they've exposed themselves more than I've seen them ever do before. It was what drew me to Italy in the first place, what made me seek out Rachel."

Gray heard the smallest wince in her voice at the mention of Rachel's name. She grew quiet after that.

Gray filled the silence. "Wallace believes that the key may be a counteragent against some early form of biowarfare. If the Guild can control the key, they can control the weapon."

"You could be right, but the Guild's interest lies deeper than that. Trust me."

Gray fought against reacting to her last words.

Trust me.

Those were two words she had no right to utter.

He was saved from responding when Wallace lifted an arm ahead and pointed down to the ground. "Here it is!"

"Just think about it," Seichan finished. "I'm going back to the tractor."

Gray continued alone to the cave. Lyle had ducked into it. The entrance was shorter than Gray's waist, but it opened into a tiny cave beyond. Kneeling, Gray pulled out a flashlight from his pack and played it over the inside. It was a natural cavern, and except for a dented beer can and a bit of trash, it was nondescript.

If this was Merlin's final resting place, he needed to complain about the accommodations. No wonder Father Giovanni never gave it a second look.

"Nothing's here," Wallace finally concluded.

Gray agreed. "Let's head over the hill."

They walked briskly back as rain began to spatter harder. Once they reached the trailer, they set off again. Lyle drove the tractor over the summit of the hill and down the far side.

Lowlands stretched ahead, again parceled out into tracts of farmland and grazing fields. But at the foot of the hill rose their destination. It was a square tower, half in rubble, rising in the middle of a cemetery. It was all that was left of Saint Mary's Abbey. A newer chapel and chapel house stood off to one side. From this height, Gray could also make out some crumbled foundation walls of the old abbey.

As they descended, Lyle pointed to a small house in the distance. "Plas Bach!" he called out, naming the place. "You can rent that place. It's also home to our famous apple tree."

Gray reached into a pocket of his coat and realized he still had the apple tossed to him by Father Rye. As he stared at the pink apple, it reminded him of the abbey's residents. Both the apple tree and the monks were described in various circles as uncommonly healthy and of amazing longevity. Had the monks of Saint Mary's known some secret? Was it the same secret they all sought now, the key to the Doomsday Book? And if so, how did they come by it?

With a final belch of exhaust, reeking of oil, the tractor ground to a halt at the foot of the hill beside the cemetery. Celtic crosses dotted the grounds, including an especially tall one in the shadows of the abbey's broken tower.

The group climbed out of the trailer bed and dusted off stray bits of straw. The downpour had mostly stopped, which was a relief. But lightning flashed to the north. Thunder rumbled a low warning of more rain to come. They had better work quickly.

Gray stepped over to Lyle. "You said Father Giovanni spent most of his time here. Do you happen to know what he was doing? Is there anywhere he concentrated on looking?"

Lyle shrugged with his whole body. "He was all over the ruins here. Mostly measuring."

"Measuring?"

A nod answered him. "He had tape measures, and what do you call it?" He pantomimed with his arms, holding them askew and eyeballing down them. "Little telescopes for figuring out how high things are and what not?"

"Surveying equipment," Gray realized aloud. "Is there any place he spent lots of time measuring?"

"Aye. Our crosses and over by the old stone ruins."

"Ruins? You mean the abbey?"

Wallace stepped to Lyle's other side. "I think the boy means the ruins of the ancients, don't you, lad?"

"That's correct, sir."

"Can you show us?"

"Of course I can." And he was off.

They followed as a group, crossing through the cemetery. Lyle pointed to each Celtic cross as he passed it. He ended at the tallest in the cemetery. It rose from a small hillock.

"This marks the grave of Lord Newborough," Lyle said. "One of our most famous Bardsey nobles and a great benefactor to the Church."

Gray craned up at it. Father Giovanni surely knew the significance of the Celtic crosses, how they were modifications of older Druid crosses, which likewise had been borrowed from the ancients who originally occupied the British Isles and carved that symbol on their standing stones. One symbol that linked all three cultures, flowing from the ancient past to the present.

Had the key followed the same path? From ancients, to Celts, to Christians?

Wallace stared across the cemetery. "Father Giovanni measured all the crosses?"

"He did indeed."

"And you said he did the same to some stone ruins?"

"Over this way." Lyle circled the rubble of the abbey bell tower and marched into a grassy field. He kicked his feet as if looking for something. "Father Giovanni searched all the ancient hut circles. Most are on this side of the island."

Wallace marched beside Gray. "No wonder the monks set their abbey here. It was common for the early Church to build on sacred sites. Stamping their religion on top of another. Both as a way of getting rid of it, but also to help the newly converted smoothly transition into the new faith."

"Here!" Lyle called out from a few yards to the right. "I think this is the one!"

Gray crossed over with Wallace. The boy stood in the middle of a crude ring of stone blocks half-buried in the turf. Gray walked its circumference.

Wallace scratched his chin. "Are you sure this is the right hut circle? The one our friend was interested in?"

Lyle suddenly didn't look so certain.

Gray stopped at one of the stones. He knelt down and parted the grasses. He stared down at the stone and knew they were at the right place.

On the crude boulder was carved a symbol.

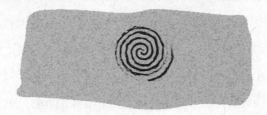

A spiral.

Gray stared across the field. He double-checked with his compass. In a direct path east from here, where the sun would rise on the new day, stood Lord Newborough's grave marker, a giant Celtic cross, whose roots traced back to the same artisans who had carved the ragged spiral on the boulder at Gray's feet.

"This is it," he mumbled.

"What's that?" Wallace asked, not hearing him.

Gray continued to study the distant cross. He didn't need any measuring tools, though he might not have figured it out so quickly if it hadn't been for Lyle telling him about the painstaking survey the priest had done here.

"I know where Father Giovanni looked," Gray said. Rachel drew closer. "Where?"

"Between the spiral and the cross," Gray said and pointed to Lord Newborough's grave marker. "Like on the stones up at your excavation, Wallace. Crosses on one side, spirals on the other."

"And like the leather satchel," Rachel reminded him.

Gray nodded. "Though Marco never had that advantage. He had to figure all this out on his own. Going by only what he saw at the excavation site. It must have finally dawned on Marco. Possibly literally. Father Rye said that Marco became agitated last June, which meant he was here during the midsummer solstice. The longest day of the year. A sacred holiday for the pagans, especially those who worshiped the sun."

He pointed to the cross and drew a line down to his toes. "I wager it would take calculations to prove it— something Marco likely did—that on the morning of the solstice, the sun's first rays would strike that cross and cast a shadow pointed straight here."

"And that led to Marco's discovery?" Wallace pressed.

"Maybe. I can pace it out to be sure, but I don't think I have to. Look what sits exactly midway between the cross and the spiral."

Gray pointed at the pile of crumbling stones.

"Saint Mary's tower," Wallace said, then turned to him. "You think whatever Marco found was hidden beneath the tower?"

"You said it yourself. That the Church built its holy buildings atop older sacred sites. The island is riddled with caves. Caves that the Druids considered sacred. And stories continue to this day of some powerful magic, personified by Merlin, buried in a cave on the island. What if they got the cave wrong?"

Wallace's voice grew hushed. "Not the Hermit's Cave, but something hidden in secret under the abbey."

Rachel asked a good question. "But how do you look under there?"

"That dead priest sure didn't bulldoze his way in there," Kowalski added.

They were both right. There were no signs of excavation around the tower ruins.

"There must be another way down there," Gray said and turned to the best source for that information. "Lyle, are there any other tunnels or caves somewhere near here?"

"Aye. Lots of caves. But none too close."

It would take them months to search them all. Gray stared over at Rachel. She stood with her arms crossed. They didn't have months.

"But I can show you what I showed Father Giovanni!" Lyle suddenly said brightly. "It's not a cave, but it's just as good."

"What?" Gray asked.

"Come see. My friends and I play down there all the time." Lyle took off like a shot. They had to run to keep up with him.

"We're not in that big of a hurry," Kowalski grumbled.

"Speak for yourself," Rachel said.

Lyle led them back around the tower. This time he headed in the opposite direction from before. He came almost full circle, but then stopped not far from the tall Celtic cross. He pointed to a square hole in the ground, framed by stones.

"What is it?" Wallace asked.

Gray dropped to his knees and stared down. The sides were stacked bricks. Near the bottom, a black niche was cut into one wall.

"Like I said," Lyle answered, "it's not a cave."

Gray grabbed his flashlight. "It's a crypt."

"Aye. Lord Newborough's tomb. Course he's not down there any longer. At least I don't think he is."

"We have to search it," Gray said.

Kowalski shook his head and backed two steps away. "No, *we* don't. Whenever you go in a hole, bad things happen."

20

October 13, 12:41 P.M.
Svalbard, Norway

Monk sent a silent prayer of thanks to the engineers who invented heated handgrips for snowmobiles. The day's temperature continued to drop as the polar storm rolled across the Arctic archipelago. Even bundled in a snowsuit, helmet, gloves, and layers of thermal under-garments, Monk grew to appreciate the advancements of modern snowmobile technology.

He and Creed rested their vehicles in a snowy val-ley below the entrance to the Svalbard Global Seed Vault. Two hundred yards away, the angular concrete bunker stuck out of the side of Mount Plataberget. It was the only evidence of the vast underground depository.

That, and the patrolling Norwegian army.

Creed's voice came over the radio in his helmet. "Got company coming."

Monk twisted in his seat. Behind them, a two-man Sno-Cat came charging around an icy escarpment. Its tracks chewed across the terrain and cast up a rooster tail of ice and snow.

For the past hour, he and Creed had been playing a cautious game of cat and mouse with the outlying patrols. They tried their best to keep a wary distance without looking as if that was what they were doing. The rental company's logo on the sides of their snowmobiles would only allow them so much latitude.

"What should we do?" Creed asked.

"Stay put."

Their smaller machines could probably outmaneuver the bulkier Sno-Cat, but to flee now would only draw the full attention of the Norwegian army upon them. Instead, Monk lifted an arm in greeting.

Might as well say hello to the neighbors.

For the past hour, Monk had been observing the soldiers, noting their behavior. They spent most of the time chatting with each other in huddled groups. He noted a few cigarettes glowing. Occasionally a bark of laughter would echo off the mountain and reach them. He recognized the general pattern: boredom. Out here in the hinterlands of the frozen north, the soldiers plainly placed their full confidence in the isolation and harsh terrain.

No reason to dispel that attitude.

"Just play it cool," Monk said into the radio.

"If I was any cooler, I'd be shitting ice cubes."

Monk glanced over at him. Was that Creed cracking a joke? Monk lifted his eyebrows. There might be hope for the kid yet.

The side door to the Sno-Cat popped open. Steam wafted out of the heated cab. The soldier didn't even bother to pull up his parka's hood. In fact, he left the coat unzipped. With his blond hair and apple cheeks, he looked like he'd just stepped out of a Ralph Lauren catalog, the Norwegian version.

See the Norwegian in his natural habitat . . .

Monk took off his helmet, to look less intimidating. Creed did the same. The soldier waved an arm at them and spoke in Norwegian. Monk didn't understand him, but the general gist was plain.

What are you doing here?

Creed answered in turn, stumbling a bit with the language. Monk heard the word *American.* The kid must be laying out their cover story. Monk supported him by pulling out a book from his parka's pocket, a field guide to birds that he'd picked up at the rental agency. He also lifted the binoculars from around his neck.

Nobody here but us bird-watchers.

The soldier nodded and tried his hand at English. "Storm coming," the Norwegian warned. He waved an arm back in the general direction of Longyearbyen. "Should go."

Monk couldn't exactly argue against that. "We'll be heading back," he promised. "Just stopping to rest."

He rubbed his backside for effect—actually he was sore after trundling all over the glacier-broken landscape.

This earned a grin from the soldier. Over by the Sno-Cat, the other door popped open. The driver hopped out, yelled a warning, then jammed a whistle to his lips and drew his sidearm. As he blew a shrill shriek, he pointed his weapon at them.

What the hell?

Both Creed and the other soldier dropped flat to the snow. Monk hesitated. The soldier fired three times. Monk twisted at the same time and spotted a large lumbering form disappearing around a cluster of boulders off in the distance. The gunman's shots sparked off the stone.

"Polar bear," Creed said needlessly as the blasts echoed away.

He and the soldier regained their feet. Creed had gone pale, but the soldier only smiled and said something in Norwegian that made his companion with the pistol grin.

They seemed not overly concerned. Like scaring away a raccoon from a garbage can. Of course, in this case, Monk and Creed were the garbage cans. The polar bear must have been stalking them since they'd stopped.

The first soldier motioned toward town, warning them off.

Monk nodded.

The two soldiers climbed back into the Sno-Cat, sharing a joke, clearly at the Americans' expense.

Creed returned to his snowmobile. "What do we do now?"

"We keep patrolling. But this time, why don't I watch the seed vault, and you keep an eye out for anything looking to eat us."

Creed nodded and put on his helmet.

Monk lifted his binoculars and focused across the valley. He hoped Painter wouldn't be too much longer. If he and Creed continued to idle around here, suspicions would begin to arise. Especially with the storm about to hit.

Adjusting the focal length on his binoculars, he brought up a clear image of the bunker entrance. He watched the door open and the slim figure of a woman rush out. One of the guards tried to engage her. Who wouldn't? Even from two hundred yards away, it was plain she put the sex back in sexy.

She snubbed the guard with a raised palm and hurried toward the parked vehicles. Apparently she'd had enough of the party—and could not get away fast enough.

12:49 P.M.

The interview quickly went bad.

Painter and Senator Gorman had followed the CEO of Viatus into the set of offices off the main vault tunnel. A staging area for the caterers had been set up in the central room with desks shoved to the walls and replaced by rolling food-tray cabinets, chafing dishes, and storage bins. Dessert was being prepared, which apparently involved a chocolate fountain. The place smelled like a Hershey's factory with an underlying hint of Norwegian cod.

They hurried through the space to a back office. Inside, a pair of computers glowed at either end of a long table. Between them, organized into neat rows, were piles of aluminum packets. Along a neighboring wall were stacked a half-dozen black plastic storage bins. One was open on the floor, full of the silver envelopes.

"Seed shipments arrive daily," Karlsen had explained, playing tour guide. "Unfortunately, now they're backlogged due to the party. But tomorrow these boxes will be sorted, cataloged, registered by country, even . . ."

That's when things went wrong.

Maybe it was the nonchalant manner of the CEO, or maybe it was clear to all that Karlsen's rambling discourse hid a well of guilt. Either way, as soon as the office door was shut, the senator lunged out and grabbed a fistful of Karlsen's shirt. He slammed him into the stacked bins.

Stunned by the sudden attack, Karlsen did not react for a breath. Then his face collapsed into a muddle of confusion.

"Sebastian, what are you—?"

"You fucking killed my boy!" Gorman yelled at him. "Tried to assassinate me last night!"

"Are you insane?" Karlsen shoved both arms out and broke free. "Why would I try to kill you?"

Painter had to admit that the guy definitely sounded shocked. But he also noted that Karlsen failed to deny the murder of the senator's son. Painter came between them. Red-faced, Gorman retreated a step. He turned his back, plainly trying to regain his composure.

Inwardly Painter kicked himself. He hadn't noticed Gorman ramping up like that. He should have reined him in sooner. They weren't going to get anything out of Karlsen by driving him into a defensive posture. The man would put up walls that they'd never get through.

Painter readjusted his strategy. With Karlsen shaken, and before the man locked down completely, Painter knew he had to strip away any attempt at pretense.

"We know about the mushroom farm, about the bees, about what was covered up in Africa." Painter hit him with charges one after the other. While Karlsen might have been able to take one blow, the rapid series of punches gave him no chance to recover.

His facade momentarily crumbled, revealing his complicity, his knowledge. He was not a pawn or a blind figurehead. Karlsen knew damned well what was going on.

Still, the man tried to backpedal. The flash of guilt vanished behind a wall of denial. "I don't know what you're both talking about."

No one was fooled.

Least of all a grieving father.

Senator Gorman flew at the man again. Painter didn't try to stop him. He wanted Karlsen off balance, hit from all sides. Morally, psychologically, physically. Painter would use all the tools he had at hand.

Gorman barreled into Karlsen, ramming a shoulder into his chest and driving the man back into the wall. Lifted off his feet, Karlsen struck the wall hard. The breath gasped out of him. The senator had been a defensive lineman in his college years.

But Karlsen was no doddering old man. He raised his arms and slammed his elbows down hard on the senator's back. Gorman was knocked to his knees.

On the ground, the senator got an arm behind Karlsen's left leg. With a roar, Gorman hugged and twisted hard. He threw the murderer of his son facedown on the floor, then piled onto his back and pinned him to the floor.

"You killed Jason!" Gorman growled at the man, his voice trapped between fury and sob. "You killed him."

Karlsen struggled to free himself, but Gorman held him down. The CEO's face became beet red. He twisted his neck, trying to get a look at Gorman. His voice spat at his accuser. "I . . . I did it for you!"

The words momentarily stunned the senator. But Painter wasn't sure if the shock came from the sudden confession or the strange statement. A part of Gorman must have hoped Painter was wrong. Now there was no illusion.

"Shut the fuck up," Gorman warned, not wanting to hear anything more.

With the one domino dropped, Painter knew he could get the others to fall. What he had thought might take a full day had been accomplished in minutes. But they were far from finished here. Karlsen could recant. He was still on home turf in Norway, with powerful ties and connections.

Painter knew he had to take advantage, to control the situation. That meant getting Karlsen out of here and keeping him in custody. For that, he would need to call in some help.

"Keep him there," Painter said.

He crossed to the computers and searched behind them. There had to be a communication trunk feeding into this room. A T1 or T3 line for Internet connectivity, but more important—

Painter's fingers found the telephone line. He pulled and traced it back to the wall. With no cell service up here, he needed to radio Monk, but buried underground, that was impossible. He would have to tap into an open line using a device known as a SQUID to boost the signal. As his fingers ran along the wire to the wall, he found some gadget already plugged into the telephone outlet. He pulled it out and immediately recognized its function.

Cell signal booster.

It wasn't that sophisticated, but the technology was above anything he'd seen here. It felt out of place. He examined it closely and recognized a short-range transmitter wired into it.

Why would someone need a short-range transmitter wired to a telephone line?

He could think of only one reason.

The door crashed open behind him.

He swung around as Copresident Boutha stormed into the room. A few other men stood behind him. Boutha frowned in confusion at the scenario he'd burst in upon: Karlsen on the floor, the senator kneeling on his back.

"Caterers reported yelling . . .," Boutha began, then shook his head. "What is going on here?"

Using the distraction, Karlsen was able to throw an elbow back and catch Gorman in the ear. Knocked to the side, Gorman couldn't stop Karlsen from rolling free.

Boutha and the others still blocked the way out. Trapped, Karlsen turned to face Gorman, only to find a fist flying toward his nose. He dodged enough to avoid a broken nose, but he took a hard punch to the eye and stumbled back a few steps.

"Stop!" Painter bellowed, freezing everyone in place with the force of his command.

All eyes turned to him.

Painter pointed an arm at Boutha. "We must evacuate this facility. Now!"

"Why?"

Painter looked down at the foreign device in his hand. He could be wrong, but he saw little reason for a short-range transmitter.

Except one.

"There's a bomb hidden somewhere down here."

Shocked reactions and questions tried to follow.

Painter cut through them. "Get everyone out!"

Unfortunately, they were too late.

12:55 P.M.

Monk edged his snowmobile through the valley, making a slow slaloming pass along the bottom. Creed followed in his tracks, watching for polar bears. Monk kept an eye on the concrete bunker that marked the entrance to the seed vault.

Overhead, the storm had rolled a mass of dark clouds over the mountain. The sky pushed lower and dropped the temperature with it. Winds also picked up, scouring through the valley in blinding gusts of ice crystals.

Monk called for a stop. He thought he had heard something, or at least felt something deep in his chest. He cut the engine. The low rumble continued, coming from the cloud layer overhead, like distant thunder to the north. Before he had a chance to question it, the rumble turned into a roar, then into a scream. A pair of jets shot out of the clouds and raced straight down the valley toward Monk and Creed.

No, not toward *them*.

As the jets passed overhead, they veered sharply back up with a shriek of acceleration. Missiles fired from their underbellies. Hellfire rockets. The missiles struck the snowy ridge where the seed vault was buried. A line of fire exploded across the mountain face. Rocks and flames shot high. The concussions pounded Monk and Creed.

Up on the ridge, men went flying, some torn to fiery shreds. Others fled on foot or slid down the mountainside. Monk watched a large Sno-Cat tumble into a crater that once was the lone road up there.

As the smoke cleared, Monk searched the ridge. The bunker still stood, but one side had been blasted black and a large chunk of it had cracked away. The missile strike had only dealt a glancing blow.

Then a new rumble grew in volume. Monk feared the jets were scrambling for another pass. But this noise was accompanied by cracking detonations.

As Monk watched in horror, the entire mountainside above the bunker began to slide. A massive section of glacier broke loose and crashed, breaking into smaller and smaller pieces, gaining speed and turning into an avalanche of ice.

It swamped the bunker and buried it completely.

More soldiers were caught and crushed in its path.

And still it kept coming.

Toward them.

"Monk!" Creed screamed.

Dropping back into his seat, Monk thumbed the ignition. His engine roared. He gunned the throttle. The rear track chewed snow, then found traction. Twisting the handle, Monk pointed an arm to the far side of the valley.

"Get to high ground!"

Creed needed no guidance. He had already turned and was flying toward the opposite side. The pair of them raced across the valley floor, trying to get clear.

Monk heard the avalanche strike behind him. It sounded like the end of the world, a detonation of ice and rock. A chunk of glacier the size of a one-car garage bounced past Monk on the right. Ice pelted his snowmobile and his back.

Monk hunkered down. He could go no faster. He had the throttle fully open.

As the avalanche's leading edge reached them, ice boulders pounded alongside their vehicles. A river of dancing pebbles washed under and around them. The smaller bits of glacial ice had been polished smooth during the grinding plunge, turning into a flood of diamonds.

Then they were headed up.

The front skis of the snow machines carved a swift path up out of the valley. The icy monster behind them tried to give chase, but then gave up and settled back into the valley.

To be sure, Monk climbed higher before calling for a stop. Keeping his engine running, he turned and surveyed the damage. A fog of ice crystals clouded the lower valley, but it was clear enough to see to the far ridge.

There was no bunker.

Just broken ice.

"What do we do?" Creed asked.

A shout answered him. They both turned to the left. A pair of Norwegian soldiers appeared, rifles on their shoulders. Only now did Monk spot the Sno-Cat parked higher up the slope.

It was the same pair as before.

But this was no friendly visit like the earlier one.

The soldiers kept their weapons up. After what had happened, they must be ringing with suspicions, half-blind with anger and shock.

"What do we do?" Creed asked again.

Ever the teacher, Monk showed him by raising his arms. "You surrender."

1:02 P.M.

Painter stood in the dark.

The lights had gone out with the first explosions. At first he thought the hidden bomb had gone off. But as the series of concussive blasts continued, echoing down from above, Painter guessed a missile strike against the mountainside.

It was confirmed a moment later when a massive grumbling roar erupted. It sounded like a freight train running over them and crashing away.

Avalanche.

Screams and shouts echoed from the tunnel as guests and workers panicked. This deep underground, the darkness was absolute and sought to smother you.

Painter remained rooted in place, taking inventory. For the moment, they were still alive. If there *was* a hidden bomb down here, why hadn't it gone off at the same time as the missile strike?

He squeezed the transmitter in his hand. Pulling the device out of the wall outlet may have saved all their lives, preventing a signal from being telephoned in and triggering the bomb.

But they weren't out of danger yet.

If Painter had planned this attack, he would've built in a secondary backup plan. Something set on a delayed timer to account for any mishap. He thought hard and fast. The transmitter had a limited range, especially with all the rock. If a bomb was planted, it had to be close, likely brought in recently.

The caterers?

No, too many and too risky. Somebody would've seen it.

Then he remembered Karlsen's earlier words as they entered the back office: *Seed shipments arrive daily. Unfortunately, now they're backlogged due to the party.*

The storage bins.

Blind, Painter stepped over to the stacked boxes. He fumbled the top off one and shoved his hands into it, all the way to the bottom. He sifted through the heat-sealed aluminum seed packets.

Nothing.

He knocked the bin aside. It crashed in the dark.

"What are you doing?" Gorman shouted, startled.

Painter didn't have time to answer. Desperation kept him silent. He found nothing in the second bin—but as he yanked the lid off the third, a glow shone from inside the box, buried under a layer of seed packets.

In the darkness, the tiny light shone as brightly as a beacon. The other men drew closer. Painter picked aside the packets and exposed what lay beneath.

Numbers on an LED display glowed back at him.

09:55

As he watched, the counter ticked downward.

The room's lights flickered, went off, then came back on. The emergency generators had finally kicked in. Out in the hall, the screaming immediately quieted. While their situation was no better, at least they would die with the lights on.

Painter reached inside and carefully lifted out the object. He doubted it had been rigged with any motion-sensing trigger. The storage bin had been shipped, likely roughly handled in transit. Still, he cautiously lowered it to the floor and knelt beside it.

The object was the size of two shoe boxes, roughly barrel-shaped. The LED display glowed on the top. A net of wires folded into the metal casing under it. Military lettering—PBXN-112—stamped into its side left no doubt in Painter's mind as to what they all faced.

Even Boutha guessed.

"It's a bomb," he whispered.

The man, unfortunately, was wrong.

Painter corrected him. "It's a warhead."

1:02 P.M.

Krista braked the four-wheel-drive truck at the foot of the mountain. As she fled down the icy road, she had watched the missile barrage in her rearview mirror.

Flames had filled the world behind her. Concussions had rattled her truck windows. A moment later, the glacial ridge of the mountain had broken away and shattered across the entrance to the seed vault.

By the time her truck came to a stop, her hands still trembled on the steering wheel. Her breathing remained hard.

She had fled immediately after the phoned warning. What if she had been delayed, been slowed up for some reason? There had been no margin for error.

Still, she *had* survived.

The terror in her was slowly transformed into a strange elation. She was alive. Her hands balled into fists on the steering wheel. A bubbling laugh of relief shook out of her. She fought to compose herself.

To either side of the road, men appeared in camouflaged polar snowsuits. A tank of a vehicle on massive treads trundled to block the road.

She had nothing to fear. Not any longer. These were her forces.

She shoved the truck door open and headed over to join them. Snow had begun to fall. Heavy flakes drifted through the air. She climbed up into the cab of the giant vehicle. The rear passenger compartment was packed with grim-faced men bearing assault rifles.

Outside, the others mounted snowmobiles.

The road into the mountains might be gone, but she still had work to do up there. There would be stragglers after the bombing, and she had her orders.

No survivors.

1:04 P.M.

"Can you stop it?" Senator Gorman asked.

In the back office, the others all gathered around Painter and the warhead on the floor, even Karlsen. He looked as sick as anyone. This must not have been his play. Especially since he was trapped with them. Painter did not have time to contemplate the significance of that.

Instead, he faced the others. "I need someone to run and check on the condition of the upper tunnel," he said calmly and firmly. "Have we caved in? Is there a way out? And I need a maintenance engineer ASAP."

Two of Boutha's men nodded and ran back out, all too happy to flee *away* from the warhead.

"Can you defuse it?" Karlsen asked.

"Is it nuclear?" Gorman followed up.

"No," Painter answered both of them. "It's a thermobaric warhead. Worse than a nuclear weapon."

They might as well hear it straight. The warhead was a form of fuel-air explosive. The casing was filled with a fluorinated aluminum powder with a PBXN-112 detonation charge buried in the center.

"It's the ultimate bunker-buster," Painter explained as he studied the device. Talking helped him to concentrate. "It's a two-stage explosion. First, detonation casts a massive cloud of fine aerosol. Enough to fill this entire tunnel. Then the powder ignites in a burning flash. This creates a pressure wave that crushes everything in its path, using up all the oxygen at the same time. So you can die four ways. Blown up, crushed, burned, or suffocated."

Ignoring the gasps around him, Painter focused on the detonator. His expertise wasn't in munitions but in electronics. It didn't take him long to recognize the tangle of lead, ground, and dummy wires. Cut the wrong one, change the voltage, trigger a shock . . . there were a thousand ways for it to blow up in your face and only one way to stop it.

A code.

Unfortunately, Painter didn't know it.

This wasn't like the movies. There was no bomb expert to defuse it at the last second. No clever ploy to implement, like freezing the warhead with liquid nitrogen. That was all cinematic crap.

He looked at the clock.

In less than eight minutes, the warhead was going to blow.

The pounding of feet alerted them to the early return of a runner.

"No cave-in," the man gasped out. "Ran into one of the soldiers coming back down. Outer blast door held. He opened it. It's just a wall of ice out there. We're buried. So thick, he said, you can't see any daylight through it."

Painter nodded. The strategy made sense. The vault had been engineered to withstand a nuclear strike. If you wanted to kill everyone down here, toss in a warhead like this and seal it up tight. If the firestorm didn't kill you, the lack of remaining oxygen would.

That left his second option.

The other runner appeared with a tall Norwegian built like a refrigerator. The maintenance engineer. His eyes spotted the warhead on the floor. He went pale. At least he was no fool.

Painter stood, drawing his attention up from the bomb. "Do you speak English?"

"Yes."

"Is there any other way out of here?"

He shook his head.

"Then those air locks for the seed rooms. Are they pressurized?"

"Yes, they're maintained at a strict level."

"Can you adjust them higher?"

He nodded. "I'll have to do it manually."

"Pick one of the seed banks and do it."

The engineer glanced around the room, nodded, then took off at a dead run. The man definitely was no fool.

Painter turned to the other men—Boutha, Gorman, even Karlsen. "I need you to gather everyone into that seed vault. Now."

"What are you going to do?" the senator asked.

"See how fast I can run."

1:05 P.M.

With his hands on his helmet and no ability to speak the language, Monk had a hard time negotiating for their freedom.

The Norwegian soldiers continued to level their weapons at the prisoners, but at least their cheeks weren't pressed as firmly against the rifle stocks. Creed pleaded their case. He had his helmet off and was speaking rapidly, a mix of Norwegian and English, accompanied by charades.

Then a voice started to rasp in Monk's ear, full of static, coming from his helmet radio. Most of the communication dropped out. *"Can you hear . . . help . . . no time to . . ."*

Despite having a rifle pointed at his face, Monk felt a surge of relief. He recognized the voice. It was Painter. He was still alive!

Monk tried responding. "Director Crowe, we read you. But it's choppy. Is there any way we can help?"

He failed to get any response. The tone of Painter's voice didn't change. The transmission wasn't reaching him.

Creed had heard Monk's outburst. "Is that the director? He's still alive?"

The two rifles focused on Monk.

"Alive but trapped," he answered. He held up a hand, struggling to listen to the radio. The transmission remained crap. There was a lot of rock to get through, even for a SQUID transmitter.

The soldier barked at him. Creed turned and tried to explain. Their stern faces shifted from anger to concern.

As static buzzed in his ear, Monk considered his options. How long would the oxygen last in there? Could they get heavy digging equipment moved up there fast enough, especially with the road bombed out?

Then a few words burst through the static. It squashed his momentary hope. Painter's words were chewed apart by the static, but there was no mistaking the threat.

"Down here . . . a warhead . . . We'll try to . . ."

Static cut off the rest.

Before Monk could relate the bad news to Creed, a rumbling echoed over the mountains, accompanied by the whining roar of snowmobiles.

They all turned.

Down the mountainside, a cluster of vehicles slowly wound up from the lower valley, heading their way.

Monk lifted his binoculars and focused on one of the snowmobiles. Men were double mounted. While one drove, the other had a rifle up on a shoulder. They were all dressed in polar suits. Snow-white, with no military insignia.

A stray Norwegian soldier had somehow made it halfway down the mountain already. He waved at the approaching party.

A rifle cracked.

Blood spattered against the white snow.

The soldier dropped.

Monk lowered his binoculars.

Someone had come to clean house.

1:09 P.M.

Painter didn't know if his radio transmission got out. He had plugged the SQUID into the wall and hoped for the best.

All he could do now was run.

He pushed a caterer's serving trolley ahead of him. Strapped on top with bungee cords was the warhead. He sprinted up the hundred and fifty yards of the tunnel.

The LED display glowed back at him.

04:15

As he ran, he watched it tick down below the four-minute mark. At last, he spotted the outer blast door at the top of the exit ramp. It had been left open by the guard who had peeked out. Chunks of ice had spilled inside, but beyond the door was a solid wall of broken glacier.

With a surge of speed, he shot up the ramp. He wanted the charge placed as close to that opening as possible. Reaching the top, Painter shoved the trolley cart toward the door, spun on a toe, and sprinted in the opposite direction.

At least it was all downhill from here.

He fled, breath gasping, trying to lengthen his stride.

If he couldn't stop the bomb, he might as well make use of it. He didn't know how thick the plug of ice was over the door, but the warhead's thermobaric payload was unique. The initial blast could help break some of the ice; then, as the cloud of fluorinated aluminum ignited, the searing heat would vaporize and melt more. But it was upon the secondary blast wave that Painter pinned all his hopes.

The biggest threat of a thermobaric bomb was its sudden and massive burst of pressure. Exploded inside caves or closed buildings, the pressure wave would travel outward and kill around corners and far down passageways. It pulverized and sheared flesh. Burst eardrums, exploded lungs, squeezed blood out of every orifice.

Painter hoped it could also blast out that plug of ice, pop it free like a champagne cork.

But, of course, without crushing them all to pulp in the meantime.

As he hit the bottom of the tunnel, he sprinted into the lower cross passage. He skidded around the corner and sped to the center air lock.

He ripped the door open, heard the pressure pop, then slammed the hatch shut behind him. Air valves in the ceiling chugged to bring the pressure back up. As Painter crossed the air lock, the door flew open ahead of him.

Senator Gorman held it and waved Painter into the seed room. "Hurry!"

Painter dove through. Gorman closed the door with a steel clang.

A crowd gathered around the door, keeping together despite the size of the vault. The seed bank itself was unremarkable, just a cavernous room full of numbered shelves. Identical black storage bins filled the racks, like a warehouse club that sold only one item.

Someone in the group was counting down loudly.

"Eleven . . . ten . . . nine . . ."

Painter had barely made it back in time. After breaking the air lock seal, he prayed the pressure had a chance to rebuild in time. Their best chance to survive the coming blast was to fight pressure with pressure.

If the air lock didn't hold, they'd all be crushed.

"Eight . . . seven . . . six . . ."

Karlsen pushed through to join Painter. His eyes were wide. "Krista's not here," he said, as if Painter knew what that meant.

Someone else did. "Krista . . . Krista Magnussen? Jason's girlfriend?"

Anger flashed in Senator Gorman's voice.

Painter shoved the two men apart. "Later."

First, they had to survive.

The countdown continued.

"Five . . . four . . . three . . ."

21

As Gray prepared to descend into the crypt, the true heart of the storm rolled over Bardsey Island. It was as if the gods themselves warned against violating the tomb.

With a crack of thunder, the skies opened up. Rain poured down in large drops that shattered like bombs upon gravestones and markers. To the north, lightning crackled in forking chains.

"I'll go first," Gray said between thunderclaps.

The boy Lyle had run to the nearby chapel house to fetch a rope. But with the rain falling so hard, Gray feared the tomb could flood before any of them had a chance to search it.

The crypt's opening was a hole in the ground about two feet wide, barely enough room for one person to climb through. It dropped seven feet to a stone floor. Below, it was wider, maybe twice as large as the opening. He couldn't see more without going down.

Grabbing the sides, Gray lowered himself into the hole. He used his legs to brace himself, then dropped the rest of the way down. He landed in a crouch and freed his flashlight.

He stared up at the others' faces.

"Be careful," Rachel said.

"Let me know what you see," Wallace added.

Both Kowalski and Seichan hung farther back.

Gray clicked on his flashlight and searched the main shaft. The sides were natural rock archways that framed brick walls, slightly inset. He imagined coffins and moldering bones behind those bricks. And perhaps one of those bodies was Lord Newborough's.

As rain sluiced down the walls, Gray took the time to examine each surface. He ran his hands over them, searching for loose stones, some indication that Father Giovanni had been here and discovered something.

"Well?" Wallace called down.

"Nothing."

Rachel pulled away, but her voice reached him. "Lyle's coming back with the rope."

Gray turned his attention to the fourth wall. Here the bricks framed a low archway, barely taller than midthigh. Crouching, Gray shone his light down into it. The space was plainly meant to hold a coffin. Afterward, the archway would have been walled up like the others. But currently the niche was empty.

He knew the hole had to be important. This wall faced the ruins of the abbey's tower. Dropping to his hands and knees in the pooled water, Gray crawled into the niche. It was deep. Beyond the opening, the bricks disappeared and solid rock surrounded him. Gray worked slowly to the back of the tomb.

He patted the sides, ran his palms over the surfaces. Nothing.

Though frustrated, he remained confident. Whatever was hidden had to lie beneath the ruins of Saint Mary's. But maybe he was wrong about the access point. Maybe it wasn't this crypt. Father Giovanni could have searched it upon Lyle's suggestion—just as Gray was doing—then moved on.

He heard a splash behind him as someone joined him in the crypt.

He retreated and climbed out of the niche. Rachel stood there. Her hair clung wetly to her face. Her eyes glowed under the shine of his flashlight, full of hope. He could not fail her.

"Dead end?" she aked.

He grimaced, not appreciating her choice of words, nor happy with his lack of success. "I don't see any sign that Father Giovanni has been down here."

"Can I try?" she asked and held out her hand for his flashlight.

How could he refuse?

He passed her the light. She crouched on one hand and sidled into the empty tomb. Her lithe physique allowed her more maneuverability in the tight space. Her flashlight swept along the walls.

"See anything?" he asked.

"No."

From above, Wallace voiced Gray's earlier concern. "Maybe we're in the wrong hole."

Rachel gave up and swung around. In a demonstration of limberness, she turned herself fully around in the niche and headed back out—then froze.

"What is it?" Gray asked.

"Come see."

Her flashlight was pointed straight back at him. Shielding his eyes, he started to crawl in toward her.

"No," she warned. "Slide in on your back."

Gray obeyed. Soaking wet, he rolled over and scooted on his elbows and pushed with his legs into the niche. Faceup *was* the proper position for lying in a grave.

"What'dya see down there?" Wallace called.

"Don't know yet," Gray answered as he shimmied deeper.

"All the way back," Rachel urged.

He kept sliding in. Eventually his head rested between her knees. She leaned over him with the flashlight. She smelled of wet wool. He was all too conscious of her breasts above his head.

"Look," she said.

He was, but she probably meant where the flashlight was pointed. He had to squirm up to his elbows and look back toward the entrance. He didn't see anything at first, just the back half of the brick wall that closed off the natural stone niche.

"Notice how all the bricks are laid horizontal, but look at the three around the lip of the opening. At the top and to either side."

Gray saw it now, too. "They're placed vertically."

The opening was a perfect half circle. The three vertical bricks marked off the 12, 3, and 9 o'clock positions.

"Do you think it's significant?" Rachel said.

Gray did. "It's like half of the pagan cross."

In the reflection off the pooled water, he could almost see the other half of the circle. He pictured completing the symbol, drawing lines to connect the stones. It would form the Druid cross they'd been following from the beginning.

"But what does it mean?" Rachel asked.

"Let me try something."

Gray crab-crawled on his elbows back out of the niche, then reversed himself and went in on his belly, feetfirst this time. He hoped he wasn't completely soaking himself for no reason.

Wallace called down, "Well?"

"Still working," Gray answered in a strained voice.

He got under the entrance and examined the three bricks. The two to the side seemed nondescript and solidly mortared. Stretching up, he grabbed the top brick. It seemed no different—until his probing fingers scraped along the top lip. There was a slight indentation, perfect for a grip.

He snagged his fingers in place and tugged.

The stone pivoted out. It caught for a moment, but as he pulled harder, a metallic *snap* sounded behind him—followed by a grinding of rock. They both twisted and glanced over their shoulders. The back wall swung open, revealing a narrow staircase leading down.

"The entrance," Rachel murmured near his ear. "We found it."

It took some maneuvering to back their way through the door and into the stairwell. Though narrow, it was wide enough to stand up in.

Rachel shone her flashlight down the short flight of brick steps. "Is that a tunnel at the bottom of the stairs?"

Gray climbed down to investigate, but as his boot hit the fifth step, he felt the stair sink an inch under his weight.

Another metallic *snap* sounded.

His heart stopped as a single word crystallized in his mind.

Trap.

Behind them, the door swung closed. Rachel yelled and leaped for the exit. She was too late. The door sealed with a distinct and final *click*.

She pounded on the stone door, but it was no use.

They were locked in.

12:42 P.M.

Seichan heard Rachel yell—then a crack of thunder deafened everyone standing over the crypt.

As it echoed away, Wallace leaned over the hole. "Didya find something down there?"

There was no answer.

Seichan also noted that the glow of the flashlight had vanished. Something was wrong. Reacting on instinct, she tucked her arms and dropped smoothly through the narrow entrance. She landed with a splash, absorbing the impact with her knees. Her fingers already clutched her lighter. She shoved her arm into the dark niche and flicked the lighter on. The flame's glow flickered all the way to the back of the crypt.

It was empty.

"What's going on?" Wallace called from above.

"They're gone."

Kowalski moved closer to the crypt, dripping wet and sullen. Lyle had gone to fetch some umbrellas. "What did I tell you . . . never go down a hole with Pierce."

"It might be a good thing," Wallace said.

Kowalski turned on him with a baleful eye.

"They must have found the secret entrance," Wallace elaborated.

But Rachel's cry had not been a happy one of discovery.

Seichan leaned into the crypt. She shouted with all her lung power. "Pierce! Rachel!"

Lightning flashed and thunder rolled, but Seichan made out a faint call. At least they were still alive. She climbed in farther.

"I can't understand!" she shouted.

A loud splash startled her. She glanced over her shoulder and saw Wallace standing behind her, one hand on the rope.

"I wouldn't do that," Kowalski warned from above.

"Be quiet!" Seichan snapped.

She cocked her head and listened. She made out Gray's voice. She closed her eyes, straining. His commands were clipped. She imagined him cupping his mouth and shouting.

"Just inside! A vertical brick! Above the entrance! Yank it!"

Needing both hands to search, she flipped her lighter closed and twisted her body fully into the crypt. Feeling blindly along the entrance to the crypt, fingering the bricks, she found one that fit Gray's description. She reached to the top, discovered a carved indentation to grip, and yanked hard.

A loud *snap* sounded.

The back wall of the crypt swung open. She spotted the panicked face of Rachel. Gray stood at her shoulder.

"Got locked in," Gray said. "Get the others, but be careful of the fifth step. It seals the door."

Behind Seichan, Wallace shone his flashlight at them. "You found the way in. Brilliant! Simply brilliant!"

After a minute of wrangling, they all made it safely down the stairs to the lower tunnel. A dark stone passageway headed steeply away.

Kowalski declined to join them, calling down from above. "You go on. I'll wait for the umbrellas."

Off to the side, Rachel spoke. "Look at this." She pointed her flashlight at a thick bronze lever in the floor near the foot of the stairs. "I think it might be a release to unlock that secret door."

"Must have been how Father Giovanni came and went," Gray said. "Still, we should keep the exit jammed open just in case."

As a precaution, he had lodged a loose chunk of headstone from the cemetery to hold open the doorway.

Seichan respected his decision. She preferred keeping a back door open in case of trouble.

Wallace pointed his flashlight down the tunnel. "Medieval monks often crafted trapdoors and hidden rooms in their abbeys and monasteries. Places were riddled with secret passageways like this. It was one of their means of hiding from marauders. Additionally, the tunnels offered a way to spy on their guests. Knowledge proved to be as much of a defense in those hard times as any shield."

"Then let's go see what these monks were hiding down here," Gray said and led the way.

The others followed. Seichan stayed at the rear.

The passageway dropped steeply, but it did not take long to reach the end. The tunnel opened into a domed space. There were no other exits.

"We must be directly under the ruins of the tower," Gray said.

Wallace ran one hand along the wall. "No chisel or pick marks. It's a natural cavern."

But the professor's eyes remained focused on the middle of the chamber. A massive sarcophagus rested in the center of the room. It stood waist high and looked like it was carved out of a single block of stone.

Beyond the casket, against the far wall, stood a Celtic cross.

As the others moved toward the sarcophagus, Seichan studied the cross. It was not as ornate as the others in the abbey cemetery. This one was stark and more crudely hewn, making it seem more ancient. The only decorations were a few spirals done in bas-relief, and the cross's circular element had been scored into tiny blocks.

Dismissing the cross, the others had turned their attentions to the stone coffin resting on the floor. The sides were featureless, its lid secured in place.

"Could it be Lord Newborough's resting place?" Rachel asked.

Wallace leaned a hand on the lid and ran his fingers over the rough side. "Too old. If Newborough's down here, he's most likely buried off in one of those other sealed crypts. This is someone else's grave. Also, the sarcophagus is made out of bluestone, same as the region's Neolithic standing stones. It must have been quarried somewhere on the mainland and shipped all the way here. Quite an undertaking. My guess is that this is the grave of one of those ancient ring-builders, possibly one of their royalty."

Rachel spoke. "Like the Fomorian queen?"

"Yes, our dark goddess," Wallace said, but he suddenly became distracted.

With a frown, he leaned down. He held his flashlight against the side of the sarcophagus and cast his light across its surface. His fingers ran along the stone. "It looks like there was once a carving here. Some type of decoration, maybe even writing. But someone ground it mostly off."

His frown deepened at such desecration.

Gray glanced up. "If this dates back to the Neolithic period, the Church could have scrubbed away the original markings."

"Aye. That would be like them. If something didn't mesh with their dogma, it was often destroyed. Look what happened to the Mayan codices, a vast font of ancient knowledge. The Church deemed them to be the devil's work, and all but a few were burned."

Seichan recognized a contradiction and moved closer. "Then why didn't they just destroy the sarcophagus? Why go to the trouble of scouring it clean?"

Wallace answered, "If it is a grave marker, they might have respected its interment. The Church, at the time, was not above its own superstitions. They might not have wanted to disturb the bones."

Gray voiced his own interpretation. "Or maybe what was stored here had value to them."

"Like the Doomsday key," Rachel said.

Seichan ignored Rachel's glance in her direction. She merely crossed her arms.

Gray bent down and examined the lid. "It looks like it was wax-sealed at one time." He lifted his hands and rubbed flakes from his fingers. "But somebody broke that seal."

"It had to be Father Giovanni," Rachel said. "Look over here." She had moved over to the old cross and pointed at the walls to either side.

Drawn in charcoal were notations and calculations done in a crisp modern hand. It looked like Father Giovanni had measured every dimension of the cross. He'd also drawn a perfect circle around it. More lines crisscrossed it in an unfathomable pattern. To Seichan, it had a vaguely arcane look.

What was Marco doing here?

Gray studied the cross. Seichan saw the calculations going on behind his expression. If anyone could find that key, it was this man.

Gray finally turned away. Seichan suspected that a part of his mind was still working on the mystery of the cross, but he pointed over to the sarcophagus.

"If Marco broke that seal, let's see what he discovered."

1:03 P.M.
It took all of them to shift the lid.

How had Father Giovanni done it on his own? Gray wondered as he braced his feet and shoved. *Did he have help? Or did he haul down some tools?*

Still, brute force proved sufficient. With a scrape of stone on stone, they pushed the top askew but kept the lid balanced on the top.

Gray shone his flashlight down into the interior of the sarcophagus. The hollow space was hewn out of the bluestone block. He had been expecting some moldering bones, but though there was room for a body, the sarcophagus was empty.

Except for one item.

A massive book, bound in thick leather, rested in the center. It stretched a foot wide, just as thick, and two feet long. It looked perfectly preserved. Most likely the tome hadn't been disturbed since it was first closed up and sealed with wax.

Gray reached for it.

"Careful," Wallace warned, his voice hushed. "You don't want to damage it. We should be wearing gloves."

Gray hesitated, sensing the age of the text.

Despite his words of caution, Wallace waved impatiently at Gray. "What are you waiting for?"

Swallowing, Gray gingerly placed two fingers on the edge of the book. Surely Father Giovanni had already opened it at least once. As Gray lifted the heavy cover, the book's binding, likely sinew and long dried, resisted opening.

"Gently now," Wallace urged.

Gray pulled the cover fully open and leaned it against one wall of the stone chest. The first page was blank, but it was transparent enough to see through to the rich colors of the next page.

Wallace shifted closer. "Dear God . . ."

The professor reached down himself and pulled back that first page. "It's calf vellum," he said, pinching the paper. But his eyes grew wider as he revealed what lay below.

Under the beams of their flashlights, the ink on the next page glowed like molten jewels. Dark crimsons, golden yellows, and purples so rich they looked damp. The illustrations on the page were meticulous and dense, depicting stylized human figures tangled with knots and wrapped in intricate scrollwork. In the center of the first page, surrounded and supported by the intensity and force of the artwork, sat a crowned and bearded man on a gold throne.

It was clearly meant to represent Christ.

"It's an illuminated manuscript," Rachel said, awed by its beauty.

Wallace turned a few more pages. "It's a Bible."

His finger hovered over the crisp lines of Latin text that ran tightly over the pages. The calligraphy was ornate, with fanciful images folded into the capital letters. The pages' margins were equally decorated with a riotous mix of mythical animals, winged children, and tangles and tangles of knots.

"The iconography reminds me of the Book of Kells," Wallace said. "An illuminated treasure of Ireland that dates back to the eighth century. It was the result of decades of labor by sequestered monks. And that book only covered the four gospels of the New Testament."

Wallace's voice trembled. "I think this book is the *entire* Bible." He shook his head. "If so, it's priceless beyond imagination."

"Then why was it left here?" Seichan asked. Even she had drawn closer to see the book.

Wallace could only shake his head. But he carefully pulled back a few more leaves of the Bible, and an answer appeared.

The turn of a page revealed a gaping hole in the center of the book. The hole sliced straight through the pages and formed a cubby three inches square and one deep.

Wallace gasped at the destruction.

Gray leaned closer. The hole was plainly meant to hold something, to keep it hidden and preserved. Without turning, Gray held his hand out to Rachel. She reached to a pocket inside her coat.

They all knew what must once have been hidden there.

A moment later, Rachel placed the leather artifact in Gray's palm. The satchel looked to be made out of the same leather that bound the book. He held the object over the cubby. It fit perfectly into the hole.

"Father Giovanni stole the artifact, but left the Bible," Gray said, picturing the mummified finger inside the pouch. "Why?"

The one word held many questions.

Wallace added another. "Why didn't Marco tell anybody about this?"

"Maybe he did," Seichan said coldly. "To be hunted and murdered, he had to have told someone."

"She's right," Gray realized. "Maybe Marco didn't reveal *all* he knew—like the discovery of the Bible—but he told someone enough to get himself killed."

"Oh, God . . ." Wallace suddenly blurted.

Gray turned to him.

"About two years ago, Marco contacted me. He needed money to continue his travels. I told him that my sponsor, the Viatus Corporation, might be willing to finance any ancillary research connected to my dig. I gave him my contact's name. A head researcher there. Magnussen was her name."

Seichan stiffened beside Gray, but she remained silent.

"But I never heard back from Marco after that." Wallace looked sickened. "I assumed he never bothered. I forgot about it until now. Oh, God, I may have led him directly to his killers."

Gray ran the scenario through his head. It made sense. Viatus would have hired Marco, especially if he had proposed looking for a potential counteragent to whatever killed those mummies. How could they say no? But then somewhere along the way, Marco found something that frightened him enough to make a run for Rome, to meet with Vigor Verona, to expose all he knew. His employers must have grown wise to what he was planning and taken him out.

Wallace held a hand pressed over his mouth, still shocked. With his other hand, he pushed the loose pages back over the hole in the Bible, hiding the book's violation as if that might lessen his own guilt.

Rachel spoke as she accepted the satchel back from Gray. "Father Giovanni stole the artifact, but the bigger questions are *who* left it here to begin with and *why*?"

Her words drew them back to the heart of the mystery. Her life depended on discovering those answers.

"I may be able to answer the question of *who* left the Bible," Wallace said and took a deep breath to steady himself.

Gray turned to the man, surprised. "Who?"

"Possibly the owner of the Bible."

Wallace pointed back to the book, toward the inside surface of the leather cover. A page of vellum had been glued there.

Earlier, Gray had been too focused on the book's contents to note the one page shadowed by the cover. He examined it now. It was as densely illuminated as the rest of the work, but the content centered on a stylized name, possibly the owner of the priceless book.

Wallace read the name so dramatically illustrated. "Mael Maedoc Ua Morgair."

The name meant nothing to Gray. His lack of knowledge must have been plain on his face.

"You can't live in these parts without knowing that name," Wallace explained. "Especially in my profession."

"Who is it?"

"One of the most famous of Irish saints, second only to Saint Patrick. His given name was Mael Maedoc, but Latinized it's *Malachy*."

"Saint Malachy," Rachel said, clearly recognizing the name.

"Who was he?" Gray asked.

"He was born about the same year as the Doomsday Book was written." Wallace let the significance of that sink in before he continued. "He started out as the abbot of Bangor but grew to become archbishop. He spent much of his time on pilgrimages."

"So he most likely came here?"

Wallace nodded. "Malachy was an interesting man, kind of a reluctant archbishop. He preferred to travel, mingling with both the pagans and the pious of the region, spreading the word of the gospels. He moved easily between both worlds and eventually brokered a lasting peace between the Church and those who adhered to the old ways."

Gray recalled Wallace's earlier belief that the last of the pagans waged a final war against Christendom, possibly using the bioweapon acquired from the ancients. "Do you think a part of that brokered peace might have been knowledge of the plague and its cure, the proverbial key to the Doomsday Book?"

"His fingerprints are definitely here." Wallace gestured toward the book. "Then there's also the reason Malachy was canonized, why he was considered worthy of being made a saint."

"Why's that?"

"Ah, now there's the rub," Wallace said. "Malachy was known throughout his life for the miracle of *healing*. A long litany of miraculous cures is attributed to this saint."

"Just like the history of Bardsey Island," Gray said.

"But I also recall another story told about Malachy. From my own bonny Scotland. Malachy came traipsing through Annandale and asked the lord of the land there to spare the life of a pickpocket. The lord agreed, but ended up hanging the thief. Outraged, Malachy cursed him—and not only did the lord die, but so did everyone in his household."

Wallace glanced significantly at Gray.

"Healing and curses," Gray mumbled.

"It sounds like Malachy learned *something* from his new Druid friends, something the Church decided to keep secret out here."

Rachel interrupted. "But you skipped over what Malachy was best known for."

"Ah, you mean the prophecies," Wallace said with a roll of his eyes.

"What prophesies?"

Rachel answered, "The prophecies of the popes. It's said that on a pilgrimage to Rome, Malachy fell into a trance and had a vision of all the popes from his time to the end of the world. He dutifully wrote them all down."

"Bloody nonsense," Wallace countered. "The story goes that the Church supposedly found Malachy's book in their archives some four hundred years *after* the man died. Likely the book was a forgery."

"And some claim it was just a *copy* of Malachy's original text. Either way, the descriptions of each pope have over the centuries proved to be oddly accurate. Take the last two popes. Malachy describes John Paul II as *De Labore Solis*. Or translated, 'From the toil of the sun.' He was born during a solar eclipse. And then there's the current pope, Benedict XVI. Described as *De Gloria Olivae*. 'The Glory of the Olive.' And the symbol for the Benedictine order is the olive branch."

Wallace lifted a hand dismissively. "Just people reading too much into cryptic snippets of Latin."

Rachel turned to Gray for understanding. "But what's most disturbing of all is that the current pope is number one hundred and eleven on Malachy's list. The very next pope—*Petrus Romanus*—is the last pope, according to the prophecy. That pope will serve when the world comes to an end."

"Then we're all doomed," Seichan said, voicing as much skepticism as Wallace.

"Well, I certainly am," Rachel spat back, silencing her. "Unless we find that damned key."

Gray kept silent. He avoided weighing in on the matter. But Rachel was right about one thing. They needed to find that key. As he stood, he contemplated the significance of finding this dead saint's Bible sitting in a pagan sarcophagus. And more important—

"Do you think it was Saint Malachy's finger inside that Bible?" Gray asked.

"No," Wallace said firmly. "This sarcophagus is too old. Much too old. My guess is that it dates to the time of Stonehenge. Someone was buried here, but not Malachy."

"Then who?" Gray asked.

Wallace shrugged. "Like I said, possibly some Neolithic royalty. Perhaps that dark pagan queen. Nonetheless, I suspect that finger bone is all that's left of whoever was first buried here."

"Why do you think that?"

"And where's the rest of the body?" Rachel added.

"Moved. Probably by the Church. Maybe by Malachy himself. But they left the bone here as was traditional back then. It was a sin to move a body from its resting place unless you left a small piece behind."

"A relic of that person," Rachel said with a nod. "So they can continue to rest in peace. Uncle Vigor talked about that once. It was considered sacrilegious to do otherwise."

Gray stared into the sarcophagus. "Malachy used his own Bible to preserve the relic. He must have believed that whoever was buried here was worthy of that honor."

Gray also remembered Father Rye's description of Marco on the day he returned from the island all upset. The young priest had spent the night praying for forgiveness. Was it because he stole the relic, thereby desecrating a grave that had been sanctified by a saint of his own Church? And if so, what possessed him to do that? Why did he think it was so important?

Rachel raised another question of significance. "Why was the body even moved?"

Wallace offered one explanation. "Perhaps to keep safe whatever was hidden here. During Malachy's time, England and Ireland were under constant attack by wave after wave of Viking raiders. The island, with no fortifications, would have been especially vulnerable."

Gray nodded. "And if this crypt was where the key was kept, it must be somehow tied to the body interred here. So to preserve the knowledge, both the body and the key had to be moved to a safer location."

"But what the hell is this key?" Seichan asked. "What are we even looking for?"

Gray looked toward the only other clue left to them by Father Giovanni. He moved over to the wall and studied the charcoal notations next to the cross. He laid a hand on the wall. What had Marco been trying to figure out?

The others gathered behind him.

He looked up at the Celtic cross. Only now did he realize something. "The cross," he said, running his fingers down it. "It's made out of the same stone as the sarcophagus. It even feels scoured like the crypt."

Wallace stepped closer. "You're right."

Gray turned to him. "This wasn't put here by Malachy or some other pious Christian to mark the grave."

"It was already here."

Gray looked at the cross with new eyes, not seeing it as a *Christian* symbol but a *pagan* one. Did it offer some clue to what the key actually was? From the notations on the wall, Father Giovanni had been trying to figure something out.

Needing to know more, Gray pointed his light at the bottom of the cross. "The set of three spirals near the base of the cross. Is there any special significance to them?"

Wallace moved over to join Gray and Rachel. "It's called a tri-spiral. But it's actually not *three* spirals. Only one. See how the three of them join and blend to form one sinuous pattern. This same triple pattern can be found marked on ancient standing stones across Europe. And like many pagan symbols, the Church appropriated this one, too. To the Celtic people, it represented eternal life. But to the Church, it was the perfect representation for the Holy Trinity. The Father, the Son, and the Holy Ghost. All entwined together. The three who are one."

Gray moved his gaze up to the single spiral that sat in the middle of the cross, like the hub of a wheel.

He remembered Painter's original briefing about the symbol. How the pagan cross and spiral were often found together, one overlapping the other. The cross was a symbol for Earth. And the spiral marked the soul's journey, rising from this world to the next, like a curl of smoke.

Gray's attention shifted to Father Giovanni's markings drawn on the wall. He sensed some meaning behind the notations and lines. He could almost grasp it, but it remained tantalizingly out of reach.

Stepping closer, Gray put down his flashlight and reached to the circular section on the cross. He ran his fingertips across the scored markings.

Like spokes on a wheel.

As the thought popped into his head, he was still staring at the spiral in the center of the cross. He had compared it earlier to a wheel hub. It even looked like it was turning.

Then suddenly he knew.

Maybe he had sensed it from the beginning, but he couldn't get past the Christian symbolism. Now, considering the cross anew and pushing aside preconceptions, he recognized what was nagging at him.

"It *is* a wheel," he realized.

Reaching more firmly, he grasped the stone circle and turned it counter-clockwise, in the direction of the curl of the spiral.

It moved!

As he turned the wheel, his eyes shifted to the calculations drawn on the wall. The cross hid a clue about the key, but to unlock it you had to know the proper code. The wheel must act like a combination lock, protecting some hidden vault where the key was once stored.

From all the calculations on the wall, Marco had been working on that proper sequence, trying to figure out the numbers to the combination.

Unfortunately, Gray realized something too late.

You only got one guess at the combination.

And he got it wrong.

A loud *boom* shook the ground under his feet. The floor suddenly dropped from under him. He grabbed for the cross and hooked his fingers onto the crossbar. Looking over a shoulder as he hung, he watched the back half of the chamber floor rise up. The entire floor was tilting—tipping away from the only exit.

The others screamed and scrambled to brace themselves.

The stone lid slid off the sarcophagus, skittered across the tilted floor, and toppled into the gaping hole under Gray's feet. His flashlight had already rolled into the pit. Its shine revealed a bottom covered in vicious bronze spikes, all pointed up.

The stone lid crashed and shattered against them.

Behind Gray, the floor continued to tip, going vertical, trying to dump everyone below.

Wallace and Rachel had managed to get behind the sarcophagus and brace themselves. The coffin remained in place, anchored to the floor. Seichan couldn't reach the refuge in time. She went sliding toward the pit.

Rachel lunged out with an arm and caught the back of her jacket as she slid past. She pulled Seichan close enough so the woman could grab the edge of the sarcophagus.

Rachel continued to hold her. At the precarious moment, each woman depended on the other for her life.

As the floor tilted to full vertical, Seichan hung like Gray.

But Gray had no one holding him.

His fingers slipped, and he plummeted toward the spikes.

22

October 13, 1:13 P.M.
Svalbard, Norway

The warhead detonated on schedule.

Even hidden behind two steel doors and walls of bedrock, Painter felt the blast as if a giant had his hands over his ears, trying to crush his skull. And yet he still heard the other two seed banks' air locks blow. From the concussive sound of it, the same giant had stamped his foot and crushed the other chambers flat.

Crouched beside their air lock, Painter heard the outer door give way and slam into the inner one with a resounding clang. But the last door held. The overpressure in the air lock had been enough to hold off the sudden blast wave.

Painter touched the steel door with relief. Its surface was warm, heated by the thermobaric's secondary flash fire.

The lights had also been snuffed out by the blast. But the group had prepared for that. Flashlights had been passed out, and they flickered on across the chamber like candles in the dark.

"We made it," Senator Gorman said at his side.

His voice sounded tinny to Painter's strained ears. The others began picking themselves up off the floor. Cries of relief, even a few nervous laughs, spread through the assembled guests and workers.

Painter hated to be the bearer of the bad news, but they had no time for false hope.

He stood up and lifted his arm. "Quiet!" he called out and gained everyone's attention. "We're not out of here yet! We still don't know if the explosion was enough to break through the wall of ice trapping us down here. If we're still stuck, rescue could take days."

Painter motioned to the vault's maintenance engineer for confirmation. He lived up here. He knew the terrain and the archipelago's resources.

"It could take well over a week," he said. "And that's if the road is still open."

That was doubtful, considering the missile barrage Painter had heard. But he kept that to himself. The news was bad enough already. And he had more to deliver.

Painter pointed to the door. "The firestorm will have burned away most of the available oxygen and turned the air toxic out there. Even if the exit is open, these lower levels will still be choked with bad air. We're in the only safe pocket down here. But it will only last for a couple of days, maybe three."

The engineer looked like he was going to shorten that projection, but Painter stemmed that with a hand on his arm. Painter also avoided telling the group the real reason for his haste.

Whoever attacked could come back.

The crowd had gone completely quiet as the sobering news sank in.

Karlsen finally spoke from the edge of the crowd. These were mostly his guests. "So what do we do?"

"Someone has to go out there. To check the door. If it's open, they're going to have to make a long run through a toxic soup. Someone needs to get out and bring back help. The rest will stay here where it's safe for the moment."

"Who's going to go out there?" Senator Gorman asked.

Painter lifted his hand. "I am."

Karlsen stepped forward. "Not alone you're not. I'll go with you. You may need an extra pair of hands."

He was right. Painter didn't know what he might encounter out there. There could be a partial cave-in, a tangle of damaged equipment. It might take a couple of people to move an obstacle. But he eyed Karlsen with skepticism. He was not a young man.

Karlsen read the doubt in his face. "I ran a half marathon two months ago. I jog daily. I won't hold you back."

The senator joined him. "Then I'm going, too."

Clearly Gorman was not letting the murderer of his son out of his sight. And truth be told, Painter didn't want to either. He had a slew of questions for the man, questions that might prove vital to avoiding an ecological disaster.

Still, he preferred both men to stay here.

But Karlsen raised a point that Painter couldn't counter. He gestured toward the door. "It's not up for debate. Whether you like it or not, you can't stop me from following you. I'm going."

Gorman stood shoulder to shoulder with the man on this matter. "We're both going."

Painter didn't have time to argue. He had no authority to have Karlsen handcuffed to one of the racks. In fact, Karlsen had more supporters here than Painter did.

"Then let's go." Painter took one of the flashlights. He used a canteen to wet some scarves and wrap their lower faces, covering mouths and noses. "Try to hold your breath as much as possible."

They nodded.

The engineer had also secured sets of safety goggles to protect their eyes from the sting of the heated, smoky air.

They were as prepared as they could be.

Once ready, Painter stood by the door. He left the maintenance engineer in charge. If they failed, the man had the knowledge to keep the others safe for as long as possible.

"When I open the door, the pressure is now higher in here than out there. It will suck away some of the oxygen. So close this as soon as we leave and don't open it unless we come knocking. If the way is blocked, we'll be right back. If not, pray for the best."

"I've not stopped praying since I saw that bomb," the engineer said with a weak grin.

Painter clapped him on the shoulder and turned to Gorman and Karlsen. "Ready?" he asked.

He got two nods.

Painter turned to the engineer. "Open it." Then to his two companions. "Take a deep breath."

The door cracked open with a disturbing hissing of escaping air and a wash of incredible heat. Painter dashed through it and into the dark tunnel. It was like diving into a sauna. But this steam burned the skin with more than just heat. Painter felt the chemical sting. The air out here was worse than he had imagined.

He heard the other men pounding behind him.

Once Painter rounded out of the seed bank passageway and into the main tunnel, he flicked off his flashlight. He held his breath both literally and figuratively.

Had the entrance been blown open?

He stared ahead into the pitch-black tunnel. He saw no evidence of any light shining back. The tunnel was a straight run. If the way was open, even a little light should stand out like a beacon.

His feet began to slow.

It hadn't worked. They were still trapped in this poisonous well.

But after a few more blind steps, his eyes adjusted more fully to the darkness as the flashlight's dazzle faded. It wasn't much, but far up the tunnel a meager glow shone back through the smoky darkness.

He let slip a small sigh of relief, allowing precious air to escape his lungs.

As hope ignited inside him, he flicked on his light and ran faster. He didn't know if Gorman or Karlsen had seen the promising glow, but they knew the plan. If there hadn't been any sign of light, they were supposed to head back. Since Painter continued, they knew what that meant.

They all sped faster, running through the ruined catering area. Tables were overturned and slammed into the tunnel's end. Anything plastic had melted. The line of ice sculptures had been vaporized. Anything combustible had been set on fire, but the consumption of oxygen by the thermobaric charge had just as quickly smothered the fires.

Residual smoke still hung dead in the air, but the farther they ran, the less dense it grew. A fine black powder covered everything, a by-product of the flash of fluorinated aluminum.

They ran onward.

Painter was forced to take his first breath. He pressed the damp scarf to his nose and sucked in a gulp of air. It stank of burned rubber and stung like acid. He didn't know how much oxygen was still in the air, but he kept running. The higher he got, the cleaner the air would be—especially with the ice plug broken away.

He reached about the halfway point, only another seventy-five yards to go. He could now see a faint glow even with his flashlight on. It drew him forward. But the more he was forced to breathe, the more the tunnel began to waver, shimmering a bit before his watering eyes. His lungs burned. His skin itched all over.

Still he did not slow.

He glanced behind him and saw the other two men falling behind. Senator Gorman looked the worst, weaving on his feet. Karlsen had a grip on his elbow and kept him steady, propelling the senator along.

Painter slowed to help. He needed both men alive.

But Karlsen waved an arm angrily at him, his command clear.

Keep going.

Painter realized he was right. He had to get out of this toxic soup, clear his head. If necessary, he could come back for them. With no other choice, he sped toward the glow and the promise of fresh air.

Finally the blast door appeared, bathed in a bluish glow. A few brighter spots stung Painter's eyes. But as he ran forward, his heart sank.

It can't be . . .

The door was still blocked.

The glow was only daylight diffusing through the ice. The blast had failed to free them. Painter ran toward the exit anyway. There was nowhere else to go. As he drew closer, he realized that some of the brighter spots in the wall were chinks in the blockage.

Hope surged again and was enough to propel him to the doorway. He crossed to one of those chinks, pressed his face against it, and sucked in air. If nothing else, it was deliciously cool. He took several breaths. His head immediately began clearing, the fogginess shredding away.

He turned and saw Karlsen and Gorman about fifteen yards away. Karlsen was now half-carrying the senator. Painter shoved off the wall of ice and hurried back. He supported Gorman's other side.

Together, they hobbled the rest of the way to the door. Painter got both men breathing through cracks in the wall, then found a third spot higher up. As he sucked air, he realized that the ice wall wasn't covered in black soot. This was *new* ice. The blast must have unplugged the entrance—but a secondary avalanche had tumbled back over it, resealing them in.

But the ice wouldn't be as thick.

Painter put an eye to the crack. He could see out.

Near the top of the door, the blockage was less than two feet thick, made up of a jumble of blocks. They were large, but with time, they might be able to dig themselves out.

Still, Painter sensed they didn't have much time. No telling when another avalanche might surge down from above and seal them in tighter.

As if hearing this thought, Painter heard a rumble.

He felt the ice shiver under his cheek.

Oh, no . . .

1:20 P.M.

From across the valley, Monk had watched the explosion. The noise was like a thunderclap inside his head. Startled, deafened, he was knocked on his butt in the snow.

Creed and the two Norwegians fared no better.

A massive eruption of ice and flames had burst out of the buried seed vault. An oily blackness roiled up into the sky.

As if offended, the storm clouds suddenly opened. Snow fell thickly. One second it wasn't snowing, the next, heavy windblown flakes filled the air. It worsened to a whiteout condition in a matter of half a minute. But before the curtain dropped, Monk saw that the explosion had exposed the concrete bunker—at least for a few seconds. A moment later, a second avalanche had slid and tumbled over the entrance.

Was anyone still alive in there?

A pair of gunshots echoed, coming from the lower mountain. Monk could no longer see the trundling force of mercenaries, but they were still coming, still cleaning house.

If anyone had survived that underground blast, they wouldn't be alive for long.

Monk had only one choice.

It took Creed's help, but he finally convinced the Norwegians.

1:21 P.M.

As the rumble grew and the ice shook, Painter prayed the avalanche wouldn't be a large one. But the rumbling grew in volume.

Then, out of the blanket of snow and wind, a Sno-Cat shot into view, rising up from below. It did not slow and sped straight at them.

"Get back!" Painter yelled.

He shoved Gorman away from the doorway, then grabbed Karlsen by the hood of his parka and flung them both bodily away from the wall of ice.

And not a second too soon.

The heavy vehicle struck the blocked doorway. Its front treads rode up the ice wall. The bumper cracked into the top half of the doorway. Ice blocks shattered into the tunnel and slid away.

The Sno-Cat backed up, likely readying itself for a second run.

Painter dashed forward. The bumper had broken a hole large enough for Painter to slide his body through. Diving into the jagged gap, he clawed and elbowed his way through the door.

The Sno-Cat suddenly halted its retreat.

The passenger door popped open. A familiar figure leaned out.

"Director Crowe?" Monk said, his face raw with relief.

"Monk . . . you are a sight for sore eyes." And Painter's eyes were sore—bloodshot and inflamed.

"I get that a lot," Monk said. "But we should get moving."

Painter turned. Karlsen clambered out of the hole, followed by the senator. "There are more people locked up down below."

"And that's where they should stay." Monk hopped out, reached back inside, and came out with an armload of rifles. "Can you shoot?" he asked the other two men.

Both Gorman and Karlsen nodded.

"Good, because we need as much firepower as we can muster."

"Why?" Painter asked.

Before Monk could answer, the distant grumble of a heavy engine echoed out of the storm.

"We've got company coming."

Painter joined Monk over at the Sno-Cat and took a rifle. He noted that the vehicle held only one man, a Norwegian soldier. He searched around.

"Where's Creed?" Painter asked.

"Left with this soldier's buddy on our snowmobiles. They've gone for help."

Painter hoped they made it back in time with the cavalry. He assessed the group left to defend the fort.

One vehicle and four men.

The Alamo had better odds . . . and look how that turned out.

23

Rachel almost dropped Seichan when she saw Gray fall from his perch. He slid down the face of the cross and caught himself on the tri-spiral bas-relief that decorated the lower leg of the cross.

He scrambled for a moment, then laced his fingers over the top of the symbol sticking out. Would it hold his weight or break away?

The same worry must have crossed his mind. He kept his body from moving too much. His boots hung over a twenty-foot drop into a pit lined by spikes.

But Gray wasn't the only one threatened.

Rachel slid across the upended side of the sarcophagus. "Hold my legs!" she shouted back to Wallace.

The professor shared her perch on the stone coffin. He clung as precariously as she did. He grabbed her ankles and helped stabilize her.

It gave Rachel some slight reassurance but not much.

She hung over the side of the sarcophagus. She had a grip on Seichan's jacket. The woman who poisoned her clung with only her fingertips to the edge of the coffin.

Neither of them could hold out much longer.

A small quake shuddered through the chamber. The apparatus was ancient. Triggering it must have upset whatever fragile balance had been established over the centuries. She pictured the ruins of the tower above. It might all come down.

Another shake rattled through the tilted floor. From inside the sarcophagus, Malachy's Bible tumbled out. It fell into the pit and was speared through the middle, impaled on one of the spikes.

Wallace groaned at the loss, but they had more immediate concerns.

Bobbled by the quaking, Seichan lost her grip. She fell without making a sound, as if she expected it, deserved it. One of Rachel's hands lost its grip, but her other fist remained twisted in Seichan's coat.

She stopped the woman's plunge with a wrench of her shoulder. But the weight dragged her over the edge of the sarcophagus. Only Wallace's grip on her ankles stopped them both from a deadly plunge.

Rachel's upper body hung upside down, her hips and legs remaining atop the coffin, pinned by Wallace. It was hard to breathe. Seichan dangled below, hanging from her coat. Her only sign of fear was how tightly she clutched that coat to her neck with both hands.

Rachel wanted to let her go, but the woman was her only lifeline.

The floor shook again. A piece of the cavern roof broke away. A large slab dropped, and shattered against the spikes.

She closed her eyes and prayed for some way out.

Her angelic answer came from the most unlikely of sources.

"What the fuck!"

The shout came from the other side of the tilted floor, where the tunnel led up to Lord Newborough's crypt.

It was Kowalski. He must have come down either out of impatience or because he had heard the booby trap being sprung.

"Help!" Rachel yelled, but with her chest stretched and her belly squeezed, it came out as a squeak.

"Hello!" Kowalski called. Plainly he hadn't heard her.

Gray bellowed as he hung. "Kowalski!"

"Pierce? Where are you? All I see is a pit and a blank wall. How did you all get across?"

From Kowalski's vantage point in the tunnel, all he must see was the underside of the fake floor—and the pit.

Gray yelled again. "Go back and pull the bar!"

"Pull my what?" He sounded offended.

"The lever! Up the tunnel!"

"Oh, okay! Hang on!"

Rachel stared down at Seichan, then over to Gray. *Hang on.* That's all they could do.

"Hurry!" Gray called out. He had begun to slip again.

Kowalski's voice came back fainter. "Quit nagging me!"

Rachel clung as tightly as she could. She closed her eyes and pictured the bar sticking out of the floor. She had spotted it earlier. It made sense that there would be a reset button for this trap. While the mechanism might kill any thieves who stumbled down here, the engineers of the trap would have needed a way to reset it. Otherwise, they'd be cut off from the key, too. Some sort of reset had to lie outside the chamber.

But was it the lever?

She prayed Gray's intuition was right.

She had her answer a moment later.

The entire floor suddenly vibrated. A great grinding of gears shook through the room. The floor began to tilt again—*but the wrong way.* It started to rotate upside down. Rachel dared not even scream as her body began to slip across the stone. They were going to flip over.

Then something caught. The floor stopped with a stomach-jarring jolt. With a harsher grinding of gears, the floor slowly reversed itself. It swung back in the proper direction.

Rachel clung hard, her lips moving as she said the Lord's Prayer.

She watched the floor's edge rise under Gray's toes and push him back up. She rolled off the side of the sarcophagus and onto the leveling floor. They all lay flat, breathing hard. Even Gray slumped to his rear beside the cross.

Kowalski came back with a flashlight. "If you're done playing down here . . ."

Rachel glared in his direction.

"I came to tell you that the storm's getting fierce. Lyle says we better move it if we want to get off this godforsaken island."

Before anyone could move or respond, another section of the roof crashed down, striking the floor like a bomb. Water and a flow of bricks came next. The tower was coming down on top of them.

"Out!" Gray yelled.

They all shot to their feet and ran for the exit. A resounding *snap* jolted the entire floor. It began to wobble, teeter-tottering as something broke in the ancient mechanism.

Off balance, Rachel tumbled to the side, but Gray caught her around the waist and rushed with her toward the tunnel. They all flew into it as more of the cavern imploded.

A last glance showed the floor tilted askew as a waterfall of bricks and rain flooded into the room. Then she was too far up the tunnel to see any more. A moment later, an earthshaking crash chased them. A flume of rock dust rolled up the tunnel and over them.

Coughing, they reached the exit and climbed up, one after the other, back into the storm. Up top, a stunned Lyle offered them umbrellas.

Rachel took one, but she kept her face turned up toward the sky. She let rainwater wash over her.

We made it, Rachel thought.

1:42 P.M.

Gray stared over at the wreckage of the abbey tower. It was now only a tumbled pile of rubble sunk halfway into the ground. Water had already begun to pool around it.

The cavern was surely gone.

A roar rose behind him as Lyle started the tractor. The storm wailed—the winds had picked up while they'd been down there. Rain pelted out of the sky, whipping horizontal at times as the winds swept off the Irish Sea and across the island. Even the lightning had grown more subdued, as if cowed by the growing intensity of the storm.

They loaded up into the trailer for the ride back over the hill to the harbor. Lyle hunched in his seat and pushed the tractor into gear. The trailer lurched as it began to move.

They all crouched low, trying to keep out of the rain and the wind.

Wallace gazed back at the fallen ruins of Saint Mary's Abbey. "First rule of archaeology," he said, then glanced sidelong at Gray. "Don't touch anything."

Gray did not blame the professor for scolding him. He had acted without properly considering the dangers. He had been so shocked to discover that the cross predated Christianity, that the wheel component actually turned. He leaped before looking. Unlike Father Giovanni. Judging by all the priest's calculations, he had gone after the puzzle in a systematic and studied way.

But then again, the priest had been trained as an archaeologist. And Father Giovanni didn't have a woman's life hanging in the balance.

His group had only another two days to solve this mystery. Gray wouldn't apologize for pushing their investigation hard, for taking chances, for eschewing caution to get results.

Still, as he pictured the painstaking notations and calculations done by Father Giovanni, he knew there was something he was still missing. The more he tried to pin it down, the more it slipped away.

Wallace shook his head. "Just think what we might have learned if we'd had more time with that cross . . ."

Gray heard the accusation behind his words. The man's usual joviality had been worn away by exhaustion, terror, and not a small amount of disappointment. With one mistake, they'd destroyed a priceless illuminated treasure and lost access to whatever the cross had kept hidden.

"What if the key is still down there?" Wallace asked pointedly.

Gray had had enough. "You don't believe that. And neither do I." The words came out more harshly than he intended, but he was tired, too.

"How can you be so sure?" Wallace asked.

"Because Father Giovanni *left*. He continued his search. I think he solved the riddle of the cross, found an empty vault that once held the key, then moved on, taking the one object he needed to continue his search."

"The relic from the grave," Rachel said.

Gray stared out into the storm. "The key is still out there. I don't think the cross offered Father Giovanni that much help. So he moved on, just as we must."

"But where?" Wallace asked. "Where do we even begin to look? We're right back where we started."

"No, we're not," Gray said.

"How can you say that?"

He ignored the professor's question and turned to Rachel. "How did you know so much about Saint Malachy?"

She shifted on the floorboards, clearly caught by surprise. "It was Uncle Vigor. The prophecies intrigued him. He could talk for hours about Saint Malachy."

Gray had suspected as much. Monsignor Verona had always been passionate about the mysteries of the early Church, seeking truths behind miracles. Such a figure as Malachy would have captured both his attention and his imagination.

"That's why Father Giovanni sought out your uncle," Gray said. "He knew the key to solving this mystery lay in the life of that saint. So Giovanni went to the best source he knew."

"Vigor Verona." Wallace sat straighter, ignoring the wind and rain.

"Maybe Marco knew about the plot by Viatus, or maybe he just had an inkling. But I suspect that the further he delved into this matter of curses and miracles, the more he knew he was in over his head. That he needed the expertise and protection of the Church behind him."

Seichan added her own bleak viewpoint from the back of the trailer. "But he sought them out too late. Someone knew of his plan."

Gray nodded. "If we're going to discover where the Doomsday key was hidden, we're going to need an expert on Saint Malachy."

"But Verona is still in a coma," Wallace said.

"It doesn't matter. We have someone who knows just as much." He turned to Rachel.

"Me?"

"You're going to have to help us from here."

"How?"

"Because I know where the key is hidden."

Wallace looked hard at him. "What? . . . Where?"

"Malachy's Bible was left in that sarcophagus for a reason. More than just to sanctify a relic. It was left behind as a symbol, a bread crumb to lead to the key's new resting place. Prior to the coming of the Romans, the key and the grave of this ancient royal were always kept together. They were bound together. And in the sarcophagus, we discovered Malachy's Bible binding a relic of this ancient person, binding it to *him*."

"So what are you saying?" Wallace pressed him.

"I think Saint Malachy has taken the place of this ancient. That he's become the proverbial keeper of the key."

Wallace's eyes grew wide. "If you're right, then the key . . ."

"It's in Saint Malachy's tomb."

Kowalski groaned and picked at a fingernail with a piece of straw. "Of course it is. But I'm telling you flat out, I'm *not* going in there."

Before they could discuss it further, the trailer jerked to a stop. Gray was surprised to see that they'd already reached the harbor.

Lyle hopped down and waved them out. "You can hole up in the old harbor house. Get yourselves out of the rain, right enough. I'll fetch my da."

As Gray hurried down the path toward the stone house, he stared out to sea. The waters rolled with frothing whitecaps. Closer at hand, the ferry rocked and teetered in its slip, even sheltered within the harbor's breakwater. It was going to be a hellish ride back over to the mainland.

But for now, the windows of the harbor house glowed and flickered with the promise of a crackling fire. They all piled through the door, shutting out the storm behind them. The room was paneled in raw pine, with heavy exposed beams. The floor creaked underfoot. The place smelled of wood smoke and pipe tobacco. Candles lit a few tables. But it was the fire that drew them all deeper inside. They gladly shed their coats over a few chairs.

Gray stood with his back to the fire, appreciating the heat from his heels to the top of his head. The warmth and the cheery dance of flames went a long way to beat back the hopelessness that had begun to settle over them.

But now they had a course of action.

A place to look next.

The door slammed open as the wind ripped the knob from Owen Bryce's fingers. He caught it again and forced it closed. Drenched, he stomped and shook off the worst of the rainwater.

"It's parky weather out, that's for sure," the boatman said with a crooked grin at his understatement. "And I'm afraid I have some good news and some bad."

Such a preamble never boded well.

Gray stepped away from the fire.

"The bad news is that we won't be able to make the crossing today. The storm has blown the seas into a treacherous state. If'n you didn't know, the Welsh name for the island is Ynys Enlli, which means 'island of bad currents.' And that's on a sunny day."

"So what's the good news?" Kowalski asked.

"I've checked and I can get you rooms here for the night at half off. Good for the entire week."

Gray felt his stomach sink. "How soon do you expect we can make it off the island?"

He shrugged. "Hard to say. Electricity and phones are down all over the island. We have to get the all-clear from the harbormaster in Aberdaron before we can even think of throwing off our ties here."

"Your best estimate?"

"We had some tourists here last year that got stranded for seventeen days due to storms."

Gray waited for the answer to his question. He looked sternly at the man.

Owen finally relented, running a hand over the top of his head. "I'm sure we can get you back to Aberdaron in two days. Three days tops."

Off to the side, Rachel sank into one of the chairs.

She didn't have that many days.

24

October 13, 1:35 P.M.
Svalbard, Norway

Monk lay flat across the roof of the Sno-Cat as it trundled through the snowstorm. Painter shared his perch. They were both tethered to the roof rack like luggage. The harder gusts of wind continually fought to rip them from the roof. Snow frosted them like icing on a cake.

Each man had an assault rifle snugged to his shoulder, and the Norwegian soldier had supplied them both with one additional piece of gear, essential for cold-weather fighting.

Monk adjusted the infrared goggles on his face. They darkened the view ahead. Not that it mattered—the blizzard's whiteout conditions had lowered visibility to mere yards. But the scopes built into the eyepieces captured any ambient heat signatures and brought them into focus. Below their perch, the hot engine of their Sno-Cat glowed a soft orange.

Out in the storm, their targets came into view. Seven or eight snowmobiles crisscrossed up from the lower mountain slopes, glowing a soft amber through the scopes. The vehicles were just now cresting into the upper valley where Monk had spent much of his time spying on the Svalbard seed vault.

It was here that Monk and the others would make their stand, using every resource available to them.

Monk patted a hand on the rocket-propelled grenade launcher next to him. Before setting out, they had scoured the avalanche's path for additional weapons and found the launcher. Along with a wooden box of ammunition.

Below, the senator and the CEO shared the cab with the Norwegian soldier, manning rifles. One pointed out the passenger side, the other out the rear.

They were armed to the teeth, but their enemy outnumbered them at least ten to one.

As the advance team of the assault party rode into the valley on snowmobiles, the Norwegian driver lunged their vehicle to the side. He was doing his best to keep a snowbank between the Cat and the smaller, faster snow machines.

Through the goggles, Monk watched a pair of snow-mobiles, double mounted by mercenary soldiers, skim past far to the right. The enemy failed to spot the Cat half-hidden behind the snowbank, suggesting that the enemy either didn't have infrared or were too focused on the seed vault ahead.

Monk and Painter let them pass without firing.

The smaller vehicles were not their primary target.

More snowmobiles shot past with a whining rip of their engines, deafening the riders to the low rumble of the Sno-Cat. Ahead, a massive vehicle loomed into view. Its heat signature was nearly blinding. It rose up out of the lower slopes and dropped heavily into the upper valley.

It was a Hagglund troop carrier.

The main body of the assault force remained inside that vehicle. It had to be taken out. Their Sno-Cat was no match for the swifter snowmobiles, but against this behemoth, the Sno-Cat would be the nimbler one. If they could take out the Hagglund, it would demoralize the enemy. Perhaps enough to encourage them to give up the assault and turn back.

Either way, Monk and the others couldn't let the assault force reach the seed vault. According to Painter, there were over forty people still alive in there.

As the Hagglund lumbered along the valley floor, Painter exchanged his rifle for the grenade launcher. They would have only one chance. Once they fired, they would draw the full wrath of the force toward them.

Monk slapped his palm twice on the roof of the Sno-Cat.

Obeying the signal, the driver slowed to a stop.

Painter swung the weapon up and aimed. Monk pulled his goggles off. The fiery flash of the launcher might blind him. Without the goggles, he could see nothing. The blizzard swirled and spun, erasing the world. It was like being trapped in a snow globe that someone had tossed into a paint shaker.

No wonder the enemy hadn't spotted them.

"Fire in the hole," Painter said and pulled the trigger.

The launcher belched out smoke and flames, and the grenade rocketed through the curtain of snow.

Monk shoved his goggles back in place. He got them seated in time to see the hot passage of the grenade slam into the treads of the Hagglund. A bloom of fiery orange marked the impact. Hit broadside, the troop carrier tipped up on one tread.

Monk willed it to topple over.

It didn't. It crashed back down on its treads. The Hagglund tried to move, but with one set of tracks ruined, it foundered in the snow, turning in place. Doors popped open, and smaller heat signatures abandoned the vehicle, diving flat against the snow. The soldiers knew they were under attack, sitting ducks in the Hagglund.

"Firing!" Painter yelled.

Monk covered his eyes, heard the launcher roar, then looked up again. Painter's aim was perfect. The rocket crashed through the front windshield of the vehicle and exploded inside. Windows blew out in a fiery ruin. Bodies tumbled through the air, blazing brightly through the goggles.

Painter dropped flat.

Bullets whined past overhead.

Firing the grenade launcher had given away their position.

With their cover blown, Monk slapped the roof, and the Sno-Cat kicked into gear. The driver quickly gained speed going downhill, then tore the vehicle to the right. The Sno-Cat lifted up off one tread.

Monk held tight. Painter knocked into him.

The Cat jumped the snowbank and went airborne for a stomach-rising moment, then slammed back down. Monk crashed to the roof and took a glancing blow to his ribs against a roof rail.

But he didn't complain.

They had only a short window of time to take advantage of the confusion. During the short run down the slope, they had gotten below the Hagglund's position. They had to attack before the assault force was entrenched.

Monk spotted heat signatures against the cold snow. He raised his rifle to his cheek and began firing. Painter did the same. They took out a few men, sending them sprawling. But aiming was a challenge as the Sno-Cat bounced and rattled over the ice and snow.

Some soldiers ran for cover. Others fled upslope.

A barrage of return fire blasted from behind the Hagglund. *Ping*s rang out as rounds spattered against the metal grille of the Sno-Cat. Monk heard the telltale crunch of the windshield being struck.

The driver didn't slow but turned, doing his best to keep the bulk of the Hagglund between them and the shooters. Other soldiers fired at them, hidden behind chunks of ice or boulders.

Still, the Cat was a difficult target in the snowstorm, and the Norwegian did his best to keep moving, to slalom one way then the other.

As they climbed the slope, a new noise intruded: the angry whine of snowmobiles. The advance team had swung back around and was headed to the aid of the others.

While the Sno-Cat might be a shark circling the Hagglund, the smaller snow machines were leaner, swifter predators.

Their position was about to be overrun.

1:41 P.M.

Through his goggles, Painter watched the swarm of ten snowmobiles dive toward the Hagglund. The small vehicles' heat signatures were bright spots against the cold snow. He and his team had no choice but to take the fight to the others.

The Sno-Cat sped upslope to meet the charge head-on.

As they neared the blasted behemoth, the enemy began to fire more furiously at them. With the approach of the snowmobiles and the promise of additional firepower, the soldiers on the ground grew more confident and secured their positions.

A fiery trail burned across Painter's shoulders.

He didn't flinch, nor did he stop firing.

Neither did anyone else.

As the Cat climbed to face the challenge, rifles fired in a continual blaze from the trundling vehicle. They had to break the back of this assault. Painter had hoped taking out the Hagglund would send the others running, but these were seasoned fighters. They didn't scare that easily.

It would have to become a fiery brawl, pitting speed, wit, and skill.

Or so he thought.

A strange new noise intruded.

A shrill whistling pierced the chatter of gunfire.

Monk slapped the roof of the Cat three times. The driver slammed to a stop. Unprepared, Painter went flying forward off the roof. His body slammed into the windshield, but the tether kept him from tumbling away.

Monk had kept his perch. He reached with a knife and cut Painter's tether, then did the same to his own.

"Get inside!" Monk yelled and pointed below.

Painter trusted the firmness in Monk's voice. As he hopped down, both doors popped open. Monk dove for the passenger side. The driver leaned out, grabbed Painter's sleeve, and dragged him in. The small Cat was only a two-man vehicle, but there was a storage compartment in back. Still, it was a tight fit.

Gunfire continued, flaring brightly through the snow. A few stray shots clipped their vehicle. But with all return fire stopped and the engine throttled down, their exact position grew more obscured in the storm.

"What's happening?" Painter asked.

Monk continued to stare intently forward. "I told you Creed went to fetch help. The Norwegian army isn't the only force defending that vault."

"What're you—?"

Then Painter saw them. Massive heat signatures bloomed out of the snow. Easily a dozen. They bounded at incredible speeds, growing larger as Painter watched. Now he understood.

Polar bears.

The sharp whistling continued, echoing down from the higher valley.

Bear whistles.

The piercing noise must be driving them on down.

"The driver's buddy grew up here," Monk said in a rush. "Knew the haunts of the bears. Over three thousand are on the island alone. He was confident he could flush out a pack, get them angry and get them moving. Sorry I didn't say anything earlier. Thought he was insane."

Painter agreed. It was insane—but it had also worked.

Polar bears hunted seals. They could sprint at thirty miles per hour, with bursts of speed even faster. And this angry pack was going downhill.

Through the goggles, Painter watched the bears overtake the snowmobiles. Massive shapes swamped the slower vehicles, unleashing their savage fury against any moving targets in their rampaging path. Painter watched one snow machine go down, then another, toppling and crashing to the side, buried under a mountain of angry muscle.

Screams broke through the slowing gunfire—accompanied by fierce roars that stood Painter's hair on end.

The remaining snowmobiles reached the Hagglund, but they didn't slow. They raced straight past, the riders hunched low. The bears followed, sweeping through the entrenched soldiers on the ground. Some fired at the beasts, but the bears were mere shadows in the snowstorm.

The shots only succeeded in drawing their fury.

Screams and roars rose in volume.

One soldier fled on foot toward the Cat, as if their vehicle might offer him some refuge. He never made it. Out of the storm, a thick paw snagged a leg. The bear continued to run. The limb was ripped from the soldier's body. He flipped high in the air, spraying blood.

Another bear bowled past the Cat, knocking its shoulder into the side as if warning them, an act of intimidation.

It worked.

Painter didn't breathe.

The pack stormed through the valley, scattering men, leaving bloody bodies behind. Then, as quickly as they came, the pack vanished back into the storm like ghosts.

Painter stared. Nothing moved out there now.

Anyone who could flee had done so, striking off in a hundred different directions. Painter had hoped to break the back of the assault force by taking out the Hagglund. It hadn't worked. But even the most seasoned veteran had to be shaken to the core when faced by such a raw display of nature's brutal force.

A new whining grew in volume, coming from up-slope.

A pair of snowmobiles blipped into existence in his goggles.

Moments later, they appeared out of the storm. Creed lifted an arm in greeting. The Norwegian driver patted Painter on the shoulder, his gesture clear.

It was over.

2:12 P.M.

Krista climbed through the snow.

She clutched her hood closed against the freezing wind. One sleeve of her parka was burned to a crisp. From the excruciating tug on that side, she knew a few patches had seared down to her skin, fusing cloth and flesh.

She had barely escaped the Hagglund. She had been halfway out a window when the second grenade slammed through the windshield. The blast tossed her end over end and slammed her into a snowbank. Her flaming arm was immediately extinguished.

Knowing they were under attack by an unknown and unexpected force, Krista had crawled, half in shock, over to the Hagglund and hid under it. There she rode out the firefight and the slaughter that followed.

She still trembled at the memory.

She remained hidden when her attackers gathered nearby. She gasped when she spotted her nemesis again. The dark-haired Sigma operative, the one named Painter Crowe. With his face now windburned, she even recognized the hint of his Native American heritage.

How many damned lives does this Indian have?

Staying hidden, she waited for them to leave. One snowmobile headed down toward Longyearbyen, going for help. The others headed back up to the seed vault, to maintain a defensive perimeter against any stray soldiers who might attempt to complete the failed mission.

She had no intention of doing that.

She crossed through the storm to an abandoned snowmobile. The driver's body covered several yards of bloody snow. In agony, she tromped through the carnage and searched the vehicle. The keys were still in place.

Swinging a leg over it, she settled heavily into the seat and twisted the key. The engine grumbled up to a whine as she engaged the throttle.

She leaned low and sped away, heading down the mountain. There was nothing she could do here now.

Except make a promise.

Before this was all over, she would put a bullet through that Indian's skull.

25

October 13, 3:38 P.M.
Bardsey Island, Wales

Gray lounged in a steaming tub of hot water.

He kept his eyes closed, struggling to settle his mind. For the better part of an hour he had argued with Owen Bryce, explaining how Rachel had a medical condition that required immediate evacuation. That she needed medicines back at their hotel on the mainland. The only concession he got from the man was that he would reconsider the request in the morning.

It didn't help matters that Rachel still *looked* okay.

So for now, they were trapped on the island.

At least for a few more hours.

They would wait for nightfall, which at least came early this time of year. Once the islanders were settled in for the night, the plan was to steal that boat. They dared not wait until morning. If Owen still refused, they would lose another day. That could not happen.

So they took the offered rooms. They could use a little downtime. They were all worn thin and needed a moment to rest.

Still, Gray had a hard time relaxing. His mind gnawed and worried on the mysteries and dangers they faced.

Thunder rumbled up into a resounding clap. It rattled the panes of glass in the window above the tub. Candlelight flickered beside the bar of soap. The electricity was still out. Before drawing his bath, he had started a small fire in the bedroom's hearth. Through his closed eyelids, he noted the rosy dance of the flames.

As he sprawled in the tub, a shadow suddenly moved across the glow.

He stiffened, sitting up suddenly, sloshing water over the floor. A figure stood in the doorway, dressed in a robe. He had not heard Rachel enter the room. The thunder had masked her approach.

"Rachel . . ."

She trembled where she stood, her eyes haunted. She didn't say a word. She shed her robe with no seduction. She simply let it drop and crossed in a rush of steps to the tub. Gray stood and caught her in his arms. She folded against him, needing him. She buried her head against his neck.

He bent at the knees, scooped an arm under her backside, and lifted her up. She was lighter than he remembered, as if hopelessness had hollowed her out. Turning, carrying her, he settled them both into the hot water.

He cradled her in the steaming bath. Her hand slid down his belly, desperate, hurting, her need raw and on the surface. He stopped her and drew her hand back to his chest. He simply held her, waiting for her to stop trembling. They had been running since the fire in the woods, since she had first learned of the betrayal. He should have known better than to leave her alone now as they waited for nightfall.

If his mind had been troubled and unsettled, what must she be going through? Especially alone. He wrapped his arms tightly and squeezed as if by sheer muscle he might keep her safe from harm.

Slowly her trembling wore itself out against his strength.

She sagged into him.

He held her for a long while more—then with a finger, he touched and drew her face up. He stared into her eyes. They shone with her desire to be touched, to feel alive, to know she wasn't alone . . . and deeper down, almost buried, the embers of old love.

Only then did he bring his lips to hers.

4:02 P.M.

Seichan waited inside her room. She stood with her back against the door and an unlit cigarette in her hand. A few minutes ago she had heard Rachel's door creak ajar, heard her footsteps pass down the hall, then Gray's bedroom door open.

Seichan listened with her eyes closed.

The door never reopened.

As she maintained her vigil, she fought against the welling mix of anger and jealousy, along with an ache she could not dismiss. It clutched her lungs and made it hard to breathe. Leaning against the door, she slowly sank to the floor and hugged her knees.

Alone, with no one to see, she allowed herself this momentary weakness. The room was dark. She had not bothered with a fire, or even a candle. She preferred the darkness. She always had.

Rocking ever so gently, she let the ache pass through her.

She knew she was reverting to a time when pain came often, growing from slaps to violations more intimate. There had been a secret closet where she would hide or seek refuge afterward. It had no windows. No one knew about it but the rats and mice.

Only there, tucked away in the darkness, had she felt safe.

She hated herself now for needing that comfort. She knew she should just tell him and end this pain. But she swore not to. It was because of *him* she had made that promise.

And no matter what the agony, she would never break it.

6:55 P.M.

Under cover of night, Gray led the others down the jetty.

The ferryboat rocked in its berth and beat itself against the bumpers. Rain poured out of the dark sky. Ahead, Kowalski stood beside the weathered catamaran. He had gone ahead and made sure that the boat was empty, the keys had been left.

Who would steal the boat in this storm?

It was a question Gray was ready to answer.

They all hurried down the dock.

"Get aboard," Kowalski said. "I'll free the ropes."

Gray helped the others clamber into the stern of the ferry. It took acrobatics and timing as the deck rose and fell.

He took Rachel's hand.

She would not look at him, but she squeezed his fingers warmly, thanking him silently. He had woken, snarled in blankets, to find her gone. He could not say he was totally disappointed. He knew the score; so did she. What had happened was sincere, deeply felt, and needed—perhaps by both of them. The momentary flash of passion was born out of fear, out of loneliness, out of mortality. Gray loved her, and he knew she felt the same. But even as they lay tangled together before the fire, buried in each other, wracked by a passion that burned away all thought, a part of her remained untouchable.

Now was not the time for anything to be reborn between them. She was too wounded, too fragile. In that room, she had only needed his strength, his touch, his warmth. But not his heart.

That would have to wait.

Gray hopped over the rail to the deck and grabbed the tossed line as Kowalski leaped into the boat.

"It's going to be a monster of a crossing," Kowalski warned them all. He hurried to the covered pilot-house. He got the engines started with a burbling roar, then signaled for Gray to let go of the last line.

With the boat freed, Gray headed across the rock-ing deck. Kowalski idled them away from the jetty and out toward the open water. They would run dark with no lights until they cleared the harbor.

Gray glanced back toward shore. No one came running. In this storm, the boat might not be missed until morning.

He turned back to face the roiling black sea. The wind howled and rain pounded. "Are you sure you can handle the boat in this weather?" Gray asked.

Kowalski's background was as a seaman with the U.S. Navy. He had the stub of a cigar clenched in his teeth. At least it was unlit.

"Don't worry," the man said around his cigar. "I only sank one boat . . . No, wait. Only *two* boats."

That was reassuring.

Gray returned to the stern deck. Wallace was passing out neon-orange life jackets from a storage locker. They all quickly donned them, clicking on the safety lights at their collars.

"Keep hold of something at all times," Gray warned.

As they passed the breakwater, lightning lit up the night. The seas looked even worse. Waves seemed to be traveling in all directions, crashing into one another and casting up geysers of seawater. The currents had turned as wild as the weather.

Kowalski began whistling.

Gray knew that was not a good sign.

Then they were into open water. It was as if they had been dumped into a washing machine. The boat rode high, then low, rocked left and right—and, Gray swore, sometimes all at the same time.

No matter where he looked, all he saw were white-capped waves.

Kowalski's whistling grew louder.

The ferry hit a steep swell. The bow lifted straight for the sky. Gray clung hard to a rail as everything loose in the boat slid toward the stern. Then they were over it and headed down the far side.

An errant wave hit them broadside at the same time. It washed over the stern like a sweep of God's hand. Gray took a mouthful and was blinded by the sting of cold salt water.

Then they were clear and rising again.

"Gray!" Rachel called out.

Coughing, he realized the problem at the same time.

Seichan was gone.

Seated on the far side, she had taken the brunt of the wave on her back. It had ripped her off the rail and flushed her overboard.

Gray stood.

He spotted her bobbing far to stern, illuminated by her lifejacket's small light—then the waves tore her from view.

Fixing her last location, Gray ran and leaped over the end of the boat. They couldn't lose her.

As he flew toward the sea, Rachel yelled to Kowalski, "Turn around!"

Then Gray hit the water, and all went black.

7:07 P.M.

Seichan spun as waves tossed her about like a leaf in a flood. The cold cut to the bone and made it difficult to draw air, which was hard enough with walls of water continuing to sweep over her.

She couldn't even see the boat's lights, only mountains of water.

She clung to her life jacket with one hand and wiped salt water out of her eyes with the other. She had to make for the boat.

Another giant wave crested ahead of her, impossibly high, leaning over her, raging white along its lip.

Then it fell on top of her.

She was slammed deep. The current churned her and spun her. She could not say which way was up. Water surged into her nose. She gagged in reflex, swallowing more stinging water.

Then the buoyancy of her jacket dragged her back to the surface.

She tried for a gasp of air, but all she could do was choke. She blinked away the salt, struggling to see.

Another wave rose before her.

No . . .

Then something grabbed her from behind.

Terrified, she screamed. The wave crashed over her. But still those arms held her. Hard legs wrapped firmly around her hips. They rode out the tumult together. She had no air, but the raw panic bled away, leaving only a steady fear.

Though she couldn't see him, she knew who had grabbed her.

They surfaced together, riding higher with two life jackets.

She twisted to find Gray clasped tightly to her, his eyes rock-hard and determined.

"Save me," she whispered, putting all she could into those two words.

Even her heart.

7:24 P.M.

The lights of the fishing village glowed through the storm. The beach lay directly ahead. Kowalski aimed toward it.

Gray kept to his side.

He had to admit the man *did* know how to pilot a boat.

While he and Seichan had been battered in the churning waves, Kowalski had found them and brought the boat around in the rough seas. A lifeline was tossed, and they were dragged to the boat and hauled back on board.

The rest of the crossing was brutal, but no one else got tossed overboard. Seichan coughed behind him, still struggling to clear the water out of her chest. She had never looked so pale.

But she would live.

Kowalski worked the wheel and drove the catamaran into the shallows. A final wave lifted the boat and shoved it onto the beach. The twin keels dragged through the sand with a violent shudder of its deck. Then at long last they stopped.

No one had to be told. They all abandoned ship, splashing into the ankle-deep water and fleeing from the last of the waves. Kowalski took an extra moment to pat the side of the catamaran.

"Nice boat."

As a bedraggled and sodden group, they climbed from the shore up toward the fishing village of Aberdaron. Like Bardsey Island, the place was shuttered against the storm. No one was on the streets.

Gray wanted to be gone before anyone discovered the beached ferry. After the dangerous crossing, he didn't want to end up locked in a local jail.

He rushed them through the dark town and up to the church of Saint Hywyn. Their stolen truck was where they'd left it, still parked near the church. Gray turned to Wallace as they headed through the church- yard.

"What about your dog?" he asked and pointed to the rectory.

Wallace shook his head, though it clearly pained him. "We'll leave Rufus be. He's better off sleeping next to a fire than traipsing about in this boggin' weather. I'll come back for him when this is all over."

With the matter settled, they all piled into the Land Rover.

Gray got the engine started, quickly headed out of the lot, and spun them away from Aberdaron. He ac- celerated as he hit the main road out of town.

But they still needed a destination.

"Saint Malachy's tomb," Gray said and glanced in the rearview mirror toward Rachel. "What can you tell us about its history?"

They'd never had a chance to discuss the matter in more detail. All he knew from a cursory inquiry with Rachel was that Malachy was laid to rest in northeast- ern France. Rachel had tried to elaborate, but at the time it had been enough. Gray had needed to concen- trate on getting them all off the island.

With a long ride ahead of them, it was time he learned more.

Rachel spoke while staring out into the storm. "Malachy died sometime in the middle of the twelfth century. He expired in the arms of his best friend, Saint Bernard of Clairvaux."

Kowalski twisted his head. "Saint Bernard? Didn't he invent those slobbering mountain dogs?"

Rachel ignored him. "Malachy was buried in an abbey that Bernard founded, the Abbey of Clairvaux. It's about a hundred and fifty miles outside of Paris. Most of the abbey was destroyed in the nineteenth century, but a few buildings and walls still exist, including its main cloister. But there's a small problem."

From the way she said it, Gray knew the problem was not small.

"What?"

"I tried to tell you before . . ." She went suddenly sheepish, as if she thought she should have pressed him harder earlier. But like Gray, she'd also had a lot on her mind.

"It's all right," he said. "What is it?"

"The ruins are protected. They may be the best-guarded buildings in all of France."

"Why's that?"

"The Abbey of Clairvaux . . . it lies at the heart of a maximum-security prison."

Gray swung around in his seat to look her full in the face. She had to be joking. From the stern and worried look on her face, she wasn't.

"Great. So now we're breaking into a prison *and* a tomb." Kowalski sank down and crossed his arms. "Nothing could possibly go wrong with that plan."

26

Krista paced the length of the ice-cold warehouse on the outskirts of Longyearbyen. Crates were stacked to the rafters. The place smelled of oil and coal. She wore a thick sweater to cover the bandages on her arm. A morphine haze clouded the edges of her thoughts. Other men were in worse shape. Two bodies on the warehouse floor were covered over by tarps.

Only eight men left.

She held the phone to her ear, waiting for instructions. She had dialed the number he had left. It rang and rang. Finally, the line was picked up.

"I've been briefed," the man said.

"Yes, sir." Krista struggled to hear any indication of the man's mood, but his words were calm and precise, unhurried.

"With the turn of events, we're radically altering our objectives for this mission. With Karlsen now in Sigma's hands, the decision is to abort all operations in Norway."

"And what about in the UK?"

"We took a chance on co-opting those outside resources to assist us in finding the key. After the current turn of events, we no longer have that luxury. We must gather our chips and leave the table for now."

"Sir?"

"The article stolen by Father Giovanni. Secure it."

"And the others?"

"Kill them all."

"But what about our—?"

"*All* have been deemed a liability, Ms. Magnussen. Make sure the same isn't said about *you.*"

Krista's throat tightened into a hard knot.

"You have your orders."

FOURTH

The Dark Madonna

27

October 14, 5:18 A.M.
Airborne over the Norwegian Sea

Painter watched the Svalbard Archipelago vanish behind them as the private jet sailed south over the Arctic Sea. They'd lost half a day evacuating the group trapped in the seed vault. Afterward, it took some fancy footwork by Kat in Washington to get them off the island before the media storm struck.

The dramatic bombing had drawn the world's eye. Already a flurry of international news crews and NATO investigators were converging on the tiny archipelago. The remoteness of the place and the fierce storm had allowed Painter just enough time to slip away.

But he didn't come alone.

Monk and Creed were sprawled over the cabin's couch. Senator Gorman sat dead-eyed in one of the chairs. Their final passenger sat across from Painter.

Ivar Karlsen accompanied them voluntarily. He could have made it difficult, if not impossible, to extract him from Norwegian territory. But the man had an odd sense of honor. Even now he sat straight in the chair, staring out the window as the islands disappeared. It was clear that he most likely had been the primary target of the bombing at Svalbard, that his former ally had turned into his enemy.

He also knew to whom he owed his life and respected that debt.

Painter meant to take full advantage of that cooperation.

The small jet lurched in the unstable air, thickening the tension in the cabin. They were headed to London. Neither Painter nor Kat had heard from Gray's team. He wanted to be on the ground in England as the search continued in the Lake District. Depending on what was found, they would refuel and continue to Washington.

But during this five-hour flight, Painter needed to wring this man dry of all he knew. Kat was investigating the sites of the seed-production fields that had been harvested throughout the Midwest. The news was grim: she'd already found multiple cases of unexplained deaths near fifteen test farms. A postmortem on one body had revealed an unknown fungal agent. And there were sixty-three more test fields still to check.

Karlsen spoke, sensing Painter's attention. "I only wanted to save the world."

Senator Gorman stirred, his eyes sparking with anger, but Painter gave the senator a hard glance. This was *his* interview.

Staring out the window, Karlsen failed to note the silent communication. "People talk about the population bomb, but they won't admit it's already gone off. The world population is racing toward a critical mass, where population outstrips food supplies. We are only a heartbeat away from global famine, war, and chaos. The food riots in Haiti, Indonesia, Africa, they're just the beginning."

Karlsen turned from the window to face Painter. "But that doesn't mean it's too late. If enough like-minded and determined people coordinated their efforts, something could be done."

"And you found those people in the Club of Rome," Painter said.

Karlsen's eyes widened ever so slightly. "That's right. The club keeps raising the alarm, but it falls on deaf ears. More trendy crises consume media attention. Global warming, oil supplies, the rain forests. The list grows. But the root of all of the problems is the same: too many people packed into too little space. Yet no one addresses that problem directly. What do you Americans call it? Politically incorrect, yes? It's untouchable, tangled in religion, politics, race, and economics. *Be fruitful and multiply,* says the Bible. No one dares speak otherwise. To address it is political suicide. Offer solutions and they accuse you of eugenics. Someone has to take a stand, to make the hard choices—and not just with words but with concrete actions."

"And that would be you," Painter said, to keep him talking.

"Don't take that tone. I know where this all ended. But that's not where it started. I only sought to put the brakes on population growth, to gradually decrease the human biomass on this planet, to make sure we didn't hit that crisis point at full speed. In the Club of Rome, I found the global resources I needed. A vast reservoir of innovation, cutting-edge technologies, and political power. So I began steering certain projects toward my goals, gathering like-minded people."

Karlsen looked at the senator, then away again.

Despite Painter's warning, Gorman spoke up. "You *used* me to spread your diseased seed."

Karlsen glanced down to his hands folded in his lap, but when he glanced up, he remained unabashed.

"That came later. A mistake. I know that now. But I sought you out because of your advocacy for biofuels, for turning crops like corn and sugarcane into fuel. It was simple enough to support such a seemingly good cause, a renewable energy source that freed us from oil dependency. But it also served my goal."

"Which was what?"

"To strangle the world's food supply." Karlsen stared at Painter with no apology. "Control food, you control people."

Painter remembered overhearing Karlsen paraphrase a line from Henry Kissinger. *Control oil and you control nations, but control food and you control all the people of the world.*

So that was Karlsen's goal. Strangle the food to strangle the growth of the human population. If done skillfully enough, it might even work.

"How did supporting biofuels help you control the world's food supply?" Painter could guess the answer, but he wanted to hear it from this man.

"The world's best croplands are overworked, forcing farmers to turn to marginal lands. They make more money growing crops for biofuels than for food. More and more good farmland is being diverted to grow fuel, not food. And it's horribly inefficient. The amount of corn needed to produce enough ethanol to fill one

SUV tank could feed a starving person for a year. So of course, I supported biofuels."

"Not for energy independence . . ."

Karlsen nodded. "But as *one* means of strangling the food supply."

Senator Gorman looked aghast, knowing the role he had played.

But Painter noted the odd bit of emphasis. "What do you mean by *one means?*"

"That was just one project. I had others."

5:31 A.M.

Monk had been following the conversation with growing alarm.

"Let me guess," he said. "Something to do with bees."

He pictured the giant hives hidden under the research facility.

Karlsen glanced over at Monk. "Yes. Viatus researched Colony Collapse Disorder. It's a global crisis that I'm sure you're aware of. In Europe and the United States, over one-third of all honeybees have vanished, abandoning colonies and never returning. Some areas have lost over eighty percent of their bees."

"And bees pollinate fruit trees," Monk said, beginning to understand.

"Not just fruit trees," Creed interjected, next to him on the sofa. "Nuts, avocados, cucumbers, soybeans, squash. In fact, one-third of all food grown in the United States requires pollination. Lose the bees, you lose much more than just fruit."

Monk understood Karlsen's interest in Colony Collapse Disorder. Control the bees, and you control another large segment of the food supply.

"Are you saying you caused the bees to die off?"

"No. But I know what did, and that's what Viatus wanted to exploit."

"Wait a second." Monk scooted closer. "You say you *know* what killed the bees?"

"It's no great mystery, Mr. Kokkalis. The media sensationalize the theories—mites, global warming, air pollution, even aliens. But it's much simpler—and proved. Only the media chooses to ignore it in favor of sensation."

"So what caused it?"

"An insecticide called imidacloprid, or IMD."

Monk remembered the codes stamped on the giant hives. They'd all had those same three letters: IMD.

"Many studies have already incriminated the chemical as the cause, along with an analog called fipronil. In 2005 France banned both chemicals, and over the course of the next years, their bees returned while the rest of the world's hives continued to collapse." Karlsen glanced around the cabin. "But did any of you hear about that?"

No one had.

"It's not newsworthy enough," Karlsen explained. "Imidacloprid, fipronil. Not as colorful as aliens. The media still hasn't reported on the success in France. Which is fine by me. IMD has its uses."

Monk frowned. "Less bees, less food."

"Eventually even the media will wise up, so Viatus continued its own research into the compounds—to incorporate IMD into our corn."

"Just like Monsanto engineered its herbicide Roundup into its GM seeds," Creed added.

"If IMD is ever banned," Monk realized, "you'll still be able to control the bee populations."

Karlsen nodded. "And in turn, the food supply."

Monk sat back. The man was a monster—but a brilliant one.

5:40 A.M.

Painter needed to fill in more blanks. He went at Karlsen from another direction. "But Viatus was doing more than just engineering insecticides into its crops."

"Like I said, we had many projects."

"Then tell me about the peat mummies—the fungus found in those bodies."

Karlsen's steady gaze grew less sure. "As a biotech company, we test thousands of new chemicals every year, drawn from the four corners of the world. But this ancient fungus . . ." His voice took on an edge of wonder. "It was amazing. Its chemical nature and genetic structure suited my goals perfectly."

Painter let the man talk to see what he'd reveal on his own.

"From the desiccated bodies, we harvested fungal spores that were still viable."

"After so long?" Monk asked.

Karlsen shrugged. "The mummies were only a thousand years old. In Israel, botanists grew a date palm from a seed that was over *two* thousand years old. And peat was a perfect preservative. So yes, we were able to grow the spores, to learn more about the fungus. Examination of the remains also showed *how* the fungus got into the bodies to begin with."

"How was that?"

"It was ingested. Our forensic pathologist determined that the mummified people had starved to death, yet their bellies were full of rye, barley, and wheat. The fungus was in all of it. It's a very aggressive crop mold, like ergot in cereal crops. The fungus is capable of infecting any vegetation. All for one purpose."

"What's that?"

"To starve any animal that eats the infected plant." Karlsen acknowledged the shocked looks on all their faces. "Crops infected by the fungus turn indigestible. Additionally, the fungus will invade the animal's gut, further reducing food absorption. It's the perfect killing machine. It starves the host to death with the very stuff that is meant to sustain it."

"So you eat and eat, yet still starve to death." Painter shook his head. "What advantage is that to the fungus?"

Monk answered. "Fungi are one of the main reasons dead things decompose. Dead trees, dead bodies. Doesn't matter. By killing the host, the fungus was creating its own fertilizer, its own growth medium."

Painter pictured the mushrooms growing in the bellies of the mummies. But he also remembered Monk's description of the discovery in the lab, of the sporulating pods that matured out of those same mushrooms. That was how it spread, casting out airborne spores that would infect more fields and start the whole process over again.

Karlsen drew back his attention. "The goal of our research was only to extract the chemical that made those grains indigestible. If we could engineer it into the corn, we'd be able to decrease its digestibility. With less digestible corn, you'd have to eat more to have the same caloric benefit."

"So once again," Painter said, "you'd be restricting the food supply."

"And in a way that gave us *total* control. By manipulating this gene, we could turn a grain's digestibility up or down like twisting a dial. That's all we intended. And it's not as if we were the *first* to seek such genetic control."

Painter focused on those last words. "What do you mean?"

"In 2001 a biotech company called Epicyte announced they'd developed a corn seed engineered with a contraceptive agent. Consumption of the seed lessened fertility. It was proposed as a solution to the overpopulation problem. All this blatant announcement got them was a huge amount of bad press, and the corn seed vanished. As I said, addressing this issue openly only welcomes retribution. It has to be kept underground, out of the public eye. That was the lesson. And I learned it."

And that was the point where everything went wrong. Painter kept his voice neutral. "But your new GM corn wasn't stable."

Karlsen gave a slight shake of his head. "The fungus proved more adept than we imagined. This organism has evolved alongside its host plants over eons. We thought we were only engineering one aspect of the fungus—its effect on digestibility—but it mutated in successive generations and returned to full potency. It regained its ability to kill, to germinate again into its mushroom form. But worst of all, it regained its ability to *spread*."

"And when did you learn about this?"

"During the project in Africa."

"Yet you had already initiated seed production in the U.S. and abroad?"

Karlsen's expression grew pained. "It was at the insistence and assurance of our project leader and chief geneticist. She said the results of preliminary safety tests were sufficient for us to move forward. I trusted her; I never checked the results myself."

"Who was this woman?" Painter asked.

Senator Gorman guessed, his voice bitter and hard. "Krista Magnussen."

5:52 A.M.

Ivar Karlsen knew he could no longer avoid the senator's fury. But it took him a moment to meet the man's eyes. Instead, he stared down. From a pocket, he had removed a coin and let it rest in his palm. It was the Frederick IV four-mark, minted in 1725 by the traitor Henrik Meyer. His reminder of the cost of betrayal.

Karlsen's fingers clenched the coin, recognizing how far he had fallen, led astray by Krista Magnussen. He finally lifted his eyes and faced Senator Gorman. The man had paid a stiff price in blood. Ivar could not deny him the truth.

"The senator is right. I hired Ms. Magnussen when we started the Crop Biogenics division six years ago. She came with a slew of recommendations from Harvard and Oxford. She was young, brilliant, and motivated. She produced results year after year."

"But she wasn't who she claimed to be," Painter said.

"No," Ivar said. "About a year ago, we began having serious problems at our facilities. Arson in Romania. Embezzlement at another. A rash of thefts. Then Krista revealed that she had access to an organization that could shore up our global security, quietly and efficiently. She described it as a corporate version of a private military contractor."

"Did this organization have a name?"

"She called it the Guild."

Painter failed to react to the name. Not even a twitch. His total lack of response convinced Ivar that the man knew about the Guild, possibly more than even Ivar did.

"It was all staged," Painter said. "The accidents, the arson, the theft . . . the Guild made those happen. They needed you. So they softened you up to earn your trust. They pulled your butt out of the fire enough times, and you began to relinquish control. You grew dependent on them."

Surely that wasn't possible. But the pattern Painter laid out . . . it was so clear, like a deadly hand of cards.

"Let me guess," Painter continued, adding to the pattern. "When things really began to go wrong . . . at the test farm in Africa . . . who did you turn to?"

"Krista, of course," Ivar admitted, his voice catching. "She reported the mutations, that some of the camp refugees were becoming sick after consuming the corn. Something had to be done. But we'd already planted production fields around the world. She said the situation could still be salvaged, but she and her organization would need a free hand. She warned I must harden my heart. *To save the world, what were a few lives?* Those were her words. And dear God, I was desperate enough to believe them."

Ivar's breathing grew harder. His heart pounded in his throat. He pictured Krista naked, kissing him, her eyes fierce and bright. He had thought he'd known the game being played.

What a fool I've been . . .

Painter continued the story, as if he'd been standing beside Ivar these past days. "The Guild razed the village and told you that was necessary to prevent the organism from spreading. They took the bodies of some of the afflicted villagers for study and justified what came next. *Let their deaths not be in vain. If more could be learned, others could be saved.* And with seed production already begun, time was essential."

Senator Gorman sat with his eyes wide, his fists clenched on his knees. "What about my son?"

Ivar answered that agonized plea. "Krista told me she found Jason copying secure data. She said he planned to sell it to the highest bidder."

Gorman pounded his fist into his thigh. "Jason would never—"

"She showed me his e-mail with the stolen files attached. I privately confirmed that the file was sent to a professor at Princeton."

"Princeton wouldn't engage in corporate espionage."

It pained Ivar to tell the man about his son. "Her organization had proof that the money trail led to a terrorist cell operating out of Pakistan. To expose him would expose us. It would also destroy your career.

Krista tried talking to him, to convince him to give up his contacts, to keep silent. She said he refused, tried to run. One of her men panicked and shot him."

Gorman covered his face.

Ivar wanted to do the same, but he had no right. He knew that the boy's blood lay on his hands. He had ordered Jason held and questioned by those brutal mercenaries.

Then Painter tore away the last of Ivar's delusions. "Jason was innocent. It was all lies."

Ivar stared across the table, dumbstruck. He wanted to dismiss what the man was saying.

"Jason was killed because he inadvertently sent the incriminating data to Professor Malloy. It was why they were both murdered. To cover up proof of the crop's instability. The Guild didn't want that exposed."

Painter stared hard at Ivar. "Once the information was leaked, they needed a scapegoat. You were to be thrown to the wolves. After they killed you in Svalbard, the Guild could safely fade away and take all the prizes with them: both a new bioweapon and the means to control what had already been unleashed. The global contamination by your crop would be blamed on the reckless ambition of a dead CEO. And with you eliminated, no one would be the wiser. To the Guild, you were no more than a pawn to be sacrificed."

As Ivar sat perfectly still, cold sweat trickled down his back. He could no longer deny it. Not any of it. And down deep, maybe he had known the truth all along but dared not face it.

"But I have one last question," Painter continued. "One I can't answer."

He slid a sheet of paper across the table. Written on it was a familiar symbol.

A circle and a cross.

Painter tapped the sheet. "I understand why the Guild would kill Jason and Professor Malloy, but why murder the Vatican archaeologist? What does this have to do with the Guild's plan?"

6:12 A.M.
Painter knew Karlsen was near the breaking point. The man's eyes were glassy, his voice a hoarse whisper. He clearly struggled with the depth of betrayal

perpetrated against him. But the Guild were masters of manipulation and coercion, of infiltration and deception, of brutality and violence.

Even Sigma had once fallen prey to them.

But Painter offered no solace to the man.

Karlsen slowly answered his question. "Father Giovanni approached our corporation two years ago to fund his research. He believed that the mummified bodies found in the peat bog were the victims of an old war between Christians and pagans. That the fungus was used as a weapon to corrupt crops and wipe out villages. And this secret war was buried in code in a medieval text called the Domesday Book. His supporting documents were impressive. He believed a counteragent existed to the spread of the fungus, a cure, a way of eradicating it from land and body."

"And you financed the search for this counteragent?"

"We did. What could it harm? We thought he might turn up some new chemical that we could exploit. But about the time we began to suspect that our new crop was unstable, we heard that Father Giovanni had made a huge breakthrough. He had found an artifact that he was sure would lead to the location of this lost key."

Painter understood. "Such a counteragent, if it existed, would solve all your problems."

"I had Krista interview him to judge the validity of his claim and to secure the artifact." Ivar closed his eyes. "God forgive me."

"But the priest ran."

Karlsen nodded. "I don't know what happened. Whatever he told her over the phone drew the full attention of her organization. And after the disaster in Africa, we had to secure that artifact. If there was even the remotest possibility of a counteragent . . ."

"But you lost it. Father Giovanni was killed."

"I never learned the exact details. After the mess in Africa, I had more immediate fires to put out. I left the matter to the Guild to pursue, to see if there truly was any validity to Father Giovanni's claim."

"And how did that go?"

He shook his head. "The last I heard from Krista was that another team was still searching for the key."

That had to be Gray, Painter thought.

"Krista assured me that the Guild had a mole on that team."

Painter went cold at his words.

If the Guild had infiltrated Gray's team—

He struggled for any way to help them, to get word to them. But he didn't even know if they were dead or alive. Either way, there was nothing he could do for them.

They were on their own.

28

A library was an unlikely spot to plan a prison break.

But they had to start somewhere.

Gray shared a desk with Rachel. Stacks of books were piled around them. Sunlight streamed through the tall windows of the modern library in the city of Troyes. Computer stations dotted rows of tables in the research room.

Despite its glass-and-steel architecture, the library was ancient. Founded in a convent in 1651, it remained one of the oldest libraries in all of France. Its main treasure was a collection of manuscripts from the original Abbey of Clairvaux. After the French Revolution, the entire abbey library had been moved to Troyes for safekeeping.

And for good reason.

"It was Napoleon who turned the abbey into a prison," Gray said, pushing back a book and stretching a kink out of his neck.

Since driving from Paris, they had spent all morning in the library, researching the abbey and its saints. They'd had little sleep, only what they could manage in the airport or on the short plane hop from England.

With the clock ticking, Gray faced two challenges: how to reach the ruins that lay at the heart of Clairvaux Prison and what to look for once they got there. With much still to learn, he had no choice but to assign tasks and split everyone up.

Gray accompanied Rachel and Wallace to Troyes. The town lay only eleven miles from the prison. Its library contained the greatest collection of historical documents about the abbey. To expedite their research, Gray divided their tasks. Rachel concentrated on Saint Malachy's life, death, and entombment at the old abbey. Wallace was off with a clerk to the restricted Grand Salon of the library to review original documents concerning Saint Bernard, the founder of the monastic order and a close friend of Malachy's.

Gray concentrated on digging up every architectural detail he could find on the original abbey. He had a stack of books equal to Rachel's. Open before him was a text that dated to 1856. It contained a map of the original abbey precinct.

A tall outer wall surrounded the property, interrupted by watchtowers. Inside, the grounds were divided into two areas. The eastern ward held gardens, orchards, even a few fishponds. To the west spread barns, stables, slaughterhouses, workshops, and guest lodgings. Between them, secured behind its own inner walls, stood the abbey itself, including the church, cloisters, lay buildings, and kitchens.

With the book open before him, Gray studied the nineteenth-century map.

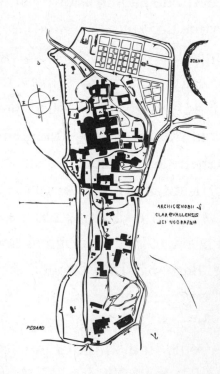

Something kept drawing him back to this picture, but the more he concentrated, the less sure he became. For the past half hour, he had used the map to pinpoint the few surviving structures of the abbey. All that still stood were a couple of barns, a few sections of walls, a nicely preserved lay building, and the ruins of the original cloister.

It was the latter—*le Grand Cloître*—that most intrigued Gray.

The Grand Cloister lay immediately next to where the old abbey once stood. And it was beneath that church that Saint Malachy had been buried.

But was he still there?

That was another worry. According to Rachel, after the French Revolution, the tomb of Saint Malachy disappeared from the historical record.

Did that mean something?

Which brought Gray back around to a question that still nagged him.

"Why *did* Napoleon turn the abbey into a prison?"

Wallace had returned and overheard the question. "It's not that unusual," he explained as he sat down. "Many old abbeys from the Middle Ages were converted into penal facilities. With their thick walls, towers, and monastic buildings, they were an easy conversion."

"But of all the abbeys in France, Napoleon picked this *one* for his prison. He picked no others. Could he have been protecting something?"

Wallace rubbed his lower lip in thought. "Napoleon was a key figure during the Age of Enlightenment. He was fixated on the new sciences but also fascinated by the old. When he led his disastrous campaign into Egypt, he brought a slew of scholars with him to scour the archaeological treasures there. If he *had* learned of some forbidden knowledge hidden at the abbey, he might well have guarded it. Especially if he thought it might threaten his empire."

"Like the curse." Gray remembered the word written in the Domesday Book.

"Wasted."

Had something scared Napoleon enough to lock it up?

Gray hoped so. If the Doomsday key had been buried in Saint Malachy's tomb, it might still be there.

Rachel didn't have time for them to be wrong.

Over the course of the past hours, she had begun to run a fever. Her brow was hot, and she was prone to chills. Even now, she wore a sweater buttoned to her neck.

She didn't have the luxury of mistakes.

Gray checked his watch. They were scheduled to meet Kowalski and Seichan in another hour. The pair had gone off to the prison, to scope it out and study it for weaknesses. It was up to Seichan to discern a way into the maximum-security facility. She had left with a doubtful expression fixed to her face.

Rachel stirred from her book, her complexion waxy and pale, her eyes red and puffy. "I can't find anything more than I have," she finally conceded in defeat. "I've read Malachy's whole life story, from his birth to his death. I still could not discover a reason why Malachy, an Irish archbishop, was buried in France. Except that he and Bernard were the deepest of friends. In fact, it states here that Bernard was buried *with* Malachy at Clairvaux."

"But are they still there?" Gray asked.

"From everything I've read, the bodies were never moved. But the historical record after the French Revolution goes blank."

Gray turned to Wallace. "What about Saint Bernard? Were you able to find anything about the man or the founding of the abbey that might be useful?"

"A couple of items. Bernard was closely associated with the Knights Templar. He even authored the Templar rules and was instrumental in getting the Church to recognize their order. He also instigated the Second Crusade."

Gray weighed that information. The Knights Templar were considered to be the keepers of many secrets. Could this be one of them?

Wallace continued, "But one item stood above all the others, the story of a miracle. One that happened here. It is said that Bernard became deathly ill from an infection, but as he prayed before a statue of the Virgin Mary, it bled milk that healed him. It became known as the Lactation Miracle."

Rachel closed her book. "Another example of a miraculous healing."

"Aye, but that's not even the interesting part," Wallace said with a sly cock of one brow. "According to the story, the statue that bled the milk . . . was a Black Madonna."

Gray took a moment to absorb the shock of it. "A Black Madonna healed him . . ."

"Sounds familiar, doesn't it?" Wallace said. "Maybe it was allegorical. I don't know. But after Malachy's death, Saint Bernard became a major advocate for the worship of the Black Madonna. He was instrumental in starting the cult."

"And that miracle occurred right here."

"Aye. Definitely suggests that the dark queen's body might have been transported here to Clairvaux—along with the key."

Gray hoped he was right, but there was only one way to know for sure. They had to get into that prison.

12:43 P.M.
Clairvaux, France

Seichan headed through the woods.

Her scouting expedition to Clairvaux had produced few results. Wearing cold-weather hiking gear, she had binoculars around her neck and a walking stick. Just a young woman out for a day's hike. Only this traveler packed a Sig Sauer in a holster at the small of her back.

The prison and former monastery lay in a valley between two wooded ridges. According to Rachel, it was common for the Cistercian order to build their monasteries in such remote locations. Preferring an austere lifestyle, the monks withdrew to woodlands, mountaintops, even marshes.

Out of the way, it also served as a good prison site.

Seichan had hiked completely around the perimeter of Clairvaux, noting the position of all the guard towers, the rows of walls, the steel pickets, and the razor-sharp rolls of concertina wire.

It was a fortress.

But no castle was impenetrable.

A plan was already building in her head. They would need uniforms and passes and a French police truck. She had left Kowalski at an Internet café in the neighboring village of Bar-sur-Aube. Through a Guild source, he was gathering a list of the names of both prisoners and guards, including their photos. She believed she could have everything ready by tomorrow. Morning visiting hours would allow one or two of them to get inside. The rest would need to come in the marked truck with fake photo credentials.

Still, there remained many variables. How long would they need to be in there? How would they get out? What about weapons?

She knew they were moving too fast, too recklessly.

Seichan suddenly ducked behind the thick bole of a white oak. She couldn't say why she felt the need to hide.

Just a prickling at the base of her neck.

She knew better than to ignore it. The human body was a big antenna, picking up signals the conscious mind often missed, but the deeper part of the brain, where instinct was rooted, continually processed them and often sounded the alarm.

Especially if trained from childhood, like Seichan, whose survival had depended on listening to those darker folds of awareness.

As she held her breath, she heard the crackle of dried leaves behind her. Ahead, a rustle of branches. She dropped into a crouch.

She was being hunted.

Seichan knew that spotters had followed them to France. Before leaving England, she had reported in with her contact. Magnussen knew their destination. The tail had picked them up again in Paris. It hadn't taken Seichan long to spot them.

But she would have sworn no one had followed her from Bar-sur-Aube after she dropped off Kowalski. She had left her car parked at a roadside rest stop and headed into the woods alone.

Who was out there?

She waited. Heard the rustle behind her again. She fixed the location in her head. Pivoting out, she took in the view in one unblinking stare. A man with a rifle, camouflaged, crept through the woods, clearly military-trained. Even before she was done pivoting, she snapped out her arm. The steel dagger flew from her fingertips. It shredded through the leaves and impaled the hunter through the left eye.

He fell back with a cry.

She rushed forward and closed the distance in four steps. She slammed her palm into the hilt, driving it deep into his brain.

Without slowing, she snatched his rifle and continued upslope.

A boulder lay near the ridge. From her earlier survey, she had the entire terrain mapped in her head.

Reaching the shelter, she slid and flipped over on her belly. She came to rest in a sniper's crouch, her eye already at the scope.

A *ping* ricocheted off the boulder near her head.

She heard no gunshot, but the round's passage had brushed through a pine branch. Needles puffed. She fixed the trajectory through the scope, spotted a solid shadow moving through a dappled one, and squeezed the trigger.

The rifle spat with no more noise than the snap of a finger.

A body crashed. No scream. A clean head shot.

Seichan moved again.

There would be a third.

She ran along the ridgeline, triangulating the most likely spot for a third assassin. She kept to the high ground. The map of the terrain overlay her vision, like the heads-up display inside a helmet.

If she had been setting up an ambush in this region of the woods, there was a tempting roost ahead. A lightning-struck dead oak with a hollowed-out trunk. If she had hiked another thirty yards, she would have moved into its field of fire. The other two assassins, sensing their prey about to stumble into the snare, must have let their guard down and closed in prematurely, foolishly exposing themselves in their haste.

Surely Magnussen would have warned them of their target's lethality.

But these were men, mercenaries with egos to match.

She was only a woman.

She came at the tree from behind, from upslope. She slipped to it without disturbing leaf or twig.

Planting her rifle an inch from the back of the dead oak, she fired through it. A cry of surprise and pain erupted as a body fell out of the tree's hollow on the far side. She came at him with her dagger.

He was burly, smelled of grease, his face stubbled with a black beard. He cursed at her in Arabic with a heavy Moroccan accent. She had the dagger at his neck, intending to interrogate him, to find out why she had been ambushed and who had sent them.

She could make him talk. She knew ways.

Instead, she dragged her knife across his throat, below the larynx, a silent kill, and kicked him in his face. There was no need to interrogate him, she realized. She already knew the answers to her questions.

Something had changed. A kill order had been sent by Magnussen. Catching her alone in the woods, they'd tried to take her out first.

She pictured Gray and the others. She ran headlong toward the parking lot. They had no idea.

She reached to a pocket and flipped open her phone. She jabbed in the number she had memorized.

As it was picked up, she let all her anger ring out. "Your operation! Just so you know, it *failed*!"

1:20 P.M.

Rachel stood with Wallace in a hotel garden at the heart of Bar-sur-Aube. She checked her watch. *Kowalski and Seichan should have been here by now.*

She stared out toward the street. The plan was to meet for lunch, to go over plans. They had rooms booked here. The hotel—le Moulin du Landion—had been stylishly converted out of a sixteenth-century water mill. The original canal still ran through the gardens, turning an old wooden waterwheel.

She should have been charmed by the place, but all she felt was ill. Her head pounded, her throat burned, and her fever was getting worse. She finally slumped and sat on one of the patio chairs.

Gray returned from the lobby. He shook his head as he approached. "No one picked up the keys." He noted her sitting, and his face tightened with worry. "How are you feeling?"

She shook her head.

He kept staring at her. She knew what he was thinking. Seichan had sketched a general plan for entering the prison. They would attempt it tomorrow morning. Gray clearly wondered if she'd make it that long.

Suddenly Seichan appeared, passing from the street through the garden gate. She searched all around. The woman, always hyperalert, seemed especially edgy now. Her eyes were rounder, her gaze more flighty.

Gray must have noted the same. "What's wrong?"

She frowned at him. "Nothing. Everything's fine." But when she noted they were missing one person, she tensed again. "Where's Kowalski?"

"I thought he was with you."

"I left him in town to do some research while I scouted the woods."

"You left Kowalski to do research?"

Seichan dismissed the skepticism. "It's all grunt work. I left instructions a monkey could follow."

"Yet we're still talking about Kowalski."

"We should go look for him," Seichan said.

"He's probably found a bar open for lunch. He'll find his way back here eventually. Let's talk about what we've all learned today." Gray motioned to Rachel's table.

Seichan didn't seem happy with that decision. She remained standing, pacing, keeping a constant vigil. Rachel noticed a muscle in her face twitch when the waterwheel squeaked.

The woman was drawn tight, but eventually she took a seat.

Gray questioned her on the plans for tomorrow. They all kept their voices to a low murmur, heads bowed together. As Seichan listed everything they would need, Rachel grew more and more dismayed. A thousand things could go wrong.

Her headache grew to a stabbing agony behind her right eye, painful enough that she began to feel nauseated.

Without missing a beat of the conversation, Gray placed his hand on top of hers. He hadn't even looked in her direction. It was an instinctual gesture of reassurance.

Seichan noted it, staring down at his hand—then she suddenly swung toward the street and tensed. She went dead still, like a cheetah before it charges.

But it was only Kowalski. He came sauntering into view. He lifted an arm in greeting, opened the garden gate, and crossed toward them. He was puffing on a cigar, carrying a pall of sweet-smelling smoke with him.

"You're late," Gray scolded.

He merely rolled his eyes.

Wallace used the interruption to voice his own concern about the plans for tomorrow. "This is a bloody long shot. It will take perfect timing and lots of boggin' luck. And even then, I doubt we'll make it to those abbey ruins."

"Then why don't we just take the tour?" Kowalski asked and slapped a brochure on the table.

They all stared down at a tourist pamphlet. It displayed a picture of an old arched colonnade with a fancy marquee above it.

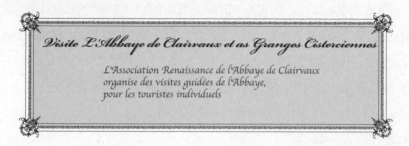

Visite L'Abbaye de Clairvaux et as Granges Cisterciennes

L'Association Renaissance de l'Abbaye de Clairvaux
organise des visites guidées de l'Abbaye,
pour les touristes individuels

Rachel translated the French. "The Renaissance Association of Clairvaux Abbey conducts tours of the prison."

They all stared over at Kowalski.

He shrugged. "What? Got that thing shoved in my face. Sometimes it helps not to blend in."

In Kowalski's case, that was an understatement. No one could mistake him for a local.

Rachel skimmed the rest of the brochure. "They conduct tours twice daily. Costs two euros. The day's second tour begins in an hour."

Wallace took the brochure and flipped through it. "Such a short tour won't allow us much time for a thorough search, but we could get a cursory sense of the place."

Gray agreed. "It'll also let us get a peek at the security from the inside."

"But on this tour," Seichan warned, "we'll be searched. We won't be able to bring any weapons inside."

"No one will," Gray said with an unconcerned shake of his head. "With all the armed guards surrounding us, we'll be safer than we've ever been."

Seichan looked far from convinced.

2:32 P.M.
So the bitch lived.

Four kilometers outside the town of Troyes, Krista crossed the grassy field toward the unmarked helicopters. The two stolen Eurocopter Super Pumas were already being loaded for the mission. Eighteen men in combat gear waited to load up. Technicians had finished equipping both birds with the necessary firepower.

A spotter on the ground reported that the targets were on the move. They had commissioned a tour of the abbey ruins and were headed to the prison. She had hoped to have dispatched Seichan before moving forward. The woman was too much of a wild card, but Krista had more than enough firepower and men to deal with her.

It just made it harder.

So be it.

Her orders were to acquire the artifact and eliminate the others. She intended to do that, but after the recent disasters, she also recognized how precarious her standing had become in the organization. She recalled the threat behind the cold words on the phone. Any failure from here would end in her termination. Yet she also knew that just *meeting* those expectations would not serve her.

After all that had gone wrong, she needed a win, a trophy to present to Echelon. And she intended to get it. If the Doomsday key was present among the ruins, she would force the others to find it for her, then eliminate them.

With the key in hand, her position in the Guild could be resecured.

Keeping that goal in mind, she left nothing to chance. Her targets had no weapons and no means of escape. Not while trapped in the heart of a maximum-security prison. Once her assault started, the prison would be locked down.

They would have nowhere to run, nowhere to hide.

She signaled her squad to board their aircraft.

It was time to crash this party.

29

Gray knew they were in trouble.

Security at the prison proved to be iron-tight, even for the private tour group. Their passports were logged in, their packs hand searched, and they had to pass through two metal detectors, followed by a full-body wanding. Guards armed with rifles, batons, and holstered sidearms held positions throughout the main facility. More men patrolled the outer yard with massive guard dogs.

"At least they skipped the cavity search," Kowalski groused as they cleared the last checkpoint.

"They'll do that on the way out," Gray warned him.

Kowalski glanced his way to make sure he was joking.

"This way, *s'il vous plaît*," their tour guide said with a wave of her mauve umbrella. The representative from the Renaissance Association was a tall, no-nonsense woman in her midsixties. She was dressed casually in khaki pants, a light sweater, and a burgundy jacket. She made no effort to mask her age. She had a weathered look to her, her gray hair pinned back over her ears. Her expression seldom mellowed from stern.

Down a hall, they came to a set of double doors that led out to an inner courtyard. Sunlight splashed over the trimmed lawns, manicured bushes, and gravel paths. After the high security, it was as if they'd suddenly stepped into another world. Sections of crumbled stone walls, half-covered in ivy, crisscrossed the two-acre expanse, along with angular mounds that marked old foundations.

Their guide led them across the yard, trailed by an armed guard. She waved her umbrella toward the walls. "These are the last remnants of the original *monasterium vetus.* Its square chapel later became incorporated into the larger abbey church with its vast choir and radiating chapels."

Gray took it all in.

On the tour bus ride there, the woman had given them a brief history of the monastery and its founder. They knew most of it already. Except for one telling detail. Saint Bernard had built the monastery on his own family's land. Because of that detail, he would certainly have been well aware of the topography, of any hidden caves and grottoes.

Had he chosen this exact spot for a reason?

Gray noted Rachel staring down at the ground, too, surely wondering the same.

Off to the side, Seichan kept her gaze higher, toward the surrounding walls of the prison and its watchtowers. The ruins were completely enclosed on all four sides. Her expression remained grim.

Seichan caught him studying her. She held his gaze as if she were about to say something. Though outwardly stoic, the tinier muscles in her face, those beyond most people's voluntary control, seemed to shift through an array of emotions, blurring into an unreadable confusion.

She finally turned away as the tour guide spoke. "Come, come. We'll move next to the beautifully preserved lay building. It offers us a wonderful example of monastic life."

She headed to the far side of the yard where a three-story stone building sheltered in the corner. It was fronted by archways and pierced by small doors and windows.

"The lower level housed the monastery's *calefactorium*, or communal day room," she explained. "Its design is ingenious, *très brillant*! Beneath the pavement ran a series of flues from hidden cellars. Fires below would warm the cold monks after prayers or night offices. Here they could also grease their sandals before they began their day."

As she went on to explain more about daily monastic life during the Middle Ages, Gray studied the stones under his feet.

So the monks were proficient engineers and tunnel makers.

He also remembered Wallace's assertion that such monasteries and abbeys were often riddled with secret passageways.

Did any of them survive?

The woman led them through more of the ruins, even out to the remains of a barn that served as an old currier's shop, and lastly she rounded them back toward the ruined walls of the old church. She ended at the massive Grand Cloister, the crown jewel of the tour.

They crossed through a huge archway and entered the cloister grounds. The structure consisted of a square walkway, covered on top and lined with columns on the inside, facing a sunny inner garden. Gothic vaults held up the roof over the walkway.

Gray ran his fingers along the neighboring wall. To have lasted for a millennium, the whole structure stood as a testament against the ravages of time and weather.

What else might have survived?

Their guide brought them out into the central garden, with its narrow paths framed by low bushes and angular flower beds. "The cloisters were built to the south of the church to take full advantage of the best sun."

She lifted her face to the sky to demonstrate.

Gray followed her out and stood beside an ornate compass that graced the center of the garden. He turned in a slow circle and studied the square of columns that surrounded him.

Of all the abbey grounds, why was the cloister so well preserved?

He sensed that if there was a way into Saint Malachy's tomb, it had to be here. A few steps away, Rachel took photographs. They would study them back at the hotel, try to discern a solution.

Still, as Gray stood there, he knew photos could not capture the ancient feel of the place. He took a moment to absorb it all. Something about the structure nagged at him. He pushed away all distractions. He ignored the others wandering the ruins, turned a deaf ear to the guide's continuing discourse.

Instead, he listened to this place.

He allowed himself to slip back in time, to hear the monks' chanting, the ring of bells in a call to prayers, the silent prayers cast heavenward.

Here was a sacred place . . .

Surrounded by ancient stone columns . . .

Then he knew.

He turned full around once more, his eyes wide. "We're in a sacred stone ring."

A step away, Rachel lowered her camera. "What?"

He waved an arm around the cloister. "These columns are really no different than the standing stones back in the peat bog." His excitement grew, his voice breathless. "We're standing in the middle of a Christian version of a stone ring."

Gray rushed to the towering columns and moved from one to the next. Carved out of massive blocks of yellow-gray limestone, each one had to weigh several tons, truly no different from the standing bluestones of England.

On his fourth column, he found it. It was faint, no more than a shadow worn into the surface of the limestone. He ran his fingers over the mark, tracing the circle and the cross.

"It's the symbol," he said.

The guide had noted his sudden attention. She joined him. "*Magnifique.* You've discovered one of the consecration crosses."

He turned to her for elaboration.

"During the Middle Ages, it was traditional to sanctify a church or its property with such symbols. Unlike the crucifix that represents Christ's suffering, these crossed circles represent the apostles. It was typical to adorn a sacred place with them. They always numbered—"

"Twelve," Gray finished for her. He pictured the standing stones in the peat bog. There had been twelve crosses there, too.

"That's correct. They mark the blessings of the twelve apostles."

And maybe something much older, he added silently.

Gray moved through an archway into the covered walkway. He wanted to examine the far sides of the columns. The standing stones back in England had spirals on their reverse sides.

He searched quickly along the cloister. The others joined him. He found no markings on the inner surfaces of the columns. By the time he had circled all the way back to where he started, his excitement had waned. Maybe he was wrong. Maybe he was reading too much into the symbolism.

The woman noted his determined search. "So you've heard the local legend," she said with a slight scoffing tone. "I think half the reason the cloister still stands is because of that mystery."

Wallace wiped his brow with a handkerchief. "What mystery are you talking about, my dear lady?"

The woman smiled for the first time, slightly smitten by the older professor. Also, Wallace had been sticking close to her, asking lots of questions, which probably contributed to the attraction.

"It's a legend only told locally. A story passed from one generation to the next. But I'll admit, it is an oddity."

Wallace returned her smile, encouraging her to continue.

She pointed to the courtyard. "As I said before, it's typical to sanctify a church with *twelve* consecration crosses. But here there are only *eleven*."

Surprised, Gray stepped back out into the garden. He mentally kicked himself for not being thorough enough. He had never thought to count the number of symbols. He had assumed there were twelve, like the standing stones.

"The story goes that the missing twelfth and final consecration cross of Clairvaux Abbey guards a great treasure. People have been looking for it for ages, scouring the grounds here, even searching the outlying barns. But it's all just silly *légendes*. *Absurdité*. Most likely the twelfth cross had been carved inside the abbey itself, joining the blessing out here to the church."

And maybe that link still existed, Gray thought.

The guide checked her watch. "I'm sorry, but we must end our tour here. Perhaps if you come tomorrow, I could show you more."

This last offer was mostly directed at Wallace Boyle.

"Oh, I'm sure we'll be back," he promised her.

Gray glanced at Seichan to see if she thought that might still be possible. She had sidled next to him. With the tour ending, she had grown visibly tense.

Before he could question her, a loud siren blared, jarring and strident. They all searched around. What was going on?

The armed guard moved closer. Rachel turned to their guide, checking her face to see if this was a normal occurrence.

"We must find cover," Seichan said at Gray's ear. Her voice was urgent, but she looked almost relieved, as though she had been waiting for something to happen.

"What's going on?"

Before she could answer, a new noise intruded. Past the siren, a heavy *thud-thud* reverberated, felt in the gut. He looked to the sky as two helicopters shot into view over the wooded ridgeline. The pair rose high, then tipped their noses and dove straight toward the prison.

From the sirens, Gray knew those two did not belong in this airspace.

The prison was under attack.

3:22 P.M.

Krista sat next to the pilot as he angled the helicopter toward the prison below. Even through the muffling headphones and the roar of the rotors, she made out the scream of the sirens below. The facility had picked up their approach, tried to hail them, but without proper call signs radioed back, the prison had sounded the alarm.

Ahead of her, the first Eurocopter swept over the prison grounds. From its belly, barrels dropped. They tumbled below and crashed with fiery explosions. The concussions cut through the chaos, booming like thunder.

Krista wanted as much mayhem as possible. She had been informed of the security protocol at Clairvaux Prison. In case of emergency, the facility would isolate the abbey ruins, both to protect a national treasure and to secure any tourists trapped there.

Like now.

The pilot from the lead helicopter radioed to her. "Targets have been spotted below. Sending coordinates."

She glanced at her bird's pilot. He nodded. He'd gotten the coordinates and banked the helicopter hard to the right. They were carrying ten men aboard their bird. Drop lines were being readied at both hatches. Once over the ruins, the men would bail out, slide down the lines, and secure the targets below.

Krista would accompany that first assault team.

She intended to handle this personally.

After the prison was bombed and burning, the other helicopter would unload its men in a second wave. The two birds would continue their patrol, ready and waiting to evacuate on her orders.

Leaning forward, Krista stared below. The coordinates marked a massive square of stone ruins around a large garden. The space was wide enough to land a helicopter inside if necessary.

The pilot came on the line. "Waiting your mark," he said.

She lifted a fist and pointed her thumb down.

Time to end this.

3:24 P.M.

Gray sheltered with the others under the cloister's covered walkway. His ears rang from the blaring sirens.

His head pounded from the concussions. Fountains of fire and smoke erupted all around them.

Gray understood the tactic of firebombing the prison.

Someone wants us trapped.

And he could guess who.

Seichan's bosses wanted them on a shorter leash. Had she informed them about how close Gray's team was to finding the key? Was this how they wanted to play their endgame?

Still, Seichan looked just as angry. Apparently she hadn't been informed of this change in plans.

"What are we going to do?" Rachel asked.

He couldn't answer. He knew there were many questions buried in that one. How were they going to get out of here? What about the promised antidote to her poisoning? Without the Doomsday key in hand, they had no bargaining chip.

They needed that key.

Just before the assault, something had begun to gel in Gray's mind. A vague idea, the whisper of a thought. But the sirens and bombs had blown it all away.

Something about the missing twelfth consecration cross.

Out of the smoke, a helicopter swooped into view. Its shadow fell over the yard as it skimmed to a hovering position. Rotorwash buffeted the enclosed space, flattening the flowers and shaking the bushes.

Gray and the others had nowhere to run.

As he faced the garden, he suddenly knew the answer. There was no calculation, no piecing it together. It formed fully in his head.

Time slowed to a crawl.

He remembered his fixation with the old abbey map at the Troyes library. He knew what had nagged at him. There had been a pagan cross inscribed on that very page. Back at the library, he had missed it, failed to recognize it in that context. In his mind's eye, he saw it clearly now.

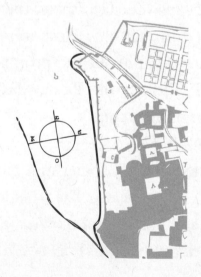

The pagan cross represented the earth quartered into its primary corners: east, west, north, south.

Just like the map's *compass*.

Gray stared into the garden—at the decoration that graced the middle of the yard. The compass was an ornate brass construction that rested on a waist-high stone plinth. The compass was sculpted with elaborate frills, each of the four cardinal directions clearly marked, along with many gradations in between.

The twelfth consecration cross—though disguised in this new incarnation—had been in plain sight all along.

If Gray had any doubt, he reminded himself of one other thing. The compass stood in the *center* of the courtyard, surrounded by stones marked with sacred symbols. Such a spot was the most hallowed ground to the ancients who raised those old stones.

Gray knew what he had to do.

He swung to the guard and pointed to the hovering helicopter as its hatches were thrown open. "Fire!"

But the guard looked terrified. He was young, likely new, assigned to babysit the tour groups. He was out of his league.

"Well, if you're not going to . . ." Kowalski grabbed the gun out of the guard's stunned hands. "Let me show you how it's done."

He sprang up, aimed, and began shooting at the helicopter. Men dove away from the open hatch. One drop line tumbled loose and writhed as the helicopter yanked up and off to the side, caught by surprise at the gunfire.

Gray knew he had moments to confirm his theory.

"Kowalski, you hold off that bird! Everyone else, with me!"

Gray ran into the garden and headed toward the compass. "Get around it!" he ordered as he gripped the large brass N.

Wallace, Rachel, and Seichan manned the other cardinal directions.

"We have to turn it! Like at the tomb on the island. Make it twist like a spiral!"

Gray dug his toes into the lawn, planted his shoulder, and pushed. The others did the same. Nothing happened. It wouldn't budge. Was he wrong? Were they turning it in the right direction?

Then suddenly it gave way. The entire compass lurched, rotating around its brass hub.

Rifle shots blasted from Kowalski's position.

Return fire peppered down from above, concentrating on the shooter. Rounds chewed into the column where Kowalski had taken shelter. He was forced to duck away.

The helicopter swung back toward the yard. The beat of the rotors pounded, deafening them.

"Don't stop!" Gray yelled to the others.

The mechanism was ancient. Turning the compass was like drilling into sand: grating, stubborn, and coarse.

The helicopter steadied into position above them.

Ropes dropped on all sides.

3:27 P.M.

"Don't shoot!" Krista screamed as one of the men aimed at the four below. "I want that group alive."

At least for now.

The soldiers' bloodlust was up. One of them had taken a stray round to the face and lay dead on the cabin floor. Whoever was firing on them knew how to handle a rifle. She'd give him that much.

She pointed to the far side of the cloister, to where the sniper had taken roost. She clapped a gunman with a grenade launcher.

"Take him out."

There was nowhere the bastard could hide.

Especially from a thermobaric grenade.

Kowalski sprinted.

He knew from the sudden cessation of gunfire that something much worse was about to drop on his head. At least the old lady and the guard had already fled the cloister when the firefight first started. They'd wanted no part of this fight.

Typical French . . .

The only warning Kowalski got was a sharp whistling that cut through everything else. He glanced back—so he didn't see the hole.

One second he had stones under his feet, then nothing but open air.

He fell headlong down a narrow set of steps.

A fiery explosion ripped past his heels. A blast wave kicked him in the rear and catapulted him down the rest of the steps.

He landed in a crumpled, dazed pile at the mouth of a dark tunnel.

Deafened, with his nose bleeding and his backside smoking, Kowalski realized two things. The steps hadn't been here a moment ago. And worse, he knew where he must be.

3:28 P.M.

Even with his ears ringing from the grenade blast, Gray heard his name bellowed, followed by a blistering string of curses.

"Run!" Gray yelled to the others.

He grabbed Rachel; Seichan snagged Wallace. They all fled from under the helicopter, dancing through the whipping ropes. The blast wave from the grenade had burst outward with a fiery slap. Even the helicopter had bobbled, which bought them just enough time to sprint for the walkway.

A large chunk of the cloister was now a blackened, smoky ruin.

Seconds before, Gray had watched Kowalski barreling away from the blast zone. Then the big man had suddenly fallen straight out of view, as if he'd tumbled down a well—no, not a *well*.

"Get your ass over here!"

Only one thing made Kowalski sound that scared.

The four of them ducked into the walkway. Gray spotted it immediately. A narrow staircase had opened in the floor. So he'd been right. Spinning the compass had unlocked the hidden passageway.

"Hurry," he said.

Behind them, the helicopter had stabilized and men in combat gear zipped down the lines. He heard the boots hitting the ground as he reached the stairs.

"Down, down, down," he urged.

The others piled through the opening. Gray went last. Out of the corner of his eye, he saw a soldier leveling a rifle. He ducked. A spray of bullets passed over his head and rebounded off the wall. Ricochets pelted like bee stings. He took one to the skull that felt like it cracked bone.

It could have been worse.

Only rubber bullets, he realized as he hurried below. Nonlethal. Someone wanted them captured alive.

He tumbled into a lower passage.

Kowalski yelled back to him. "There's a lever over here! Should I pull it?"

"Yes," they all shouted in unison.

Gray heard a scrape of metal. The stairs began rising behind them. Each step was really a slab of rock, staggered to make a staircase. Each slab rose vertically to reseal the opening above.

Darkness fell over them completely.

A scratch of flint sounded, and a small flame flickered to life. It illuminated Seichan's face as she held up her lighter.

"Now what?" she asked.

Gray knew they only had one chance. Rachel's life— *all* their lives—hung on one hope. "We must find that key."

30

October 14, 3:33 P.M.
Clairvaux, France

Krista stalked across the cloister's garden. The day had turned to twilight as smoke choked the sky, occasionally stirred by a passing helicopter.

Throughout the prison grounds, hundreds of fires burned. Sirens continued to blare, punctuated by gunshots and men's screams. The prison guards had enough to manage with loose prisoners, raging fires, and utter chaos. They wouldn't bother with the ruins for the moment. But to ensure their continuing privacy, she had the second assault team set up a perimeter, guarding all access points to the area. Overhead, the helicopters with their gun mounts added air support.

An especially loud explosion drew Krista's gaze to the west. A fresh curl of flame shot into the sky.

An exploded fuel tank off by the small heliport, she guessed. The area had been one of their first targets.

Krista had wanted the prison as isolated as possible, for as long as possible. Before the strike, she had the major phone and communication trunks severed. She had the one road out to the prison planted with mines. Eventually a response would reach here, but she planned on being gone before that happened.

Or so she hoped.

Her second-in-command met her in the walkway. He was a hulking black Algerian named Khattab. He scowled and shook his head. "Still no contact with the targets."

She had a team scouring beyond the ruins of the cloister. A soldier had shot at one from the group; from the description, it had been Grayson Pierce. But where did they all go? The shooter's report made no sense. He had shown her where the others had vanished. But Krista found no window or door. The walls were solid. Had they slipped through the shadows and escaped?

So far they had not been spotted again.

All they'd found were a scared guard and an old woman out in the ruins. She had questioned them, but they didn't know anything.

She stood in the walkway with Khattab and stared at the brass compass in the middle of the garden. They'd been doing something over there when her team flew in.

She pointed. "Get two men on that compass. See if there is anything unusual."

"And what about the targets? Do our orders remain the same?"

"I have new orders." She had hoped to secure the Doomsday key, but she recognized that was one brass ring beyond her reach. "Shoot to kill."

As she stepped away, her boot heel skidded on some sand. It drew her eye to the stones underfoot. She knelt down. She had missed it before in the shadows, but a sandy line of grated limestone delineated a rectangle on the floor. Half-hidden behind a pillar, the location was where the shooter had seen their escaping targets vanish.

Krista pinched some of the crushed stone. She rubbed it between her fingers. Her eyes narrowed.

"Khattab, scrub those orders. I want men over here. Someone with demolition experience."

Maybe that brass ring wasn't quite so far out of reach.

3:34 P.M.

With his flashlight in hand, Gray led the others down a brick tunnel. It descended steeply in a straight course. As well as Gray could get his bearings down here, it seemed to be leading them beneath where the old abbey had once stood. By now, they had to be four stories underground.

No one spoke.

They all knew everything depended on finding that key.

Gray followed the beam of his flashlight. The sides of the tunnel vanished up ahead. Despite the urgency, he slowed everyone down. He remembered the booby trap he had inadvertently activated. Now was not the time for a careless mistake.

Holding his breath, he edged down the last of the tunnel. His flashlight's beam diffused into a much wider space. He stepped to the opening and gazed out at the chamber beyond.

His first impression was of a subterranean cathedral. Brick walls lined by four giant pillars supported a massive circular dome. The structure was similar to the vaults along the edges of the cloister. But here the dome was really one massive vault. Arched ribs rose from each of the four pillars and crossed at the top. Viewed from below, Gray knew what the pattern must look like: a circular dome quartered by crossed ribs.

It formed the pagan cross.

The quartered circle.

If there had been any doubt about the symbolic representation, he had only to look below for confirmation. Sculpted in bronze and embedded in the limestone floor lay a massive design. It stretched thirty yards across. It curled in one continuous pattern, sweeping out, then back in again, forming three perfect spirals, all entwined together.

It was the ancient tri-spiral, the ubiquitous symbol found carved across the standing stones in England, illuminated in old Irish Celtic texts, and absorbed by the Catholic Church to represent the Holy Trinity.

The circle above, the spiral below.

And between them stood one object. It was the chamber's only feature.

"A Celtic Cross," Rachel said, her voice awed.

The others joined Gray as he entered the domed chamber.

The cross rose from the center of the tri-spiral. Sculpted also of bronze, it was plain, unadorned, only seven feet tall. It was constructed of two bronze poles crossed up high with a circular crosspiece.

Gray led the way.

Only Kowalski hung back by the tunnel. "I'll stay here," he said. "I remember what happened the last time you messed with a cross."

The four of them continued into the chamber.

Wallace commented on the simplicity of the religious sculpture. "Cistercian monks always preached against excessive adornment. They believed in austerity and minimalism. Everything in its place and serving its function."

Gray carefully crossed to the bronze spiral. He wasn't sure such a massive floor design could be classified as *austere*. But the professor was correct about the cross. In form and size, it seemed insignificant. In fact, it looked more like an industrial tool than a religious symbol.

Still, no one could deny its importance.

Rachel commented on it, looking up. "It stands between the spiral and the quartered cross."

Gray took a moment to shine his light across the dome. As his beam washed over the roof, he recognized something he'd missed. The dome, divided into four quarters, was not unadorned. His light reflected off raw chunks of quartz crystal imbedded in the ceiling.

As he cast his light around the dome, he knew what he was looking at.

"It's a starscape," Rachel said.

Gray agreed. He recognized constellations formed out of bits of quartz. The crystals varied in size, creating the illusion of three-dimensionality.

But they didn't have time to appreciate the artistry.

Seichan reminded them. "What about the key? Back at Bardsey Island, you thought the cross held the combination to unlock its vault. Could it be the same here? Look."

She pointed to the circular element hanging on the cross. The bronze wheel was scored with deep lines, similar to those on the stone cross on Bardsey.

Like the marks on a combination lock.

Gray suspected she was right, but there was a problem.

He didn't know the combination.

And the last time he'd tried, he'd almost gotten them all killed.

From everyone's worried expressions, they hadn't forgotten either.

"We have to attempt it," Wallace said.

"And if you trigger the booby trap," Seichan said, "we can have Kowalski yank that lever like last time."

He shook his head. "Even if it worked, we would still be screwed. Pulling the lever might haul our butts out of the fire here, but it could also reopen the stairs."

He eyed the others, letting the significance sink in. Commandos would flood down here.

"Out of the fire and into the bloody frying pan," Wallace concluded sourly.

Gray turned back to the cross. "We get one try. One mistake, and we're doomed."

Rachel offered the only solid reason for attempting it. "But we're just as doomed if we do nothing."

Kowalski added his own opinion. He grumbled it under his breath, but the acoustics carried it across the chamber.

"One more person says *doomed* and I'm out of here."

3:48 P.M.

Krista stood next to Khattab as the team's demolition expert finished packing the last hole with C-4 plastic explosive. He worked it with his fingers and shaped the charge with the deft skill of a sculptor. Once satisfied, he inserted a spark detonator tied to a wireless transmitter.

He waved everyone back.

They retreated out into the garden.

No one wanted to be under the walkway when it blew. The expert had warned that there was a chance the blast could collapse the walkway and bury the secret entrance.

"Ready?" Khattab asked.

She waved impatiently.

With a nod from Khattab, the demolitions expert lifted his transmitter and pushed the button.

3:49 P.M.

The blast dropped Rachel to one knee—not from any concussion, but from sheer fright. Already tense, she was caught off guard by the explosion. The meters of rock muffled the blast, but it still sounded like a gunshot.

"They're trying to blow their way inside," Seichan said, staring back at the tunnel.

"On it!" Kowalski called and ran with his rifle up the tunnel. But he was only one man against an army.

Already on one knee, Rachel slumped and sat on the floor. Her fever had grown worse. Chills shook through her. Her head pounded, as if her brain were expanding and contracting with each beat of her heart. She also could no longer ignore the nausea.

Gray stared over at her. She waved for him to continue his study of the cross. He had spent the past ten minutes examining the cross without touching it. He circled around and around. Sometimes he leaned close; other times he pulled back and stared off into space.

They had noted a few oddities about the cross. The horizontal crosspiece was hollow. And behind the cross, Wallace had discovered a long string pinned to the middle of the cross. It was dried sinew braided into a thick cord and weighted down at the end by a triangular chunk of bronze.

No one knew what to make of it—and no one dared touch it.

A pounding of boots announced Kowalski's return. "They didn't make it through," he shouted with relief. "We're still locked up tight."

"They'll keep trying," Seichan warned.

Rachel stared over at Gray. They were running out of time.

For the moment, Gray had stopped. He slowly sank to the floor, as if giving up.

But she knew him better than that.

At least she hoped she did.

3:59 P.M.

Krista held the phone to her ear. She hadn't wanted to take the call, but she had no choice. A palm was clamped hard over her other ear. The sirens still blared. And the firefight had grown louder from the prison yards. It sounded like an all-out war. She knew the fighting threatened to spill at any time into their isolated oasis.

"We know where they are!" she yelled into the phone, trying to keep the desperation out of her voice. "We'll have the passage blown open in the next ten minutes."

She glanced over at the walkway. Khattab monitored the demolition expert's handiwork. The Algerian noted her attention. He held up ten fingers, confirming her guess.

It was their second attempt. They had blasted a crater into the walkway and exposed a buried set of limestone slabs. She knew they were close and cursed the caution of their explosives expert.

Still, from the blackened wall and columns, she recognized the need. If they accidentally collapsed the walkway over the hidden entrance, they would never get down there.

The man on the line finally spoke. His voice was gratingly calm, unhurried. "And you believe they've accessed some vault that might hold the Doomsday key?"

"I do!"

At least she hoped like hell they had.

There was a long pause on the phone, as if she had all the time in the world. Off to the side, sharper rifle blasts erupted. They came from her own team. That could only mean one thing—the war was beginning to break through to them.

"Fair enough," the man finally said. "Secure the key."

There was no need to threaten.

The line clicked dead.

She stared over at Khattab.

He held up nine fingers.

4:00 P.M.

Father Giovanni must have known something.

That was all Gray had to go on.

He sat with his eyes open, but he was blind to everything around him. He placed himself back in the crypt beneath Saint Mary's Abbey on Bardsey Island. He pictured the charcoal markings on the wall. In his mind, he again read the notations scribbled by the priest and studied the large circle drawn around the cross. Other lines bisected and sectioned the circle.

At the same time, he pictured the cross here. He remembered his first impression, trusting it. He had thought it looked more like an industrial tool than a religious symbol. Like a bronze timepiece, a device crafted for purpose, not decoration.

Wallace's description of the Cistercian order echoed in his ears.

Everything in its place and serving its function.

He craned his neck and stared up at the quartz star-scape. Breathing through his nose, he felt something rising up inside, some understanding that he couldn't quite put into words.

Then he was on his feet. He never remembered rising. He stepped back over to the cross. He stared at it from the side. The bronze sculpture was only a bit taller than Gray. It required him to crouch to peer through the hollow crosspiece.

"It's not a cross," he mumbled.

"What do you mean?" Wallace asked from the other side.

Gray shook away any response. He didn't understand, not completely yet. He bent down and stared through the hollow arm.

Seichan stood at his shoulder. "It's almost like a telescope."

Gray straightened, stunned.

That was it.

That was the one piece he needed.

Inside, a dam suddenly released, understanding flowed through Gray's head. Images flashed across his mind's eye faster than he could follow, but still, somewhere beyond reason, they came together.

He stared up at the roof.

Like a telescope.

He turned and grasped his enemy in a hug. Seichan stiffened, unsure what to do with her arms.

"I know," he whispered in her ear.

She jolted at his words, perhaps misinterpreting them.

He let her go. He dropped to the floor and checked the base of the cross. It sat on a half sphere of bronze. He felt around the edges. It wasn't flush. There was a wafer-thin gap between the stone and the bronze.

He sprang back to his feet and ran for the pack he'd abandoned on the floor. He dumped it out and found a black marker. He knelt down, needing to see it for himself. He worked quickly, his marker flying across the stone.

As he worked, a part of his mind traveled back to Bardsey. He recognized the partial calculations on the wall now. The circle with the lines. Father Giovanni was smarter than all of them. He had figured it out. The circle was a representation of the earth. His notations—

"They were calculations of longitude and latitude."

The others gathered around him.

"What are you talking about?" Wallace asked.

Gray pointed to the bronze sculpture in the center of the room. "It's not a cross," he repeated. "It's a navigational tool. One tied to the stars!"

He finished his drawing.

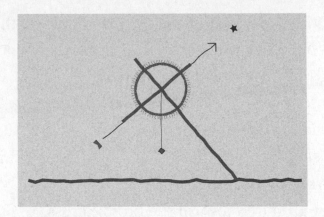

His sketch showed how the cross could be tilted, how its arm could be pointed at a star, how the weighted sinew could act like a plumb line, and the turning wheel of the device could measure degrees.

"It's an early sextant," he explained.

"Oh my God." Wallace fell back in shock. A palm rose to his forehead. "For the longest time, archaeologists have debated how the ancients were so accurate in positioning their stones. How precisely they were able to align them!" He stabbed a finger at the drawing. "Bloody hell! That device could even be a theodolite!"

"A what?" Rachel asked.

Gray answered, recognizing it now, too. "A surveying tool, used to measure horizontal and vertical angles. Used in engineering."

"The worship of the spiral and the cross," Wallace said. "The symbols truly do represent the heavens and the earth."

Gray stared down at his sketch of the earthbound cross pointed at the stars. "It's more than that. The symbols also represent the worship of secret knowledge, *the secrets of navigation and engineering.*"

Seichan brought them back down out of the stars with a sobering question. "But what does all this have to do with the Doomsday key?"

They all stared toward the bronze cross.

Gray knew the answer. "In ancient times, only the priest classes had access to such powerful knowledge." He glanced at Wallace for confirmation.

The professor nodded.

"To unlock the Doomsday key, we have to demonstrate that same knowledge."

"How?" Rachel asked.

He remembered what Father Giovanni had been calculating at Bardsey. "We have to use the stars above and calculate a navigational coordinate. I'm guessing we have to dial in our location here. An approximate longitude and latitude." He faced the others. "That's the combination."

"Can you calculate it?" Wallace asked.

"I can try."

Gray returned to the floor. The Celtic cross functioned differently from a sextant, which used mirrors and reflections to discern latitude and longitude. But it wasn't that dissimilar.

"I need a fixed constant," he mumbled and stared up at the quartz starscape. It had been put there for a reason.

"The north star," Seichan said. She crouched and pointed to the chunk of quartz that represented the pole star, used over countless ages for navigation.

That would do.

He worked quickly. He knew the approximate coordinates for Clairvaux from using his GPS during the drive here. He pictured the reading from the unit:

LAT 48°09'00"N
LONG 04°47'00"E

Longitude and latitude measurements were broken down to hours, minutes, and seconds. Just sweeps around a clock. Like the lines scored into the spinning wheel of bronze on the cross. It was all proportional.

In under a minute, he had what he believed were the correct assignments using the ancient tool and their current location.

He memorized them and stood up.

Rachel stared at him, her eyes hopeful.

Gray prayed he was equal to that hope. "In case I'm wrong, you all might want to retreat back to the tunnel."

He hurried over to the cross. As he reached it, he suddenly grew less sure. He would have only one chance.

If he was wrong, if he miscalculated, if he failed to manipulate the ancient sextant correctly, the others were all dead.

He stopped and stared at the device.

"You can do it," a voice said behind him.

He glanced over his shoulder. Seichan stood there. The others had joined Kowalski in the tunnel. "Get back," he said harshly.

She ignored him, not even reacting. "It may take two people. One to hold the cross steady at the proper angle, the other to dial the combination with the wheel."

He wanted to argue, but he recognized she was right. A part of him also had to admit that he didn't want to be alone.

"Let's do it then," he said.

Gray again crouched to peer through the hollow arm of the cross. *Like a telescope,* he thought, remembering how the words had unlocked the knowledge inside him. They had come from Seichan.

He knew what had to be done. He reached to the cross and pulled the arm down. The entire sculpture tilted, pivoting on the spherical base. As soon as he moved it, a massive *clank* echoed up from under the floor.

There was no turning back.

Gray swung the arm so it pointed north. Staring through the barrel of the armpiece, he searched the starry dome. Seichan helped by keeping her flashlight pointed at the chunk of quartz that marked the north star.

After a moment of searching, he spotted the star and centered the scope on it. As he did so, a loud gong sounded. It came from overhead and reverberated through the space.

What did that mean?

From the roof, hundreds of stone plugs popped free and rained down. One struck Gray on the shoulder. Startled, he almost dropped the cross. Seichan swore and pressed a hand to her forehead. Blood seeped between her fingers.

She continued to stare up.

Gray followed her line of sight. From the roof, bronze spikes pushed out of a hundred holes. They lowered swiftly on long poles toward the floor. Behind them, a slab of stone dropped over the tunnel exit.

Gray and Seichan would never make it to the door in time.

It was a reverse of the trap at Bardsey. Instead of being dumped atop a sea of spikes, they were to be impaled from above.

Either way, the meaning was the same.

Gray had failed.

31

"Are you sure this will blow that secret passage open?" Krista asked.

The demolition was taking longer than expected. After further calculations, the munitions expert had wanted to drill more holes into the crater, to spread the charges out for a more controlled blast.

The man shrugged as he worked. He was using an awl to hand drill the last of his mouse holes. The cubes of C-4 still waited to be molded and packed. He answered in Arabic. Her second-in-command translated.

"He says that it will blow open only if Allah wishes it."

Krista had her hand clutched on her holstered pistol. *Allah had better wish it, or that bastard was going to get a bullet through his skull.*

"How much longer?" she asked instead.

"Still another ten minutes."

Krista wanted to scream, but she simply turned and strode away.

Overhead, one of the helicopters swept past. Its rotors stirred the thick pall of smoke. Sunlight dappled brighter, then sank back to a murky twilight. The air reeked of oil fires and cordite.

She heard the helicopter's guns chatter as it sped toward the skirmish line. Her forces fought to keep the prison war from spilling over them. Orders were bellowed. Men cried and screamed. The fighting was unusually brutal. She watched one of her commandos drag a fellow soldier into the cloister. The man on the ground writhed, pressing his guts into his belly with a fist.

Like the fallen soldier, they couldn't hold out forever.

She turned to Khattab.

He raised nine fingers.

She took a deep breath to calm herself. They could last that long. Once the tunnel was opened, she was going down that hole and laying waste to all that stood between her and the key.

She glanced down to the suitcase at her feet.

Nothing would stop her.

4:05 P.M.

Seichan steadied Gray with a hand on his shoulder. He had stepped away from the cross, but he continued to hold it with one arm. She knew what he was thinking as he stared up at the spears sweeping down from above. Lines of agony etched his face.

"Should I yank the lever?" Kowalski hollered. He was on his knees, yelling under the closing slab of rock as it sealed the only exit.

"No!" Gray called back.

The others were safely in the tunnel, out of immediate danger from the impaling spikes. Only she and Gray were at risk. She knew the choice Gray had to make. If the lever was yanked, the trap would reset, but it might also open the secret door, allowing the soldiers to flood inside. If they saved themselves, the others would die.

There was no winning here.

All Gray's decision did was buy the others a slim chance. If Krista's forces were chased off before the door was blown open, the others might still live.

It was long odds, but it was a chance.

She stared upward.

She would take those odds right now.

Seichan stopped and faced Gray. She drew his eyes from the death descending on them. He had to know the truth.

What did secrets matter now?

But Gray suddenly twisted away. "What if I wasn't wrong?"

"What?"

"Hold the cross steady while I turn the wheel," he ordered.

She obeyed, baffled.

"Maybe it's *not* a booby trap. Maybe it's a timer. Once you attempt to solve the combination, you're allowed only a certain length of time to complete it." He motioned to the roof of spikes.

"So we're not allowed to guess. No trial and error."

"Exactly."

Gray reached to the weighted string of sinew and made sure it draped smoothly. He ran his fingers along the wheel of the cross. His lips moved as he counted the marks. He reached a spot that must have corresponded to his calculation.

"Here goes," he whispered.

He gripped the wheel and turned it until the spot he marked drew even with the weighted plumb line. He stopped and held his breath, his lips stretched thin with tension.

A gong sounded like before.

"That's got to be it!" he said.

Unfortunately, the spikes dropped even faster now. They plummeted toward the floor.

"Gray!"

He saw and counted quickly. Out loud this time. "Eight, seven, six, five, *four.*"

Reaching the proper mark, he held his finger there and spun the wheel the other way. It required turning it almost a full circle.

Seichan ducked as a spike headed for her face. They were both driven to their knees. Seichan held one arm high, supporting the cross. Gray had both limbs up: one to hold the marked position, the other to spin the wheel.

As she watched, a spear point sliced along her arm.

Gray cried out as a spike stabbed into the back of his hand and pushed his arm off the wheel.

Kneeling in a slightly different position, Seichan snaked her arm between two spikes and got her hand on another section of the wheel.

"Tell me when to stop turning!" she gasped out.

It required shifting up to gain leverage. The wheel was hard to spin. She pressed her cheek into a spike. It pierced all the way through. Blood filled her mouth, flowed down her neck.

She struggled to turn the wheel, but it was too tight.

Panicked, her eyes caught Gray's. She couldn't talk with her cheek impaled. Agony wracked her. She willed all her grief and agony into that one glance, bared herself to the man, hiding nothing for once.

Not even her heart.

His eyes widened, perhaps truly seeing her for the first time, recognizing what lay hidden between them. A hand crossed that gulf and found her leg. He squeezed her knee and whispered three words that no one had ever uttered to her and meant.

"I trust you."

What pain failed to do, his words accomplished. Tears welled and flowed down her cheeks. She pushed into the spear, driving it deeper. Her fingers gripped harder. She tugged on the wheel. It slowly turned.

Time stretched to a razor's edge.

Pain tore through her.

She felt the spear tip on her tongue.

Still, she turned.

"Stop!" Gray finally called out.

She let go. She slumped, sliding off the impaling spear and onto the floor. Distantly, a third gong sounded.

Three spirals, three gongs.

Her vision darkened at the edges, but she saw the spikes pull back, retracting slowly toward the roof.

With her skull on the floor, she heard huge gears turning below, like listening to God's pocket watch.

Closer at hand, the cross straightened and righted itself.

Gray was suddenly at her side. He scooped her up and dragged her onto his lap. She curled around him, hugging him. He held her tight.

"You did it. Look."

He lifted her higher in his arms. She stared out across the room.

As the gears wound below, each of the three spirals began to flip, revealing false floors. The sections rotated full around. The spiral sides vanished, turning upside down to reveal what had been hidden for all these centuries.

Bolted to the underside of each floor was a glass cradle.

As the three floors settled to a stop, the three cradles swung in their stanchions.

Even from here, Seichan knew they weren't *babies* in those oversized cradles, but *bodies*.

The cradles were actually caskets.

"It's the tombs," Gray said.

Across the chamber, the door unsealed, and the slab pulled back up. The others rushed into the chamber.

Wallace's eyes were huge. "You did it!"

"Gray . . .?" Rachel called out.

Tears streamed ˙down her face. She must have thought he was dead. Relief and horror mixed in her expression at finding him alive but covered in blood.

Seichan tried to stand but was too weak.

Gray lifted her to her feet. He supported her with one arm. Blood still flowed from her stabbed cheek, but not as heavily. Wallace offered his handkerchief. She balled it up and pressed it to her face.

Gray stared at her, his eyes questioning. She nodded and took a stumbling step out of his arms. It was the hardest thing she'd ever done. But she didn't belong there.

Rachel rushed to him and helped bind Gray's hand.

Wallace came with Kowalski. "They're glass coffins . . ."

"Of course they are," Kowalski said.

Gray gave his bandage a final cinch. Blood still dripped from his fingertips as he pointed toward the tombs. "We need to find that key."

4:08 P.M.

Gray knew where to look first.

He led the others to the one casket that was unlike the other two. Fine dust covered the glass, but the motif was clear. Flashlights focused on it, their glows igniting its brilliance.

The sides and top of the coffin were forged out of intricately designed panels of stained glass. The colors were as bright as jewels, and the images all too familiar. Sculpted out of shards of glass and slivers of gems were rows of tiny hawks, jackals, winged lions, beetles, hands, eyes, feathers, along with angular stylized symbols.

"They're Egyptian hieroglyphs," Wallace noted with a gasp.

"Formed out of stained glass." Rachel sounded equally awed.

Wallace leaned closer. "The glyphs, though, are very old. Early Egyptian. Old Kingdom, I imagine. The Church must have copied them from some original funeral stele. Perhaps they were once carved on that sarcophagus in Bardsey. Before scrubbing them off, some monk must have kept a record, then re-created them here in stained glass."

"Can you read it?" Gray asked, hoping it held some clue to the key.

Wallace ran a finger through the dust. " 'Here lies Meritaten, daughter of King Akhenaten and Queen Nefertiti. She who crossed the seas and brought the sun god Ra to these cold lands.' "

By the time the professor was done, his hands trembled as much as his voice. "The dark queen." He turned, his eyes wide with shock. "She's an Egyptian princess."

"Could that be possible?" Rachel asked.

Gray stared through the stained glass. He remembered Father Rye's tale of Bardsey Island, of the claim that the wizard Merlin was buried there in a glass coffin. Was this the true source of that myth? Had word whispered out of the entombment here, confusing the name *Meritaten* with *Merlin*?

Gray ran the mythic history of the British Isles through his head. He remembered the priest's description of the war of the Celts against a tribe of black-skinned monsters, the Fomorians. To the Celts, a tribe of displaced Egyptians would have seemed foreign and strange. And according to those same stories, the Fomorians shared their abundant knowledge of agriculture, a skill well honed by the Egyptians along the Nile.

Wallace straightened, deep in thought. "Some historians claim the ancient stone builders of England might have been Egyptian. At a Neolithic burial site at Tara in Ireland, they found a body decorated with ceramic faience beads, a skill not known to such people—but the beads were almost identical to those found in the tomb of Tutankhamen. And in England, near the city of Hull, massive boats were discovered preserved in a peat marsh. They were distinctly Egyptian in design and dated to 1400 B.C., well before Vikings or any other seafaring people came to our shores. I myself viewed an ancient stone at the British Museum, unearthed by a farmer in Wales. It shows a figure in Egyptian garb with pyramids in the background."

Wallace shook his head, as if still struggling to believe it himself. "But here . . . here's true proof."

"And the key?" Seichan reminded them, coughing hoarsely, still holding a bloody cloth to her cheek.

Beyond the glass, a figure lay in the coffin. A bronze clasp closed the hinged lid. Gray knew they had to disturb the rest of this Egyptian princess. He reached and undid the clasp. He pulled the lid up and leaned it back.

A sweetly sick scent wafted out.

"My God!" Rachel exclaimed.

Though withered and desiccated, the body was still strangely preserved. Long black hair draped the reclining figure. Her dark skin was stretched smooth. Even her eyelashes were intact. Fine cloth wrapped her body from toe to neck. A gold crown topped her head, clearly Egyptian in design from the decorations in lapis lazuli.

The only other exposed parts of her body were her hands. They were folded over her chest, clutching a stone jug carved with more hieroglyphs. The jar was sealed on top with a gold lid in the shape of a hawk's head.

"Look at her right hand," Rachel said.

Gray noted the missing index finger.

Wallace's attention fixed on the stone-and-gold jug. "The design looks like a canopic jar. Used to hold the embalmed organs of a king or queen."

Gray knew they had to look inside. The Doomsday key had always been connected to the body of the dark queen. He reached into the casket and slipped the heavy container from the queen's withered fingers.

"I wouldn't do that," Kowalski mumbled and backed up a step. "No way, no how. Thing's got to be cursed."

Or it's the cure, Gray thought.

With their skill in agriculture, the Egyptians must have discovered some type of fungal parasite that could wreak havoc and lay waste to a village. A form of bio-warfare. But did they also possess the counter-agent?

Gray cradled the jar, gripped the hawk's head, and tugged the lid off. He cringed inwardly, not knowing what to expect.

Curse or cure?

Wallace held a flashlight steady as Gray tipped it over.

From inside, a snow-white powder spilled out, so fine it poured like water. He remembered the story of Bernard and the Lactation Miracle, how the Black Madonna wept milk and cured him.

Gray knew what pooled in his palm. "It's the cure," he said, knowing it to be true. "This is the key."

He poured the powder back into the canopic jar and sealed it tight.

"You might want to see this," Seichan coughed out. She had moved to another of the caskets and opened it.

They joined her.

She pointed her light into the glass casket. A body lay wrapped in cloths, wearing a simple white robe with a cowl. His hands were also folded, clutching a small leather-bound book.

But it was the body's face on which Seichan focused her light. The man looked as if he could have died yesterday. His skin, while slightly sunken, was unblemished, his lips red, his eyes closed as if in slumber. His brown hair looked freshly combed and trimmed straight across his brow.

"He's not decayed at all," Seichan said.

Rachel placed a hand to her throat. "The bodies of saints are said to be incorruptible. They don't decay. This has to be Saint Malachy"—she glanced at the third coffin where a vague outline of another body could be seen—"or Saint Bernard."

Wallace had another thought on the miraculous nature of the body's incorruptibility. He stared over at the jar in Gray's arms, then back to the remains.

"Canopic jars didn't always hold embalmed organs." He nodded toward the jug. "Sometimes they just stored embalming compounds. Oils, unguents, powders."

Gray understood. "If the key was a curative, specifically against the fungal scourge, the powder must possess strong antifungal properties . . . possibly antibacterial, too." He stared at the face of the saint. "And the main sources of bodily decay are fungi and bacteria. Embalm a corpse with such a compound, seal the coffin tight, and it would appear incorruptible."

He also remembered the unusual health and longevity attributed to the monks of Bardsey Island. Such a powerful curative would have protected the monks against the usual pathogens that swept through the Middle Ages. No wonder the island had a reputation for healing.

Wallace's eyes widened. "So the key . . ."

"It must originally have been an embalming compound. Perhaps one brought from Egypt or discovered in their new land. Either way, its medicinal use must have quickly been recognized. Back in those times, such a cure must have seemed miraculous."

Wallace nodded. "And when paired with a deadly pathogen, it was a powerful combination. A bioweapon and its counteragent."

"And the knowledge passed from the Egyptians, to the Celts, to the early Church. Where it was eventually bottled up and hidden here."

"But that wasn't the only knowledge passed along that historical line." Wallace turned to face the Celtic cross. "For the longest time, archaeologists have debated how the Egyptians built the pyramids with such precision, such alignment. They would have needed a powerful surveying tool."

Gray studied the cross with new eyes. Could this have been it?

Behind him, Rachel let out a small gasp of surprise. She had remained at the casket. She and Seichan were bent over the body. They had opened the book held in the saint's hand.

"The name inside," Seichan said grimly. "Mael Maedoc."

"Saint Malachy," Rachel concurred. She flipped pages of the book. "It's his journal. Look at these numbers and the scribbled bits of Latin . . ."

She glanced back at Gray. "This is Malachy's *original* prophecy of the popes. In his own handwriting." Her voice grew even sharper. "But there's more written! Pages and pages of it. I think the journal contains hundreds of additional prophecies. Divinations never reported by the Church."

And maybe rightly so, Gray thought. The Church must have been frightened enough by the prophecy of the popes, of predictions about the end of the world. No wonder the journal was hidden away.

Before Rachel could explore the writings in more depth, Seichan reached to the book and flipped back to the front page. A symbol was drawn there. It was Egyptian. She glanced over at Gray. He recognized it. They had all seen it before.

He now knew why the Guild had grown so excited. The group had always been fixated on the roots of ancient knowledge, especially Egyptian. Father Giovanni must have suspected an Egyptian connection and let it leak out, sparking the Guild's sudden interest.

He stared down at the symbol, one they'd encountered before while dealing with the Guild years ago: conical depictions of a sacred meal.

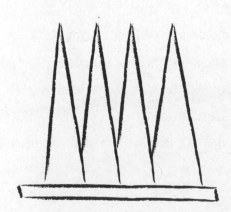

The symbol represented what was called shrew-bread, or the bread of the gods. It was fed to the pharaohs to open their minds to divinity. Had the dark queen Meritaten brought more than just a miraculous embalming compound from Egypt? Had she carried forth some of the shrewbread? Had Malachy consumed it, touched the divine, and experienced his visions?

Gray stared down at the symbol drawn in the front of the book.

Before any of them could explore it further, a blast rocked down from above. This explosion was louder. It stung his ears. Smoke and rock dust swept out of the tunnel and into the chamber.

"They're through," Seichan said.

Gray swung to Kowalski. "Get your rifle and—"

But before the big man could move, Wallace deftly plucked the weapon out of Kowalski's hands. The professor swung the rifle at them. He backed in a shuffle of steps toward the tunnel.

"I don't think so," Wallace said.

From the passageway, six soldiers rushed into the chamber, followed by a tall woman with a Sig Sauer pistol held in her hand.

Wallace glanced back. " 'Bout time you got down here, lassie."

32

Krista appreciated the shocked looks on their faces. Especially the Eurasian woman's. Even through the blood, her fury shone back at Krista like an open flame. The anger only warmed Krista further. After all the hardships in getting here, this moment was almost worth it.

Almost.

"You didn't think you were my only asset out here?" Krista asked calmly. "What's trust without an extra bit of insurance?"

Wallace joined her with his rifle.

She nudged her elbow in his direction. "Wallace and I have been a good team from the start. Back since he first discovered that pathologic fungus. The professor was also kind enough to warn us about Father Giovanni's betrayal. The priest should have been more careful to whom he made his confession."

A small laugh escaped her, unbidden, bubbling forth from a mix of elation and raw-edged relief. She fought it back down, hating the moment of weakness. Anger took its place and helped anchor her.

She steadied her voice and glanced at Wallace. "What about the key? Is it here?"

Wallace grinned. "Aye, and we found it. It's in that jar over yonder."

Gray Pierce backed up a step. "We had a deal."

She didn't have time for such foolishness or naïveté. "Khattab, go get it."

To discourage any last-minute treachery, Krista kept her pistol pointed at the Italian woman. With no choice, Gray handed over the stone jar.

In turn, Khattab left them something in exchange. As she had arranged, he placed the steel suitcase on the floor and retreated back with the key.

Gray stared down at the case. From his expression, he already guessed its contents.

She elaborated. "An incendiary bomb using kinetic fireballs. New design out of China. Burns for a very long time. Hot enough to incinerate the bricks off the walls. Can't leave anything behind."

Gray stepped forward. "At least take Rachel with you," he pleaded. "Honor that much."

She shook her head and felt an odd twinge of respect for the man. Along with a trickle of sorrow. She recognized the pain in those eyes, along with the wellspring from which it rose. Would anyone ever make such a sacrifice for her?

With an exasperated sigh, she offered the only bit of consolation she could. "I'm afraid it wouldn't do any good. I wasn't entirely truthful. The vial of toxin Wallace left in that drop box for Seichan has no cure. It's a hundred percent fatal. She's likely experiencing its effects already. Dying here will be swifter, less painful."

Krista retreated from the shocked expression on his face. The Italian woman turned away and buried her face in Gray's chest.

Krista turned to Khattab. "Let's go. Make sure your man blows the entrance to the tunnel before evacuating."

She was done here.

Or almost.

She turned and pointed her pistol at Wallace. His eyes widened. She pulled the trigger and shot him in the stomach. He didn't cry out, just gasped and fell on his backside.

His face screwed up in a mask of pain as he supported himself with one arm. "You don't know what you're doing."

She shrugged and shifted the pistol toward his head.

"I'm Echelon," he spat at her.

She froze, shocked. She struggled to make sense of the claim. *Could it be true?* Only a few people alive even knew the name *Echelon*.

She kept her pistol leveled. She remained unsure, but she knew one thing for certain. The only way to move up in this organization—there had to be room at the top.

She squeezed the trigger.

Wallace's head cracked back, then forward. He collapsed to the floor.

She swung around and headed toward the tunnel. She expected no repercussions. Her orders had been to kill everyone.

All of them, she remembered.

"Let's go!"

She hurried with the others up the tunnel. Khattab kept to her side with the stone jar cradled under one arm. Sunlight flowed ahead and drew them forward. A rubble pile led to freedom through the blasted door.

She wanted to be out of there as soon as they were aboveground. The prison was growing too hot. Gunfire echoed down to them.

She followed the soldiers topside. They scrambled as a group out of darkness and into sunlight. It took her an extra moment to realize how loud the gunfire was. It wasn't until Khattab fell to one knee, then down to his side, that she recognized the danger.

Half his face was gone. The stone jar rolled from his dead arms out into the sunlit garden.

More men fell around her as she spun and dove behind a pillar.

The war had reached them.

Overhead, a loud eruption of flames drew her eye. She watched one of their helicopters explode in a fireball of smoke and flaming debris. It spun and slammed to the ground.

Her heart pounded.

What was going on?

Then across the garden, she spotted who was firing, who had ambushed her team. Men in French military uniforms. But more than that, she recognized the man in the lead.

Impossible.

It was that damned Indian.

Painter Crowe.

Her heart pounded—not with fear, but with a rage that burned away all reason. She reached into a pocket and pressed the transmitter. The ground bumped under her, and the explosion blasted. Smoke rolled up out of the hole in the ground.

There would be no rescue for his teammates.

Using the distraction and smoke, Krista fell back into the shadows. She didn't fool herself. Trapped in the prison with her team overwhelmed, all was lost. She had only one objective left. She had made a promise to herself before she left Norway, a promise she intended to keep.

4:20 P.M.

The firefight ended as suddenly as it started.

Painter's group had been caught off guard by the sudden appearance of a contingent of hostiles pouring out of a hole in the ground. His team had failed to spot the tunnel opening buried in the shadows of a blasted section of the cloisters.

But the last of the enemy had fallen.

The French soldiers spread out and through the garden. They kept rifles on their shoulders, moving swiftly and purposely.

Painter dropped back. He let out a shuddering breath. He searched the grounds. Where were Gray and the others?

Monk crossed toward him down the walkway. His rifle still smoked. His expression remained grim, worried for his friends.

The only warning was a shift of shadows. A woman rolled into view at a narrow doorway to Painter's right. From a foot away, she had a pistol pointed at Painter's chest.

She fired four times.

The blasts cracked like thunderclaps.

Only one shot grazed Painter's shoulder. At the same time she fired, he was tackled to the side.

He landed hard on a knee and twisted around.

He watched the impact of the bullets pound John Creed out into the garden. The man toppled onto his back.

The woman screamed and came at Painter, bringing her gun to his face. He lunged up at her. He'd freed the blade from his boot and stabbed it deep into her belly.

Well trained, she ignored the pain and got the gun under his chin. Her eyes said it all. The blade could not stop her before she killed him.

"Think this is yours," Painter said savagely and pressed the button on the WASP dagger's hilt.

The explosion of compressed gas ripped into her belly. It pulverized and flash-froze her internal organs. Shock and pain burst through her, paralyzing her.

He shoved her away with both arms. She flew and crashed onto her back. Her mouth stretched into a silent scream of agony—then her body went limp. Dead.

Monk rushed past Painter into the garden. "Creed!"

Painter leaped to his feet and followed.

Creed lay on his back. Blood flowed from his lips, bubbled from the three shots to the chest. His eyes were huge, knowing what was coming.

Monk fell to his knees next to him. He tore off his jacket and bunched it up, readying a compression. "Hang on!"

All of them knew there was nothing to be done. Blood had pooled and spread over the hard-packed ground. The rounds must have been hollow-points, shredding on impact.

Creed fumbled blindly for Monk's hand and gripped it tight. Monk covered it with his other palm.

"John . . ."

One last breath escaped. Creed's hand slipped away. Monk tried to grab it back, as if that might help, but the man's eyes went glassy.

"No," Monk moaned.

Painter leaned down to offer what could only be cold comfort—but a new noise intruded. He swung around, dropping low. It came from the smoky hole.

He watched a group crawl into sight, climbing out of the hole, coughing and staggering.

One figure searched around, then stumbled out into the garden.

"Gray . . ."

4:22 P.M.

They'd only had seconds.

Gray had known the woman would blow the incendiary charge as soon as she was outside. So as the last soldier vanished up the tunnel, he had sprinted over to the Celtic cross and spun its wheel. The monks would have engineered some mechanism for sending the tombs back into hiding.

It was a natural enough guess.

Spin the wheel, spin the floors.

He had been right.

Turning the wheel flipped the tombs back below and rolled the spiral designs up.

As the floors rotated, Gray yelled for Kowalski to toss the suitcase bomb down into the cavity below. He wasn't sure if it would be enough protection, but they had no other option. Afterward, they fled to the walls and dropped to their stomachs.

When the explosion blew, the circular plates of the floor jumped up, dancing on flames—then crashed back down. The heat seared like a blast furnace. Smoke choked, but most of it got sucked up the tunnel as up a chimney flue.

It was the conflagration below that remained the danger.

The fires baked the stones under them. Off to the side, the bronze spiral began to glow through the smoky pall.

Gray called for them to retreat to the tunnel.

Crouched there, Gray heard a firefight echoing down from above—then the gunfire suddenly ended.

He didn't know what was happening. He heard a few more shots and then someone yelled. He knew that voice. He almost shook with relief.

Monk.

As the heat grew worse, Gray had led the others up the tunnel and back out into the open. Bodies lay everywhere. French soldiers surrounded them. He stumbled into the garden.

"They're with us!" Painter shouted, pushing forward.

Gray struggled to understand what his boss was doing here, *how* he could be here. But explanations would have to wait. Searching around, Gray spotted a familiar stone-and-gold object rolled up against a bush.

The canopic jar.

Relieved, he rushed over, dropped to his knees, and collected it up.

The lid was still in place.

Painter joined him.

"It's the Doomsday key," Gray explained.

"Keep it safe." Painter turned as Seichan joined them. Gray's boss seemed unsurprised at her being there.

Seichan faced Painter and shook her head.

"We had to attempt it," he told her cryptically.

"It still failed. I warned you from the start that the Guild would never trust me fully again." Seichan turned her back and stared into the garden toward the one victim who hadn't truly escaped. "And I shouldn't have trusted the Guild."

Rachel stood numbly, her face turned up to the sky. They were all free, but she was still trapped.

Even now, as Gray watched, her legs trembled.

The heat, the stress, it had worn her body past endurance.

With her face still in the sun, she went boneless and collapsed.

10:32 P.M.
Troyes, France

Hours later, Gray sat on a bench in the corridor outside Rachel's hospital room. Monk and a French internist were inside. Rachel had been hooked to an intravenous drip and pumped full of a cocktail of antibiotics. Though she was out of danger, it had been a close call. She'd had to be evacuated by helicopter to the medical facility in Troyes.

But at least she was awake again.

Gray picked at the bandage around his hand. His wounds had been debrided, stitched up, and wrapped. But he knew he was far from healed.

A door opened down the hall. He watched Seichan step out of her room. She wore a hospital gown and carried a pack of cigarettes. She glanced down the hall, clearly wondering where she could smoke in a hospital. She turned in his direction and suddenly froze.

She didn't seem to know what to do with herself. He suspected she would have to get accustomed to that state. The Guild would be hunting for her. The United States still had orders to capture her. It had taken all of Painter's skill to keep her presence secret. He was still off putting out a thousand fires, holding the world at bay.

But they couldn't hide forever.

None of them.

Gray patted the seat next to him.

For half a minute, Seichan remained standing, then finally walked over. Half her face was in a bandage. She didn't sit. She stood with her arms crossed. Her eyes were slightly glazed by morphine. She stared toward Rachel's door.

"I didn't poison her," she said in a hoarse whisper. So soon after surgery, it wasn't good for her to talk. But Gray knew she had to.

"I know," Gray said. "She's got double pneumonia. Too long in the rain, too much stress, a low-grade viral infection."

Seichan sank to the bench.

Painter had already explained most of the story. A month ago he had approached Seichan, tracked her down using the implant. She hadn't discovered the bug on her own. In fact, according to Painter, she'd been shocked, angry, and hurt by the betrayal when he finally told her. But he offered her a chance, convinced her to work for him, to attempt one last time to infiltrate the Guild. Painter had caught wind of the pending order to haul her in for interrogation. He knew she still offered the best chance to discover who ran the Guild.

She had agreed and waited for the right mission to arise to prove herself to the Guild, to try to insinuate her way back into their fold. She never suspected it would drive her into conflict with Gray. But once committed, there was no turning back.

"I had to maintain the ruse," Seichan said, referring to both the poisoning and her overall subterfuge. "I switched thermoses in Hawkshead. I pretended to dose Rachel, but then afterward I destroyed the biotoxin. I knew there were spotters watching our every move. My phone was being monitored. Plus I already had suspicions about Wallace Boyle."

Gray imagined that those suspicions had less to do with any insight about the professor and more to do with her usual state of constant paranoia, but in this particular case, they were well placed.

"It was only when we reached France, when we all split up, that I had a chance to get away from Wallace, to steal a disposable phone. After I killed the assassins in the woods—"

"You called Painter. You knew then the mission was a bust and let him know it."

She nodded. "I had no choice but to break cover. We needed help."

That they did.

During the same phone conversation, Painter had asked her to continue her charade. With Wallace still an unknown and the death count climbing in the Midwest, the world needed that key. Even if it meant staying in bed with the devil.

A long stretch of silence rose between them. It was awkward and tense. She fingered her pack of cigarettes and looked ready to bolt.

Gray finally broached a subject he'd brought up before.

He turned to her. "You told me long ago that you were one of the good guys, that you were really working *against* the Guild as a double agent. Was that true?"

She stared at the floor for a long time, then glanced sidelong at him. A hardness crept into her voice and her eyes. "Does it matter now?"

Gray studied her, matching her gaze. He tried to read her, but she was a wall. In the past, during missions where their paths had crossed, she had ultimately helped him. Her methods were brutal—like murdering the Venetian curator—but who was he to judge? He had not walked in her shoes. He sensed a well of loneliness, of hard survival, of abuse that was beyond his world.

He was saved from responding by the creak of a door. Monk pushed out into the hall, followed by the hospital's internist. Monk's gaze swept between Gray and Seichan. The residual tension must have felt like a cold front.

Monk waved to the internist as he departed, then pointed to the door. "She's tired, but you can visit for a few minutes . . . but *only* a few minutes. And I don't know if you've heard, but her uncle is out of his coma. Vigor woke up this morning. And won't shut up, I hear. Anyway, I think the good news went a long way toward perking her up."

Gray stood.

Seichan rose, too, but she turned toward her hospital room.

Gray stopped her with a touch on her arm. She visibly flinched. "Why don't you come inside, too?"

She just continued to stare down the hall.

Gray's fingers tightened on her arm. "You owe her. You put her through hell. Just speak to her."

She sighed, responding to the necessity and taking the offer as a punishment. She allowed herself to be led to the door. Gray hadn't meant the invitation as a chastisement, but at least it got her moving.

Seichan had been standing outside long enough.

Inside the room, Rachel was sitting up in bed. She smiled when she recognized Gray, but a flash of anger lit her eyes when she saw who followed him inside. Her smile faded.

"How are you feeling?" he asked.

"Well, I'm not poisoned."

Seichan knew the barb was directed at her. But she took it without comment. She walked past Gray and took the seat next to the bed.

Rachel leaned away.

Seichan sat quietly, her fingertips resting on the bed rail. She didn't say a word. She just sat there, letting Rachel's silent anger wash over her. Slowly Rachel sank back into the bed.

Only then did Seichan whisper, not tearfully, not coldly, just plainly, "I'm sorry."

Gray hung back. He suspected that Seichan needed to speak those words as much as Rachel needed to hear them. They spoke haltingly, quietly after that. Gray drifted back toward the door. He knew it was a conversation he had no part in.

He returned to the corridor and found Monk still seated on the bench. Gray joined him and noted that Monk clutched his cell phone between his two palms.

"Did you speak to Kat?"

Monk slowly nodded his head.

"Is she still angry with you for putting yourself in harm's way?"

Monk just kept nodding, not stopping.

They remained quiet for a few breaths.

Gray finally asked because he knew his friend well. "How are you doing?"

Monk sighed. A longer stretch of silence followed before he spoke. His words were calm but masked a well of pain. "He was a good kid. I should've been watching over him better."

"But you couldn't—"

Monk cut him off, not angry, just tired. "You know, I'm not sure I'm ready to talk about it yet."

Gray respected that. Instead, they just sat quietly in each other's company. And that was enough for both of them.

After a time, a familiar whistling arose down the hall. Kowalski appeared. Somehow his partner had come through everything without a scratch, but for security reasons he was still restricted to the hospital.

As he sauntered toward them, Gray saw that he held something in one of his large mitts. Once Kowalski spotted them on the bench, he hurriedly shoved his arm behind his back. Gray remembered a certain fixation Kowalski had back in Hawkshead.

As he drew abreast of them, Gray called over. "So is that a gift for Rachel?"

Kowalski stopped, suddenly sheepish. Caught, he pulled the teddy bear into view. It was white, plushy, and dressed in a nurse's uniform. He stared down at it, over to Rachel's room, then finally glared at Gray and shoved the bear at him.

"Of course it is," he growled.

Gray took the bear.

Kowalski stomped off heavily, no longer whistling.

"What was that all about?" Monk asked.

Gray leaned back. "You know, I'm not sure I'm ready to talk about it yet."

33

They all met at Senator Gorman's office on Capitol Hill.

Painter was seated next to General Metcalf. On his other side, Dr. Lisa Cummings sat with her legs crossed.

One toe of her shoe lightly brushed Painter's pant leg. It was not done casually. He and Lisa had been apart for too long. And since she had returned from vacation, she had been busy, often red-eyeing out to the Midwest to oversee the medical crisis out there. The two of them captured whatever spare moments they could together.

Metcalf continued reporting on the manufacture of the antifungal compound. Painter had already reviewed the report.

Instead of listening, he watched his girlfriend's reflection in the window behind the senator. Lisa had her hair up in a French twist and wore a conservative suit to match the mood of the meeting. He daydreamed about undoing that twist, unbuttoning that shirt.

"We're spraying all the production fields," Metcalf continued, "covering a safety zone of fifteen miles around each site. The EPA has mobilized with the National Guard to monitor and continue testing samples of surrounding vegetation for another thirty miles out."

Gorman nodded. "On the international front, all the planted fields have been scraped and sprayed. We can only hope we've stamped this out in time."

Lisa spoke up. "If not, we'll be ready. The initial human trials have been successful. Minimal adverse reactions. The early cases have responded well. It will be a boon to medicine across the board. While we have a slew of powerful antibiotics, our arsenal of antifungals, especially for systemic infections, has been limited and is burdened by high toxicity levels. With such a new compound readily available—"

"And free," Painter added.

She nodded. "We'll keep this disaster in check."

"Speaking of free," Gorman said. "I dropped in on Ivar Karlsen after visiting the Viatus production plant for the drug."

Painter drew his attention back. Karlsen was in a Norwegian penal facility, still awaiting trial. He continued to oversee business from his cell. As partial restitution, the man had voluntarily turned over the full resources of his corporation's biotechnology infrastructure to manufacture the compound. It was shocking how quickly they were able to start mass-producing it.

Lisa had tried explaining to Painter that the antifungal compound was derived from a genus of lichen found only in sub-Saharan Africa, that its chemical structure attacked a unique sterol found only in fungal cell membranes, making it both effective and safe for treating both mammals and plants.

Painter glazed out after further details. All he needed to know was that it worked.

"You should have seen his prison cell," Gorman said. "It's practically a suite at the Ritz."

"But it's a suite he won't be checking out of any time soon," Painter added. *If at all, considering the man's age.*

Metcalf stood. "If we're all done here, I still have matters to address back at DARPA headquarters."

Gorman stood and shook his hand. "Whatever I can do to help, I'm in your debt." The words were spoken to Metcalf, but Painter noted Gorman's glance in his direction.

After events in Norway, they'd been forced to reveal Sigma's existence. The senator would have kept digging anyway and only made matters worse. The knowledge also gave them a powerful ally on Capitol Hill. Already Painter had noted a change in sentiment regarding Sigma among the various U.S. intelligence agencies. For once, the wolves at their door had been dragged back. Maybe not leashed completely, but it allowed Painter more freedom to fully secure Sigma.

And he knew they would need it.

The Guild would come gunning for them.

After saying their good-byes, Painter and Lisa walked with General Metcalf through the halls of power. Painter was still waiting for confirmation from the general on one extremely sensitive matter.

"Sir . . .," Painter began, meaning only to remind Metcalf.

"She's your problem," the general said instead. "I can't countermand the order to have her apprehended. Her crimes are too tangled internationally. She'll have to stay low, and by low, I mean crawling through the sewers." Metcalf stared over at him. "But if you think she'll be an asset?"

"I do."

"So be it. But it's on your head."

Painter always appreciated such enthusiastic support. With a final few words, Metcalf headed off toward another meeting on the Hill. That left Painter alone with Lisa as they crossed into the morning sunshine.

He checked his watch. The funeral service started in another hour. He had just enough time to shower and change. Despite the bright day, a somberness settled through him. John Creed had died saving his life. Since Painter had sent men and women into harm's way all too often, he had honed a level of detachment. It was the only way to stay sane, to make the hard choices.

He couldn't do it here.

Not with Creed.

A hand slipped into his. Lisa tugged and leaned into his arm.

"It'll get better," she promised him.

He knew she was right, but somehow that only made it worse. To move past meant *forgetting*. Not all of it, but some of it.

And he never wanted to forget John's sacrifice.

Not any of it.

3:33 P.M.

Monk wandered through the rolling hills of Arlington Cemetery with Kat at his side, hand in hand, bundled in long coats. It was a crisp fall day with the massive oaks fiery in their splendor. The funeral service had ended an hour ago. But Monk hadn't been ready to leave.

Kat had never said a word.

She understood.

Everyone had shown up. Even Rachel had flown in from Rome for the day. She headed back tomorrow morning. She didn't like leaving her uncle alone for long. Vigor had just gotten out of the hospital two days ago, but he was recuperating well.

During their slow walk, Monk and Kat had wandered in a full circle and ended up back where they had started. John Creed's grave sat atop a small knoll under the limbs of a dogwood. The branches were already bare, skeletal against the blue sky, but come spring they'd be full of white blossoms.

It was a good spot.

Monk had wanted everyone gone for a moment of privacy at the gravesite, but he saw that someone still knelt there, both hands gripping the headstone. The posture was a sigil of raw grief.

Monk stopped.

It was a young man wearing army dress blues. Monk vaguely recognized him from the funeral. The man had sat as stiffly as everyone else. Apparently he'd also wanted an extra moment to say good-bye.

Kat tightened her fingers on Monk's hand. He turned to her. She shook her head and drew him away. Monk gave her a questioning look, sensing that she knew more than he did.

"That's John's partner."

Monk glanced back and knew she wasn't referring to a business partner. He hadn't known. He suddenly remembered a conversation he'd had with Creed. Monk had teasingly asked him what had gotten him drummed out of the service after two tours in Iraq. Creed's answer had been two words.

Don't ask.

Monk had thought he was just telling him to mind his own business. Instead, he was answering Monk's question.

Don't ask, don't tell.

Kat urged Monk away, allowing the man to grieve in private. "He's still in the service," she explained.

Monk followed. He now understood why the man had sat so stiffly earlier. Even now, the depth of his grief had to be kept a private matter. Only alone could the man truly say good-bye.

Kat leaned into him. He put his arm around her. They both knew what the other was thinking. They never wanted to say that particular good-bye.

9:55 P.M.

Gray stood under the spray of the shower. He had his eyes closed and heard the telltale clank from his apartment's plumbing. He was about to run out of hot water.

Still, he didn't move, enjoying every last bit of steam and blistering heat. He stretched kinks and rubbed knots. He'd had an intense workout and now paid the price. After being bruised and battered, he should have used more restraint. He'd just had the stitches out of his hand two days ago.

With a final rattle, the water quickly turned cool. Gray turned the faucet off, reached for a towel, and dried himself in the steamy warmth.

The brief cold spray took him back to the storm on Bardsey Island. Earlier today he had talked to Father Rye on the phone, to make sure Rufus was settling in as a church dog. Gray had also called to make certain Owen Bryce got the wired money to cover any repairs to the ferry they'd stolen.

Life was settling back to normal on Bardsey after a hard series of storms.

On the phone, Gray also questioned Father Rye about dark queens and Black Madonnas. The good father was certainly a font of knowledge. Gray suspected this month's phone bill would be sky-high. Still, he had learned something interesting, that some historians believed the Black Madonna might have its roots in the worship of the goddess Isis, the queen mother of Egypt.

So there again was that Egyptian connection.

But after the explosion beneath the cloister, all further evidence had been destroyed: the glass caskets, the bodies, even Malachy's lost book of prophecies.

All gone.

And probably just as well. The future was best left unknown.

But Malachy's prophecies of the popes ended with a bit of a foggy mystery. According to Rachel's uncle, Malachy had numbered all the popes on his list, with the exception of the very last one, *Petrus Romanus*, the one who would see the end of the world. This last apocalyptic pope had been assigned no number.

"This suggests to some scholars," Vigor had explained from his hospital bed, "that perhaps an unknown number of popes remain unnamed between the current pope and the last. And that the world might go on for a little bit longer."

Gray certainly hoped so.

Finally buffed dry, he wrapped a towel around his waist and headed into the bedroom. He discovered he wasn't alone.

"I thought you were leaving," Gray said.

She lay tangled in the sheets, one long leg bared to the hip. She stretched like a lithe lioness waking, one arm over her head, exposing a hint of breast. As she lowered her arm, she lifted the bedsheet. Her body still lay hidden in folds and shadows—but the invitation was plain.

"Again?" he asked.

An eyebrow tipped higher, followed by a shadow of a smile.

Gray sighed, undid his towel, and tossed it aside.

A man's work was never done.

Epilogue

Painter headed down the last flight of stairs to the nethermost region of Sigma Command. It was only a few minutes before midnight, an inauspicious moment to be visiting a morgue.

But the package had arrived only an hour ago. The work had to be done swiftly. Afterward, all evidence would be destroyed, cremated on site. He reached the morgue.

Sigma's head pathologist, Dr. Malcolm Reynolds, was waiting and led him inside. "I have the body ready."

Painter followed the pathologist to the neighboring room. The smell struck him first: overcooked meat gone bad. A figure lay under a sheet on the table. Wheeled next to it was a coffin. The casket's diplomatic seal had been sliced open by Dr. Reynolds.

It had taken Painter a huge effort to get the body released in secret from France and delivered here with false papers.

"It's not pretty," Malcolm warned. "The body sat in that makeshift oven for several hours before someone thought to move it."

Painter was not squeamish—at least not much. He pulled back the sheet and exposed Dr. Wallace Boyle's corpse. The man's face was bloated, blackened on one side, a purplish red on the other. Painter imagined the charbroiled side had been facedown on the brick floor of the subterranean chamber. He remembered Gray's description of the incendiary charge and how it had baked the stones.

"Help me roll him on his stomach," Painter said.

Together, they got Wallace over on his belly.

"I'll need something to shave him."

Malcolm disappeared.

As Painter waited, he stared down at the gaunt corpse. Wallace had claimed to be a member of Echelon, and according to Seichan, that name was rumored to denote the Guild's true leaders. She had no other information, except for a darker rumor, a story she'd only heard once.

Malcolm returned with an electric clipper and a disposable razor. Working quickly, Painter used the clipper to remove the hair from the back of Wallace's head, then shaved it smooth.

As he dragged the razor, he proved the rumor was true.

A small tattoo, about the size of Painter's thumbnail, had been inked at the back of the skull. It depicted the tools of a mason: drafting compasses straddling an L-square.

The symbol represented Freemasonry, a worldwide fraternal organization. But the image in the center of the symbol was wrong. The square and the compass usually framed the letter *G,* standing for God or Geometry.

But sometimes it stood for Guild.

Painter knew Seichan's terrorist organization had no real name, at least not spoken below the level of its leaders. Was this symbol and its connection to the Free-masons the source of the more commonly used name?

Painter studied the tattoo. In the middle of the symbol were inked a sickle moon and a star. He had never seen anything like it. Whoever these people were, they weren't Freemasons.

With the symbol exposed, Painter grew more edgy. He had found what he needed.

"Burn the body," he ordered Malcolm. "Down to ash."

Painter didn't want anyone to know what he'd learned. Much remained unknown about Seichan's former masters. But he had two pieces to the larger puzzle.

The name *Echelon* . . . and the strange *symbol.*

For now, that would do.

But it wasn't over—not for either side.

Malcolm asked him a question as he left. "What does it mean?"

Painter answered, knowing it to be true, "A war is coming."

Author's Note to Readers: Truth or Fiction

Everything in this book is true, except for what's not. I thought I'd end this adventure by splitting those hairs. First, two elements gave birth to this story. I came upon each independently, but I knew there had to be a connection and that Sigma would need to investigate.

The History of the Celtic Cross. There is an intriguing and startling analysis of the history of the cross and the possibility that it was used as a navigational tool in ancient times. For a slew of details, diagrams, and analyses, I refer you to the fascinating book *The Golden Thread of Time* by Crichton Miller.

The History of Neolithic England. The details in this book about the possibility of Egyptians setting up colonies in England are true. For a more thorough study, I suggest reading *Kingdom of the Ark* by Lorraine Evans. Also, in regard to the Fomorian tribes found living in Ireland by the invading Celts, some historians have theorized that their descriptions (dark-skinned and skilled at agriculture) might refer to a lost tribe of Egyptians.

Ancient Symbols. The novel describes a number of symbols and the way these images were often transformed and reimagined across the centuries. Such theories have a basis in fact, including the story of the consecration crosses found carved in medieval churches.

Saints. As mentioned at the opening of the book, Malachy was an Irish saint who lived during the twelfth century and is said to have performed many miraculous healings, along with recording his famous prophecies of the popes. He was indeed buried in a tomb at Clairvaux Abbey, and the ruins of that abbey do oddly enough lie within the grounds of a maximum-security prison (a prison started by Napoleon). There are weekly tours of the ruins for two euros a head. The stories concerning the life of Saint Bernard (the Lactation Miracle, his association with the Knights Templar, and his support for the cult of the Black Madonna) are historical. For more about the Celtic saints and culture in general, I recommend *How the Irish Saved Civilization* by Thomas Cahill and *The Quest for the Celtic Key* by Karen Ralls-MacLeod and Ian Robertson.

As for the prophecies, here are Malachy's descriptions of the last few popes in history:

a. **Pope Paul VI (1963–1978)** is described with the words *Flos Florum,* or "flower of flowers." His heraldic coat of arms bore three lilies.

b. **Pope John Paul I (1978)** is named by Malachy as *De Medietate Lunae,* or "of the half moon." His papacy lasted one month, crossing from one half moon to the next.

c. **Pope John Paul II (1978–2005)** is designated as *De Labore Solis,* or "from the labor of the sun," which was a common metaphor for a solar eclipse. The pope was born on the day of a solar eclipse.

d. **Pope Benedict XVI (2005–)** is described as *De Gloria Olivae,* or the "glory of the olive." The Benedictine order, from which the pope took his name, has the olive branch as its symbol.

e. **Then there is the last pope, the one who would oversee the world's end:** *Petrus Romanus.* His description is the longest of them all.

In Latin:

In persecutione extrema S.R.E. sedebit Petrus
Romanus, qui pascet oves in multis tribulationibus:
quibus transactis civitas septicollis diruetur,
et Iudex tremendus iudicabit populum. Finis.

Translated:

In extreme persecution, the seat of the Holy
Roman Church will be occupied by Peter the
Roman, who will feed the sheep through many
tribulations, at the term of which the city of seven
hills will be destroyed, and the formidable Judge
will judge His people. The End.

But as Vigor mentioned to Gray, this last pope is not
numbered as the others were before him. Some have
interpreted this to mean that there could be more popes
between Pope Benedict XVI and the last pope. I guess
only time will reveal the truth.

And Sinners.

  a. **Biofuels:** The amount of corn needed to fill an
     SUV tank full of ethanol would indeed feed a
     starving person for a year. And it is believed

that the shift from farming *food* to farming *fuel* has resulted in a spike in food prices.

b. **Genetically Modified Foods:** Volumes of material, both pro and con, have been written about GM foods. For some disturbing reading on this topic, I can recommend two books. In regard to the lax regulation of the industry, *Seeds of Deception* by Jeffrey M. Smith should be required reading. As to some more sinister aspects, I found *Seeds of Destruction* by F. William Engdahl to be frightening (specifically regarding the contraceptive seeds mentioned in the novel).

c. **Bees:** Do we know what is killing all the bees? According to the well-documented book *A Spring without Bees* by Michael Schacker, it seems there is an answer, one that has been both suppressed and ignored. And France's bees *are* coming back.

d. **Weapons of Destruction:** In this novel, I use WASP daggers, thermobaric warheads, and kinetic fireballs to cause much mayhem. The weapons are all real.

Overpopulation. The Club of Rome is a real organization that does a lot of great work. And in their report titled *The Limits to Growth,* they do lay out the doomsday scenario described by Ivar Karlsen, in which, if left unchecked, the world is headed toward a tipping point where 90 percent of the population could be wiped out.

The Doomsday Book. As mentioned in the introduction, it is a real historical tome. And some entries are indeed cryptically listed as "wasted." It was compiled during a time when friction continued between Christians and pagans, especially in the borderlands.

Location, Location, Location. Most of the places in this story are real, as are the stories associated with them.

a. **Akershus Fortress** does lie at the edge of Oslo's harbor, and cruise ships do dock near there. As to its history of executions, those are also true, including the story of the mint master Henrik Christofer Meyer, who died for his crimes and whose forehead was branded by King Frederick IV.

b. **Svalbard Global Seed Vault** is a real depository that has gained the nickname "The Doomsday Vault." All the details of the facility are accurate, including one of its main means of defense: polar bears.

c. **Bardsey Island** truly is Avalon. All the stories and mythologies of the island are accurate, including Merlin's Tomb, Lord Newborough's Crypt, and the twenty thousand buried saints. Also, the Bardsey apple continues to grow, and cuttings can now be purchased of this ancient tree. As to those nasty currents around the island, those are also real. So make that ferry crossing only in the best of weather!

d. **The Lake District of England** is indeed a land of enchantment, dotted by rings of standing stones, and, of course, is the home of the industrious Fell Ponies. There are also many, many peat bogs in the region, though nothing as forested or as fiery as in this book. But subterranean peat fires have been known to burn for centuries, even through snowy winters. And such fires are still used to make the finest Scotch (but that's a whole other story). As to the bog mummies, they are also real—as is the retail shop in the hamlet of Hawkshead that exclusively sells teddy bears (Sixpenny Bears).

So go buy Kowalski a bear . . . I guess he deserves one.

HARPER LUXE

THE NEW LUXURY IN READING

We hope you enjoyed reading
our new, comfortable print size and found it
an experience you would like to repeat.

Well – you're in luck!

HarperLuxe offers the finest in fiction and
nonfiction books in this same larger print size and
paperback format. Light and easy to read, HarperLuxe
paperbacks are for book lovers who want to see
what they are reading without the strain.

For a full listing of titles and
new releases to come, please visit our website:

www.HarperLuxe.com